Horror Mystery SCIENCE FICTION Fantasy 2

Overlook Connection
2007 CATALOG
Bookstore of The Fantastic!

Jack
Ketchum

Mick
Garris

Christopher
Fahy

Ellen
Datlow

Bev
Vincent

Thousands
of Items!
Books
Magazines
Video
MORE!

Rob
Zombie

Brett
Savory

J. F.
Gonzalez

Fiction

News

New OCP
Releases!

ORDER
CATALOG
ONLINE!

Stephen King Section Inside!

Postscripts

SPRING 2007   NUMBER 10

Contents

Peter Crowther,
Editor and Publisher

Nick Gevers
Assistant Editor

Alligator Tree Graphics
Design and Layout

Postscripts is published quarterly by PS Publishing Ltd. Unsigned edition £6/$12 per copy. Signed edition £25/$50 per copy. Postage £2 within UK; £4/$8 outside UK. Four-issue subscriptions: Unsigned edition–£26 postage-paid within UK; £30/$60 outside UK. Signed edition–£100 postage-paid within the UK; £110/$220 outside the UK. (*Occasional larger issues–such as this one–will be double the normal price for the unsigned edition. These bumper editions will, however, be sent to subscribers at no additional cost.*)

Printed in the UK by Biddles.

THE A TO Z OF FANTASTIC FICTION

Fiction (continued)

The following stories were previously published as noted: "Night Falls, Again,"
Michael Marshall Smith, Embrace The Mutation, *Subterranean Press 2002;*
"This Rich Evil Sound," Steven Erikson, Revolvo and other Canadian Tales,
TSAR Books 1997; "The Luxury of Harm," Christopher Fowler, The British
Fantasy Society: A Celebration, *BFS Publications 2006; "Distress Call,"*
Connie Willis, The Berkley Showcase Volume 4, *Berkley 1981.*

Cover art by John Picaccio

Illustrations by Wayne Blackhurst (pages 39, 165, & 306), *Randy Broecker*
   (pages 154 & 271), *Les Edwards* (pages 70 & 131), *and James Hannah*
   (pages 177, 204–205, 233, & 325), *and David Kendall* (pages 116
   & 348).

PS Publishing Ltd / Grosvenor House / 1 New Road /
Hornsea / East Yorkshire / HU18 1PG / ENGLAND

e-mail: editor@ pspublishing.co.uk   **Internet:** http://www.pspublishing.co.uk

Stephen Jones is the winner of three World Fantasy Awards, four Horror Writers Association Bram Stoker Awards and three International Horror Guild Awards, as well as being a Hugo Award nominee and a seventeen-times recipient of the British Fantasy Award. One of Britain's most acclaimed anthologists of horror and dark fantasy, he has more than eighty-five books to his credit. You can visit his website at www.herebedragons.co.uk/jones.

Editorial: Is There Anybody Out There?
Stephen Jones

Does anybody read horror short stories any more?

That may seem like a strange question to ask in the Introduction to a short fiction genre magazine, but for the past few years I have been genuinely concerned that horror stories are fast heading the way of the Dodo and Passenger Pigeon.

When I was growing up in London during the 1960s and '70s, there was a bewildering array of books and periodicals readily available featuring short stories. Herbert van Thal's perennial-seeming series *The Pan Book of Horror Stories*; *The Fontana Books of Great Ghost Stories* and *Great Horror Stories*, ably edited by R. Chetwynd-Hayes and Mary Danby, respectively; August Derleth's superior paperback anthologies and Lin Carter's compilations of the classics for his Ballantine/Pan "Adult Fantasy" imprint.

Although I was too young to have purchased any pulp magazines off the newsstands, I could still find their digest-sized successors in the form of *Amazing, Fantastic, Galaxy, Analog* and *The Magazine of Fantasy and Science Fiction* at my local newsagents, along with such home-grown titles as *Science Fantasy* and John Carnell's innovative *New Worlds*.

These were heady days, when you could read literally hundreds of new short stories, in all genres, each and every month.

However, that all changed in the mid-1970s, with the success of William Peter Blatty's *The Exorcist*, Peter Benchley's *Jaws*, Stephen King's *Carrie* and James Herbert's *The Rats*. Suddenly, the novel was king, and with the emergence of the "blockbuster" or "best-seller" concept in the publishing industry, the writing was on the wall (so to speak) for the lowly short story.

Publishers and the reading public simply lost interest in short fiction. Anthologies and single-author collections were "no longer commercial" according to the industry on both sides of the Atlantic. (Thus neatly creating a self-fulfilling prophecy—if you don't publish it, nobody will read it, thus there is no demand for it.)

Over just a few years, series titles began to disappear from the bookstores. One-by-one the digest magazines closed down, merged their titles or changed their formats.

By the time David Sutton and I started publishing *Fantasy Tales* in 1977, there were almost no markets for short fantastic fiction in the United Kingdom. The same was basically true across the pond, with only *Weirdbook* and *Whispers* welcoming original weird fiction around the same time.

Yet in many ways, this became a blessing for us. It meant that our publications attracted some of the finest writers that the genre had to offer; writers who had nowhere else to place their fiction. As a result, we found ourselves working with such luminaries as Fritz Leiber, Robert Bloch, Manly Wade Wellman, Hugh B. Cave, Karl Edward Wagner, Charles L. Grant, Dennis Etchison, Ramsey Campbell, Brian Lumley and numerous others. For a while, short fiction flourished again in such small press publications, as later collections from these authors ably testify.

Because the independent presses also began to realise that there was a market (although admittedly small but loyal) for anthologies and short fiction collections, pretty soon they began picking up the slack and issuing handsome volumes by all the above writers, and many others besides, containing the cream of their work.

With a few notable exceptions, the so-called "mainstream" publishers continued to ignore shorter works, unless forced to issue a collection in order to secure a multi-book deal for an author's next novel, or grudgingly issuing the occasional anthology so long as it was based around some spurious "high concept".

Even the infamous "crash" of horror fiction around the late 1980s failed to change this long-ingrained prejudice. When they could no longer push their shelves full of embossed and foil-covered clichéd horror novels, publishing houses continued to recite their mantra that "short fiction doesn't sell".

Luckily, some people couldn't hear them or simply ignored their recurrent mutterings. When I entered the professional publishing industry around this same time as an editor (nobody ever said that I had good business acumen), I quickly realised that there was still an audience that read and enjoyed short stories, albeit perhaps smaller and more selective than previously enjoyed by my illustrious predecessors.

And there were still some discerning publishers—admittedly the smaller ones—who were willing to give that audience what it wanted.

Over the next decade or so, collections and anthologies, if not flourished, then at least survived. Despite a few spectacular missteps (mostly involving publishers believing the hype of agents and editors and paying way over the odds for a particular "high concept" or "Big Name" anthology), a number of mainstream imprints dipped their toes in the water with anthology series and single-author collections. Independent publishing houses such as Subterranean Press, Cemetery Dance, Fedogan & Bremer, Nightshade Books, MonkeyBrain Books and Earthling Publications have filled their lists with collections and anthologies and novellas that would most probably not have found a home anywhere else. And, for the most part, they have been successful doing so.

Giving up a lucrative career in New York publishing, Gordon van Gelder has almost single-handedly kept *The Magazine of Fantasy & Science Fiction* going when some of his better-known and more prestigious rivals have long since fallen by the wayside. If not for the tireless efforts of editors such as Ellen Datlow, Mike Ashley, Peter Haining, Martin H. Greenberg, John Pelan and others of their ilk, as readers we would not enjoy the many anthologies they collectively produce and writers would be all the poorer without their markets to sell to.

And chief amongst these names, I should also mention Peter Crowther, a polymath writer/editor/publisher who has staked his own money on creating PS Publishing, a burgeoning independent imprint that enthusiastically embraces all forms and lengths of genre fiction.

And chief amongst his highlights and successes is the magazine you now hold in your hands—*Postscripts*.

It is a bold and innovative (some may say "foolhardy") step to launch a short fiction magazine at a time when literacy levels are falling and the general public has more than enough gadgets to keep themselves blissfully distracted and removed from the written word.

Yet in a few short years *Postscripts* has firmly established itself as a dynamic and eclectic market for some of the finest short fiction being published in the genre today. In every issue you will find science fiction, fantasy and horror authors rubbing shoulders with each other, along with purveyors of "slipstream" and other unclassifiable branches of short fiction. And, in my role as an editor of one of the annual "Year's Best" anthologies, I can confirm that the overall quality of each issue is amongst the highest the field has to offer.

Yet, despite all this, is anybody taking any notice? Is anybody actually purchasing copies? Buying subscriptions?

It is no secret that people are reading less and less. Not just books, but also magazines, newspapers, even cereal packets. These days our news has to be served up to us in "lite"-sized chunks, and fiction is packaged in slim-line volumes that will not tax the brain and still match the décor.

Meanwhile, publishers are producing more and more product to try to capture that elusive and progressively shrinking market of people who actually buy and read books. The fact that much of this increased output consists of so-called "celebrity" biographies, life-style guides and media tie-in volumes all destined for the early remainder shelves doesn't seem to matter. This is what most people consider "reading" these days, and every one of these deeply discounted tomes clogging up the shelves in bookstores (and, even worse, supermarkets) is denying a slot to something more worthwhile and perhaps a little more challenging.

And the biggest loser in this sea of mediocrity is short fiction. Collections and anthologies (admittedly along with the mid-list and debut novel) are being inexorably squeezed out. And my concern is that there are not enough independent imprints out there to pick up the slack anymore.

Hence my initial, somewhat rhetorical question: Does anybody read horror short stories any more?

Actually, I'm delighted to say that, yes, apparently they do.

The subscription figures for *Postscripts* are gradually increasing, which is always a very good sign with any short fiction magazine. And there is a multitude of short story collections and anthologies currently being published or forthcoming from a wide variety of imprints on both sides of the Atlantic.

As a full-time editor, whenever I announce a new anthology project I am deluged with manuscripts from writers who simply want to see their work in print. I know that it is no different for my colleagues, and we all do our very best to get as many stories into print as we can.

Also, short fiction can work as an excellent training ground for new and up-and-coming authors to learn their craft and increase their exposure. It may be almost impossible to have a full-time writing career by only turning out short stories, but repeated appearances in various anthologies and magazines is an effective way of getting your name out there and recognised when it comes to pitching your first novel. It doesn't hurt for established writers to keep their creative hand in with the short form, either.

And as our recreation time gets ever shorter with the demands of work, family life and modern living, the short story format is a perfect literary medium to dip in and out of when you have an hour or so spare and crave a little escapism.

This particular issue of *Postscripts* is being published to tie-in with the World Horror Convention being held in Toronto, Canada. For those readers not familiar with conventions, they are an excellent opportunity to meet and learn from your favourite authors, editors and artists. For the would-be writer, they are a golden opportunity to not only network with industry figures and your peers, but also to learn about your craft and business practices in relaxed and convivial surroundings.

Any genre needs new blood to survive, and ours is no exception. For the field of fantastic literature to grow and flourish, we need continually to encourage new writers to enter the marketplace and develop their own distinctive voices.

As an editor, I have worked with several generations of writers, and there is no greater thrill than finding a previously unknown writer or obscure story that you can include in a book. For the secret of being a good editor is not the stories you accept; it is the ones you reject that make the book or magazine you are compiling all the stronger.

I cannot imagine the quality of the stories that Pete Crowther had to reject in order to bring us the line-up he has assembled for this very special issue of *Postscripts*. I certainly don't envy the work it must have involved and the time it would have taken.

So, if you're reading this at the convention in Toronto, I strongly urge you as a reader to take out a subscription to this magazine immediately and get as many of the writers and artists in this edition to sign your magazine. If you are a writer, I commend these stories to your attention as examples of how to craft exemplary short fiction and recommend that you buy a drink for as many editors and publishers as you can find in the bar and tell them all about your own work.

And if you are reading these words long after World Horror Convention 2007 has come and gone, then remember what I said in the previous paragraph and follow those same instructions as soon as you have the opportunity. I promise that you won't regret it.

So . . . does anybody read horror short stories any more? You bet. As this volume—and all the others—of *Postscripts* so ably affirms. Short fiction is flourishing in the most unlikely and unexpected corners of literature, especially where our particular genre is concerned. And with your continued support or involvement, long may it continue . . .

"In the year we got married, my wife and I undertook a drive across the United States from Boston to Los Angeles. We took our time, and a far from direct route, and wound up covering over five thousand miles in a month. It was, without question, one of the very best things I've ever done. Through design, happy accident, and as a result of my having (according to Paula) a flawed understanding of what constitutes a "holiday", we saw many ruined, half-ruined or soon-to-start-being-ruined structures and communities along the way. This story was inspired by some of them, together with the ghosts of lost hope that each of these wildernesses-in-waiting represented."

The Handover
Michael Marshall Smith

Nobody moved much when he came into the bar. From the way Jack shut the door behind him—quietly, like the door of a cupboard containing old things seldom needed but neatly stored—we could tell he didn't have any news that we'd be in a hurry to hear. There were three guys sipping beer up at the counter. One of them glanced up, gave him a brief nod. That was it.

It was nine thirty by then. There were five other men in the place, each sitting at a different table, nobody talking. Some had books in front of them, but I hadn't heard a page turn in a while. I was sitting near the fire and working steadily through a bowl of chili, mitigating it with plenty of crackers. I'd like to say Maggie's chili is the best in the West, but, to be frank, it isn't. It's probably not even the best in town: even this town, even now. I wasn't very hungry, merely eating for something to do. Only alternative would have been drinking, but just a couple will go to my head these days,

and I didn't want to be drunk. Being drunk has a tendency to make everything run into one long dirge, like being stoned, or living in Iowa. I haven't ever taken a drink on important days, on Thanksgiving, anniversaries or my birthday. Not a one. This evening wasn't any kind of celebration, not by a long chalk, but I didn't want to be drunk on it either.

Jack walked up to the bar, water dripping from his coat and onto the floor. He wasn't moving fast, and he looked old and cold and worn through. It was bitter outside, and the afternoon had brought a fresh fall of snow. Only a couple of inches, but it was beginning to mount up. Maggie poured a cup of coffee without being asked, and set it in front of him. Her coffee isn't too bad, once you've grown accustomed to it. Jack methodically poured five spoons of sugar into the brew, which is one of the ways of getting accustomed to it, and stirred it slowly. The skin on his hand looked delicate and thin, like blue-white tissue paper that had been scrunched into a ball and absently flattened out again. Sixty-eight isn't so old, not these days, not in the general scheme of things. But some nights it can seem ancient, if you're living inside it. Some nights it can feel as if you're still trying to run long after the race is finished. At sixty-four, and the second youngest in the place, I personally felt older than God.

Jack stood for a moment, looking around the room as if memorising it. The counter itself was battered with generations of use, as was everything else. The edges of chairs and tables were worn smooth, the pictures on the walls so varnished with smoke you'd had to have known them for forty years to guess what they showed. We all knew what they showed. The bulbs in the wall fixings were weak and dusty, giving the room a dark and gloomy cast. The one area of brightness was in the corner, where the jukebox sat. Was a big thing when Pete, my old friend and Maggie's late husband, bought it. But only the lights work these days, and not all of them, and none of us are too bothered about it. Nobody comes into the bar who wouldn't rather sit in peace than hear someone else's choice of music, played much too loud. I guess this comes with age, and anyway the 45s in the machine are too old to evoke much more than sadness. The floor was clean, and the bar only smelt slightly of old beer. You want it to smell that way, a little, otherwise it would be like drinking in a church.

Maggie waited until Jack had caught his breath, then asked. Someone had to, I guess, and it was always going to be her. She said: 'No change?'

Jack raised his head, looked at her. 'Course there's a change,' he muttered. 'No-one said she weren't going to change.'

He picked up his coffee and came to sit on the other side of my table. But he didn't catch my eye, so I let him be, and cleared up the rest of my food, rejecting the raw onion garnish in deference to my innards. They won't stand for that kind of thing any more. It wasn't going to be long before a cost-benefit analysis of the chili itself consigned it to history alongside them.

When I was done I pushed the bowl to one side, burped as quietly as I could, and lit up a Camel. I left the pack on the table, so Jack could take one if he had a mind to. He would, sooner or later. The rest of the world may have decided that cigarettes are more dangerous than a nuclear war, but in Eldorado, Montana, a man's still allowed to smoke after his meal if he wants to. What are they going to do: come and bust us? The people who make the rules live a long ways from here, and the folk in this town have never been much for caring what State ordinances say.

One of the guys at the bar finished his beer, asked for another. Maggie gave him one, but didn't wait for any money. Outside, the wind picked up a little, and a door started banging, the sound like an unwelcome visitor knocking to be let out of the cellar. But it was a ways up the street, and you stopped noticing it after a while. It's not an uncommon sound in Eldorado.

Otherwise everyone just held their positions, and eventually Jack reached forward and helped himself to a cigarette. I struck a match for him, as his fingers still seemed numb and awkward. He still hadn't taken his coat off, though with the fire it was pretty warm in the room.

Once he was lit, and he'd stopped coughing, he nodded at me through the smoke. 'How's the chili?'

'Filthy,' I confirmed. 'But warm. Most of it.'

He smiled. He rested his hands on the table, palms down, and looked at them for a while. Liver spots and the shadow of old veins, like a fading map of territories once more uncharted. 'She's getting worse,' he said. 'Going to be tonight. Maybe already.'

I'd guessed as much, but hearing it said still made me feel tired and sad. He hadn't spoken loudly, but everybody else heard too. It got even quieter, and the tension settled deeper, like a dentist's waiting room where everyone's visiting for the first time in years and has their suspicions about what they're going to hear. Maybe 'tension' isn't the right word. That suggests someone might have felt there was something they could do, that some virile force was being held in abeyance, ready for the sign, the right time. There wasn't going to be any sign. This night had been a while in coming, but it had come, like a phone call in the small hours. We knew there wasn't anything to be done.

Maggie pottered around, put on a fresh jug of coffee. I started to stand up, meaning to get me a cup, but Jack put his hand on my arm. I sat back, waited for him to speak.

'Wondered if you'd walk with me,' he said.

I looked at him, feeling a dull twinge of dread. 'Already?'

'Only really came back down here to fetch you, if you wanted to go.'

I realised in a kind of way that I was honoured. I took the heavy coat from the back of my chair and put it on. A couple heads raised to watch us leave, but most people turned away. Every one of them knew where we were going, the job we were going to do. Maybe you'd expect something to be said, the occasion to be marked in some way: but in all my life, of all the things I heard that were worth saying, none of them were actually said in words.

And what could anyone have said?

Outside it was even colder than I expected, and I stuffed my hands deep in my pockets and pulled my neck down into my scarf like a turtle. The snow was six inches deep in the street, and I was glad I had my thick boots on. The moon was full above, snow clouds hidden away someplace around a corner, recuperating and getting ready for more. There would be more, no doubt of that. The winters just keep getting colder and deeper around here, or so my body tells me. The winters are coming into their prime.

Jack started walking up the street, and I fell in beside him. Within seconds my long bones felt like they were being slowly twisted, the skin on my face like it was made of lead. We walked past the old fronts, all of them dark now. The hardware store, the pharmacy, the old tea rooms. Even in light of day the painted signs are too faded to read, and the boardwalk which used to run the length of the street has rotted away to nothing. It happened like a series of paintings. One year it looked fine; then another it was tatty; then finally it was broken down and there was no reason to put it back. Sometimes, when I'd walked up the street in recent years, I would catch myself recalling the way things had once been, working my memory like a tongue worrying the site where a tooth had once sat. I could remember standing or sitting outside certain stores, the people who'd owned them, the faces of the people I'd spied from across the way. The times all tended to blend into one, and I could be the young boy running to the drug store, or the youth mooning over the younger of two sisters, or a man buying whiskey to blur the night away: switching back and forth in a blink, like one man looking out of three sets of eyes. It was like hearing a piece of music you grew up to, some tune you had in your head day after day until it was as much a part of your life as breathing. It was also a kind of time travel, and for a moment I'd feel as I once had, young and empty of darkness, ready to learn and experience and do. Eager to be shown what the world had in store for me, to conquer and make mistakes. To love, and lose, and love again. Amen.

Eldorado was founded in 1850 by two miners, Joseph and Ezekiel Clarke: boys who came all the way from New Hampshire with nothing but a pair of horses and a dream. Sounds funny now, calling it a dream, probably even corny. People don't think of money that way any more. These days they think it's a right. They stay where they are, and try to make it come to them, instead of going off to find it for themselves. The brothers came in search of gold, like so many others. They were late on the trail, and worked through the foothills, finding nothing, or stakes that had already been worked dry, and then climbed higher and higher into the mountains. They panned a local river, and found nothing once more, but then one afternoon came upon the seam— just as they were about to give up and move on, maybe head over to Oregon or California and see if it was paradise like everyone said. It must have seemed like magic. They found gold. When we were young we all heard the story. A kind of Genesis tale. A little glade, hidden up amidst the mountains at over three thousand feet: and there for the taking, a seam of money, a pocket of dreams.

The brothers stayed, and built themselves a cabin out of the good wood that grew all around. But news travelled fast, even in those days, and it wasn't long before they had company. A lot of company. The old mine workings have gone to ruin now, but it was a big old construction, I can tell you that. Was a few years when Eldorado was home to over four thousand people, producing five million dollars a year in gold. The town had saloons and boarding houses, a post office and a fistful of gambling rooms, even a grand hotel. Almost all have fallen down now, though until ten years ago people still used the hotel to board their animals in, when it got real cold. Two walls are still more or less there, hidden amongst the trees, though I wouldn't want to stand underneath them for long. I once showed the site to a couple of tourists who came up all this way in a rental car, having seen the town sign down the road. They seemed a little disappointed to find there was still people living here, and were soon on their way again.

That was near ten years ago, and no-one's come up to look since, though the town sign's still there. It says 'Eldorado, 15 miles', and stands on a turn of the local road from Giles to Covent Fort, though lately I swear the trees around it have been growing faster. Neither Giles nor Covent are much to brag about themselves these days, and the road between them isn't often used. If it weren't for that town sign, there would be no way of knowing we were up here at all.

When the gold ran out there was zinc for a while, and a little copper. The gold fever died away, but Eldorado continued to prosper for a time. There was a Masonic lodge built, and two banks, and a school house with a clock and a bell—the fanciest building in town, the symbol there was a community here, and that we were living well. I can't even remember where the lodge was now, the banks are gone, and the school

closed in 1957. I went to that school, learned most of what I know. Everybody did. It was the place where you turned into a grown-up, one year at a time, back when a year was as long as anyone could imagine, when two seemed like infinity. Probably that was why, for a long time, folks would stop by the abandoned school every now and then, by themselves and on the quiet, and do a little patching up. Wasn't any sense in it, because it wasn't going to re-open, not least because there were no new children—but I know I did it, and Jack did, and Pete before he died. Had to be that others did too, otherwise it would have fallen down a lot earlier than it did.

Now it's gone, and even on the brightest Spring day that patch of the mountain seems awful quiet. I guess you could say that no-one here has learned anything since then. Certainly what you see on television doesn't seem to have much application to us. I stopped watching a long time ago, and I know I'm not the only one. TVs don't last forever, and there ain't no-one around here knows how to fix them. And anyway they just showed a world that isn't ours, things that we can't buy and wouldn't want to, so what use was it, anyway? We've got quite a few books, spread amongst us. That's good enough.

Eventually the copper ran out, and though people looked hard and long, there wasn't anything else useful to be found. The gambling dens moved on, in search of people who still had riches to throw away. The boarding houses closed soon afterwards, as those who hadn't made Eldorado their home moved on. Plenty people stayed, for a while. My folks did, in the 1920s. Never got to the bottom of why. But anyhow they came, and they stayed, and I followed in their footsteps, I guess, by staying here too. So did some others.

But not enough. And nobody new.

Halfway down to the end of Main, Jack and I turned off the road and made our way as best we could up what used to be Fourth Street. I guess it still is, but you'd be hard pressed to find the first three, or the other eight, unless you'd once walked them, and gone visiting on them, or grown up in a house that used to stand on one. Now they've gone to trees and grass, just a few piles of lumber dotted around, like forgotten games of giant pick-up-sticks. You'd think people might have made an effort to keep the houses standing, even after people stopped living in them. But it's not the kind of thing that occurs to you until far too late, and then there doesn't seem a great deal of point. Spilt milk, stable door, all of those.

The grade has always been kind of steep on Fourth, and Jack and I both found the going hard. Jack had already made the trip once that night, and I let him go in front, following his footprints in the snow. There was another way of getting up to the house, a little less steep, but that involved going past the town's first cemetery, now overgrown, and the notion wasn't even discussed. Ahead of us, a single light shone in one of the upper windows of the Buckley house, which sits alone right at the end,

a last stand against the oncoming trees. I felt sick to my stomach, remembering times I'd made the walk before, towards that grand old house hunkered beneath the wall of the mountain. Hundreds of times, but a handful of times in particular. My life often seems that way to me now. So much of it was just landscape I passed through, a long open plain with little to distinguish the miles, or like some indifferent movie that went on for a long, long time. But then there's something inside me like a satchel, or a little box, where I keep the *real* things.

A few smells, and sounds, touches like a faint summer breeze. Some evenings, a couple afternoons, and a handful of dawns, when I woke up somewhere I was happy to be, coddled warm with someone and protected from the bright light of day and tomorrow. It's nights I remember most. Some bad, some good. You fall in love at night, and that's also when people die. Even if their last breath is drawn in daylight, by the time you've understood what's happened, the darkness has come to claim the event as its own. Nights last the longest, without doubt, both at the time and afterwards. They contain multitudes, and don't fade as easily as the sun. They're there, in my bag, and I'll take them with me when I go.

When we got to the house we stomped the snow off our boots on the porch, and then let ourselves in. Over the last few weeks of visiting I had gotten used to the dust, how it overlaid the way the house had used to be. She'd kept it up as well as she could over the years, but now you could almost hear it running down, like the wind dropping after a storm. The downstairs was empty but for Naomi's cat, who was sitting in the middle of the hall, looking at the wall. It glanced up at us as we started on the stairs, then walked slowly away into the darkness of the kitchen.

I knew then that it was already over.

When we reached the upper landing, we hesitated outside the doorway to the bedroom, as if feeling we had to be invited in. The interior was lit by candles, with an old kerosene lamp by the window. The Doc was sitting on a blanket box at the end of the bed, elbows on his knees. He looked like an old man, very tired, waiting for a train to take him home. Not much like someone who'd once been the second-fastest runner in town, after me, a boy who could run like the wind. He'd gone away, many years ago. Left town, got trained up, spent some years out there in the other places. Half the books in town were his, brought with him when he came back to Eldorado.

He looked up, beckoned us in with an upward nod of the head. We approached like a pair of children, with short steps and hands down by our sides. I kept my eyes straight ahead, knowing there'd be a time to look after the words had been said.

Jack rested a hand on the Doc's shoulder. 'She wake at all?'

He shook his head. 'Just died. That's all she did.'

'So that's it,' I said.

The three of us sighed then, all together. Just an exhalation, letting out what had once been inside.

The Doc started to speak, faltered. Then tried again. 'Maybe it's not going to happen,' he said, trying for a considered tone, but coming out querulous and afraid. 'After all, how do we know?'

Jack and I shook our heads. Wasn't any use in this line of thought. Nobody knew how we knew. But we knew. We'd known since the children stopped coming.

We walked around on separate sides of the bed, and looked down. I don't know what Jack was looking at, but I can tell you what I saw. An old woman, face lined, though less so than when I'd seen her in the afternoon of the previous day. Death had levelled the foothills of her suffering, filled in the dried stream beds of age. The coverlet was pulled up to just under her chin, so she looked tucked up nice and warm. The shape beneath the blankets was so thin it barely seemed to be there at all: it could have been just a runkle in the sheets, covering nothing more than cooling air. Most of all she looked still, like a mountain range seen from the sky.

Wasn't the first time I'd seen someone dead, not nearly. I saw my own parents laid out, inexplicably cold and quiet, and my wife, and many of my friends. There's been a lot of dying hereabouts over the last few years, every passing marked and mourned. But Naomi looked different.

It's funny how, when you first know someone, it will be the face you notice most of all. The eyes, the mouth, the way they have their hair. Everybody has the same number of limbs, but their face is all their own. Then, over the years, it's as if this part of them leaves their body and goes into your head, crystallises there. You hardly notice what the years are doing, the way people's real faces thicken and dim and change. Every now and then something brings you up short, and makes you see the way things have become. Then you lose it again, almost as quick as it came, and you just see the continuity, the essence behind the face. The person as they were.

I saw Naomi as she and her sister had once been, the two brightest sparks in Eldorado, the girls most likely to make you lose your stride and catch your breath—whether you were fifteen, same as them, or so old that your balls barely still had their wits about them. I saw her as the little lady who could shout loudest in the playground, who could give you a Chinese burn you'd remember for days. I saw her as I had when Pete and I used to hike up Fourth with flowers in our hands and our hearts in our throats, when Pete was cautiously dating Naomi, and I was going with her sister Sarah, who was two years younger and much prettier, or so I thought back then.

It's that year that many of the nights I keep in my bag came from, that brings faint memories of music to my head. Sarah and I came to a parting of the ways before Thanksgiving, and she eventually married Jack, had no children but generally seemed content, and died in 1984. Pete and Naomi lasted a couple more months than we had, and then Pete met Maggie and things changed. Five years later, both on rebounds from different people altogether, gloriously grouchy and full of cheap liquor, Naomi and I spent a night walking together through the woods which used to stop on the edge of town. We looked for the stream where the Clarkes first panned, and maybe even found it, and we didn't do anything more than kiss, but that was exciting enough. Then the morning came, and brought its light, and everything was burned away. We'd never have been right for each other anyhow, that was clear, and it wasn't the way it was supposed to be. Of course a decade or two later, when I first started to look back upon my life and read it properly, like a book I should have paid more attention to the first time, I realised that this might have been wrong. When I thought back, it was always Naomi's face that was clearest in my mind, though she'd been Pete's and I'd been Sarah's and anyhow both of those futures were long in the past and dead and buried half a lifetime ago. By then Naomi was married, and when we met we were polite. Almost as if that current which can pass between any two people, the spark of possibility, however small, had been used up all in that night in the woods, under-used and thrown away, and now we could be nothing but friends. Naomi never had children either, nor Maggie. None of us did.

Even now, when the forest has started to march its way right up Main Street, I can remember that night with her as if I'm still wearing the same clothes and haven't had time to change.

Remember also the way the sisters always seemed to glow, all of their lives, as if they were running on more powerful batteries than the rest of us, as if whoever had stirred their bodies into being had been more practised at the art than whoever did the rest of us. I loved my wife a great deal, and we had many good years together, but as I get older it's like those middle years were a long game we all played, a long and complex game of indeterminate rules. Those seasons fade, and we return to the playground like tired ghosts coming home after a long walk, and it's how we were then that seems most important. I can't remember much of what happened last year, but I can still picture those girls when we were young. On the boardwalk, in the big old house their father built, around the soda fountain when they were still little girls and we were all sparkling and young and blessed, a crop of new flowers bursting into life in a field which would always be there.

Almost all of those people are dead now. Distributed amongst the two cemeteries, biding their time, like broken panes in the windows of an old building. A few of the windows are still intact, like me and Jack and Maggie and all, but you have to wonder why. There's nothing to see through us now.

When Jack and I had looked down on Naomi a while, and nothing had changed, we turned away from the bed. The Doc had quietly gotten his things together, but didn't look ready to leave just yet.

'There's something me and Bill have

to do,' Jack said. 'Only stopped by for the truck. And, well, you know.'

The Doc nodded, not really looking at us. He knew what we were going to do. 'I'll stay a while,' he said. Back in '72 there'd been something going on between him and Naomi. He probably didn't realise that we knew. But everybody did. Then after her husband died in '85, oftentimes the Doc had taken his evening meal at the Buckley table. I'd always wondered if it might be me who did that. Didn't work out that way.

'What are we going to do about her cat?' I asked.

'What can anyone do about a cat?' the Doc said, with the ghost of a smile. 'Reckon it'll do pretty much what it wants. I'll feed it, though.'

We shook his hand, not really knowing why, and left the house.

Jack's truck was parked around the side. It wasn't going to be a picnic getting down the hill, but it was too far to walk. We got it started after only a couple of tries, and Jack nosed her carefully out into the ruts of the street. Fate was kind to us, and we got down to Main without much more than a spot of grief. Turned right, away from the bar, away from what's left of the town.

When we drew level with the other cemetery, Jack slowed to a halt and turned the engine off.

We sat with the windows down for a while, smoking and listening. It was mighty cold. Wasn't anything to hear apart from wind up in the mountains, and the rustle of trees bending our way. Beyond the fence the stones and wooden crosses marched away in ranks into the night. Friends, parents, lovers, children, in their hundreds. A field full of the way things might have been, or had been once, and could never be again. Folks are dead for an awfully long time. The numbers mount up.

Jack turned, looked at me. 'We're sure, aren't we?'

'Yes,' I said. 'We've been outnumbered for a long, long while. After Naomi, there's only fifteen of us left.'

It felt funny, Jack turning to me, wanting to be reassured. I still remembered him as one of the big kids, someone I hoped I might be like one day. I did grow up to be like him, then older'n he'd once been, and then just old, exactly like him. Everything seemed so different back then, everyone so distinct from one another. Just your haircut can make you a different colour, when everyone's only got ten years of experience to count on. Then you get older, and everyone seems the same. Everybody gets whittled away at about the same rate. Like the '50s, and '60s, and '70s and '80s, times that once seemed so different to each other, but are now just stuff that happened to us once and then went away; like good weather or a stomach ache.

Jack stared straight out the windshield for a while. 'I don't hear anything.'

'May not happen for hours,' I said. 'No way of telling. May not even happen tonight.'

He laughed quietly. 'You think so?'

'No,' I admitted. 'It'll happen tonight. It's time.'

I thought then that I might have heard something, out there in the darkness, the first stirring beyond the fence. But if I did, it was quiet, and nothing came of it right then. It was only midnight. There was plenty of darkness left.

Jack nodded slowly. 'Then I guess we might as well get it over with.'

We smiled at each other, briefly, like two boys passing in the school yard. Boys who grew to like each other, and who could never have realised that they'd be sharing such a task, on a faraway night such as this.

Later we'd drive back up into town, park outside Maggie's bar, and sit inside with the others and wait. She was staying open for good that night.

But first we went down the hill, down a rough track to an old road hardly anyone drove any more. We got out the truck and stood a while, looking down the mountain at a land as big as Heaven, and then together we took down the town sign.

☒

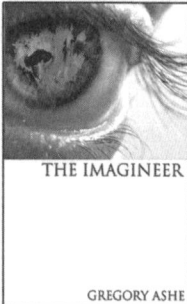

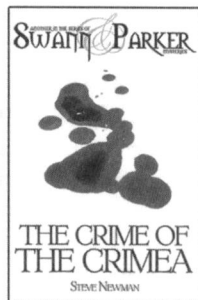

"Those of you who are familiar with the process of (occasionally) drinking too much beer may recognise the psychological process at the heart of this story: that of a split between the sober and non-sober parts of the mind. I've actually just realised that this idea has been taken and developed further in the novel I've recently finished, The Intruders. *Anyway, this story was conceived for an anthology entitled* Chiaroscuro, *to feature fiction inspired by the school of painting of which Caravaggio is perhaps the best-known exponent, in which the interplay between light and dark areas is accentuated. The anthology never got published, sadly, but the odd thing was that at the time I'd also been trying to come up with an idea for a different book, based around the artwork of J. K. Potter. I'd had my picture for this propped up by the computer monitor for weeks, and eventually realised that 'Night Falls, Again' had been as much inspired by that picture as anything else . . . and so the story went there instead."*

Night Falls, Again
Michael Marshall Smith

I'm not thinking about where I'm going to sit. I'm not thinking about anything at all. No sir. Not me. My mind is a total blank. I'm just walking into a bar to have a drink, which is a perfectly reasonable ambition. People do it, all the time. Everywhere. That's what bars are for. For people to just walk into. People like me and you. Otherwise they wouldn't be there, on every street.

The bar in question is called Tony's and takes up most of a small block a little north of Duval Street. It's split roughly in half, in terms of area. You can hang inside amongst the dark wood and neon beer signs, planting your elbows on tables sticky with last night's margaritas; or there's a covered patio outside, with twisted vines overhead and a good view of the street and its passing mildlife. The tourists mainly opt for the outside—the Europeans, especially, who like the warmth. The locals head for the interior, where it's cooler. They can get heat anytime— plus the bar has televisions, so they can keep up to speed with the incessant burbling of the news and sports and the soaps. Especially the soaps. People sit there for hours on end, heads tilted back, mouths hanging open, drinking the fiction by the glass: not wanting to miss a moment in the lives of these shadow friends, the narratives of whose existence are barely more deranged than our own.

I steer a course through the tables outside, and head through the double-door portal to the interior. It's late afternoon and neither area is crowded. I could sit wherever I want. I've lived in Key West for nearly two years now, and so the heat is no big novelty to me either, but I decide that once I've sourced a drink I'll come sit with it outside. Inside is for night time, when it's dark. During the day you might as well be out in the light: while it's there; while it lasts. The only problem with the outside is the waitress service. They do their best and are cheery as all hell, but drinks can still be slow in arriving. I know that I shouldn't let the first one take too long. I don't want to get panicked. I'm not good with temptation when I'm panicky. Later on, outside will be great. I'll take up residence at a table with a view, and sip my drink, waiting patiently for the next one to arrive. I'll watch the people as they amble up and down the street, and make up half-stories about where they've come from: the families and the couples, the children growing tired and fractious, the oldsters holding hands. It'll be sedate and civilised and grown-up.

But for now, speed is of the essence.

I walk into the dim inner sanctum and walk straight up to the bar. A television is on stun directly above my head, two coifed ladies in tight sweaters accusing each other of fell deeds, the nature of which I can't make out. One of them has slept with the other's husband, or daughter, or is her long-lost neurologist, or something. The sound is loud and crackly, the picture an oversaturated bleed of interlacing. I've seen the show before but can't remember what it's called. Sometimes I'll let one or other of them welter in front of my eyes for a while, for old times' sake, but I begin to lose a grip on the difference between what I'm watching and what is real. I find myself expecting friends, people I haven't seen in a while, to pop up in the next scene. They never have,

but I'm not sure whether this is good or bad.

The two guys behind the bar are busy, but one nods to show he'll be with me real soon. I light a cigarette and lean back against the counter, still firmly not thinking. I scan the other customers instead, the husbands and wives, the girls and their guys. The day is unusually hot, and a few tourists have made it inside. Most have foreheads that are at least blushing; some look like they should be sitting in a burns unit. If you're not used to it, the breeze off the harbour will fool you. There'll be a few couples wincing in their hotel rooms tonight, carefully putting lotion on each other and making injured hissing sounds. Sleeping under the same sheet later on, but not getting any closer than that, musing that tomorrow they'll maybe buy a hat, and wishing they'd had the thought twenty-four hours previously.

After a minute or so I turn to check on progress, but the drink jockeys are still pouring and stirring. I have an impulse to just walk out, but it's only mild and I beat it down with little effort.

I notice that another man has entered the bar, and is now standing at the counter. I frown. I know the guy. At least, I think I do. It feels like I've seen him before, anyway. He's tall with ragged dark hair, and is dressed in a dark suit with a tie pulled down, the top button of his shirt undone. His shirt is also dark. I don't know what he thinks he's playing at. In Key West, for Christ's sake. In *summer*. There are places around here where you can dress like an advert in GQ if you really want to—in the *evenings*—but stand around looking like that in the afternoon and not only will you be hotter than hell but you're going to look like you've been up all night.

I watch the guy for a while, trying to work out where I know him from. At one point he sweeps his eyes around the counter, probably trying to work out how many are ahead of him in line for a drink. This gives me a better look at his face, but even that doesn't help. It isn't like I can think "Oh yeah, that's . . . oh, what's his name?", or "Doesn't he work in such and such a store?"

Just a face I know, in some context or other.

The bar people are still shaking cocktails but none of the contents has my name on it. I abruptly decide this isn't the place for me. Not today. It isn't working out. I turn and walk away from the counter. I'm going to go back out through the doors and out into the day. And that's when I get caught.

Between the inside and outside doors of Tony's there's a corridor about four feet deep. As I enter it, a bunch of tourists are already in place. An extended family, or a distended one: each looking as if they've had been unevenly but enthusiastically inflated with a pump. They start to move, then change their minds and return to the bill of fare, shipwrecked in Gap casuals, mired in space, worrying. Is this a *good* place, or are they going to get ripped off? Are they going to get *value*? Those extra couple of cents make all the difference, and never mind that in the search for value nirvana you waste irreplaceable hours of your life. My grandmother used to say that if you look after the cents then the dollars will look after themselves. This has a nice ring to it, but on the other hand Grandma's dead and has been for a long time, so it evidently didn't help her with the bigger things in life. She did leave behind a vast jar of small change, I'll admit. It added up to two hundred and eighty bucks, or about a hundred and fifty instances of not having quite what she wanted, but something slightly cheaper instead.

The point is, I got stuck. Tourists to the left of me, tourists to the right, a hot and frowning mass of indecision. I can't get past. If this hadn't happened, I would have just walked straight out and into the heat, turned right, walked across the patio and through the gate and into the street. There's a strong chance that I might have headed out to the harbour and drunk an ice tea; sitting watching the birds until people started to gather for the sunset, at which point I would have gone home and watched the tube or read a book or held something else in front of my eyes until they started to close. My mission in Tony's had been very specific. A single idea had been allowed to surface, and it was this I was following through. It's possible that . . . well, whatever. It doesn't happen that way. Instead, as I try to be polite about cutting my way through the blubbery mass in front of me, I happen to glance out onto the patio. To the left.

And I see her.

She's sitting at one of the tables outside, wearing a long white cotton skirt and a T-shirt that doesn't have a slogan on it. There's an empty seat opposite her. She has mid-length blond hair and skin which has been carefully sheltered from the sun, and she is exactly the person I most don't want to see.

I take a step back, using the tourists as a screen. My heart misfires, a spastic double-thud. I wait, hot and nervous enough to feel a little sick. Eventually the tourists move, like iron molecules in a bar stroked long enough that all of the magnetic poles finally started to point in the same direction. They decide against what's on offer, and go back out into the light.

I still don't move. For a moment I neither go outside, nor back the way I've come. I don't know what to do. Whichever way I turn seems bad. I've lost faith in being inside, but I don't want the woman to see me. I can't cope with her today. I'm just not in the mood.

I glance inside the bar. One of the barmen is putting a Manhattan in front of the man in the dark suit. The man lays some bills down on the counter, payment for it and against any future brethren it might have.

Outside, the woman is still without a drink. A waitress walks right by her, but she doesn't try to flag her down. She's settled in for the duration, and will wait until the staff deign to see her of their own volition. She's like that, I know. Willing to wait, marinating you in her displeasure until you're good and softened up, ready to be flash-fried.

That's harsh, in fact. She isn't like that often, and it's usually justified. Enough light is filtering down through the vines in the trellis to pick out the white and blond in her hair, like a fistful of pretty fibre optics. She looks beautiful, and far away. But not far enough. There's no other route out of the bar. I have to jump one way or the other, face one music or other.

I can't handle the woman.

I turn and go back inside. This time both barmen come to attention immediately, as if wondering what has taken me so long. I ask for what I want and I hand over the exact amount. I don't leave a wad on the bar. I'm not staying. I don't even sit on a stool, but drink slowly, standing up. I'm shaking, but only a little.

When half of the beer is inside me, I feel steadied enough to look around the room. The tourists are happily sipping and wincing. Two new women in sweaters are on television, baying two sides of some story editor's idea of trauma. The guy in the dark suit is still in place at the counter. As I watch, he pushes his pile of money toward the barmen in mute request. I turn away, still bothered about where I recognise him from. It's not like I think he's trouble, or that he sparks trepidation in me. It just bugs me, not remembering things. It's getting worse. Either that, or more selective.

When I'm halfway through my drink I go to the john. On the way back I glance out of the doors. The woman is still sitting out there, still waiting for a drink. Something big and fruity, probably, a non-drink that will take an age to wade through.

I walk bad-temperedly back to my position at the counter and start sipping again. On the screen above my head the voices crackle and spit, clichés put on pedestals by ominous musical stings. My drink gets finished. The barman hovers, waiting to see if I want another. I hold up my hand for him to wait a second, turn to peer out of the door. She's still out there, waiting. I turn back and nod.

I drink slowly for a while. Pretty slowly. Midway through the fourth beer I go to the john again. It's that way with me. Suddenly the alcohol starts trickling through my system like clockwork. You become a conduit, experience entering and leaving almost immediately, barely touching the sides. Afterwards I wash my hands with cold water and rub them over my face. I look in the mirror for a while. My hair looks a mess. But my eyes look a little better. Warmer inside.

Back at the bar, the other man is still drinking. Sometimes you'll be sitting in a place like Tony's and two of you will get talking, rationalising a lonesome task into sociability. Not this time. I don't want to talk to him. He doesn't want to talk to me. We aren't communicating. Don't need to. Everything's cool. It's fine all round. He just keeps ordering and being served, and by now I'm doing the same, though I'm settling up each time as if this is going to be the last. I still don't have a tab running. I'm still only there for a couple of quick ones. Until she goes.

Maybe an hour passes. It's late afternoon by now, but still sunny outside. Sunset is an hour or so away. The tidal movements in the street outside have started to run in both directions: some people on their way out to the harbour already, others going home to change first. I am dimly aware that I'm being stupid. Instead of standing in here with people who don't know me and don't care, I should go outside and get on with what's planned. It's childish, like breaking a toy instead of dutifully putting it away. It's been suggested that what I'm doing is a bad thing to do, and so naturally that means I have to do it. Reaction, instead of action. Always. Bits of you want different things, and it's so hard to tell which is right unless you're presented with something you know for damn sure that you don't want to do. Why is that, for God's sake? It shouldn't be that hard. It should be obvious what you want. If there's genuinely someone there inside you, some one person, then he or she *must* want something in particular, must have specific desires they wish to see realised. But you still hit that wall, locked in a doorless courtyard, caught in silence between two opposing shouts. Sometimes working out what you want is the most difficult thing in the world, and then you go ahead and get it wrong anyway.

The john and I are old friends by now. I've started muttering things to myself as I look in the mirror, in that way you do. Drawing yourself closer, mixing the strands together, stroking your own magnet. Telling myself I look okay, that I'll sort myself out. A kind of tension, enjoying standing there looking at my reflection because I know that when I go back out I have a drink sitting waiting for me. The comfort of short-term futures, of immanently satisfiable desires.

I come out again. Look through the open door. She's still waiting. She's patient, I'll give her that. Of course . . . maybe she shouldn't have been. Sometimes indulgence is not the greatest thing.

I creep a little nearer to the door this time, take a longer look. She too is watching the people as they walk in the street, her hands folded in her lap. Her nose, which I liked but which she thought too big, has finally caught a little sun. Her hair is pushed back and behind her ears. A drop of blood is running from above the hairline, down her temple. She puts her hand up to tuck a stray hair back, and the drop is smeared.

I go sat back on my stool—I have a stool by now—and signal for another beer.

Another couple drinks, and more time passes. Finally it just becomes stupid, and the man and I acknowledge each other. Upward nods of the head. That's the way it's done. When I finish my drink I raise my eyebrows at him. He nods, moves his stuff over. That's also the way that it's done. You have to invite them in.

"Same again," I tell the barman. "And one for my friend." Barman only brings one drink, but that's okay. The man in the suit already has one. We sit,

not talking, just watching the people with their beers and cigarettes, their smiles and plans. They have all become a little fuzzy now. I finish my pack of Marlboros, slide off the stool to buy more. Decide I might as well go to the john again, while I'm on my feet. Up and down, up and down: it's a tough life if you don't weaken. I caroom off the door frame on the way in, but that's okay. You expect to pay one way or another. Nobody saw.

Mirrors in bar toilets are always so dirty. They make you look ways that you're not. Sometimes better, mainly worse. Different, anyhow. Sometimes it's hard to recognise yourself. The face you see in front of you doesn't look like the one you're expecting. Just slightly familiar, and rather strange. It's like living in a house painted purple, when everything is white inside. You think: I wonder who lives in there? What is he like, and what does he want? And why is he wearing that suit?

I stumble back out again and take a look through the door, and she's still out there. Still sitting, so fucking stoic. A few lines running down the face now, tracks of vibrant red. One down each cheek. Coming down the forehead too, out of the hair line. The reddening on her nose is not from the sun, I realise. It's a graze. Blood is dripping off it onto the table, and down the front of her t-shirt.

What we could have done, of course, had she not been so obsessed with keeping up with The Young and the Brainless, was go out and have a couple drinks in the afternoon *together*. Do the sunset. *Together*. Go back, get changed. *Then* I would have been happy to go straight out to dinner. It just seemed a waste, that's all. A waste of what we'd come down for.

Stool. Raised hand. Another beer. I'm sensing that the barman is viewing me differently with each repetition of this cycle. It doesn't really matter, so long as he keeps doing his job. I've got a friend sitting next to me now. I'm an army of two. That's enough.

I didn't mean for it to happen. I just didn't want to be bossed around. I wanted to have a few drinks before we went out for the evening. We were due to have dinner with some people, locals we'd met at the harbour while watching fish in the bay. They lived twenty miles away, up on the next Key. They'd seemed nice enough, but a little wealthier than we were: and so I wore the only suit I'd brought with me and felt kind of an ass because it was so dark and formal and people don't dress like that around here. Our car was parked outside Tony's. She hadn't wanted to stop, didn't understand what I was so het up about. Looking back, I'm not sure that I do either. I was merely trying to maximise the vacation, fitting in stuff wherever we could. That was my thinking. I just thought it'd be fun to stop in for a couple of cocktails before we went to dinner. Start the evening right. She didn't want to. She thought it was rude. Probably it *was* rude. It's difficult to judge now. Being rude seems a very small issue. Like good value. Who cares?

Every drink is a coin in a dusty jar.

When I eventually came out, she left the remains of her fruity drink and got up. We didn't argue. We never did. We just did whatever I said. I'd had maybe five, six Sweet Manhattans. Large ones. I drove.

When I go to the john now I'm careful not to look in the mirror. I am feeling not bad but have reached the stage where thinking is difficult. Words don't seem to mean very much. Even the letters which make them up feel awkward and unformed, and have to be remembered one by one. The paper I got from the barman is getting wet and I'm running out, but I don't really want to ask him for more because he looked at me kind of weird last time and it's important he stays on my side. This ballpoint is shit too. And it's all a waste of time. I have told it a hundred times, to people and pads of paper and to a bird which sometimes comes and perches on the balcony outside the room I rent. Mary would have known what type it was. I don't. Instead of making more sense, everything means less and less each time. It doesn't work, the telling. Maybe I'll try it on the man in the suit. Maybe he can make it untrue.

I drove, that night. Into another car.

She's still sitting out there, but she'll be gone soon. Gone for a while. Someone blurry has taken the place opposite her. In fact, someone is sitting in her seat too. Mary's face is wholly red now, the back of her head broken open. Blood is spattering softly onto the floor through the slats of chair, out of bad places.

She is looking right at me.

It doesn't matter. The barman is my friend and will keep giving me what I need. He likes me now, I think: likes me very much. The man in the suit has gone, but not far. He came and sat on my stool with me.

Later I'll have to leave, but by then she'll have gone. For a while. She will stay away as long as I stay this way, and I can stay this way as long as I can find what I need, and pretend it's what I want.

Stay this way, stayaway, it's okay— and getting better. You don't have to wait until night falls. You can go find it, by yourself, at any time.

It's always dark somewhere.

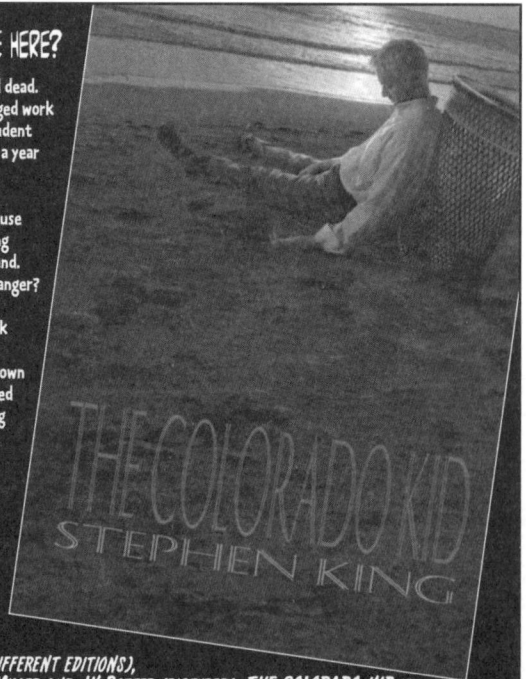

"This is a recent story, and concerns anxiety, I guess. As I've got older I've watched most of the people I know find their lives more and more plagued by this form of neurosis. Friends developing phobias, or finding aspects of everyday life harder to deal with, and my own tendency to follow habitual rather than chosen courses of behaviour. I believe the human mind is fundamentally flawed, over-clocked far past its native capacity and stumbling over the tasks we demand of it, and that anxiety is often a by-product of the countless little crashes that take place in it every day—the smoke rising from the overheating of our brains' beleaguered components. As a result we all end up with about the same amount of anxiety, and the only questions are how it manifests, what we attach it to, which coping strategies we develop—and how all may ultimately miss the target.

"I think this story is largely about that, along with the idea that the chaotic fates are out there waiting to get us, regardless of how we try to cheat them of their fun."

One One Three
Michael Marshall Smith

"**B**e careful," was all he said.

I was waiting for a train. I'd been up to Manchester for the day, and was standing at Piccadilly station for my ride home. I was surrounded by mid-afternoon crowds who were staring with intent supplication at boards designed to tell them where to go and at what time—or, more likely, how big a delay there would be before they could schlep to a different platform to that which had originally been implied. There were harassed women, a child hanging from each arm, bleating urgently about sweets. Young, pasty-faced couples, too, each wearing sweat pants and eating burgers that could be neither lunch nor an evening meal. Shaggy-haired antipodeans with unfeasibly large backpacks, exhausted by freedom. Men in suits, of course, guys like me—and other, less archetypal travellers, individuals going to and fro on impenetrable journeys. I stood in the middle of all this nursing a sub-Starbucks latté, nice and warm in my long coat, briefcase safely upright between my feet.

People moved restlessly all around me, fretting and chasing time, but I was the calm at the centre of their storm. I wanted my train's departure to be punctual because I had a further meeting back in London, but otherwise I was relaxed. I had a First Class seat reserved and so was confident of a comfortable journey back to civilisation. I had enough work to make the time pass quickly. The only mild inconvenience in prospect was something I'd grown used to, and which I could address right now. I pulled out my pack of Marlboro Lights. Two and a half hours is manageable interval between

27

cigarettes, for all except the most addicted—but a top-up never does any harm, and it passes the time.

So I stood a little longer, sipping a coffee which had marginally improved now I'd got down to the hazelnut, taking luxurious drags on my cigarette and feeling in reasonable accord with the world.

Aha—there we go: Platform 11.

Around me people were immediately in motion, scrambling toward the platform, ready to club their fellow humans to the ground for the chance at a table seat. I watched them indulgently, took a final pull on the cigarette, and then dropped it on the floor to step it out. I judged the weight of my coffee cup—there was enough left to make it worth bringing on the train, to tide me over until someone brought hot sludge in a china cup—and bent down to pick up my briefcase.

"Be careful," somebody said.

I looked up mildly, knowing I wasn't in anyone's way or in danger of spilling my coffee or anything else that required urgent remedial action. The speaker's tone had been confidential, and the information or advice he'd been seeking to impart was for me alone.

All I saw was the back of a man, disappearing into the melee coursing towards Platform 6. Dark coat, suit underneath, unremarkable brown hair above. I wasn't even sure it was him who had spoken, but I couldn't see any other candidate. It had been a male voice, certainly.

I turned around to check there was no trolley or other vehicle headed my way. No, just other travellers, darting this way and strolling that. No sign of anything that anyone—specifically me—might need warning about.

Odd, but hardly headline news. I started to make my way toward Platform 11. As an afterthought, and against my usual practice, I fumbled out an extra cigarette to smoke on the way.

When the train pulled out of the station I was looking out of the window. I have a habit of doing this at the start of rail journeys. There's something stirring about the gargantuan nature of railway architecture, a mythic emptiness that puts me in mind of the landscapes of dreams. I find it restful to sit and watch for a few minutes, tucking the past hours away and starting on the next section of the day. It was getting dark outside. The lights within the carriage were warm and muted, and the compartment was largely empty, another plus. I had my desired seat, number 3. It was at a one-each-side table, and the place opposite was empty—better still. I could hear the clank of a trolley heading up the aisle. Hot drinks were coming. All was well.

And yet I didn't feel comfortable.

I watched out of the window for longer than usual—ignoring the work ready on the table, sipping the first cup of coffee-coloured sludge but barely noticing it. I watched the city fall back and the countryside begin, waiting for restfulness. It failed to arrive.

Absurdly, the two words from back in

the station were working at me. I'd heard them clearly, almost as if they'd arisen within my own head. The man must have been right beside me when he spoke.

Be careful.

What had he meant? Wasn't that an odd thing to do—to speak, then move on without pausing to clarify or explain? It struck me I'd been smoking at the time. Maybe the man was wearing a new coat and was worried I'd catch it. Civilians can be very paranoid about that kind of thing, not realising that decades of practice make smokers pretty good at judging where the tip of a burning cigarette is at any given moment.

Perhaps that was all it had been: the unnecessary advice of an uptight man.

I accepted another cup of coffee from the steward and turned to my work. A thick proposal from the morning's meeting, and a thinner but slicker one from the afternoon. Both demanded considered attention. Between their laminated covers they held potentially life-changing courses of action, signposts leading to different and lucrative places. And yet . . .

Annoyingly, I couldn't seem to focus on them. I knew part of the problem. There used to be a time when you could smoke where the hell you liked. I can remember when you could light up on the Underground, for God's sake, and when walking into shops with a cigarette wasn't particularly frowned upon. Amazing really, and I don't mind it's not that way any longer. I can go a couple of hours without a cigarette.

Anyone can . . . so long *as you're not thinking about them.* The man's message had started me thinking about them. The idea works away at you like a little mental tapeworm, nibbling at your thoughts. But unless I was prepared to hop out of the train at the first stop (only about fifteen minutes away now) I was nicotineless until London. Getting out on platforms, even when it's not freezing cold, is far more stress than it's worth. You're never sure you won't suddenly hear a whistle and see the train pulling away, stranding you in the middle of nowhere without your briefcase. So you suck down half the cigarette and hop back on the train feeling nauseous and unsatisfied.

I clamped down firmly on the idea. Not going to happen. But then another thought occurred to me.

Maybe the man *had* been talking about my cigarette, in a different way. I was forty four years old. In my teens I'd cheerfully assumed I would give up smoking in my mid-twenties, by thirty at the latest. This hadn't happened. I looked after myself moderately well otherwise. Drank a lot of coffee, true, and the exercise regime I'd started on my fortieth birthday went through long fallow stretches. I watched what I ate, however, for the most part. A little too much wine, perhaps, especially recently—and for the last few months I'd also been eating out more than usual, and it's not always easy to avoid the pâté or the side dish of saffron-mashed potato.

Could *that* have been what he meant? Don't assume because you've done it with apparent impunity all these years—I'd never developed a smoker's cough, and remained reasonably fit—that it will always be this way? Possibly, I supposed. Odd thing to say to a stranger, but it could be something he simply felt very strongly about. Maybe he'd undergone a recent health scare himself. Or his chain-smoking mother had just died.

Or his wife. Louise wanted me to give up smoking. Never silent on the subject, she was becoming strident. This was having the opposite of the desired effect, naturally. With her hectoring and the background anxiety of my current circumstances, I was actually smoking more. I wouldn't normally have grabbed an extra last one before getting on a train, for example.

I stared out at dark shapes on the platform while the train sat in the first station stop. There would have been plenty of time for me to get off and have a cigarette, but by then I'd moved on to other thoughts. When the man had spoken I'd been drinking a latté, too, a big milky coffee with a shot of syrup. I liked them. But I'd already worked out, in an idle moment, that those shots added up to an extra meal's worth of calories each day. Never mind all the fat in the milk, as I kept forgetting to specify semi-skimmed. It was hard to believe the man had been warning me about this, of course, but perhaps he'd been referring to the combination? Coffee and a cigarette? Hardly meths and a crack pipe, but could you call it the businessman's equivalent? A lazy middle-aged diet, a constant drip-drip

of caffeine and nicotine that some day might just . . .

No of course you couldn't. Bloody stupid idea.

It would be worth cutting down on the cigarettes, though. And being stricter at sticking to salads in restaurants, and dropping the syrup in lattés. And why not take the weekend trousers off the exercise machine and start using it again? A new broom. A fresh start.

Excellent.

Satisfied, and with the train now pulling out of the station and into the next section of whooshing twilight, I finally bent forward to do some work.

Half an hour later I was becalmed once more. I'd now read the proposals. Both were very good. That was the problem. I'd travelled up expecting that one or other of the day's meetings would present me with a no-brainer. Far from it. I'd never seen two propositions so equally matched. I excel at that kind of decision, and often simply flip a mental coin. The inner voice always knows more than you, seems almost to be looking back at you present position from the future, with the benefit of hindsight. You just have to know how to listen to it.

I couldn't do that this time. It was too important. This wasn't just business. This was my life.

I've worked in advertising for a long time. Started in the '80s—still the heydays, so far as most of us are concerned. God, we had fun back then. Barely remember 1987 at all, in fact. During the next decade the wheat was sorted from the coke-addled chaff, and everything settled down. In this stern new millennium the business is as grimly corporate as everything else, especially if you've risen above the level of short-hair-and-marker-pens, and into senior account management. I didn't mind this for a while because the money's very good and you get to do the shouting, instead of being shouted at.

But in the last nine months I'd found myself restless. Missing the cut and thrust, the danger—stupid word, I know, it's not as if lives are at stake: but you try walking into an agency-critical client while carrying a left-field pitch (on which you've massively overspent) and tell me your nerves aren't on fire. Other areas of my life had unexpectedly woken up, and I wanted to feel that excitement during working hours too. And the money could be better. Louise and the boys had everything they needed, and we had an extremely nice house. But there are always those things that need just a little more. Those additional expenses. Especially now.

The proposals concerned setting up brand new agencies. Both were from up-and-coming Manchester firms who wanted to put a big foot down in London. They were predicated on me being the guy with the Vast Corner Office, bringing major clients with me. I knew I could pull this off. I've developed excellent relationships over the years. It was time to capitalise on them. But as I tried to reach a decision—one I could present to Louise for rubber-stamping, stepping over the general to the partic-

ulars—I found myself prey to an unusual degree of uncertainty. For a really stupid reason, too.

That man. The one in the station.

Be careful, he'd said.

He'd been dressed as a professional in some creative trade. Very similarly to me, in fact. It was a ludicrous idea, but what if he worked for one of my present company's clients, and had spotted me with the new boys at lunch? Or later, with the other crew, over coffee and cognacs in the Malmaison bar—which was, after all, just a hundred yards down the road from the train station? I knew my "boss" down in London well enough to know he was a sneaky son of a bitch. It was his one area of genuine competence. Was it even possible that he might have sent someone to *follow* me up here, to . . .

No, for Christ's sake. It was not. Come on, Robert. Easy, tiger. Let's not let things get out of hand.

I was just nervous about the idea of the new agency. That was all. Who wouldn't be? I'd hauled myself into a well-nigh impregnable position in my current company. Starting over was a huge risk, even as the main man/head honcho/big cheese. *Especially* as that, in fact. A family-sized risk, you could say. Louise sort-of had a job but didn't generate net income. Meanwhile we had two sons at public school, the middle-aged man's equivalent of a massive cocaine habit. Say I set up with either of the northern crews, bringing dealmaker clients with me, and eventually the whole thing went tits up. Both documents on the table had clearly-stated terms under which financial backing would be withdrawn.

What then? My old agency would have made an effigy of me, set fire to it, and sent it floating on a boat down the Thames. The word would have spread.

Shit creek/no paddle, bottom line.

I'd known this before, but suddenly it seemed a lot more real. Perhaps it was the prospect of making a decision after months of covert preparation. Or maybe it was the idea of talking to Louise about matters which had been floating safely around my head for some time. It's a scary moment when you rip dreams from the womb and trust them to take their first scream in the real world.

Or maybe it was . . . that *bloody man.*

I didn't seriously believe he was a spy sent from London. That was ridiculous. But maybe he'd just spotted in me another man of a certain age, a man of a particular type. Men with their first flecks of real grey, who find they want to mix it up a little, to reassure themselves this isn't all there is to life. Perhaps he'd merely wanted to send a gentle warning, to remind a fellow traveller that risk is not always good, nor change, and that it's worth remembering what you already have.

I shook my head firmly, irritated to find myself even considering this kind of nonsense. The movement inadvertently signalling the steward, who'd evidently been hovering behind me wondering whether I wanted more coffee. He walked off, taking the flask with him. This was annoying because I *did* want another cup.

Though . . . caffeine = bad, right? So let's start the cut-down tonight. And watching the food more carefully. And exercising. All that. Good plan. As discussed.

I grabbed the proposal on top and sat back to read it again from the beginning. I noticed that at some point in the last ten minutes I'd doodled something on the cover in ballpoint. A series of interlocked circles, and in the centre something that looked a little like two numeral 1s, and a 3. What, if anything, had I meant by that?

Christ, I wanted a cigarette.

And there was still an hour to go.

But there was something else working at me now.

I was getting closer to London, and my next meeting. It wasn't actually a "meeting", in the conventional sense. I was due to latch up with Jess for an hour, at the pub we used around the back of the station. Not a terribly romantic location . . . but actually, of course, that meant that it was. When you're having an affair—and after nine months, I now used the word without much qualm in my own head—you end up in the kind of places you normally wouldn't go. Because they're safest. Because they're a place the other person knows. Because they're there. The Swan was a grotty but nonetheless cosy pub in Riddick Street, a couple of turns from Euston station. The kind of place only locals know, with very little passing trade. Not in a million years would Louise happen to walk in, even assuming she still ever wanted to go to pubs, which she did not. Jessica's husband was likewise barred by the fact he worked over in the City, and they lived south of the river in Butler's Wharf. It was safe, a haven, secluded in the heart of a big city. We could hunker down in our double seat in the back near the fireplace, and do the kind of things people do when there isn't the time to go somewhere private.

Murmur, smile, and touch, reassuring each other that feelings remained as they did, that this small, secret fire still burned very bright.

The prospect of seeing Jess always made me a little jumpy. I'd been a faithful husband for twenty years. This had only changed because . . . well, a number of reasons. My age. The quiet cul-de-sac of prolonged marriage. A need for something which forced you to wake up and define yourself, to feel real and active once more, through the choices and decisions you make, the lies you have to tell. Jess was undeniably cute. Funny, too, and bright, and engaged with the world in a way Louise simply wasn't any more. I still loved my wife, very much. But Jess, in addition to being herself and valuable for that, was thirty. Nearly fifteen years younger than my wife. Yes, it makes a difference. Not just because of the younger body, as women always sourly assume: it's more that young women retain a vestige of openness and optimism, a belief that life is there for the finding, and fun for the taking. The confidence that comes with middle age can be an empowerment to a smug, dispiriting

cynicism, a jaded stasis. With someone younger, the universe—and you, personally—have not yet been found wanting.

Being with someone who finds things cool, and who has exciting plans that she doesn't yet realise will come to nothing, someone who doesn't always remember or bother to take her make-up off before bed . . . these things can be a reminder that you were that way yourself once too. Apart from the make-up part, naturally. It was a little disquieting to realise that a woman of thirty now counted as significantly younger than me, but time will do that to you, I suppose.

I was looking forward to seeing my particular woman of thirty. To offering her the drink she always chose, only to discover she'd randomly decided on something else. To sitting close with someone whose proximity affected me physically, to seeing her looking at me in that way she did. All this could last a maximum of an hour and fifteen minutes—Louise had invited the neighbours for dinner, and I had to be home on time. That was okay. Just as the grotty and nondescript can become romantic, snatched moments feel so much longer and deeper than those you can have every day, and for free.

But as I sat on the train, now less than half an hour from The Swan, the prospect seemed far more complicated. I'd managed to seal Jess in a box in my head. She was no keener than me on having the situation blow up in our faces. But regardless of how careful we were, the potential for disaster remained. Isn't that the point, on some level? The first kiss of an affair, that irreversible step: how dangerous it is. So why does it happen? Is it actually the sexual or emotional drives at work here, or are we drawn to the catastrophe-in-waiting itself? Is it this danger of breaking the world that gives the moment of first contact such stunning power—and if so, why? Is this what it takes to make us feel *alive* now? Are our adrenal glands so under-used in the modern world and middle age, left crying out for something to do, some crisis to respond to? Do we miss—from the harder, darker days of our species—the constant threat of the-end-of-it-all?

More to the point: did I personally want to run these risks? It made my life *so* complicated. Expensive, as well—a steady outlay of cash in out-of-the-way restaurants and discreet (and thus wildly expensive) hotels. I had to maintain two mobile phones, to avoid disclosure from the bills. There were other dangers, too. Louise and I texted each other on a regular basis. Only a few days before she'd noted how I'd always done a smiley one way— :-) —but had now started doing it differently— :D. I passed this off as a time economy.

In fact I'd picked it up from Jess.

It was trivial, but it rattled me. Disaster didn't have to come from Louise happening to glance through a restaurant window to see her husband holding another woman's hand. It could come insidiously, through an unremarkable sequence of small changes, from her unconsciously picking up disturbances in the ether.

I'd never thought of it this way before, that the end could come not with a bang but with a whimper. Suddenly the prospect scared me a great deal. I was good at dealing with crises. But slow breakdown? Entropy? A gradual emptiness coalescing between me and the woman I'd loved for half my life? Didn't I turn a degree away from her every time I did something she would hate to know about? When you put yourself first, aren't you always doing it at the expense of someone else?

In my case, at the expense of a woman who—I was oddly proud to realise—remained strong enough to simply not stand for it if she found out?

As I sat staring into space, feeling somewhat panicky, I realised I was clutching one of the agency proposals in my hands. We were on the outskirts of London already and I hadn't got anywhere with making the decision. I was feeling very stressed about the situation with Jess, too, the one thing which got me out of bed with a possibility of joy. What was going on in my head? Why was...

Abruptly I got it.

It was that fucking man again.

"Be careful," was all he'd said—and here I was telling myself to stop drinking coffee, and smoke less. Half-convincing myself he'd dropped a hint to warn me about screwing with my career, too. So what now? Did I also believe he was part of a covert relationship-monitoring team, the KGB of Clandestine Affairs? That he'd given

35

me a discreet prod to stop me risking everything on a woman who, if the truth was told, could be a little self-centred? Who had a husband at risk, but not a whole family? Who didn't always seem to remember when she could call, and when she could not—and who really didn't understand what a big deal it had been when the Sex Pistols sang *Anarchy In The UK*?

My heart was beating hard now, and I realised I was having something like a panic attack. I'd been effectively doing two jobs at once since I started putting the new potentials in place, and living two emotional lives too. Patiently enduring brain-dumps about Louise's day or endlessly helping Sam or Max with their homework, all the while knowing I was going to be late meeting Jess and that she wouldn't always hang around (but also that her being cross when we met often worked out just fine, actually a lot better than fine, if we could find somewhere private to prolong the discussion).

But where was that situation going? Was there *any* chance it was headed somewhere positive? And did either of the two companies up North give a damn about me, or were they just going to asset-strip me of clients and then throw me back out into the cold? Was the little doodle I'd made on one of the proposals supposed to warn me I was over-reaching myself, adding one and one and making three? I was now busting for a cigarette too, but would the one I lit after getting off this bloody train be that which finally flipped a switch in a cell deep in my lungs, trig-

gering the cancer which would kill me dead?

And then, far later than it should have done, an idea occurred to me. Something that could explain all of this.

This alleged man I'd seen, the one I believed had delivered a message so it had been like it came from my own head. A man who had been dressed like me, too . . .

Maybe he *was* me, eh?

Perhaps I'd delivered this message to *myself*, speaking within my own tired thoughts, and then selected a random commuter to pin it to. Perhaps there was a part of me which knew I was taking too many risks in too many areas at once, and was getting totally freaked out. A part that was saying:

Look Robert, be careful. You've only got one life. Don't fuck it up. Stop smoking. Stick with the perfectly good job you've already got. And with your very, very good wife. Be careful.

Just be careful, for Christ's sake.

I checked my watch. It was seventeen minutes past six. Jess would be in the pub already—she had been heading there straight from her work. I could call her on her mobile, tell her the train was delayed, that I wouldn't be able to see her tonight. Make this the start of down-sizing the relationship, gradually backing out of it for good. I'd miss her—I really would, and God knew I'd miss the sex—but it would be for the best. Excitement wasn't everything. And if I couldn't choose between the agencies up north, perhaps that was because there was no way of selecting between two methods of making the same mistake. So why not just go home tonight and have dinner with your nice wife and nice friends, and on Monday go back to work and stay on track?

And when I got off the train I could just *not have* that first cigarette, couldn't I? Buy some gum or patches right there in the station. It would be hard, but it was an option.

Wasn't it?

No, I thought. *I can't do that. Any of it.*

I put the phone back in my pocket. Whether this was a warning from my own mind or someone else, it remained the siren wail of middle years, withered advice from a soul which had started to flag, to lose heart, to look for safety at all costs. That wasn't who I was.

I could start exercising again, of course, but the occasional cigarette or coffee wasn't going to kill me. And yes, I could stick with my job and watch the halfwit who owned the company getting fatter on the proceeds of my hard work: or I could trust my feet to carry me to a future in which I sat in his place. And in a pub nearby was an attractive young woman, slim and wry and full of beans. She was waiting to hold my hand, for me to lean forward to bite her lip.

Did I *really* not want to be that man? Could I make that call and walk away forever from her smiling, upturned face, or from the prospect of a professional life under my own direction, from the tang of cigarette smoke on autumn air?

So I'd been warned, fair enough. And I'd thought about it, give me credit, thought about it hard. But now I was going to do what was right for *me*, the individual living my life.

Be careful of what? Of being alive?

No. Not me, bro. Thank you and goodnight.

I shoved the proposals in my briefcase. I'd flip the mental coin later, trust that inner voice.

I spent a minute in the carriage toilet brushing my teeth up to kissing standard, then sat and watched as the train pulled into the station. I enjoyed the feeling of it pulling me home but also into the future, relishing its invitation to make the most of everything. I had before. I always would.

When I got off the train, before I set off in the direction of a certain public house, I reached into my jacket and pulled out a cigarette. I lingered a moment, enjoying the taste of the smoke after I'd lit up, and the prospect of the next hour and the upcoming weeks.

Then I set off up the platform, smiling to myself. Yes, you can be careful.

Or you can have a life.

FATALITY NO. 113:

ROBERT JOHN MURRAY. *Killed on south side of main concourse during terrorist bombing of Euston Station at 18:28 on 24/11/2007. Identified from remains of wallet and mouth.*

꒯

"Feng Shui—at least as understood and dispensed by short-haired interior decorators and time-on-their-hands-householders—is utter nonsense. You heard it here first. By all means try to ensure that your sofa is not positioned on the edge of a precipice, but making sure the lid of the toilet is down does not, as claimed by a wife of my close acquaintance, stop money from flooding out of the house. What it does *do is ensure that the lid of the toilet is down, which—while a preferable state of affairs—doesn't tap into especially dark secrets of ancient wisdom.*

"Nonetheless there are unquestionably ways of arranging objects and living spaces which do (for reasons both obvious and obscure) make life seem a little easier. This story is, I suppose, a case of taking that idea to its illogical conclusion."

And A Place For Everything
Michael Marshall Smith

A t last, Metcalfe saw it. It was very *hard to concentrate by then, and the speck was very, very small. But in the end he spotted it, and knew where it should be.*

Careful not to alter his own position, he reached out to it.

The book on Feng Shui had not been the beginning; more the beginning of the end. He'd known for years that his environment, and the positioning of the objects within it, could affect his state of mind. He couldn't seem to settle if a room was untidy. The papers strewn on the table, the mug left on top of the television set, would impinge on his field of vision and affect his ability to work. He had to get up and move them. It was one of the reasons that he'd had to stop living with Susan. Her tendency to leave things where they dropped meant countless wasted minutes tidying up before he could get down to work. Not just work: he

couldn't relax properly either, unless everything was just right.

He'd come across the book by accident, browsing in a second hand bookshop off Charring Cross Road. Metcalfe had selected the volume at random, and had been inclined to dismiss it without another glance: Feng Shui, so far as he'd gathered, seemed largely a mechanism for charlatans to relieved the gullible middle classes of their money. But he soon saw he was holding no gaudy pamphlet, but a well-produced old book, and after perusing the text on the back cover he bought it and hurried home.

The ancient Chinese, he was reminded, had developed a science around the relative placing of natural land formations and man-made objects. Originally applied to the positioning of graves, it had come to be an all-encompassing system which issued guidelines on where best to place a house, or a business, and how to arrange furniture and other internal objects to best direct the flow of "ch'i"—The life force. Although he was not terribly convinced of the existence of a life force, Metcalfe quickly saw there were parallels between the habitual tidiness he'd developed, and the advice given in the book. A lot of it was common sense, of course, and possibly no more. A carefully-placed plant brought a corner into a room, a wind chime or mobile broke up empty space and seemed to bring the air to life. Some of the remedies, however, were less easy to discount. Metcalfe moved the position of his bed to bring it into better conjunction with the shape of the room and the location of the door, and immediately found that not only did he feel more at home in his rather bleak bedroom, but he seemed to sleep better too. He rearranged the furniture in the living room too, also working from guidelines in the book, and hung a mirror on the wall to counter the building opposite, the corner of which pointed aggressively through his window directly toward where he usually sat. He even made such changes as were possible to his office at work, and while the slightly eccentric layout caused some of the others to look at him oddly, they seemed to make the long days spent selling his time easier to bear.

The shaft of light coming through the window was obscured for a moment by a passing cloud, making the speck of dust harder to see. Metcalfe paused, waiting for it to come back into clear view again.

He'd quickly learnt all he could from the book, and outgrew it. He knew where it was—he knew the position of every object in the flat—but hadn't referred to it in weeks. It had been useful as a source of rough principles, but Metcalfe soon realised that close-enough wasn't sufficient. Although he was less distracted in his rearranged room, it wasn't perfect. Now the major objects were in the right places, and the disturbing influences from the outside world were deflected or absorbed, it became easier to see small imperfections that remained. His desk was in the correct position relative to the wall, and his armchair angled well in relation to the table, but while the books on the bookcase weren't right and the curtains slightly too long, the overall effect remained marred. Not only that, but while an ashtray could be positioned correctly so as not to jar with the table it rested on, it might be out of alignment with a mug on the desk. There was more than one level, more than one set of relationships.

It would have been easier if straight lines and consistent angles were involved, but they weren't. It was often, at least to start with, a matter of trial and error, distance and angle and bearing and height all having to be experimented with. Although Metcalfe found that he was now getting even less work done in the evenings, and that he was spending hours fine-tuning the positions of everything in his room, it was worth it. The new relations created a much better atmosphere, and he found himself feeling more and more relaxed,

less distracted, less prone to doubt and anxiety.

Leaving the house in the morning started to become difficult. Giving up the serenity and calm of his carefully arranged room, and having to undergo the jumbled chaos of the outside world, increasingly made him almost cry out in discomfort. Fighting the noise and unreason of London, of the office and its endless meaningless demands, eventually became too unpleasant to contemplate—and one morning Metcalfe simply failed to put himself through the trauma of leaving the front door. He didn't know if the office had ever tried to contact him. The phone's irregular shape had proved impossible to align satisfactorily with the rest of the objects in the room, and Metcalfe had thrown it away with little regret.

The sun came out from behind the cloud again, and he reached slowly towards the speck. It was very hard to move his arm now, and he could feel its correct position crying out to it, but he persevered, believing that the effort would be worth it.

The breakthrough had come less than a week ago. Sitting one evening in his armchair, facing across the room, Metcalfe had forced himself to concentrate. He knew that he still had more to do, but was finding it increasingly hard to puzzle out what it might be. The initial position he'd found for the desk, though an improvement, had turned out to be wrong. Now it stood on its

end, partially obscuring the door to the hall, and that was perfect. He could feel the correctness of that corner of the room, as he could of all the others. The pile in the carpet was brushed in the correct directions, and a thin white line he had drawn at a certain angle on one wall had been, he was sure, a conclusive touch. After painting it he'd had what he could only describe as a blackout: for half an hour he'd lost all sense of time and place, even of self. Everyday thoughts and worries had left him, and for that brief period it was almost as if he'd become simply an object.

Coming to, taking back his customary relationship to the world, had felt like an unwanted weight settling back onto his mind. It was while remembering this feeling that Metcalfe realized it was not enough simply to arrange objects in relation to each other. Harmony between them was most of the work, but not all. They were not the only things in the room. There was one more, and its positioning was just as important as the rest.

Carefully, Metcalfe wiped his finger on the carpet to pick up the speck of dust. As he moved his arm closer to where he knew the mote should go, he felt the proof of what was coming, the quiet joy of knowing he'd been right. He dropped the speck.

An easy thing to forget, his body. Thirty years of believing that the thing he lived in was somehow different, somehow special, had blinded him to its essential similarity to everything else in the world, all the other things that took up space. As he experimented over the following week, first finding his ideal position within the room, then readjusting other objects in line with the altered relationships this caused, he came to realise what a sham the body's individuality was.

As he fine-tuned, and got closer to the truth, it became harder and harder to think of himself as different, more difficult just to think, in fact. His mind relaxed, relinquished its accustomed difference to the outside world, and slowly felt its way towards dissolution.

If he could bring himself to believe it still important, he would have liked to tell someone what he'd discovered. That all things have a place, and that a man is just a thing.

Metcalfe watched with wonder as the speck fell into position, everything becoming white before his eyes. His breath slowed, the movement of his lungs and other organs ceasing to beat a rhythm. As the mote came to rest, he simply stopped, became still; merely one object among many, in an untidy room.

$\boxtimes$

Old Flame
Michael Marshall Smith

The day had finally given way, reached saturation point with heat and burst, leaving the evening cool. The only problem was that it was now gone eleven, and time to go to bed. And when it was time to get up again, it would be hot.

Susan shut the windows one by one, wishing she wasn't so paranoid and could take advantage of the slight breezes that might come during the night. But Mill Road was Mill Road. Of course she knew it wasn't really necessary, but when you're a girl alone in a flat at night the creaks of trees and clunks of central heating are quite enough if you *know* that's all they are.

The punitively expensive flat was the upper floor of a terrace house, with the landlord entrenched below. There was a double lock on the door at the bottom of the stairs which marked off her territory, and a lock on her bedroom door. Comfortingly secure. She smiled at herself. It wouldn't be so bad if it wasn't so bloody *quiet*: late at night the slightest noise leapt out of the silence, hard-edged and threatening.

After turning all the lights off, trying not to look at the desk at which not enough work had again been done, Susan retreated into her room and locked the door. Climbing into bed with her cup of tea she avoided the file on management accounting which was trying to catch her eye, and read a few pages of her novel instead. As Peter had always said, there was no point revising last thing at night: it simply wound her up and stopped her sleeping properly. Peter had been good at advice like that: it was a shame that he hadn't been better at not sleeping with girls who had longer legs than hers.

Stubbing her cigarette out in the ashtray on the bedside table, she put the packet next her novel, ready for tomorrow morning. Smoking wasn't the worst of Peter's habits, by any means, but it was still one she wished she hadn't picked up. For a moment she sat, turning the wheel on her lighter and watching the flame kick into tiny life. Click: flame. A present from Peter, a celebration of her collusion. Click: flame. The sound of wheel against flint was harsh, bitter in the silence.

Shoving all the bedclothes down to her feet, apart from the top sheet,

Susan flicked the light off and sank back, relaxing at last, glad that finally it was too late to be supposed to be working. Okay, she hadn't done nearly enough that evening, but now it was time for sleep, and there was no point feeling guilty. Tomorrow. She'd get it all done tomorrow.

At least tonight she genuinely felt drowsy. For the last couple of weeks as soon as Susan lay her head on the pillow her mind had suddenly surged into overdrive, not following thoughts so much as simply racing around her skull, swooping and diving, running on a repeating loop for what seemed like hours before belting off at a tangent towards another cycle. Not having another phone call from Peter had probably helped: despite his lies, his sweat smeared across someone else's face, he called her and talked about his unhappiness. Sometimes she had to talk aloud to herself afterwards, reminding herself that *he* had been the one who'd left.

Turning on her side, one hand flat in the cool beneath the pillow, Susan drew her legs up, mind and muscles already melting away. Tonight it was going to be okay.

M oments or minutes later she stirred from half sleep, noticing that her nose was wrinkled as if in distaste. Slowly the smell, which was pungent but not unpleasant, filtered far enough into her mind to be familiar. As her conscious mind slowly surfaced Susan tried to identify it more accurately but her mind seemed to slide away from the problem back towards sleep.

Then suddenly she was absolutely awake, with a clarity she seldom experienced during the day.

She'd heard a noise. A tiny noise: but it was very close.

It was in the room.

Her body still in foetal position on her left side, she slowly swiveled her eyes, her ears feeling like inch-wide holes, full of the sound of falling air.

The smell was stronger, its identity almost within reach. There was a tiny sound again.

As her eyes became slightly more accustomed to the darkness, she rotated them toward the end of the bed, crawling inch by inch. Just before they registered that the darkness was deeper there, her body ran like cold fluid and then froze again.

There was someone standing by her bed.

For a moment the inside of her head was the only place she knew, and it was very, very cold. Slowly her body came back to her through the pain in her clenched jaw, the tendons in her throat, the clench of her fists. And there was still someone there, just further along than her eyes could reach. There was someone by the bed.

A dip of the head, just one inch, would bring him within the range of her eyes, painfully screwed round as far as they would go. But that was an inch Susan had no intention of traveling. She didn't want to see what lay there, more than she'd ever not wanted anything in her life. More than she didn't want to hear a cold footstep behind her in a midnight alley, more than she'd not wanted Peter to continue after he'd told her there was something she ought to know: more, almost, than she wanted to live.

Petrol. The smell was petrol.

There was a tiny movement in the shadow at the edge of Susan's vision, enough to break the inertia of terror, the instinctual belief that becoming a piece of stone would somehow make it all go away. Behind the identification of the smell came another thought, a less concrete and substantial one.

He wants me to look at him. He wants me to see him.

A logic born of the knowledge that she was alone in the night, that there was no help for her anywhere in the world, grasped the thought and turned it round. He's not moving. He wants me to look at him. He *needs* me to look at him. Susan shut her eyes, and closed them tight.

Inside, the idea was gaining strength, the only leader among thoughts that wanted to flee. If she didn't look at him, maybe he would go away. If shredding her face or putting his hand through her throat was all he was after, he could have done it already. But she believed he needed her to look at him. It was part of why he was there. So she wouldn't look at him, and he would go away. Please God let him go away.

Susan knew terror was still in the wings, biding its time, and felt naked lying there, only a millimeter of flesh

and an inch of pivot away. He needs me to look at him, she thought, and I'm not doing that. And so far, I'm alive. What can I do now, what can I do that's *more*? He wants me to look: how can I do that even less?

It came almost immediately. She could turn away.

She could roll over in a ball until her back was towards him, until her head was between her eyes and him. Then she couldn't *possibly* see him. It wasn't a plan that made a huge amount of sense, but some protective instinct knew sense wasn't really the issue. When the mind could count the steps towards death, when it could see that it really was just over *there*, then "No" didn't mean anything anymore. All you could say was "Yes", and hope.

Slowly she gathered her body, feeling every part of it, and readied herself.

She felt the muscles in her back move as she slowly began to turn, bringing her cheek off the hot pillow, less than a millimeter at a time. She was asleep, she was in a coma. Look, she mimed, I'm turning over in my sleep. I have absolutely no idea you're there, and so you are not. You are alone, whoever you are.

As her face slowly turned, her body following, the smell of petrol got even stronger. She didn't know what it meant. Had he come by motorbike? Was the bike red, or black: was it tucked away by the wall outside? Where had he bought the petrol, were the notes he paid with crumpled or new? She didn't actually want to know. She didn't want him to be that real.

The more she turned, the more exposed she felt, a rising panic as she presented her stomach to him. Her eyes must now be facing him, she could almost feel him the other side of the lids.

Her body itched and crawled, begging for protection, a warning at least. *Open your eyes*, it said: *if it's going to happen, at least let me know, let me flinch*.

It was several minutes before she made it onto her back, and still the smell and the need: *look at me*.

She'd thought it would be easier after that, like going downhill, but it wasn't, and after a few seconds she just turned, quickly, onto her side. It's alright, she thought, people do that in their sleep. As soon as her cheek reached the pillow she braced herself, but there was no blow, no movement, only the smell of petrol and the feel of a very faint breeze from the window.

Having her back to him was very nasty too: despite the purpose of her maneuver Susan felt her eyes trying to crawl round her head. Her back felt a hundred yards wide and very flat: an expanse of pale wood waiting for an axe. But it must be working. The room was very, very quiet as she waited, praying.

Then very softly, a voice spoke. "Susan."

The voice was one she knew, soft, and hushed, with an intimate lilt as it called. "Susan."

A pause. "I'm going to set fire to myself."

Susan began to cry, and in the silence there came the sound of a rasping wheel, and then a click.

⬚

It is the year 2176. The world has survived a catastrophic 21st Century, emerging from oil depletion, climate change, and epidemic disease with a drastically reduced population. And in the United States, it's an election year.

Young Adam Hazzard lives in rural Athabaska, one of the sixty States of the Union. His hometown of Williams Ford is—or seems to be—safely distant from the conflicts of the day: an ongoing war with European powers for possession of Labrador and ever-simmering rivalries among the military, the civilian government, and the theocratic Church of the Dominion. But that illusion of safety is quickly coming to an end.

Adam has been befriended by Julian Comstock, a young aristocrat his own age, sent to Williams Ford by his family to protect him from the jealousy of the reigning President: his uncle Deklan. Adam, struggling to come to terms with Julian's religious apostasy and the near-forgotten truths he has discovered in an antique book called *The History of Mankind in Space*, faces a wrenching decision about his own future . . . and there is much more at stake than he realizes.

"I don't write non-fiction often. It seems to involve a very different set of skills, to require a mindset and style all of its own. Too often writers of excellent fiction lapse into jaunty, short-paragraphed and mawkish prose when confronted with the task of describing reality, and I'm no exception. I hope I've largely avoided it in this piece, however, in which everything is true. I wrote it a few years ago now, and have still never seen the man in question."

A London Story
Michael Marshall Smith

We had a tramp, once. A tramp of our very own.

I realise as I write those words that it's been a long time since I heard someone use the expression "tramp". People are "homeless" now: it is no longer a position in society but a condition, like illness, politicised and commodified and removed from the pantheon of elective ways of being. But the man I'm talking about wasn't homeless, literally or in archetype. He was a tramp, old skool, and he was ours. My wife and I didn't need to leave the house to confront edgy proof of the gulf between us and other residents of the neighbourhood. Our reminder was delivered right to our door, on a regular basis—like stopping going to the supermarket and using a home delivery service instead. It was all very modern and convenient.

It started like this. One weekday autumn afternoon about seven years ago, we were in the house going about our self-employed duties when the doorbell rang. My wife opened the door to find a gentleman of the road. He was wearing a battered suit, and his grey hair and beard had been cut in the fairly recent past. His face was ruddy but gave off an only mild aroma of alcohol. He was, nonetheless and without question, a tramp.

"Yes?" my wife said, in the eerily cut-glass accent she develops when confronted with the unexpected.

The man observed that the six by three feet rectangle of our so-called front garden was full of leaves, and asked if we'd like him to clear it. My wife, somewhat surprised, agreed to the notion.

He asked for and was given a brush, and made a decent job of tidying up the area. Having belatedly realised this was not done as a public service but in hope of remuneration, she gave him a couple of quid. He thanked her and toddled off down the road.

When we discussed it later, we decided this was a Good Thing: a man of reduced circumstances earning a crust not by sitting down by the tube station with his hand out, but patrolling the neighbourhood doing odd jobs. It appealed to our self-satisfied work ethic, and perhaps also to a smug liberal paternalism—here were two poles

47

reaching across a chasm of socio-economic difference and scratching each other's backs. We returned to our computers (worth a minimum of £1200 apiece) and got back on with our gilded lives, well pleased with our success at the sharp end of inequality.

Three weeks later he was back. Few leaves had fallen in the meantime, and our scrap of garden really didn't need clearing again. I explained this to the man—whose name, we were to discover in the fullness of time, was Brian. He held his ground cheerfully and asked if he could have a quid anyway—in a manner that was somehow different to begging.

I gave it to him, and he winked and wandered off.

A pattern established itself. If the garden needed tidying, he'd do it. If not, we'd give him a quid anyway. It was the same arrangement people have with domestic help, under which the cleaner gets paid even when the householders are on holiday. It's not the indentured employee's fault if the work isn't there. We would very occasionally spot Brian on the streets of Kentish Town, in the distance, but usually it was at our house—and we never spoke except in that environment.

As the year went on, Brian's visits gradually became more frequent: every two weeks, every ten days—and the question of doing the garden faded into memory. Sometimes he would be dishevelled and nearly incoherent; at others sober and fairly spruce. However drunk and down at heel, he was seldom anything but polite. At Christmas we let him clean up the garden even though it really didn't need it, and he affably accepted a mince pie, a cup of tea and a fiver. A few months later he appeared one morning with a small and battered wooden box. It looked like the kind of thing that rather average bottles of Port are packed in to make them look like a proper present. This, it transpired, was exactly what it was. Brian proudly revealed he had retrieved it from rubbish outside an off licence. He contrived to *sell* it to my bewildered wife, as a *bargain*, on the grounds that her husband would be able to turn it into an effective rat trap. No matter that, so far as we knew, there was no pressing rat problem in the area—and that if there were then we'd be yelping at the council about it, not running up Heath Robinson solutions from second-hand packaging materials. The price for the potential trap was two pounds, which—given that a quid had by now become Brian's well-established "turning up" fee—seemed very reasonable. Or acceptable. Or something. Either way, he got his money. And we, very briefly, owned a wooden box.

At least, I'd thought our ownership of it had been brief. I later discovered that the box was still in our possession three years later, my wife not having had the heart to throw it away.

Over those years Brian's visits became weekly, or more frequent still, and it became the case that we didn't always answer the door. The front step was visible from my study window—if I was careful, and skulked—and there would be occasions on which we'd decide Brian would go unpaid. At first this was because we just didn't have change, or the time for what was often a somewhat protracted dialogue: Brian had decided that if we weren't going to let him clear anything up, then he would earn his fee through conversation.

Or perhaps, I realise now, he just wanted to talk. His response to a failure to see him was that he would turn up again the next day. If we didn't open the door then, he would come back twenty four hours later—until he caught us visibly in, or we bowed under pressure and just opened the door to have it done with. In my case, occasionally, slightly bad-temperedly.

Sometimes the pattern became fractured; he would go two, three weeks without visiting, then turn up again a couple of days after being paid, expecting to be paid again. Sometimes, if his summons was unanswered, he would ring six or seven times, at five minute intervals, standing weaving outside the house. I would wait, cringing and hunched, until he went away.

After a time this began to sit a little sourly with us: he was not, after all, our responsibility. The fact that a ritual had been established—solely through his persistence—did not mean we were in his debt. This is what we told ourselves, anyway, though of course it felt otherwise—especially when something brought home the reality of our positions.

Once, for example, in exchange for his pound, he gave me a piece of advice.

If I wanted to see a good film, I should go see that *Gladiator* (which had just come out). Oh yes, I asked, without thinking, had he just seen it? No—he'd watched the trailers on the television. It looked very good. I should go and see it.

When he'd gone I remained in the doorway for a moment, berating myself for not realising (a) that London prices meant it was *inconceivable* he'd seen the film in a cinema; and (b) the managers of such places wouldn't welcome him even if Brian had decided it was a good way to blow over two months' worth of cash earned by pitching up at our door. People like Brian aren't welcome to buy nachos and sit in the second row. They smell sour, and behave unpredictably, and cannot be trusted to leave after one or even two or three screenings. They do not see films until they are on television, and probably rarely even then, slumped in the ash-covered chairs of day rooms in facilities I wouldn't even know where to find. They do not go to bars, restaurants or Starbucks either.

They live in the city without access to city things—except, of course, for the pollution and high prices and anomie and the selective blindness of the people who live there.

There was a period when things became subtly different. As part of a long chat with my wife—who was often better at listening to him than I—Brian revealed he would soon be leaving us. We'd realised it was unlikely that he actually lived on the streets, and he'd mentioned a hostel more than once.

He'd even written an address down for us, though we'd been unable to make out a single word of it, or even the number. Now he declared that he wouldn't be able to visit us much longer, because in a couple of months he'd be moving to Banbury.

We accepted the news with an odd mixture of emotions, half-way between relief and abandonment.

For the next year he mentioned the impending move every now and then, counting down the weeks until he went to Banbury. We probably answered the door a little more often as a result.

Then he stopped mentioning it, and still he came.

I opened the door one Spring morning, for example, half-expecting it to be him, a pound ready secreted in my hand. I was busy, and not really in the mood. He blindsided me immediately, as he sometimes did, by saying something wholly unexpected.

On this occasion it was: "What about that then, eh?"

"What about what?" I asked, and he pointed out he was wearing a new jacket. I hadn't noticed. Should I have done? Was it rude or uncaring of me not to spot this kind of thing; or was he, after all, simply a tramp who turned up periodically to extract a guilt levy from the two easiest touches in our road? We had already established he didn't visit anyone else in the neighbourhood. This was both because no-one else would have kept paying him, and also because he—and we too, by now—understood that there was a connection between us.

He was our tramp. We were his householders. That was the way it was.

I admired the jacket, and observed he'd had his hair cut as well—belatedly realising this was the kind of thing you say to a bright but very young child. He accepted the compliment with more grace than it had been given.

"Now then," he said, when this chit-chat was concluded, "I know you're going to give me a pound, but I'm going to ask you for three. I need it to get something."

Somewhat thrown by this matter-of-fact mention of the Turning Up Fee—which had never been explicitly recognised before—I scrabbled around for extra change, but genuinely only had another seventy pence. I gave him what I had and regretfully added that I was in the middle of lunch. I wasn't, of course. I'd finished a few minutes beforehand. I could have stood and listened to him for a while, but—what can I tell you? I just didn't want to.

He nodded, gave a wink which said he understood perfectly without necessarily condoning my attitude, and went away.

Six further months passed, in the usual fashion, and according to the well-established routine.

And then, less than a week after we'd been to view a new house half a mile away, and had decided to buy it, one morning Brian turned up.

He arrived earlier than was his custom and didn't seem himself. He wasn't drunk, especially. Mainly tired, and a little overwrought. He said he was leaving. For Banbury. That he just couldn't take London any more. Finally, he was going to Banbury.

By this time the Banbury relocation had acquired in my mind the flavour of a quest to some fantasy realm: the symbolic expression of a desire to move on to pastures new and better, to a land which no-one was sure was real, but where it was believed things would be different in a good way. (I have since been to Banbury, and realise this is not an entirely accurate description).

Something about Brian's manner convinced me this time, however, and I stood and talked with him for ten minutes, and I gave him four quid. He thanked me, and asked that I pass on his good wishes to my wife.

I promised I would, and we said goodbye. He vanished off around the corner.

He didn't come again. Ever.

Four weeks later, we moved house. In the four years since then I have never seen Brian on the streets of Kentish Town, or anywhere else. He has gone. Somewhere.

A couple of nights after the move, lying in bed in an unfamiliar room and house, it suddenly occurred to me to hope that his Banbury actually *was* real, not semi-mythical, and that he got there safely: and most of all that it hadn't been a euphemism for another place one can go when the world gets too much, that place from which there is no returning. I hope that I didn't just misjudge the whole episode, cocooned in comfort, swaddled in career stress and mundane anxiety. I hope he's really in Banbury now, or somewhere like it, and that the people there are better at listening, and that their front gardens need sweeping more often. I hope that if I ever find myself in Brian's position, people have more time for me than I did for him.

I hope he really meant he was going to Banbury.

🖂

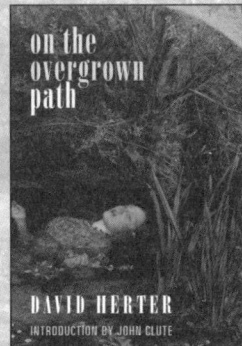

REMtemps™
Michael Marshall Smith

I got into it the same way as most people, I guess. By accident.

I was staying the night in Jacksonville, much as anything because I didn't have anywhere else to be. I arrived in town late and tired, pissed at winding up there again. It seemed like whenever I couldn't find a road to take me anywhere new, I wound up back in the city, like a yo-yo bouncing back to the hand that threw it away in the first place. I was planning on getting out of State the next day, and after my ride set me down I headed for the blocks round the bus station, where everything is cheaper. Last time I'd worked had been over a week ago, at a bar down near St Augustine. They didn't like the way I talked to the customers. I didn't care for their attitude towards pay and working conditions. It had been a short relationship.

I walked through the neon and cars, crawling kerb, until I found a place in my exalted price range. It went under the inspiring and evocative name of 'Pete's Rooms', and the guy behind the desk was wearing one of the worst shirts I've ever seen. I didn't ask him if he was Pete, but it seemed a fair assumption. The shirt looked like a painting of a road accident done by someone who had no talent, but an awful lot of paint to use up. A sign above the desk said the rate was twenty dollars a night, and that there was net access in every room.

Very reasonable. Extremely so, in fact—yet the shirt, unappealing though it was, looked like it had been made on purpose. Maybe I should have thought about that, but it was late and I couldn't be bothered.

The room was on the fourth floor and small. It wasn't as horrible as it could have been, but the air smelt like it had been there since before I was born. I pulled something to drink from my bag, and dragged the room's one tatty chair over to the window. Outside was a fire escape the rats were probably afraid of using, and below that just yellow lights and noise.

I leant out into humid night and watched people walking up and down the street, all looking for action of some kind. You see them in every big city, the mangy dogs trying to find a trail their instincts tell them must start around here someplace. I wished them well, but not with much hope or enthusiasm. I've tried most types of action, and they don't get you very far. Stealing physical possessions isn't as easy as it sounds, and they're always disappointingly heavy and difficult to sell. Drugs are either too dangerous or too organized. Ripping credit card numbers or running hacker scams can make money, but not much, and not for long. The Feds have the cash to ensure that the net runners they hire are better than those on the street. It's my opinion you're probably better off looking for regular work, but I've just never been very good at keeping it.

I stared out the window until the bottle was done, wondering where I was going next. It felt like everything had ground to a halt, as if I needed something pretty major to get my life started up again. It's felt that way before, but not quite so bleakly.

I was thirty five, with no money, no family, and all the prospects of a sand castle. It was the kind of situation that could get you down.

So I lay on the bed and fell asleep.

I woke up early the next morning, feeling strange. Tired. Spacey. Hollow-stomached, and as if someone had put little warm balls of crumpled paper inside my eyes. My watch said it was seven o'clock, which didn't make sense. Only time I see seven is when I've been awake straight through. Waking voluntarily at that time is unheard of.

Then I realised an alarm was going off, and turned my head slowly and carefully to see the console in the bedside table was flashing. 'Message' it said.

I screwed my eyes up tight and looked at it again. It still said I had a message. I rolled over to reach the keyboard and hit the RECEIVE button. The screen went blank for a moment, and then fed up some text.

'You could have earned $367.77 last night,' it read. 'If you're interested in learning more, come by 135 Highwater today. Quote reference PR43.'

I sat up, reached for a cigarette, squinting at the message. I'd never seen one like it before, and I've slept in a lot of different rooms, in motels all over the country. The amount mentioned was very specific, and it didn't take me long to remember that my room number was 43. Chances were the 'PR' stood for 'Pete's Rooms'.

Rather than just saying 'Earn $$$ fast', it seemed to be targeted directly at me.

Intriguing.

$367.77 is a lot of nights' bar work. I changed my shirt and left the hotel.

By the time I was nearing the address I was already losing interest. It was likely just a scam of some kind, and I'd done my time in the minor crime mines and I was still waiting for my Gold Card invitation. My head felt fuzzy and worn, as if I'd spent all night doing math in my sleep. A big part of me just wanted to score breakfast somewhere and go sit on a bus, watch the sun hazing across window panels until I was somewhere else.

But I didn't. I have a kind of shambling momentum, once I'm started. I followed the streets on the map, surprised to find myself getting closer to the business district. The kind of people who spam consoles in cheap hotels generally work out of holes in the wall. Highwater was a long road with a lot of big office buildings on either side, and when I found 135 I stood on the pavement for a moment, finishing the cigarette I knew they wouldn't let me have inside.

135 was a mountain of black plate glass with a revolving door at the bottom. Unlike many of the other buildings I'd passed, it didn't have videowall panels displaying with tiresome thoroughness the business and success of the people who toiled within. It just sat there, not giving anything away. The lobby was similarly uncommunicative, and likewise decked out all in black. It was like they'd acquired a job lot of the colour from somewhere and were eager to use it up. I walked across the marble floor to a desk at the far end, my heels tapping in the cool silence. A woman sat there in a pool of yellow light, looking at me with a raised eyebrow.

'Can I help you, Sir?' she asked, her tone making it clear she thought it was unlikely.

'I don't know. I was told to come here and quote a reference.'

Her face didn't light up, but she did reach to tap a button on her keyboard and turn her eyes toward the screen. 'And that is?'

'PR43.'

She scrolled down through some list for a while. 'Okay,' she said, eventually. 'Here's how it is. Your potential earnings for last night were $367.77, which is quite impressive.'

'Thank you.'

'You have two options. The first is I give you $171.39, and you go away with no further obligation. The second is that you take the elevator on the right and go up to the 34th floor, where Mr. Rabutni will meet with you presently.'

'And you arrive at the $171.39 how, exactly?'

'Your potential earnings less a twenty five dollar handling fee, divided by two and rounded up to the nearest cent.'

'How come I only get half the money?'

'Because you're not on contract. You go up and meet Mr. Rabutni, maybe that will change.'

'And in that case I get the full $367?'

She raised an eyebrow again. 'You're kind of smart, aren't you?'

The elevator was very pleasant. Tinted mirrors; quiet, leisurely. It spoke of money, and lots of it. Not much happened during the journey.

When the doors opened I found myself faced with a corridor done out in—you guessed it—black. Maybe the architect had been blind. A large chrome sign on the wall said 'REMtemps'. I walked the way the sign pointed and fetched up at another reception desk. The girl told me in turn to take a seat. I walked a couple paces from the desk, but didn't sit down. I hate sitting in receptions. I read somewhere it puts you in a subordinate position right off the bat. I'm great at the pre-hiring tactics—it's just a shame it goes to pieces soon afterwards.

'Mr. Stone, good morning.'

I turned to see a man in a sober suit standing behind me, hand held out. I stared at it for a moment, then shook it.

'You must be Mr. Rabutni. How'd you know my name?'

The man smiled. He looked just like anybody else, but more polished: as if he was a release standard human instead of the beta versions you normally see wandering around. His handshake was firm and dry.

'We ran a check on you. We need to know who we're dealing with before we hire them.'

'Yes, fine—but how? I paid cash at the hotel.'

Rabutni just smiled again. I guessed it didn't matter. They obviously had their methods.

I was shown into a small room off the main corridor. Mr. Rabutni sat behind a desk, and I lounged back in the other available chair.

'So what's the deal?' I asked, trying to sound relaxed. There was something about the guy opposite which put me on edge. He was charming, suave and obviously very rich. But behind the ever-present smile it was also clear he wasn't someone to fuck with. Plus there was the matter of how he'd been able to run a make on me without any credit card information. Maybe there'd been a video camera hidden in the elevator, and they'd used a frame-grab of my face. That implied he was wiring to some top-of-the-line information systems. I don't like people like that. They give people like me The Fear. We don't want to be known about. We just want to be left alone to scratch out our little lives in peace.

'Dreams,' he said.

'What about them?'

He leant forward and turned the console on the desk to face me. 'See if there's anything you recognize,' he said, and pressed a switch.

The console chittered and whirred for a moment, and flashed up 'PR43 @ 18/5/2015'. The screen bled to black, and then faded up again to show a corridor.

The camera—if that's what it was—walked forward along it a little way. Drab green walls trailed off into the distance. On the left hand side was another corridor. The camera turned—and showed that it was exactly the same. Going a little quicker now, it tramped that way for a while, before making another turn into yet another identical corridor. There didn't seem to be any shortage of corridors, or of new turnings to make. The floor went on for ever. The walls were featureless, and looked like they were made out of metal. Occasional chips in the paint relieved the monotonous olive, but other than that it just went on and on and on.

I looked up after five minutes to see Rabutni watching me.

'Ring any bells?' he said.

I shook my head. Rabutni made a note, and then typed something rapidly on the console's keyboard.

'The imagery of that one wasn't distinctive,' he said. 'I don't think the owner was very imaginative. And you lose a lot, of course, just getting the visual without the emotional content. Try this one instead.'

The image on the screen changed, and showed a pair of hands holding a piece of water. I know 'piece of water' doesn't make much sense, but that's what it looked like. The hands were nervously fondling the liquid, and a quiet male voice was relayed from the console's speaker.

'Oh, I don't know,' it said, doubtfully. 'About five? Six and a half, maybe?'

The hands put the water down on a shelf, and picked up another bit. This water was a little smaller.

The voice paused for a moment, then spoke more confidently. 'Definitely a two. Two and a third at most.'

The hands placed this second piece down on top of the first. The two bits of water didn't meld, but stayed separate. One hand moved out of sight and there was a different sound then, a soft metallic scraping.

That's when I got my first twitch of memory.

Rabutni noticed. 'Getting warmer?'

'Maybe,' I said, leaning to get a closer look at the console. The point of view had swiveled slightly, to show a battered filing cabinet. One of the drawers was open, and the hands were carefully picking up pieces of water—which I now saw were arrayed all around, in piles of differing sizes—and putting them one by one into different drop files. Every now and then the voice would swear to itself, take out one of the pieces of water and return it to a pile—not necessarily the one it had originally come from.

The hands started moving more and more quickly, putting water in, taking water out, and all the time there was this low background noise of the voice reciting different numbers. I stared at the screen, gradually losing awareness of the office around me and becoming absorbed. I forgot that Rabutni was even there, and it was largely to myself that I eventually spoke.

'Each of the pieces of water has a different value. Somewhere between one and twenty seven. Each drawer in the filing cabinet has to be filled with the same value of water, but no-one told him how to work out how much each piece is worth.'

The screen went blank, and I turned my head to see Rabutni grinning at me.

'You remember,' he said.

'That was the one just before I woke up. What the fuck's going on?' I reached unthinkingly into my pocket and pulled out a cigarette. Instead of shouting at me, Rabutni simply opened a drawer and pulled out an ashtray.

'We took a liberty last night,' he said. 'The proprietor of the hotel has an arrangement with us. We subsidize the cost of his rooms, and provide the consoles.'

'Why?'

'We always need new people. This is the best way of finding them. I'd like to offer you a job as a REMtemp.'

'You're going to have to unpack that for me.'

He did. At some length. This is the gist.

Five years ago, as I knew, someone had found a way of taking dreams out of people's heads in real time. The government wasn't keen on the idea, and it's still not strictly legal, but a covert industry was born. A device placed near the head of a sufficiently well-off client could keep an eye out for dreams of particular types, and—when they came— divert them out of the dreamer's unconscious mind and into an erasing device.

At first the main trade was in nightmares. After a while this changed, for two reasons. Nightmares don't happen very often, and clients balked at buying systems which would only help them out once every two or three months. They would only pay piece rate on a dream-by-dream basis, and the people who'd patented the technology wanted more return on their investment. Also, nightmares are generally giving you information you could do with knowing. They're giving you news. If you're scared crapless about something, there's a good reason for it.

So instead of nightmares the market shifted to anxiety dreams. Kind of like nightmares, but not usually as frightening, these are the dreams you get when you're stressed, or tired, or fretting about something. Often they consist of minute and complex tasks which the dreamer has to go through endlessly, often not really understanding what they're doing and constantly having to start again. Then just when you're starting to get a grip on what's going on, you get slid into something else, and the whole cycle starts again. These kind of dreams usually happen just after you've gone to sleep—in which case they'll fuck up your whole night—or in the couple of hours before waking. In either case you get up feeling tired and worn out, in no state to start a working day when it feels like you've already just been through one.

Anxiety dreams are much more frequent, and tend to affect precisely the kind of middle and high management executives who were the primary market for dream disposal. The guys who owned the technology changed their pitch, reprinted their brochures, and started making some serious money.

But there was a problem. It turned out that you couldn't just erase dreams after all. That wasn't the way it worked. Over the course of eighteen months the company started getting more and more complaints, and in the end they worked out what was going on.

When you erased a dream, all you destroyed was the imagery, the visuals which had played over the dreamer's inner eye. The substance of the dream, an intangible quality which seemed impossible to isolate, remained. The more dreams a client had removed, the more of this substance was left behind: invisible, indestructible, but carrying some kind of weight. It hung around in the room where the dream had been erased, and after a hundred or so deletions the room would become uninhabitable. It was like walking into a thunderstorm of subconscious impulses: absolutely silent, but impossible to bear. After a few weeks the dreams seemed to coalesce even further, making the air so thick that it became difficult to even enter the room at all.

Unfortunately, the kind of client who could afford dream therapy was exactly the type who was turned on by litigation. After the company had paid a few huge out-of-court settlements on bedrooms which were now impassable, they turned their minds to finding a way out of the problem. At first they tried diverting the dreams into storage data banks, instead of just erasing them. This didn't work either. Some of the dream still seeped out of the hard disks, regardless of how air-tight the casing. Also, dreams take up a phenomenal amount of storage space. Then finally it clicked. The problem was that the dreams weren't being used up.

They gave something else a try. A client's receiving machine was connected to a transmitter placed near the bed of a volunteer, and two anxiety dreams were successfully diverted from the mind of one to the other. The client woke up nicely rested, ready for another hard day in the money mines.

The volunteer had a shitty night of dull dreams he couldn't quite remember, but was paid for his troubles. No residue was left in the room. The dream was gone. Problem solved, and the cash started flowing again.

'And that's what you did to me last night?' I asked.

'Yes. And I think you'll be glad we did. People have varying ability to use up other people's dreams. Most can handle two a night without much difficulty, three at the most. They get up feeling ragged, and drag themselves through the day. Usually they only work every other night—but they still make eight, nine hundred dollars a week. You, on the other hand, are different.'

'How's that?'

'You took four dreams last night without breaking sweat. The two you've seen, and another two—one of which was so dull I can't bear to even watch just the visuals. You could probably have taken a couple more.'

'Nice to find something I'm good at.'

'That's what we're all looking for, Mr. Stone. I don't know why you can do this when other people can't, but it's rare. If you sign up with us, you could make a lot of money.'

'How much money?'

'We pay according to dream duration, with bonuses for especially complex or tedious ones. Last night you pulled down over three hundred dollars' worth—and that doesn't factor in a bonus for the dullest. In an average week, depending how often you worked, you could be earning somewhere between one and three thousand dollars.'

I coughed.

He closed the pitch. 'And we pay cash. Our business is still in a slightly unstable state with regard to legality, and we find it more convenient to disguise its true nature to some of the authorities. Paying cash is good for us. And, I assume, for you.'

I looked at him, biting the inside of my lower lip. Three thousand dollars is an *awful* lot of bar work.

'It's up to you,' he said, shrugging and smiling that smile.

It wasn't a difficult decision.

I signed a non-disclosure contract, and that's the way I spent the next two years. I was given a receiver with a REMtemps logo stamped on the side, and had it explained to me. Basically the deal was that I could go anywhere in the continental United States, so long as I kept the machine within six feet of my head while I was asleep. I didn't have to go to bed at any particular time, because the dreams booked to me were spooled into memory. When the device sensed I was in REM sleep it fed the backlog into my head. The next morning I'd wake up and check the device to see how much I'd earned. When I slept somewhere with a console I could connect it up to the device and my nightwork would appear on the screen like a list of email messages: how long the dreams were, when they started and finished, whether they qualified for bonus payment or were just hack work.

And at the bottom of the list, the good news. A figure in dollars.

Rabutni had been right about my capacity, and I found I could take six or seven dreams a night without much difficulty. Some days I'd be really groggy and find it difficult to concentrate on anything more complex than smoking, but when that happened I'd just take the following night off. After six months I was recalled to REMtemps' offices and asked if I'd like to volunteer for a higher proportion of bonus dreams. I said 'Hell, yes', and my earnings took another jump upwards. I set up accounts with a number of different banks, hired a street coder to write me a daemon which would keep the cash on the move so it was more difficult to trace, and concentrated on having fun during my waking hours.

It was a good life. I traveled from place to place, this time as a person with cash instead of some loser looking for a score. After a while it came to seem natural to wear expensive clothes, to head for the uptown hotels, to wonder which Gold Card to charge things to. I got used to the things that money also gets you, like respect, and a better class of bed companion. Every now and then the IRS or some other ratfinks would close in on one particular account, but I was making enough by then that I'd just cut the money loose and set up another stash somewhere else.

There were occasional downsides. The exhaustion which came after a night full of bonuses, or after a day chain-snorting cocaine to iron out the bumps. Being forever on the move, and never having a relationship which lasted longer than a few days. There were periods when I'd go a little wobbly, and I came to realise that was because I'd spent so many nights having other people's dreams that I hadn't had time for any of my own. When that happened I'd clock off for a week or so, let my mind catch up. Those periods were like holidays, a chance to catch up with what my own subconscious had been up to, and I came to kind of look forward to them.

But the problems were few and far between, and for the most part I was having exactly the kind of life I'd always dreamed of and never really believed I'd have. I'd found some action which was safe, which I was good at, and which paid big time money.

That should have been enough.

One morning I got a call from Rabutni. I was crashed out in a king-sized bed on the top floor of a hotel in New Orleans, the debris of a hard evening's pleasure spread all around me. I couldn't remember the name of the woman beside me, but she was a whiz at answering the phone. By the time I'd realized it was ringing she already had it up out of its cradle and by her ear.

When she passed it over to me I sat up, head foggy and full of half-remembered tasks and confusions. I suppressed the urge to look at the dream receiver to see how much I'd earned. From the way I felt I knew it was going to be considerable.

'Mr. Stone,' said that voice, and I instantly became more awake. I'd only been phoned by him once before, the time they pulled me in for promotion. 'Who was that who answered the phone?'

'I don't know,' I said. 'I mean, why? What difference?'

'I assume she's someone you've met 'recently'?'

'You could say that.' I glanced across the room to where the woman was standing. Candy, I think her name may have been. She seemed nice, and I was wondering whether she might be interested in hooking up with me for a while. At that moment she was making coffee. With no clothes on. I was hoping Rabutni would cut to the chase.

'When we're done I want you to get rid of her. Immediately.'

'*What?*'

'You met her last night, right? And she's in *your* hotel room. But she answered the phone after a single ring.'

'So?'

'She may be working for someone.'

I watched as she stirred just the right amount of sugar into my coffee. 'Don't talk crap.'

Candy winked at me and slipped into the john.

'Get rid of her, then come to the office. I have a proposal for you.'

The line went dead.

I got out of bed and put the device in my suitcase. The readout said I'd earned over a thousand dollars. Then I got dressed, and when Candy came back out, spruced and fresh and ready to play, I said I had to go out for a while.

She took it badly, and then well, and then badly again. She tried a lot of things to get me to stay. When it was clear that wasn't working, she said she'd hang out in the room and wait for me. For however long it took.

Call me someone with low self-esteem, but women don't usually behave that way after a single night in my company. It wasn't proof, but it was enough to make me gather my things and walk out the door, leaving her shouting after me. In the elevator I did what I'd been told to do in such circumstances, and pressed a button on the side of the dream receiver.

There was a soft 'crump' sound from within and the readout panel went black. The unit was now dead, logic board fused into inexplicability.

On the plane it occurred to me to wonder why—if Candy had been some kind of government agent—she hadn't just done whatever she needed to do while I was sleeping. If there was one thing a REMtemp was guaranteed to do most nights, it was catch some zeds. Maybe she'd needed to talk to me, get names or something. I couldn't work out what had been going on—if anything—and it didn't make much difference. I had to go back to the REMtemps office anyway, to pick up a replacement receiver.

I caught some breakfast before heading for REMtemps, sitting slumped over a table in an upmarket diner round the corner. I wondered how many bonus dreams I must have had to earn a thousand bucks, but couldn't get my mind to work well enough to figure it

out. It had to be a lot. Usually the fog faded to a soft confusion after a couple hours, but this morning it felt like I'd never slept in my whole life. I didn't want to meet with Rabutni until I felt together enough to cope.

A gallon of coffee and half a pack of cigarettes wired me to the point where I was ready to face him, and I left the diner and staggered into the big black building. The smile I got from the REMtemps receptionist was patronizing rather than respectful, but that's receptionists for you. I guess they'd probably look down their noses at the President if he happened by.

This time we didn't meet in a side office, but in Rabutni's own den. It was no bigger than your average football pitch, but luckily we sat at the same end so we didn't have to shout. I told him I'd done what he told me, and he smiled. I added that I'd fritzed the machine, also as per instructions, and that I'd need another one. He smiled again.

Then he pitched it to me.

He was pleased—very pleased—with the work I'd been doing. He did everything short of offering me a cigar. Though I didn't know it, a number of the company's most important clients now asked for me, apparently because I dreamed their dreams better than anyone else. Some REMtemps left little vestiges behind, elements personal to the dreamer which they couldn't assimilate. I got the whole lot, every little shadow and whisper. Hence the bonuses. Hence also the fact that he wanted to offer me a chance at a different—and more lucrative—line of work.

Memories.

As soon as he said the word I started shaking my head. Dreams were one thing. Though not exactly legal, they weren't a big deal. Kind of like smoking dope: every now and the cops would target someone, but most of the time they turned a blind eye. Probably a fifth of the Upper House was using REM-temps' services anyway. And smoking dope, for all I knew.

Memories were different. Though it had been known for a couple of years that they could be externalized in the same way as dreams, doing so was absolutely and completely illegal. Divesting people of their memories was very bad news for the authorities. For a start, it meant that polygraphs—which had been admissible as evidence for ten years—didn't work. If a suspect genuinely had no memory of committing a crime, fooling the polygraph was a breeze. In a way, it wasn't even deception: as far as the guy was concerned, the incident had just never happened.

Plus this: people are their memories. Pure and simple. What has happened to you is what you are. If you start taking bits of that away, you become a different person. If you remove the childhood incidents where someone learnt right from wrong, you end up with a guy who's kind of difficult to deal with. He doesn't have second thoughts about anything any more. He just doesn't care. Such people don't understand why they shouldn't steal, or rape, or murder—and that makes them better at it. And in the event they do get caught,

another memory dump just before the polygraph will blank that line of evidence straight away.

A test case eighteen months before had settled the issue. A freelance proxy dreamer who'd agreed to carry a criminal's memory of a certain incident was sentenced to two life terms—exactly half what the real culprit would have received had he been convicted.

In other words, memories weren't a trade you wanted to get involved in. I said as much to Rabutni.

He heard me out, and when I'd ground to a halt, he let a silence settle. When it had gone on long enough that it seemed like what I'd said had been to another person on some other day, he began.

'Yes,' he said. 'Memory temping is illegal—and rightly so. If it was legal the criminal justice system would fall apart, and none of us want that.'

'Good,' I said. 'That's settled then. Where do I pick up my new receiver?'

'However,' Rabutni continued, as if I'd said nothing at all, 'The kind of memories I'm referring to do not relate to criminal activities. I'm talking about little things, and only temporary transferals.'

'If they're that little, let the clients deal with them,' I suggested. 'And if they're only getting rid of the memory temporarily, tell them to take a valium instead. Or go out and get steaming drunk.'

'And miss out on a chance for us to make more money?' Rabutni asked, eyes ironically wide. 'I'm not just talking about the company either, Mr.

Stone. This new service is going to pay its employees *very* well.'

'The answer's still no.'

He kept looking at me, hands folded over one another on the desk in front of him. '*Exceedingly* well.'

'Nope, and no thank you. Also, no.'

'Ten thousand dollars a memory,' he said.

I stopped speaking before my mouth had even framed the next word.

He kept talking. 'And the memory can be a single instant, an individual fact. When the client base is built up you could earn a quarter million dollars every two months. All for holding memory fragments for no more than a week.'

He let that sink in for a while, and I thought about it. About pulling in seven figures a year. Wealth has a way of operating on a sliding scale. When you've bought all the things you can at your current level, you start noticing the things you still can't have. And start wanting them too. Or looked at another way: a couple more years' work and I'd never have to lift a synapse again. I could retire, fuck off down to Mexico and just do what the hell I liked.

'No,' I said. I knew where I was, and I was doing okay. Dreams were do-able. They faded. Though I'd never tried one, I suspected that memories didn't— even if they were only supposed to be temporary.

'I think you'll find the answer's 'yes',' Rabutni said, 'When you next ask me where you pick up your new receiver.'

My mind was still dulled from the night's work, and I didn't get what

he was driving at. 'Where *do* I pick it up?'

'Unless you accept my offer, you don't,' he said. 'You take memory work, or you're fired.'

'You're a fucker, aren't you,' I said.

His smile didn't waver, and I realized it wasn't a smile and never had been. 'I have heard that opinion expressed.'

I looked out the window, more to keep him waiting than any other reason. I wondered about Candy, whether she'd been paid by Rabutni. He would have known that I'd just woken up when he called, and that I'd be unable to judge properly after a night full of bonuses. Maybe he'd even set it up that way. Didn't make much difference. He had me, and he knew it. Without dreamwork I was back on the streets. I had money squirreled away, but not enough. Too much of it had been pissed away.

With the memory work I could buy my own bar, if it came to it.

'Okay,' I said.

In some ways, the work was pretty much the same. I could still go anywhere, do anything—though I took a lot more trouble to cover my tracks. I ditched my old credit cards, got some more under fake ids, and started shifting money out of the country. I was a lot more cautious about who I woke up next to. I worked maybe one, two nights on dreams, just to keep my hand in. Then a couple of times a week I'd get a call and be told to be somewhere secluded, with my new machine, at a particular time.

A tickle in the back of the mind, a momentary blackout, and then someone else's memory was mine. I kept it for an hour, a couple of days, a week at the most, and then a similar session would take it away again.

Most of the memories were straightforward. Once a week a woman would lose the fact she was married, so she'd feel less guilty about spending the afternoon with her lover. An executive would forget what his mother taught him about right and wrong, so as to make fucking over a colleague a little easier. Another woman would pass me a memory of being touched up by her dad when she was a kid, to make a Christmas spent with her folks more bearable.

Others were stranger.

Fragments, like a cat walking along a wall, jumping safely to the ground, and then turning a corner and disappearing. A girl's face, laughing. The sound of a stream gurgling past an open window in a bedroom at night. I never got any context, just those little pieces of remembrance, and had no way of working out why someone might pay ten k for a holiday from them.

It didn't matter. After the allotted time the client got them back, and they were gone from my head. I could remember what it was that I briefly had a memory of, but there was no confusion. I could tell, once it had gone, what was my experience and what had been someone else's.

It was kind of weird to spend an afternoon, once a week, convinced I could remember getting married to someone called David. But most of the memories were already used to being shunted to the side, and didn't really fuck me up. I could generally hem them in with enough self-awareness to cope with the truths they purported to tell. I don't know if there were any side effects. Maybe a few. I found myself getting tired more easily, and misbehaving less, but that could have been down to a number of factors. I was nearing forty, been traveling all my life. Maybe the time was coming when I needed to buy somewhere and settle down. But doing that would mean giving up the memory work, because a still target would be easy for the police to find. I knew what I did was harmless, but they'd be likely to see it another way. I didn't know if I was ready to stop earning yet, and I didn't know whether Rabutni would let me.

So I carried on, caretaking moments of other people's lives, and wishing that once in a while someone would lend me a *good* memory. I toyed with a little smack every now and then, just to dull the noise of other people's bad times in my head. I got occasional headaches. But for the most part it was okay, and if I needed a reason, I just watched the money flowing into my account. This went on for nearly a year.

Until about a month ago, in fact.

The guy's name was Chet Williams, and he was a regular client. Four or five times since I'd been doing memory work I'd held a particular one of his for a couple of days. The memory was of his mother, many years ago, when he was very small. He'd been standing in the back yard of the house where he grew up, a yard which faded into a small patch of forest. The day was hot and it was late afternoon, and little Chet had come out of the forest knowing it was going to be supper time soon.

Then suddenly there'd been a shadow over him, and he'd looked up to see his mom standing there, saying his name slowly and softly. She was a tall woman, thin, with a lot of reddish brown hair. In the memory Chet had looked slowly up until he'd found his mother's face. What he needed a break from every now and then was the expression he saw there. A look of fury, hate and disgust—mixed in with a little glee.

The memory always ended abruptly at that moment, and I don't know what the look meant, or what had happened afterwards. I'd always been kind of glad I didn't. Mr. Williams' memory was one of the ones I could understand someone wanting to get away from once in a while.

I came back from lounging round a hotel pool one morning to find I had an email message from an address I didn't recognize. Before I even read it I ran a check on the source. The domain code didn't set any alarm bells ringing with my software, but even so I got the console to hardcopy it without technically opening it.

The mail was from Mr. Williams. We'd never been in contact before—all transactions were brokered through REMtemps on a double-blind principle—and the only reason I even knew his name was because it was contained in the memory itself. The message said he wanted to meet with me. He had something he wanted me to carry, and he would make it worth my while.

I stared at the piece of paper for a few moments, then set fire to it and let it burn out in an ashtray. I spent the rest of the day round the pool, and the evening in a bar playing pool and talking shit with the locals.

When I got back I had another message. I went through the same procedure and found it was from Mr. Williams again. It sounded a little more desperate and listed a phone number. It also mentioned a figure.

One hundred thousand dollars.

I watched a movie on the in-house system for a while, but you know how it is. The back brain makes a decision instantly, and no matter how long you put it off, you know what you're going to do.

At about midnight I left the hotel room and went back to the bar. There was a phone box round the back, out of sight, and I called the number from the message.

A nervous-sounding man answered the phone. He took a while to settle down, and had me describe in detail the memory he usually left with me, to make sure I was who I said I was. Then he started sounding more confident, and told me what he wanted.

He had another memory, one which wasn't usually a problem. In fact, it was one of his favorites. Ten years ago he'd gone on vacation with a woman he'd just met, to some place on the beach he'd known for years. They stayed there for a while, hanging out, eating seafood, having a good time. Then he'd come back.

'That's it?' I asked.

'That's it,' he said. 'But now it's got a little more complicated.'

He'd recently met another woman. He liked her a lot. In fact, he was thinking of getting married to her. But before he asked the question, they were going to go away together, just to make sure. He wanted to go to the same town he'd taken the other woman all that time ago.

I still didn't see the problem, and said so. He said they had to go to this exact same place, because it was his favourite in all the world. But he didn't want to go back remembering what it had been like with the other woman, the one from a decade back. He thought it wouldn't be fair on the new one, that it might make him see things differently, screw things up. He really loved this new person, didn't want to take the risk of soiling what could be a make or break vacation.

Okay, I said. I could understand that: many clients had far weirder reasons for forgetting something for a while. In a way I sort of respected his attitude, and wished I had a woman who made me feel that serious. But why couldn't he go through the normal channels?

Because he wanted me, he said. I was the only person he'd used who could soak up every little bit of memory, blank it utterly, like it had never happened. He'd tried using other REMtemps on little things, as an experiment, and they

always left something—however tiny—behind.

I still didn't see why we were doing the cloak and dagger stuff. All he had to do was specify me when he booked the storage.

Then he told me.

He was going to be away for ten days.

Rabutni wouldn't accept a booking for more than seven days, I knew that. I suspected he was paying off someone in government somewhere. If they heard he was extending the time limit, all bets would be off. Also, the memory Mr. Williams wanted to leave wasn't a fragment. It was for the whole period, from the moment he and the other woman had got on the plane to when the vacation was over. A whole week.

No-one had ever tried anything remotely that long before.

I thought I was going to say no, but instead I found myself telling him the money wasn't enough. I would have to go on leave from REMtemps for a week and a half. If I wanted to I could earn a hundred in that time anyway, without risking pissing Rabutni off.

'Two hundred grand,' he said.

I thought for a moment.

'Two fifty,' he said.

'This means a lot to you, doesn't it?' I asked.

'It means everything.'

Three days later I sat in my room mid-afternoon and waited for the transmission. Williams had found some hacker with a lashed-up transmitter, who'd somehow been able to acquire the code of my receiver. I made a mental note to find some way of hinting to Rabutni, when this job was done, that the receivers weren't as impregnable as he thought. If he wasn't careful then the black market was going to start cutting into his business. Worse than that, memory temps could find themselves stuffed with all kinds of shit they weren't expecting or being paid for. The money for this job was already in my hands, however, and on its way to three different accounts.

We spoke on the phone and arranged a time for him to take the memory back. It was a different number to the one he'd originally given me: presumably the home of the freelance. Then I closed my eyes and got myself ready to receive.

It came moments afterwards. A pulse of noise and smell that filled my mind like the worst headache you've ever had, magnified a thousand fold.

I grunted, unable even to shout, and pitched forward out of the chair onto the carpet, hands and legs going into spasm. I seemed to go deaf and partly blind for a time, but that was the least of my problems.

I thought I was going to die.

After a few minutes the shaking lessened—enough that I could crawl to the bedside table and grab a cigarette. I hauled myself up onto the bed and lay face down, waiting for the pain to go away.

It started to, eventually. Half an hour later I was sitting up and drinking, which helped. My sight was clearing and I could now hear once more the sound of people horsing around by the pool down below my window. I still felt like shit, but had started to believe I was going to be alright.

I just hadn't really considered the difference between getting a quick, single fragment of someone's life, and taking over a week's worth of experience in one hit. The brain is designed to accept life piece-meal, moment by moment—not to get a week full of sounds, sights, feelings and tactile impressions condensed into a single bullet of remembrance. If I hadn't already spent years exercising my mind I'd probably have been slumped in a corner, drooling and staring into nothingness.

As it was my head was still humming and thudding, trying to wade through what it had received, to sort it into chronology and types. I could feel countless threads of sensory information squirming over each other like worms, trying to find some kind of order. Sunburn on my shoulder; salt on my lips from a Margarita; someone else's tongue in my mouth; a flash of sunlight on a car window; the sound of water rolling up sand; coolness; a shout. A thousand sentences all at once, some of them leaving my head, others coming in. My brain was lurching under the weight, miss-firing like a heart on the verge of arrest.

I reached unsteadily for the phone. Large amounts of room service was what was on my mind, but first I had to call Williams and let him know the transmission had gone okay. I'm professional about these things.

I dialed the number and waited as it

rang, holding the cold glass of my drink up against my forehead and panting slightly. There was no answer. I tapped the pips and redialed. This time I gave it thirty rings, before putting the phone back again.

I knew he wasn't going away for two days, so it was no big deal. Probably he was out, making arrangements—or maybe he'd gone home. By then it was forty minutes since the dump.

I munched slowly through a burger delivered by an offensively self-confident bellboy, keeping half an eye on what was going on in my head. It felt like a hard drive running optimization software, without enough slack to swap all the data around. I seemed to be having real trouble ordering the mass of impressions which I'd been given. Bits from the start of Williams' golden holiday were lodging into place, but parts were still missing, making the recollection hazy and fragmented.

When I was done with the food I called the number again. I let it ring for a long time and was about to put it down when someone answered.

'Mr. Williams,' I said.

'Hello,' said a voice I didn't recognize. 'Who is this?' There was a weird sound in the background.

'It's Mr. Stone,' I answered, slightly taken aback. 'Is Mr. Williams there?'

'How the fuck do you expect me to know, dickweed?' snarled the voice, and the connection was severed.

Sudden very bad feeling.

I tried the number again, immediately. No answer.

Then I called the operator. She told me there was no fault on the line but wouldn't give me the address.

I called the guy who'd set up my account daemon. He said he could check some sources and would call me back. I stumbled around the room for ten minutes, gobbling weapons grade aspirin like candy.

The phone call came. The number was from a booth in the first class departure lounge of Miami airport.

I called the other number I had for Williams. The line was dead.

Then I blacked out.

It had been really hot that week, the rare breeze as welcome as the brush of cool, slim fingers across your neck. It was clear he had been happy, and excited, but I was still surprised at how much he remembered. Conversations, her laugh, the smell of the sea through the window she insisted on keeping open in the car despite the fact the air-conditioning was on. The sound of the back of her thighs squeaking across the hot car seat. Some old song playing on the car radio, and hands tapping against the steering wheel in ragged time.

That's the bit I return to, when I can. The very beginning.

When I came to after the blackout, the first couple of hours of the memory were more or less in order. The woman was in her mid-twenties, thin, with long black hair. From the moment the plane landed, and all the way through the drive to the hotel, you could feel the joy coming off her in waves. When the car turned into the drive of the motel she squealed, like she'd never seen the sea before. You knew that everything she ever experienced would be like that, time after time: a constant surprise, a discovering. Her name was Naomi.

There were a few moments which seemed two dimensional, but whether that was because my brain was still unsure of them or it was just the vagaries of memory I couldn't tell. The rest of the memory unraveled into a white noise of data my mind was still trying to process.

I spent ten minutes in the bathroom wiping off the blood which had tipped out of my nose as I lay passed out on the hotel room floor. Then I checked out and drove up to Miami, where I bullied and lied flight registers out of the airlines. Williams wasn't listed on any of them.

I traced the first number Williams gave me, flew to Gainesville and kicked the door down.

The house was empty, unfurnished—the cupboards and wardrobe bare. The phone sat in the middle of the floor. It was obvious no-one had lived there in a while because there was no food anywhere and no sheets on the bed so you couldn't lie down and rest your head.

Three days had passed by then, and the first half of Williams' memory was in order in my mind. Even through the haze of a headache no amount of Tylenol would budge, I came to look forward to remembering more about what they'd done. I envied Williams the time he'd had with Naomi, could

understand how she'd be difficult to forget.

Another week went by. I'm not sure where I was during that time. I wrote some of it down in a book but I didn't put enough letters in some of the words, and then I forgot where I'd put the book. Williams didn't come back.

After two weeks I went to Rabutni.

I had to. I'd tried going back to work, because I knew I couldn't keep stalling him forever: but a normal, fragment memory job left me unconscious for twelve hours. When I woke up I couldn't even order room service because I'd forgotten a whole slew of new words. They're still gone. I don't know whether they just got overwritten, or if part of my brain simply blew out. Probably the latter, because one of my hands shakes a lot of the time now. Rabutni let me trace back through the records to find who'd fed me the memories of a young boy confronted by his mother in a back yard. Williams didn't seem to be his real name, and no, he didn't live where he said he did.

Then Rabutni fired me.

Most days I drive around, up and down, trying to find the town where they went ten years ago. Twice I've thought I've found it. I know it's somewhere on the West Coast of Florida, but that's an awfully long stretch of beach, with lots of people and places. It could take me all year at this rate. The headaches get worse and worse, and I keep losing things. Ways of using words, to say things like 'Look,

there is a boat' or something. It comes and goes like the water you find at the edge of land, but in general it's getting worse. I'm too full, I suppose, or something happened when the bullet hit my brain.

Oh, and the man I'd hired to hide my money hid it from me too. He thieved it from me. I know because one day when I could think pretty well I went into a bank and they said they had no accounts there under any of my names, none at all, not even little ones.

I think Naomi would have liked me too. I'm not trying to find the town because I think Williams or whatever his name is will be there. I'm looking for something else. Why I want to find it I don't know, because it's too late.

Maybe somewhere in the world is Mr. Chet and his new lady wife friend and they're having fun and still walking in the sand somewhere by big water. I hope so, even though he has been very bad to me, and not just to me. Of course it's a maybe that the memory he gave to me wasn't even his in the first place, but someone did the same to him. And maybe back and then back again until they'll never find who went on their holidays with Naomi.

Very slowly the rest of it moves into position. At the end of the memory everything is dark and loud, and what takes place happens on a bit of beach hidden round a corner and out of sight, in the night time.

There's blood everywhere and he buried her where people would never see her again. But if anyone can, I can. I am him now. I was there.

Maybe I can find her and say sorry.

◩

"This is a chapter from my upcoming novel, coming from Harper UK in April and Morrow in August. As both of my loyal readers will know, the last three novels have been published under the name "Michael Marshall" and have—very largely—been based in consensual reality. I greatly enjoyed writing the Ward Hopkins novels, and hope they take up worthwhile space on the planet. I've for a long time wished, however, to broker some kind of deal between the kind of thing I write about in my short fiction, and the material of the novels. The Intruders represents a first step in that direction.

"This chapter, which does not come at the beginning of the book, introduces one of the main characters. It's set in Cannon Beach, in Oregon, one of my favourite places in the world—though in reality, a lot of it is inspired by Crescent Beach in Florida, somewhere I often went with my family as a child. Both have very happy associations, and yet from this starting point, Madison's life is about to get very dark and complicated. That, I suppose, is the writer's strange gift—the power to dispense from a box full of shadows.

"Hopefully, sometimes, there are good things to be found in the box too."

(Further biblio- and biographical information on Mike can be found at www.michaelmarshallsmith.com.)

The Intruders

Michael Marshall Smith

A beach on the Pacific coast, a seemingly endless stretch of sand: almost white by day but now turning sallow-grey and matt in the fading light. The afternoon's few footprints have been washed away, in one of nature's many patient acts of erasure. In summer kids from inland spend the weekends here, gleaming in the sun of uncomplicated youth and pumping default-value music out of baby speakers. They are almost never picked off by sharpshooters, sadly, but go on to have happy and unfulfilled lives making too much noise all over the planet. On a Thursday a long way out of season the beach is left undisturbed but for the busy teams of sandpipers who skitter up and down at the waterline, legs scissoring like those of cheerful mechanical toys. They have concluded the day's business and flown to bed, leaving the beach quiet and still.

Half a mile up the coast is the small and bespoke seaside town of Cannon Beach, with its short run of discreet hotels, but here most of the buildings are modest holiday homes, none more than two storeys high and each a decent distance from their neighbour. Some are squat white oblongs in need of re-plastering, others more adventurous arrangements of wooden octagonal structures. All have weathered walkways leading over the scrubby dune, down to the sand. It is November now and almost all these buildings are dark, the smell of tan lotion and candle wax sealed in to await future vacations, to welcome parents who each time glumly spy a little more grey in these unfamiliar mirrors, and children who stand a little taller and a little farther from the adults who were once the centre of their lives.

There has been no precipitation for two days—very rare for Oregon at this time of year—but this evening a thick knot of cloud is coalescing out to sea, like a drop of ink spreading in water. It will take an hour or two to make landfall, where it will turn the shadows rich blue-black and strip the air with relentless rain.

In the meantime a girl is sitting on the sand, down at the tide line.

Her watch said it was twenty-five minutes before six, which was okay. When it was fifteen minutes before six she had to go home, well not home exactly, but the cottage. Dad always called it the beach house but Mom always said the cottage, and as Dad was not here it was obviously the cottage this time. Dad not being here made a number of other differences, one of which Madison was currently considering.

When they came to spend a week at the beach most days were exactly the same. They would drive up to Cannon Beach to have a look around the galleries (once), to get groceries from the market (twice), and see if there was maybe something cool in Geppetto's Toy Shoppe (as often as Madison would make it happen, three times was the record). Otherwise they just lived on the sands. They got up early and walked along the beach, then back again. The day was spent sitting and swimming and playing—with a break midday in the cottage for sandwiches and to cool down—and then around five o'clock a long walk again, in the opposite direction to the morning. The early walk was just for waking up, filling sleepy heads with light. At the end of the afternoon it was all about shells—and sand dollars in particular. Though it was mom who liked them the most (she had saved all the ones they'd ever found, in a cigar box back at home) the three of them looked together, a family with one ambulatory goal. After the walk everyone showered and there were nachos and bean dip and frosted glasses of Tropical Punch Kool-Aid in the beach house and then they'd drive out for dinner to Pacific Cowgirls in Cannon Beach, which had fishermen's nets on the walls and breaded shrimp with cocktail sauce and waiters who called you ma'am even if you were small.

But when Madison and her mom had arrived yesterday they had been sailing under different colours. It was the wrong time of year, and cold. They unpacked in silence and dutifully walked up the beach a little way, but though her mother's eyes appeared to be on the tideline Madison didn't see her bend down once, even for a quartz pebble that was flushed rose pink at one end and which she'd normally have had like a shot. When they got back Maddy managed to find some Kool-Aid from last time in the cupboard but her mom had not remembered to buy Doritos or anything else. Madison had started to protest but saw how slowly her mom was moving and so she stopped. Cowgirls was closed for winter renovations so they went somewhere else and sat by a window in a big empty room overlooking a dark sea under flat grey clouds. She had spaghetti, which was okay, but not what you had at the beach.

That morning it had started out freezing and they had barely walked at all. Mom spent the morning near the bottom of the walkway over the dunes, huddled in a blanket, wearing dark glasses and holding a book. Mid-afternoon she went back inside, telling Madison it was all right for her to stay out but she had to remain within forty yards of the cottage.

This was okay for a while, even kind of fun to have the beach to herself. She didn't go into the sea. Though she had enjoyed this in the past, for the last couple of years she had found herself slightly wary of large bodies of water, even when it wasn't this cold. She built and refined a castle instead, which was fun. She dug as deep a hole as she was able.

But when it came close to five o'clock her feet started itching. She stood up, sat down. Played a little longer, though the game was getting old. It was bad enough skipping the walk in the morning, but not doing it now was really weird. The walking was important. It must be. Or why else did they always do it?

In the end she walked down to the surf alone and stood irresolute for a few moments. The beach remained deserted in both directions, the sky low and heavy and grey and the air getting cool. She waited as the first strong breeze came running ahead of the storm, worrying at the leg of her shorts and buzzing it against her leg. She waited, looking up at the dunes at the point where it hid the cottage, just over the other side.

Her mother did not appear.

She started slowly. She walked forty yards to the right, using the length of a big stride as a rough guide. It felt strange. She immediately turned around and walked back to where she'd started, and then another forty yards. This double length almost felt like walking, nearly reached the point where you forgot you were supposed to be going anywhere—because you weren't—and instead it became just the wet rustle of waves in your ears and the blur of your feet swishing in and out of view as your eyes picked over shapes and colours between the curling water and the hard, wet sand.

And so she did it again, and again. Kept doing it until the two turning points were just like odd, curved steps. Trying to make the waves sound like they always had. Trying not to imagine where they would eat tonight, and how little they would talk. Trying not to . . .

Then she stopped. Slowly she bent down, hand outstretched. She picked something out of the collage of seaweed, driftwood fragments, battered homes of dead sea-dwellers. Held it up to her face, scarcely believing.

She had found an almost complete sand dollar.

It was small, admittedly, not much bigger than a quarter. It had a couple of dinks around the edges. It was a grottier grey than most, and stained green on one side. But it would count. Would have counted, that is, if things were counting as normal. Things were not.

What should have been a moment of jubilation felt heavy and dull. She realized the thing she held in her hand might as well be as big as a dinner plate and have no chips in it at all. It could be dry, sandy-golden and perfect like the ones you saw for sale in stores. It wouldn't matter.

Madison sat down suddenly and stared at the flat shell in her hand. She made a gentle fist around it, then looked out at the sea.

She was still sitting there ten minutes later when she heard a noise. A *whapping* sound, as if a large bird was flying up the tide line towards her, long black wings slowly beating. Madison turned her head.

A man was standing on the beach.

He was about thirty feet away. He was tall and the noise was the sound of his black coat flapping in cold winds from a storm now boiling across the sky like a purple-black second sea. The man was motionless, hands pushed deep in the pockets of his coat. What low light made its way through the cloud was behind him, and you could not see his face. Madison knew immediately the man was looking at her, however. Why else would he be standing there, like a scarecrow made of shadows, dressed

not for the beach but for church or the cemetery?

She glanced casually back over her shoulder, logging her position in relation to the cottage's walkway. It was not directly behind, but it was close enough. She could get there quickly. Maybe that would be a good idea, especially as the big hand was at quarter to.

But instead she turned back, and once more looked back out at the dark and choppy ocean. It was a bad decision, and partly caused by something as simple as the lack of a congratulatory clap on the shoulder when she'd found what she held in her hand; but she made the call and in the end no one else was to blame.

The man waited a moment, and then headed towards her. He walked in a straight line, seemingly unbothered by the water that hissed around his shoes, up and back. He crunched as he came. He was not looking for shells and did not care what happened to them.

Madison realized she'd been dumb. She should have moved straight away, when she had a bigger advantage. Just got up, walked home. Now she'd have to rely on surprise, on the fact the man was probably assuming that if she hadn't run before then she wouldn't now. Madison decided she would wait until the man got a little closer and then suddenly bolt: moving as fast as she could and shouting loud. Mom would have the door open. She might even be on her way out right now, come to see why she was not yet back. She should be— she was officially late. But Madison knew in his heart that her mother might just be sitting in her chair instead, shoulders rounded and bent, looking down at her hands the way she had after they got back from the restaurant the night before.

And so she got ready, making sure her heels were well-planted in the hard sand, that her legs were tensed like springs, ready to push off with everything she had.

The man stopped.

Madison had intended to keep looking out at the grey waves until the last second, as if she wasn't even aware of the man's presence, but instead found herself turning her head a little to check what was going on.

The man had came to a halt earlier than Madison expected, still about twenty feet away. Now she could see his face she could tell he was way older than her dad, maybe even past Uncle Brian's age, which was fifty. Uncle Brian was always smiling, though, as if he was trying to remember a joke he'd heard at the office and was sure you were going to enjoy. This man did not look like that.

"I've got something for you," he said. His voice was dry and quiet, but carried.

Madison hurriedly looked away, heart thumping. Unthinkingly protecting the flat shell still in her left hand, she braced her right palm into the sand too now, ready to push off against it, hard.

"But first I need to know something," he said.

Madison realized she had to reach maximum speed immediately. Uncle Brian was fat and looked like he couldn't run at all. This man was different that way too. She took a deep breath. Decided to do it on three. One...

"Look at me, girl."

Two...

Then suddenly the man was between Madison and the dunes. He moved so quickly Madison barely saw it happen.

"You'll like it," he said, as if he had done nothing at all. "I promise. You want it. But first you have to answer my question. Okay?"

His voice sounded wetter now and dismally Madison realized just how stupid she had been, understood why moms and dads said children had to be back at certain times, and to not stray too far, and not talk to strangers, and so many other things. Parents were not just being mean or difficult or boring, it turned out. They were trying to prevent what was about to happen.

She looked up at the man's face, nodded. She didn't know what else to do, and hoped it might help. The man smiled. He had a spray of small, dark moles across one cheek. His teeth were stained and uneven.

"Good," he said. He took another step towards her, and now his hands were out of his coat pockets. His fingers were long, and pale.

Madison heard the word "Three..." in her head, but it was too quiet and she did not believe in it. Her arm and legs were no longer like springs. They felt like rubber. She couldn't even tell if they were still tensed.

The man was too close now. He smelt damp. There was a strange light in his eyes, as if he had found something he'd been looking for a long time.

He squatted down close to her, and the smell suddenly got worse, an earthy odour on his breath, a smell that spoke of parts of the body normally kept hidden.

"Can you keep a secret?" he said.

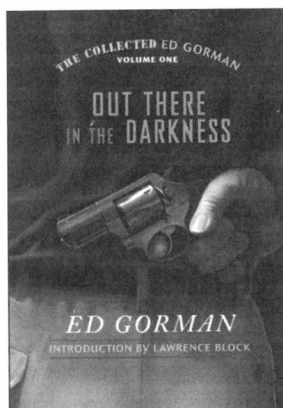

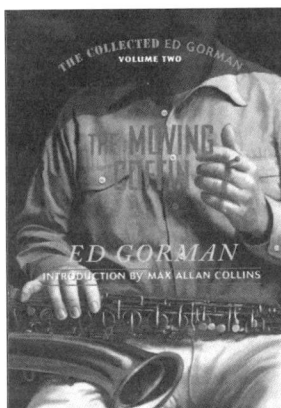

⬚

With this projected multi-volume set of the complete collected short stories of Ed Gorman, PS Publishing has provided a wonderful opportunity for discerning readers to sample the man whose work has been translated into eleven languages and won praise from sources as divergent as *The New York Times* and *Penthouse*. These first two volumes plus volume three will concentrate on Gorman's crime and mystery stories.

Reviewers and readers alike praise Ed Gorman for the originality of his stories and their sometimes heartbreaking, sometimes violent conclusions. Killers and conmen, hookers and hucksters, robbers and rogues . . . plus a dizzying array of everyday joes and jills who just happen to be in the wrong place at the wrong time—Gorman's characters will stay with you long after you've turned over the final page.

"Gorman's writing is strong, fast and sleek as a bullet. He's one of the best."
    —Dean Koontz

"His novels and short stories provide fresh ideas, characters and approaches."
    —*The Oxford Book of American Crime Stories*

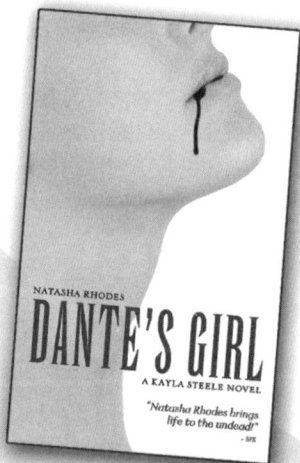

"A few years ago," Lucius Shepard tells us, "I spent some time in Diamante, Italy, a small town on the Tyrrhenian Coast, and while there I had a dream that the sea had undergone a startling transformation during the night. That was the genesis of this story. Sometime later, I was watching CNN and it struck me that the world couldn't possibly get this screwed up unless it had help from, possibly, someone even madder and more incompetent than George Bush and peers..." Lucius's latest novel is Softspoken *and his new story collection,* Dagger Key and Other Stories, *is forthcoming from PS this summer.*

Dinner at Baldassaro's

Lucius Shepard

Though she herself was not beautiful, Giacinta had a beautiful sneeze. Scarcely more than a musical sniff, it seemed to restate the cadence of her name and was followed, in short order, by a giggle as she wiped a residue of white powder from the rims of her nostrils. She was thick-waisted, heavy in the thighs, with an undershot chin and breasts no bigger than onions. But her eyes were shots of dark rum, her pale olive skin held the polish of youth, and her thin face had a desperately merry quality. For all her flaws, I considered her quite a prize.

"This . . . " She scowled dramatically and pointed to the little heap of cocaine on the mirror in her lap. "No good! But I like! I like too much!" She made to hand me the mirror and a straw—the same she had used—and adopted a mischievous look designed to tempt me. I declined temptation and, in faltering Italian, explained that drugs were not beneficial to my health.

"*Salute*," she said, correcting me—I had used the Spanish word for health, *salud*. Her eyes flicked across my body,

as if inspecting me for signs of frailty. "*Va bene.*"

She dipped her head again to the mirror, face obscured by the fall of her chestnut hair.

We were sitting in the offices of the Villa Ruggieri, where Giacinta worked as a receptionist and I had taken a suite. A showplace in the eighteenth century, its high-ceilinged rooms and muraled walls reverberating with the strains of archlute and cello, by the early twenty-first it had matured into a seedy relic of the Late Baroque, a hotel whose best two weeks came during the annual chile pepper festival (just ended), when all the shops of Diamante, the Calabrian seaside village it overlooked, featured fanciful decorations in their windows contrived of chile peppers, and tourists promenaded along the Via Poseidone wearing chile pepper T-shirts and chile pepper hats. Now in October, both the hotel and the village were in the process of shutting their doors, and, that evening, as Giacinta and I walked down the cliff trail and along a narrow, meandering street, we encountered only a few shopgirls hurrying home.

We stopped at a sidewalk café on the corner of the Via Fiume and the Via Poseidone, where we were to meet Giacinta's friend, Allessandra, for a drink before going to dinner. Incapable of other than the most primitive conversation, we endured an awkward silence of considerable length. She studied the wine list, wrinkling her nose as if responding to the various bouquets, and I examined the mural adorning the facade of the building across the street—it depicted several Renaissance children, elegantly clothed, chasing each other about the columns of a room in a palace, all done in sepia tones. There were hundreds of murals in Diamante. At least half a dozen were visible off along the block. I was mildly curious regarding the reason underlying such a proliferation, but I did not inquire about them, having no wish to endure a labored explanation couched in fractured English, with table objects used for demonstration purposes. The night air was growing cool. Giacinta threw on a light sweater over her yellow summer dress. She smiled anxiously at me, and I smiled in return.

Allessandra, who arrived twenty minutes late, was a willowy brunette who had spent a great deal of time and money at the hair salon to achieve a fabulously tousled and frosted look. She wore a leather mini that showed off her long legs and enormous gold hoop earrings through which, it seemed, a toy poodle could have jumped. She bussed Giacinta on the cheek, lit a cigarette with scarcely an interruption to her rapid-fire chatter, and began to interrogate me as might an anxious mother on the occasion of her daughter's prom, asking first how old I was.

"I'm forty," I told her.

"Gia is twenty-six," she said.

"It's a lovely age."

Giacinta looked to Allessandra, and Allessandra translated, apparently accurately, for Giacinta ducked her eyes and blushed.

"Are forty and twenty-six incompatible?" I asked. Allessandra failed to grasp the word *incompatible*, so I presented her with alternatives. "Unsuitable? Ill-matched?"

"No, no! I was pointing out that for you, Gia is much less, uh ... sophisticated."

"Ah! I see."

Giacinta wanted to know what was being said, but Allessandra told her to wait and asked my occupation.

"I do some travel writing," I said.

"For the magazines?"

"Books, mainly. I own a travel agency with offices in Rome, Paris, London, New York ... and elsewhere. The business more-or-less runs itself, and I've been at loose ends the past few years. So I've taken up writing."

Allessandra paused to translate. Her perfume overwhelmed the less aggressive aura of Giacinta's scent. Within the café, under a bilious yellow bulb, two waiters in white shirts and aprons were playing backgammon at the bar, while the bombastic pop stylings of Zucchero leaked into the street, seeming to empurple the air. The lights along the Via Poseidone marked the curve of the shore, otherwise the darkened coastline would have been all but indistinguishable from the sea. Two elderly men in caps and bulky jackets strolled along the sea wall; one threw his right arm over the other's shoulder and, making repetitive forceful gestures with his right hand, appeared to be offering advice.

"Maybe," Allessandra said, "you write the article about Diamante?"

"No, I'm here to meet some friends. We try to get together every year somewhere in Europe. This year it happens to be Diamante." I leaned forward and touched Allessandra's cigarette pack, resting by her elbow. "May I?"

"Of course."

"I quit years ago, but I still get the urge on occasion." I lit up and exhaled a plume of smoke that a breeze swept toward the sea wall. "I'm meeting my friends for dinner tonight. At Baldassaro's. They're all bringing someone, and . . . well, I didn't want to come alone. I thought Giacinta would make a charming dinner companion."

Hearing her name, Giacinta again asked for a translation and, following a brief exchange, Allessandra said, "There is a thing I don't understand, Mister . . . You . . . "

"Taylor," I said. "Please."

"Very well. Taylor." She stressed the T with a flick of her tongue, crossed her legs and lit another cigarette. "You are a man of wealth, of experience. And very handsome. Many beautiful women would be happy to take dinner with you. Especially at a place of elegance

like Baldassaro's. So why have you choosed this one?"

I had a sip of wine. "I assumed that Giacinta invited you for drinks so she could ask questions through you and make a judgment on my character. But this is your question, isn't it?"

Allessandra made a wry shape with her mouth and gave the slightest of nods.

"Perhaps you would care to go to dinner with me?"

"Another night . . . " She gave her hair a toss. "It's possible."

A Vespa with a pair of young men astride passed along the street—I allowed the angry rip of the engine to fade before continuing.

"You're a beautiful woman, Allessandra. I'm sure any man would be delighted to have you as a companion. However, I'm looking for a certain type of beauty. Beauty that falls short of the ideal. Innocence that's been corrupted, but only just. A woman who's been slighted by the world, perhaps treated roughly, yet maintains a belief in romantic possibility."

Giacinta, seeming to recognize that Allessandra was flirting with me, plucked at her friend's sleeve. Her purpose in having me meet Allessandra had less to do with ascertaining my good character than with showing me off, and now she was afraid that she had made a mistake.

Allessandra told her to wait a second and said, "Your picture of . . . What you say about the woman . . . uh . . . "

"Description. Is that the word you're looking for?"

"Yes. Your description . . . it fits every woman."

"Yes, but Giacinta possesses this quality in a way you do not. If I were to send her to a spa, have experts counsel her on matters of diet and exercise, perhaps get some work done to her chin, her breasts, she'd be very much the kind of woman you are. As it is, she's the absolute embodiment of the quality I'm seeking. Her body and mind flavored by a precise degree of sadness."

Allessandra's frown took the measure of some poignant indelicacy, as if she detected a bad smell. "It seems you are a connoisseur, a . . . I don't know how to say. Your feeling for Gia is not . . . " She snapped her fingers in frustration.

"You're suggesting that my appreciation of Giacinta's charms may be perverse? Like a preference for dwarves or the morbidly obese? Why don't you tell her that?"

Once again Allessandra had to hold off Giacinta's demand that she be filled in, saying forcefully, "*Aspetta!*"

"I'm attracted to plain women," I said. "Physical beauty bores me. I'm talking about what's generally considered beautiful. And now that beauty's become affordable . . . " I made a disparaging noise. "That qualifies me as jaded, not perverse. Still, it may be a phase I'm going through. Tomorrow night, for instance, I may feel differently."

For a second or two, Allessandra looked puzzled. Then she shook her finger at me in mock chastisement and laughed. "You fool with me!" she said. "I know!"

She turned to her friend and delivered herself of a lengthy pronouncement detailing our conversation or, more likely, a fictive version of it, darting sideways glances at me as if to affirm an unstated complicity. Judging by Giacinta's tremulous smile, I suspected Allessandra was informing her that I'd been attracted to her mental and spiritual qualities, that she could consider herself safe while in my company, and that she could expect nothing more threatening to her virtue than a fine meal at Baldassaro's—in sum, diminishing the importance of the evening, so that when I asked Allessandra out, something both women were certain I would do, Giacinta would not be so distressed.

Shortly afterward, Allessandra took her leave, seizing the opportunity of a perfunctory embrace to slip her business card into my jacket pocket, and, once she had rounded the corner, an act preceded by a wave, coquettishly fluttering her fingers, Giacinta's mood grew instantly sullen and uncommunicative. I caressed her forearm, asked if she was all right, and she shook her head, refusing to look at me. "Giacinta," I said softly, making the name into a form of adoration, and held her hand, pressing my lips to the inside of her wrist, to the rapid pulse beating there, the smell of blood and lemons. With palpable reluctance, she swung about to face me and, after I laid my hand along her cheek, letting her lean into it, only then did she relent and favor me with a wan smile.

Toward the southern extremity of the Via Poseidone, an ancient stone causeway extended several hundred yards out into the sea, connecting the mainland with a small island, almost invisible against the night sky, picked out by the lights of Baldassaro's. In addition to a four-star restaurant, the island was home to some nondescript Roman ruins that attracted a few tourists, but no one had lived there for over a century, thus it was ideal for our meeting. The causeway itself, however, was populated by a number of young couples who had come for a twilight stroll and stayed to exploit the anonymity of the dark. Every few yards we passed a shadowy couple locked in an embrace or whispering with their heads together. I had slipped a drug into Giacinta's wine back at the café, a hypnotic designed to lower inhibitions, and, upon finding an unoccupied stretch of railing, when I suggested we take our ease along it, she raised no objection. Perhaps she would have raised none in any case. If she had, I could have persuaded her with a mental nudge; but I never have liked manipulating them in that way—it tends to damage them and it might have cost me some effort. These Italian girls, whether due to Catholic fear or fleshly anxiety, were capable of reconstituting their virginity at a moment's notice. And so I trusted the drug to liberate her from such impediments.

We gazed out across the Mediterranean, lying flat beneath a salting of dim stars. I asked Giacinta to talk, telling her I liked the sound of her voice, although I understood little of what she said (a message that required some considerable time to convey, due to its relative complexity). She hesitated, but I urged her on and soon she started in reciting poetry like a schoolgirl regurgitating memorized verses on cue. After three poems she faltered, but then began speaking rapidly in a husky tone of voice. To my amusement, I recognized several vulgar words, words such as "*pompino*" and "*cazzo*", that I had learned from a woman in Bologna. I put my right hand on the join of her waist and hip, and her breath caught; she half-turned so that my hand slid up onto her rib cage, very near the swell of her breast. Her voice thickened and her speech became peppered with crudities, particular emphasis being laid on terms like "*. . . mi fica . . .*" and "*. . . mi culo . . .*" and so forth, references to portions of her anatomy upon which, I assumed, she wished me to lavish attention.

I was delighted to play a game with her, with someone so similar to and yet so vastly different from the women with whom I was accustomed to playing a more involving game. I kissed her, tasting wine and licorice from her tongue. My hand engulfed a breast, squeezing it a trifle hard, perhaps, for I felt her mouth slacken momentarily. I lifted her by the waist, boosted her up to sit upon the stone railing, and pushed her skirt up around her hips. She protested, of course, pushing feebly at my chest and saying, "*No, Taylor! Non in questo!*" But the distinction between passion and its counterfeit had blurred for us both. I fingered her panties to one side and, finding her ready, entered her. She clung to my shoulders, gasping with each thrust. I forced her to lie back, suspending her over the drop—twenty feet, I reckoned it. All that prevented her from falling was our genital union and my hands supporting her waist. She cried out . . . not loudly. Modesty was still a concern. She did not want to be caught, yet she needed this validation so desperately, this romantic violence in the service of her self-image, that she was willing to risk her reputation, not to mention her life, and entrust herself to a stranger's whim.

"*Non preoccupe, Giacinta,*" I said, and then repeated it. She gradually relaxed. Her head drooped, her arms dangled toward the dark water. Gleaming palely in the ambient light, her face was serene, enraptured, lips parted, slitted eyes directed to heaven, to a pattern of stars that exhibited the workings of a divine intellect and transformed our rutting into a mating of angels. God knows what fantasies populated her head! Perhaps she saw herself as a goddess suffering a vile martyrdom, or as a twenty-first century Leda. I gave passing thought to the notion of letting her fall, but though I am not known for my generosity of spirit, neither am I the cruelest of my kind, and I must admit to having some trivial affection for every creature who shares with us their inch of time. Yet the scent of her despair and desperation, the fact that she was surrendering herself in the faint hope that her ardor might persuade me to love her, to sweep her up into a moneyed

life, one wherein she could afford the procedures I had mentioned to Allessandra, those that would make her uninteresting to me—all this yielded a fine perfume that stirred my emotions to such an extent, I believed I loved her more purely than those who had previously used her, and it occurred to me that I might want to keep her around for the winter, that I might, for my own amusement, if nothing else, grant some of her wishes.

Afterward she brushed stone dust off her dress and cleaned herself with a tissue, casting furtive glances at lovers less bold than we; and when she was done with her toilette, she rested her head on my chest, as if sheltering there. I tipped her face toward mine and kissed her brow, an affectionate gesture unalloyed by irony. A worry line creased that kissed brow. She pushed me away and began berating me—that much was evident from her tone, but she spoke too rapidly for me to catch a single word until I heard ". . . *profillatico* . . . " The poor girl was rebuking me for not having worn a condom, a fact to which she had just awakened. I could have eased her fears on this score, but in the spirit of the scene I acted out my own concern, expressing that I had been swept away by passion, pledging that everything would be all right, that together we would find our way whether or not a little troglodyte had started its journey lifewards in her belly. At length I made myself understood and, mollified, she allowed me to guide her toward Baldassaro's. We had scarcely gone ten paces when she quickened her step, allowing the hint of a smile to touch her lips, and latched onto my arm with a proprietary grasp.

It was the last night of the season but one at Baldassaro's and we had rented the entire restaurant for a party of nine. A waiter led Giacinta and me through the main dining area and along a corridor to a large room, where a table had been set with a white linen cloth, crystal, and gold utensils. The cream-colored walls bore a mural of Roman galleys engaged in battle with a fleet of sleeker ships manned by soldiers with Persian-style beards. At one end of the room were French doors that opened onto a balcony overlooking the water. Jenay, a brunette this year, resplendent in a blue business suit tailored to accentuate her statuesque figure, smelling of flowers, greeted me with a kiss and introduced her companion, a German furniture salesman named Vid, a pop-eyed little monster in a houndstooth jacket who might have been her pet frog. When I introduced Giacinta, Vid performed a jaunty bow and Jenay whispered to me in the Old Tongue, "She's exquisite! I'm certain you'll win this year."

"What were you going for?" I asked her. "Comic relief?"

"I thought I'd give the rest of you a fighting chance."

"Just because you won last year doesn't mean . . . "

"I've won the last two out of three," said Jenay with mock indignation. "And it should have been three in a row."

"What language are you speaking?" Vid asked. "It's familiar, but I can't place it."

"It's an archaic French dialect," I said. "From the Aquitaine region."

"We belonged to one of those secret societies in college," said Jenay. "Learning it was required for membership."

"Aquitaine," said Vid. "I would have thought farther west. It reminds me of Basque."

"My, you're quite the linguist, aren't you? But then . . . " Jenay made suggestive play with her tongue and smiled. "I suppose I already knew that."

Vid, I swear before God, puffed out his chest, like a male bird fanning its plumage, and explained that in his undergraduate days, he had studied the French language and its origins; a family crisis had forced him to give up his studies.

"May I have some wine?" Giacinta looked at me crossly—she was feeling left out.

I hastened to serve her, also pouring Vid a glass, which he downed in a gulp, and the four of us began talking about Diamante, the only subject with which Giacinta seemed conversant. The town's many murals, she told us, were the result of a contest held each year—artists were invited from all over the world to paint a wall and the best of their work became part of Diamante's permanent exhibition.

Next to arrive was Elaine, also a brunette, more slender than Jenay, her perfume more subtle, with darker hair and piercing blue eyes, her pale, classical features rendered saintly by a cowled evening gown of a shimmering beige fabric. She had in tow a leather-jacketed street hustler named Daniele, his chiseled chin inked with stubble, who challenged me with a stare and otherwise exhibited a cool indifference that doubtless accorded with the personal style of some cinematic tough guy. Both Jenay and I took the position that Daniele was far too handsome and self-assured. Elaine defended her choice by saying that his pathos was inherent to his fate, which was so precisely de-marked as to be obvious, but Jenay reminded her that, pitiful though Daniele was, our contest was judged on appearances and behavior, not potential.

"What do you expect?" said Elaine. "I only had a few hours to find someone."

"You could have arrived sooner," said Jenay. "Everything is always so last-minute with you."

Elaine made a dismissive noise.

"No, really," said Jenay. "It's tiresome. You've never taken your responsibility seriously."

"This hardly qualifies as a responsibility." Elaine pushed back her cowl and I saw that she had left a white streak in her hair. "This is a pig party. It cheapens us. Though I must say . . . " Coquettishly, she touched my chest. "Yours is wonderful! Where you did find her?"

"She found me," I said. "She more-or-less fell into my lap."

Elaine smiled. "Repeatedly, no doubt."

I had grown weary of Lucan's dramatic entrances, as had we all, this mostly a reaction to his overabundant personality, which was redolent of a gay *maitre de*; yet I must confess that I also anticipated them. Music preceded him, piped in over hidden speakers: Verdi's *March from Aida*. Next came Professor Rappenglueck, Lucan's lover for a term, now reduced to a familiar, and a guest at our dinners for nearly thirty years: a diminutive man, once handsome, his looks severely diminished by age and a slovenliness attributable to mental deterioration. He shuffled forward, gray and shrunken, like a piece of fruit left too long in the icebox, mumbling as he came, absently stroking his beard, and stood at the end of the dinner table, his voice increasing in volume and waxing lectoral, addressing the empty chairs as if they were a vast assembly, holding forth in an erratic fashion on the subject of Cro-Magnon sky maps in the caves of El Castillo.

". . . the Northern Crown," he was saying. "Remarkable in its accuracy. Of course, these maps are not the great-est . . . the greatest secret of El Castillo."

The professor fell silent in mid-ramble, and Lucan stepped into the doorway, his white hair combed back from his face and glowing like a flame, lending him a leonine aspect. He swirled his opera cape with a magician's flair, as if making himself reappear after an occult disappearance, then bowed to each of us in turn, reached into the corridor and drew forth not a rabbit, but a rabbity, stoop-shouldered girl. Liliana (so Lucan introduced her) was at least six feet tall, no older than eighteen or nineteen, with dark circles under her eyes, possessed of a morose expression and a flat chest that seemed hollowed due to her posture and loose-fitting blouse. Everything about her testified that here was a girl who had contemplated (and perhaps attempted) suicide more than once, and was likely to do so again, possibly before the evening was over. A distinct threat to Giacinta in our competition, but one I was confident that she would withstand, for although Liliana's presentation offered a complex palette of disaster, she was long of limb and doe-eyed, and neither bad skin nor poor posture nor the attrition caused her flesh by the poisons of depression hid the fact that she was a real beauty who, but for the indifference of chance, might have been walking a runway in Milan. Lucan, who had not spoken a word other than her name, presented her to Giacinta with an ornate gesture, and Liliana put out her hand.

"We've met," Giacinta said, and turned away, ostensibly to select an appetizer from the table; but the insult was clear.

Liliana snatched back her hand and held it clenched at her waist, looking crushed. I suspected, if given the opportunity, she would brood over this slight the rest of the evening and later memorialize it with a cutting or some other form of self-punishment.

Lucan winked at me and said, "I'll bet those two become a lot friendlier before the night is done."

"If you say so."

"Oh, I absolutely do." Lucan removed his cape, folded it over the back of a chair. "It's a natural pairing,

you see. Liliana has gotten the better of this one"—he indicated Giacinta—"in an affair of the heart. Nothing else could have provoked such a reaction. It's our duty to heal the breach between them." He lifted a glass of wine, held it to the light to judge the color. "Lovely little town, don't you think? Have you seen the murals?"

"A few."

"Liliana took me on a tour this afternoon," he said. "Really spectacular, some of them. But I feel they need a centerpiece, something monumental to provide them with an overall context."

"Talk English!" Giacinta slapped my arm, demonstrating once again her shrewish side, a flaw she hastened to cover by conveying her frustration with being unable to understand what I was saying. She wanted to understand, she said, because . . . well, I understood, didn't I? She gazed up at me adoringly. Lucan rolled his eyes and, taking Liliana's arm, escorted her to the table.

At dinner, the four guests were seated all on one side of the table, Vid and Daniele bracketing Liliana and Giacinta; our side had a similar arrangement, Elaine and Jenay separating me and Lucan. By the time the seafood course had been served, Vid and Daniele were sneaking glances at one another over the top of the women's heads, and Liliana was casting shy looks at Giacinta, who was grumpily toying with her shrimp risotto. They struck up a conversation during the main course, an excellent veal marsala, and, when next I noticed, while the waiters cleared away the dishes, the women were chatting amiably, as if there had never been the slightest bitterness between them—it was clear that someone had influenced Giacinta to be receptive to Liliana. Recognizing this, I was incensed. An overreaction, perhaps, but I had grown fond of Giacinta and felt protective of her.

"Now that Taylor has overcome his reluctance for the game, we can proceed," said Lucan, dropping back into the Old Tongue. "I'd like first . . . "

"It's not reluctance," I said. "I simply find it jejune, this business of having guests at our dinners."

Lucan arched an eyebrow. "Yet Giacinta carries your scent. You had sex with her. You had sex with the one you brought last time . . . and the time before that. You enjoy that part of it."

"I'm prone to the same perversity as the rest of you," I said. "I fuck them because they're there to be fucked. Because their helplessness encourages me in some fundamental way. However, I don't make a big deal about it. And more to the point, I haven't used my influence on her tonight." I pointed to Giacinta, who, unaware of our attention, was leaning toward Liliana, touching her forearm as she spoke. "This is someone else's work."

"Why, that's damned impolite!" Lucan said, not trying to hide his smile. "Interfering with another man's . . . what shall we call it? Dinner date? Catch of the Day? A cross between the two, I'd reckon. It verges on the criminal."

"I know it was you, Lucan," I said.

"You've always abused your authority, even in trivial matters."

"Very well! I admit it!" With a theatrical display, Lucan made as if to bare his chest so it might more readily accept my blade. "I'm the guilty one! The poor creatures looked so lonely, I felt compelled to give them a push."

"Whatever," I said.

"You don't need my permission," Lucan continued, "to return them to something approximating their former state. But you'll be denying them pleasure, and there's so little pleasure in their lives."

I refused to look at him. "Degrade them however you wish. I won't take part in it."

"Let me make sure I understand you," Lucan said. "It's not our behavior in general you're objecting to; it's the formalization of that behavior. Yes?"

"That's it basically," I said. "Though we might do well to examine the entire range of our relationships with them. It seems we're not doing ourselves much good by . . . "

"Must we always have this conversation!" Jenay threw down her fork in disgust. "You or Elaine trot out the same tired argument every time. It's become as much a part of our dinners as Rappenglueck."

At the sound of his name, the professor began mumbling—Lucan hushed him with a snap of his fingers.

"Are you insane?" I said to Jenay. "We never have this conversation. Each time we start to have it, you complain how tedious it's become. I was thinking about this the other night. We haven't done more than touch on the subject since Torremolinos, and that was nearly sixty years ago."

"Is there anything new to say?" Jenay attempted to make the question rhetorical by framing it in an indifferent tone.

"I don't know! Is there?" I put down my napkin and stood, stepping around to the opposite side of the table, walking behind the guests, who took incidental note of me, but not so as to subtract from their attentiveness to one another. "Let's find out. Does anyone have anything new to add to the conversation that we never have?"

"We've tried to help them—that hasn't worked," said Elaine. "And they've thwarted our best efforts at destroying them."

"That goes without saying . . . though it's been centuries since we made a concerted effort in that regard," said Jenay. "They're like roaches in their perseverance."

"We don't have the strength of will we once had. I'm sure that's due in part to my leadership, but I won't accept all the blame." Lucan shook his head ruefully. "I wish you could have known Furio. If ever a man was suited for a time . . . ."

"My mother knew him," said Jenay. "In fact, he sent a gift on the occasion of my birth."

"Furio was perfectly suited for the Dark Ages," Lucan went on. "He was as decisive as an ax, and as pitiless. When it came time for his release, he . . . "

"We know," said Elaine with heavy sarcasm. "It woke volcanoes, knocked down walls a hundred miles away,

and created a symphony in the process."

"You've never attended a release," Lucan said. "If you had, you might not be so disrespectful."

Elaine wrinkled her nose in distaste. "Nobody I know would be so vulgar as to perform such a ritual. It makes you wonder at the sensibilities of our ancestors. The pyrotechnic release of one's life energy to entertain a crowd of drunks. It's . . . " She cast about for an appropriate word. "Primitive!"

"Being primitive has its uses," said Jenay. "There's a reason for the persistence of these cultural relics."

"That's how it's come to be viewed," said Lucan. "A cultural relic. I prefer to see it as something more vital. When Furio knew death was upon him, he gathered his friends so they might witness the vigor of his passing and celebrate the potency of his days."

"For all his potency, he failed to destroy the humans," I said.

Lucan scowled. "The *animals*. They outbred the plague. That's all. The one thing they do well is breed."

"They outbred us, to be sure. If we hadn't found our little French thistle, we'd have gone the way of the wooly mammoth." I paused, tamping down my annoyance with Lucan. "Yet if they hadn't outbred us, if it were a choice we'd been presented, a trade-off, giving up procreative dominance in exchange for long life and the enhancement of our mental gifts, who here would have it otherwise? We should view our survival as a gift, not a privilege. They *earned* their right to survive. They . . . "

Lucan snorted. "Next you'll be telling us their survival is God's will."

"My problem is," Elaine said, "I don't enjoy it anymore."

"Enjoy what?" Jenay asked impatiently.

"Exploiting them." Elaine half-turned to her. "Taylor's right. This ritual dominance, this antiquated behavior, colors our lives. It's a debased practice, no different from a release. And I don't like how it makes me feel."

"How *does* it make you feel?" asked Jenay, archly.

"Taylor's not right!" Lucan said. "Not in the way you mean, at any rate."

"Uneasy." Elaine met Jenay's challenging stare. "Uncertain of myself. You know."

"I'm sure I *don't* know," said Jenay.

I saw that Liliana had let her head fall back, exposing the arch of her throat, and Giacinta was pressing her lips to it, feathering her tongue along a vein that showed beneath the skin. The sight infuriated me.

"This is ridiculous!" I said. "The entire conversation."

"You insisted on having it." Jenay signaled to a waiter that he could remove her plate.

"We're not having the conversation I wanted. Far from it." I paced to the end of the table. "Look. We've established that we can't exterminate them, not without killing ourselves in the process. Now, despite our best efforts to save them, they're on the verge of destroying themselves . . . and us. We're the superior beings. Can't we come up with a scenario other than one that involves mere containment or their destruction?"

Without bothering to excuse themselves, a silent communion having been reached, Vid and Daniele left the table and, soon after, the room. His expression bemused, Lucan started to speak, but I cut him off and said, "We have to examine the possibility that our intervention is stimulating their urge toward self-destruction."

"Not this again," said Jenay.

"Yes, we've mentioned it," I said. "But always as a drollery. We need to take it seriously. If these dinners have any purpose, they remind us how easily we can damage them. One touch and they start to come apart. Look at their leaders, the ones whom we've influenced most frequently. They're pathetic. The majority of them can't even muster coherent speech."

"Pish-posh," said Lucan.

"Look at Rappenglueck," I said.

The professor lifted his head and belched, and Lucan said, "Let's not make this personal, shall we? The thing is, our affairs are inextricably mingled with theirs. We can't afford to take the chance that Taylor may not be right." He pointed at the door. "Someone should check on the boys. Elaine?"

Elaine lowered her head. "Somebody else go."

Lucan turned to Jenay.

"They're just off to have sex," she said.

"We don't want that, do we? Not with the staff still here. And the manager. Why complicate things?"

"Oh, all right. I'm sick of this blather,

anyway." Jenay stood, adjusted the fit of her jacket, and strode from the room.

"You have a point, Lucan. We can't change course abruptly," Elaine said. "At the same time, we shouldn't be overcautious. We've been acting within narrow parameters. Too narrow, if you ask me. We've been trying to maintain the status quo. It's like trying to stop a two-ton boulder from rolling downhill by jamming a doorstop beneath it. Given we're stuck with the situation, what I'm suggesting is, let's change what we can safely change and see what happens. This, the dinners, is one area in which we can experiment."

"That's not all you're suggesting." Lucan pretended to be concerned with shooting his cuffs. "What you're suggesting has larger implications."

"I realize that," Elaine said. "Changing our attitude toward them during these dinners may have a ripple effect. Perhaps it'll engender cultural change and one day we may find ourselves in partnership with them. As things stand, we only weaken ourselves with this kind of interaction."

"Partnership," Lucan said. "You mean, reveal ourselves to them?"

"Not right away," she said. "Eventually, perhaps. We're not so different from them, after all. Our superiority is based on a plant, for heaven's sake. An accident of biology."

"And we're not certain that the thistle can't be of benefit to them," I said. "We've only done the most primitive of experiments in that regard. It's quite possible . . . "

"You're talking about our enemy." Lucan enunciated his words precisely, as if speaking to a child. "Surely you comprehend that much. Our natural enemy. They very nearly destroyed us. We're at war with them. How can you forget?"

"When's the last time we took a casualty in that war?" I asked. "They're more our victims than enemies. Our governance of them sets the model for terrorism. We've become invisible, yet if we lift a finger, the earth shakes. As for our nature, I'd like to think we've risen above it."

Jenay re-entered the room. "They're fine," she said as she sat down. She glanced along the table. "Did I miss anything?"

Lucan gave a limp wave, as if commenting on the hopelessness of our impasse. "Taylor was saying he thinks we've risen above our natures in respect to the animals. I won't bother detailing how incredibly stupid I find that presumption." Then, addressing me: "If we reveal ourselves, you know what will happen."

"It would be nasty," I said. "No doubt. But if we prepare the way, who knows? And if worst comes to worst and there's a war, we'll win it."

Lucan studied me, as if weighing what I had said, but then he brought his hand down on the table, giving everyone a start . . . except for Giacinta and Liliana, who remained intent upon one another. "This is absurd! It's like listening to children prattling on about their favorite puppy."

"If you'll just listen—" I began.

"No." Lucan came to his feet. "I won't waste any more time with this shit. If Elaine and Jenay want to discuss..."

"Leave me out of it," said Jenay.

"If they want to discuss it, do it another day. As eldest, I determine the agenda for this meeting. It's time we got down to business."

Vid and Daniele wandered back into the room and stopped by the door. Daniele's mouth was agape and there was spittle on his chin; Vid's lips moved silently.

"Damn it!" Elaine spun about to confront Jenay. "You didn't have to ruin them!"

Jenay took in the scene by the door. She gave an amused sniff. "Sorry."

Elaine clenched her fists. "If you think I'm going to clean up after you..."

"Be quiet!" Lucan shouted it. "Jenay. Get them seated. And you..." He glared at me. "Sit. We've got work to do."

Jenay herded Vid and Daniele toward the table and, after returning Lucan's glare, I sat. Lucan refreshed his wine glass and said, "State the concerns of the clans you represent."

"China," said Jenay. "China, China, and China."

"Agreed, the question of China troubles us," said Elaine. "Iran remains an issue. And Africa."

"Africa?" Lucan laughed derisively. "That's not a problem. Taylor?"

"We'd like to accelerate the imposition of an overtly Fascist government in the United States," I said. "We need stricter immigration controls, surveillance policies. And we need those things now. The timetable that's been established is, in our view, dangerously slow. They've got so many black agencies within their government, no one knows what the other is doing, and I'm not certain we know. We have to get a handle on that immediately,"

"Skyler Means will take care of it," he said. "I have complete confidence in him."

"Means and his people are stretched too thin," I said. "We're all stretched too thin. Cracks are starting to show, especially in the States."

"All right," he said. "We'll discuss it. Is that all?"

"For the moment."

"Isn't that odd? I'm not hearing anything about a redefinition of our relationship with the animals." Lucan built a church-and-steeple with his fingers. "We'll begin with China. I believe it's time to consider another thinning of the herd."

It was past eleven before we concluded our business. The waiters brought in the cheese cart; the manager put in an appearance, thanked us for our business, and then they withdrew. Vid and Daniele occupied one end of the table, carrying on a faltering conversation that, judging by what I heard, made sense only to them. At the other end, Lucan sat with the professor, prompting him in his ceaseless lecture, rewarding him now and again with a wedge of cheese. Their political differences set aside for the moment, Elaine and Jenay chatted and laughed by the door, while Giacinta had followed Liliana out onto the balcony. She had unbuttoned Liliana's blouse and they were embracing.

We had that night made significant decisions that would affect millions of lives, but I was more interested in Giacinta's well-being, in repairing the damage Lucan had done, than I was with assessing my evening's work, second-guessing the compromises I had made and weighing them out against what I had won. Goaded by Lucan's tampering, encouraged by Jenay-and-Elaine's validation of my choice, but mainly due to the thrust of my own peculiar tastes, I had developed an affection for Giacinta during the brief span of our relationship and I felt no small jealousy toward Liliana—though Giacinta's attraction for her was a contrivance, a falsity, mine for Gia was equally false, equally contrived, and the only way I could deny this was to steer her away from Liliana and immerse both of us in an illusion I created. But manipulating a human mind is like entering a room filled with mist and fashioned of fragile crystal, and you must step carefully or else you will break everything. Restoring a mind is still more difficult—it was nothing I could accomplish without a degree of concentration difficult to achieve at Baldassaro's. And so, deciding that repairs would have to wait until we were back at the Villa Ruggieri, I went to refill my wine glass, coming within earshot of Lucan and the professor.

"One might reasonably conjecture," Professor Rappenglueck was saying, staring at the cheese cart, "that the great turns in human history were accomplished by force of arms, by inventions that caused society to evolve, and so forth. Who could imagine . . ." His features twisted as he sought to complete the sentence.

"Come on, Rappy." Lucan waggled a wedge of gouda in front of the professor. "'That for all intents and purposes . . .'"

"Who could imagine," the professor went on, "that for all intents and purposes our history ended in the mid-Paleolithic with the discovery by Cro-Magnon man that a variety of starthistle, when attacked by *rhinocyllus conicus* . . ."

"'. . . yielded a chemical,'" Lucan prompted.

". . . a chemical . . ." The professor licked his lips. ". . . that slowed the rate of . . ."

Lucan clicked his tongue in annoyance and fed Rappanglueck the cheese.

I pulled back a chair and sat, stretching out my legs. "Doesn't your pet mouse know any other tricks?"

"It's a synaptic response," Lucan said absently. "He senses the importance of these gatherings, and he tends to think he's back in Geneva, giving the address he prepared for the IGY conference."

"The one you prevented him from giving," I said. "By destroying him."

Lucan's face hardened, yet he refused to rise to the bait. He cut another wedge from the wheel of gouda. The professor was still nibbling on the previous wedge, yellow crumbs in his beard; he chewed faster on seeing the fresh wedge.

"A year ago," said Lucan wistfully, "he could have recited entire paragraphs. Now he can barely get through a sentence. He's falling apart." He fed the professor the second wedge, stroked his hair, and spoke to him as though to a precious child. "But you were almost famous, weren't you, Rappy? You might have been as famous as Newton or Leakey."

"Tell me. Do you still fuck him?" I asked, repulsed by Lucan's display of intimacy.

"You know, I think I'll answer your question. One day the information may come in handy." Lucan resettled in his chair. "At home, Rappy's almost his old self some days. On those days, sometimes the illusion of wholeness suffices and we're affectionate with one another. Is there anything more you'd care to know?"

The professor made a complaining noise; he had finished his gouda.

"No," I said. "I think I've got the picture."

"You really are an astonishing fool!" Lucan hacked at the cheese. "For someone who became a clan leader in so short a time, you have the most appalling blindness. You can't see yourself at all."

"And you can, I suppose?"

"See you? Oh, yes. The fact is, I've always recognized your potential. One day you'll be my successor, and I have the highest of hopes for your term. If a cure for your blindness is found, that

is." He tipped his head to the side. "Would it surprise you to learn that I espoused attitudes similar to yours when I was young? Regarding the animals, I mean."

"I'd be more surprised if you didn't make that claim," I said. "The elderly are prone to react that way when confronted with the logic of the future. 'Ah, yes!' they say. 'Once I thought as you, but experience has cured me of such enthusiasms.'"

Lucan fed another wedge to the professor. "Forget it."

"Wait! Aren't you going to tell me? I'm dying to hear. Let me think. What would you say?" I sat beside Lucan, affecting the pose of someone in deep study. "When you were younger, you were afire with possibility. You had a vision of the world based upon trust, upon accords, not on the hard-won wisdom of your elders. The long centuries armored you against such foolishness, but in your dotage you took a lover from among the animals. You'd had many such lovers, but this one . . . he was special. A professor who had stumbled across the secret of our primacy, of our very existence. After you were forced to destroy him, you continued to love him. Of course, it wasn't altogether love you felt. Part of your emotional commitment was a tribute to the youthful philosophies you once embraced. It may be you understood now that they were not so foolish, after all. But it was too late in life, your position was such that you couldn't publicly espouse them. So in a sense, your love became an emblem that demonstrated you bore the gene of caring. The taint of the animals, our cousins, whom we detest and love . . . it's a crutch we have to carry. We must proclaim it, wear it like a lapel pin in order to testify that, though we assault them with AIDS, with endless warfare, with pollutants to which we are immune, we *love* our deficient cousins. What a tragedy we're forced to poison them like rats!" I leaned back, crossed my legs. "Perhaps one day even someone as blind as I may come to adopt this posture."

"One day," said Lucan distantly. "Even you."

It was unlike him to be so docile—he had always been fierce in his arguments. He went back to grooming Rappenglueck, cleaning the crumbs from his beard. In hopes, perhaps, of receiving more cheese, the professor said, "On the shoulder of the buffalo, if you'll note the slide, there is a pattern of dots."

"It's all right, Rappy," Lucan said.

The professor tried again. "Unlike similar patterns in the other paintings, this does not represent a constellation, but the starthistle. Its position relative to the Northern Crown, appearing directly over the bull's shoulder, leads me . . . leads . . . "

"That reminds me," I said. "We haven't discussed the project."

"There's nothing to discuss." Lucan wiped Rappenglueck's lips. "No progress."

"We were told to expect a breakthrough."

"Do you really believe we'll abandon them? That we'll just slip off through some sidereal door and leave them to heaven?"

I was shocked to notice that tears had collected in Lucan's eyes . . . so shocked that I failed to respond.

"There'll be no breakthrough," Lucan went on. "The science is there, but there's no will for a breakthrough. If we inadvertently stumble upon one, we'll only use it as a last resort."

". . . leads me to suspect," the professor said triumphantly, "that Cro-Magnon man associated the thistle in a most specific way with the stars of the Northern Crown."

Lucan patted his hand.

"Am I to infer from what you say that the project staff is slacking?" I asked. "Because if that's . . . "

"Not at all. I'm saying we're bound by the patterns of the past. We're enslaved by our natures. Our hatred of the animals, our love for them . . . it's the same emotion. That's why our only recourse is extermination. We're capable of killing something we love, but abandon it? Never." Lucan made a show of cracking his knuckles. "Our ambivalence toward them has caused our current troubles. Over the millennia, it's developed into a weakness. A terrible weakness. We need something to rouse us from our stupor."

"I've heard this song far too many times," I said. "I'm sick of listening to it."

"Oh, I understand. Really, I do. You need a lesson to drive it home. I don't know if I'm the one to teach you, but tonight I'll teach you at least one small lesson. You'll learn that mercy is more of an indulgence than a grace."

"What are you talking about?"

"For one thing, your companion for the evening. Giacinta." Lucan had completed the professor's toilette and now he set about adjusting the knot of Rappanglueck's tie. "I'm afraid I left her in a rather delicate condition. As it stands, she'll likely live out her years in excellent mental health. But any further interference with her mind, if you attempt, let's say, to sway her from her passion for Liliana... They're so flimsy. She won't be able to withstand another alteration. You'll spend the rest of her life trying to restore her. Not the happiest of choices, as you can see." He put a hand on the professor's shoulder. "You could kill her. That would be the simplest course. I can tell you're smitten and I know that makes things difficult. But it would spare you a lot of grief."

Furious, I wanted to strike him, and I would have done so had we been elsewhere, engaged in less public business. I made for the balcony, intending to ascertain the extent of the damage he had done to Gia.

"Oh, Taylor!" he called.

I looked back to where he sat plucking at Rappanglueck's clothing.

"My compliments on your choice of a companion." Here Lucan offered a final florid gesture, one of such ornate, ironic precision, it seemed a summing up of the evening. "As eldest, it's my pleasure to declare Giacinta the winner of our competition. She, more than anyone I've seen in recent years, em-bodies the frailty and strength of the human weed. You have my sincere congratulations."

I shooed Liliana away from the balcony, closed the French doors after her, and examined Giacinta. It was as Lucan had said. Having been altered, the stability of her mind, of that crystal, mist-filled room, had been compromised and any further alteration would cause the walls to crack, only a little at first, but the cracks would spread, leading inexorably to collapse; yet I found myself altering her even before I had decided to do so, obeying an impulse I was unable to resist. Steeped in her thoughts, discernable as might be glints and movements, the dartings of fish in a murky bowl, I could not abide the notion that her passion, the focused product of all that indistinct energy, be directed toward anyone aside from myself for an instant longer. When I pulled back from her, I felt drenched, dripping with her, droplets of pure need, her sweet yearnings, her sour greed, her sullen ambition, her tangy lust, her bloody hungers. Her face, tilted up toward me, was once again adoring, heartbreakingly plain. But absent was that accent of desperation. My restoration having been clumsier by necessity than Lucan's alteration, I knew I would never again glimpse the original Gia.

My good-byes were perfunctory and once out on the Via Poseidone, I hailed a taxi and had the driver convey us to the Villa Ruggiere. Giacinta giggled and clung to me as we rode the ancient elevator up to my suite, where, in an immense teak bed with sheets marbled by moonlight, dappled with shadow, beneath a high frescoed ceiling, and under the regard of pale torturers and poisoners and assorted monsters of the ruling class who glowered from decaying tapestries on the walls, their rich velvets and silks reduced to a brownish ferment by the centuries, I made love to her, wanting as much of her as I could gather before she began to decline. After she had fallen asleep, I put on a shirt and trousers, went into the sitting room and lay down upon a sofa. I thought briefly of the evening, of the business we had done, and then I thought of Gia and what I intended to do about her.

She was irretrievably broken and thus unattainable, at least in her original form, the form that had initially attracted me, and I saw the trap into which I was about to walk, entering into a relationship that could be no more than a heterosexual copy of Lucan's with Professor Rappenglueck. However, her unattainability was half her charm. Love in all its forms, I supposed—love between the animals, between us, love between the subspecies—followed a similar development, beginning with a flirtatious glance, a dash of pheromones, thereafter progressing to doting looks, then to sex, and at every step along the way a decision was involved: you decided to take the first step, to walk the next step farther; you contrived the illusion that this was it for you, this was the ultimate;

and once past its peak moment, you decided whether you wanted to stick around for the tragedy, whether that suited your notion of love, whether you were going to attempt to create the illusion of unconditional love, to believe that there was more to love than your contrivance of it, that it was not your creation but a powerful universal force that swept us along. These little dramas in which we cast ourselves so as to inspire our lives, to give us reason to persevere . . . They would be amusing if not for the fact that, no matter how often our faith is proven unwarranted, we believe in them.

The cynicism of these thoughts and their underlying naïvete should have been sufficient to persuade me to rid myself of Giacinta. They seemed proof of her negative effect upon me. Yet I continued to debate the matter. An enormous face, counterfeited by shadows and the visible portions of a fresco, stared down at me from the ceiling, and I was contemplating that face, thinking it superior in design to the sylvan scene actually depicted, when I heard a chthonic rumbling, followed by a tremor that shook the building for more than a minute, toppling a clock from the mantel, sending ashtrays scampering across tabletops, overturning a chair, bouncing me onto the floor. I staggered up, knowing at once what had happened, having a clear perception of it, though I tried to persuade myself that I must be wrong, and hurried into the bedroom. Gia was still on the bed, poised on all-fours, her eyes wide with fright. I convinced her to lie back, gentled her, and told her she would be all right if she stayed in the suite, but that I had to go.

"Please!" She put her arms about my neck. "You take me."

"I can't," I said. "Wait here. Two hours. I'll come back in two hours. I promise."

My cell phone rang. Elaine. I switched it on and said, "Yes, I know."

"I can't believe the son-of-a-bitch . . . "

"Have you called Rome?"

"No, I thought you . . . "

"Call Rome. Now. Tell them to send helicopters. We have some in Palermo. Seal off the area. You coordinate from the hotel. Have you heard from Jenay?"

"No. Shouldn't you coordinate?"

"That's your job now."

Following a silence, she said tremulously, "I guess it is."

"Find out which satellites are passing over southern Italy and blind them. Knock them down if you have to."

"God, what a mess!"

"Call Rome. I'll get back to you."

Gia renewed her pleading after I switched off, but once again I rebuffed her.

"Stay. Here you be secure," I told her in fractured Italian. "*Due oras.* Okay?"

She put on a sad face, but she drew the blankets up to her neck. "Okay."

I kissed her and backed from the room, reassuring her with a smile. Then, not trusting the elevator, I raced down the stairs, ignoring the hotel guests and staff that I encountered, and descended the hill into the ruins of Diamante.

There was a tremendous amount of dust in the air. It coated my tongue, the membranes of my nostrils, got into my eyes. In the upper reaches of the town, the buildings were some of them intact, others partially demolished, yet I saw no one on the streets and I assumed Lucan's release must have killed everyone in an instant. His mental signature, which had been palpable at the hotel, boiled like steam from the wreckage, overwhelming all other sensory impressions. My cell phone rang. It was Elaine again. She told me the helicopters were on their way, the satellites had been dealt with, and our operatives within the Italian government were busy attempting to defuse the situation. As I listened, I began to feel the weight of my new responsibilities.

"Where are you?" she asked and, when I told her, she said, "I'm on top of the hotel. Wait until you see the waterfront. We're going to play hell cleaning it up."

"Call Skyler Means. Find out how much the Americans know. They're certain to have picked up something on satellite. Tell him to do whatever he has to."

I told her to continue checking in with me and switched off.

Shortly after Elaine's call, I found the body of a young woman lying under some bricks, but I did not pause to examine her, nor did I allow her death to disturb me—there were many dead that night, and I had no time to ponder my emotional state. As I descended through the town, the devastation increased. Buildings were flattened and the rubble in the winding street provided a surreal accent to the scene. Portions of Diamante's murals lay everywhere. Here a chunk of stucco bearing the pointillist rendering of an elephant's foot; here a sunrise broken into five sections; here a child's arm, a little dog trotting, a piece of a carousel, the bell of a tuba; half a Madonna's face was intact—the other half was pitted and unrecognizable. It was as if the pretty shell of the world had been blown apart to reveal its true disastrous nature.

Because of the extent of the destruction, I was able to see the waterfront long before I reached the Via Poseidone. The sea wall and the causeway had been obliterated, and, surrounding the islet on which Baldassaro's was situated, the water had been transformed into glass or something like, and the glass twisted into hundreds of tortured, translucent shapes, some diminutive, others towering thirty feet into the air, gleaming in the moonlight. The island itself was burning with a strangely steady, reddish flame, marking Lucan's grave and that of his lover. From where I stood, the entirety of the scene resembled an enormous, complicated blossom with a fiery stamen and irregular stiff petals.

The burning came to me as a faint windy sound. I was too far off to discern what the translucent shapes were, but when I stepped out onto the Via Poseidone, I realized they were heroic figures, none of them complete, yet all the more heroic for their lack of completion. Had they been finished figures, correct in every detail, they would have looked cartoonish; unfinished, mired in webs of glass, leaping out of glass waves, trying to shrug off glassy shrouds, charged with moonlight, like silver blood flowing through their limbs, they seemed more what Lucan would have had in mind: ancient warriors, both succumbing to and struggling to break free of the moonstruck glass that gave them substance. How long, I wondered, must he have trained himself in order to produce so complex a result at the moment of release? Decades, I reckoned. And I had no doubt that he had achieved his intent—the imagery and its incompleteness spoke to his obsession with the old days, to his belief that we had repressed our warrior instincts, restrained them beneath a decadent veneer. Confronted with the visible expression of those beliefs, I was moved a ways toward agreement with them.

I walked toward that barbaric sculpture garden, to the crumbling verge of the Via Poseidone, and examined a figure with a half-formed face and flowing hair, the muscular torso straining, with a two-handed grip on a club. As I inspected it from various angles, light glided back and forth inside it like the shiftings of a spirit level, bringing up bits of detail. Hulking just beyond, one of the larger figures appeared to be effortfully rising from a crouch, its head lowered, using a spear to push itself up, weighed down by a glass robe. I was about to call Elaine, thinking to modify my previous orders, when I spotted Jenay off along the street, standing beneath the immense figure of a woman depicted in the act of slashing at an invisible enemy with a knife. She was approximately a hundred feet away, anonymous at that distance, but it could only be Jenay. I hailed her and, as I approached, I saw that she had changed into jeans and a short jacket. Her hair was loose about her shoulders; she wore no make-up. She might have been the sister of the sculpted woman, who was also buxom, her wide hips flowing up from a glassy wave. They shared the same calm expression.

"Did you see it?" she asked as I came up. "The light he made?"

I told her I had been otherwise occupied.

"It was magnificent," she said. "He ruled the sky for nearly a minute."

Her poised demeanor and admiring tone aroused my suspicions. "You knew," I said.

"A few years back, he told me he wanted to die with Rappy. He only had about fifty years left, he thought, but he was emotionally spent. He said he was contemplating a release."

"And you knew he would do it tonight."

"I didn't *know*. Perhaps I suspected. He didn't seem himself."

I tried to turn her, wanting to search her face for signs of a lie, but she knocked my hand aside.

"You watched for the light," I said. "You must have known."

"I wasn't watching, I happened to be looking out the window," she said defiantly; then she put a hand to her forehead and blew out a breath, as if trying to steady herself. "Perhaps I knew."

"You should have told me, even if it were only a suspicion." Agitatedly, I opened and closed my cell phone several times. "He's left us a hell of mess."

"Is that all you take from it?" She shot me a hard look.

"I don't have time to appreciate Lucan's artistry now that I'm in command."

"Are you . . . in command? We'll see."

"You're challenging my authority?"

"If I'm challenging anything, it's your willingness to exercise authority."

"So you are challenging me. Do you want to formalize the challenge?"

"Not at this point," she said.

She glanced up at the sculpture and I, too, glanced up—the flame of the burning island brightened, and the fall of the woman's hair glowed redly. Jenay strolled off a couple of paces, her attention gathered by a smaller figure, a bearded, transparent, ax-wielding barbarian. The cell phone made a chilly noise in the empty street. I switched on and, keeping an eye on Jenay, said, "Yes."

"I can't reach Skyler," said Elaine.

"Try him in New York."

"I've tried all his numbers. Everybody's tried. The whole network is down. We haven't been able to reach any of our people on the east coast. It's Rome's opinion we've been compromised."

"That's obvious." I came a step toward Jenay. "What action do they recommend?"

"They recommend we go to a war level," said Elaine.

"Not yet." I closed to within arm's length of Jenay. "Go to Bronze . . . but tell them to go to Iron if they don't hear from me every half-hour. And tell the helicopters to fucking clean-up and get us out of here. If the Americans are going to react locally, it'll take a while, but there's no point running a risk. Jenay and I are down by the water, about seventy-five yards north of where the causeway used to stand."

"This is no coincidence," said Elaine. "Lucan and Skyler, both the same night."

"No," I said. "It's no coincidence."

Jenay's face betrayed, I thought, an almost undetectable trace of amusement. I shaped the words, You knew, with my mouth and said to Elaine, "Tell Palermo to prepare a nuke. We may be able to pass Diamante off as some sort of terrorist incident. I doubt it, but it's worth a try."

"What's happening?" Jenay asked as I switched off.

"Don't treat me like an idiot. You know very well what's happening."

She was silent a moment. "Lucan's forced your hand."

I chose not to reply.

"It follows that he would," she said. "Once he made his personal decision, he wouldn't have let the opportunity pass. And if the Americans are involved . . . Are we facing war?"

I folded my arms, scarcely able to contain my anger.

"You have to tell me," she said.

"If you want to continue with your pretense, call Elaine," I said. "She'll fill you in."

Jenay put her hands on her hips. "I realize you'd like to think of me as an element of a conspiracy, but there's no conspiracy. You're our leader now. People are going to watch you, they'll judge you by your actions. If I hesitate to give you my absolute approval, you shouldn't assume that's due to a conspiracy."

"Judge all you want. I won't be pressured or coerced any further. I've been maneuvered into a bad situation, but I may not do what Lucan wanted."

"What Lucan wanted was for someone to take decisive action. Action he couldn't bring himself to take, except in the way he did. He was well aware of his weaknesses. He used to tell me you were our hope. He saw in you a leader capable of making the kinds of decisions that we needed." Jenay touched my forearm. "Whatever he's done, he did it in part for you."

"This? This selfish, indulgent act? This treason? Yes, I can see that."

"Don't be obtuse! However you perceive it now, it's an opportunity to prove that Lucan was on the mark about you."

"Right. He created this fucking disaster just to make my leadership skills bloom." I went nose-to-nose with her. "He's killed Skyler! And probably hundreds more! Once they were taken, I'm certain Skyler and his people did what was necessary to preserve our position. But that they *were* taken, an entire network, it implies the Americans have a means of defeating our mental control. Skyler's people may not all be dead; a few may be in rooms somewhere spilling our secrets."

"Well, then. You have your work cut out for you." She said this flatly, as if to suggest it proved her point.

"Once this gets sorted out," I said, "if it can be sorted out, I promise there'll be an investigation."

Jenay shrugged. "And you'll have my full support."

A searchlight swept over the nearby figures, bringing them to flashing life, and a helicopter descended out of the night, its rotors swirling the dust that lay everywhere and making conversation a chore. Jenay and I moved apart, waiting for it to land.

From directly overhead, the burning island and its immediate surround looked even more like a blossom. I thought of those gigantic Sumatran flowers. Corpseflowers. The helicopter veered inland, and we began passing over the darkened Calabrian hills. My headset crackled. The pilots' helmets were silhouetted against the lights of the control array. Beside me, Jenay gazed out the window as I plotted the next days. Sleeper cells would have to be activated throughout the United States. Hundreds of individuals would be terminated, dozens of hard targets neutralized. I could feel the constrictions that Lucan had devised closing in around me, limiting the scope of my actions, enforcing a restructuring of my attitudes, leaving me to orchestrate the parameters of a new and improved holocaust. Thanks to him, we were entering a dangerous phase of history, one in which we would be more visible, thus more imperiled, than at any time since the Iron Age. This enlisted my paranoia and I imagined, not for the first time, that—unbeknownst to us—another group was monitoring our activities, and, above them, another group, and another, and so on and so forth. The universe as terrorist. Conspiracies of angels and demons. God the infinite suicide bomber.

"I've got Palermo on," said the co-pilot. "The package is ready for delivery."

"Have we reached a safe distance?" I asked.

"Yes."

"Patch them through to me."

I hadn't had a moment to think of Giacinta since rushing out of the hotel. I wondered if she had gone back to sleep, or if she had disobeyed my admonition and was wandering the streets, terrified and confused by the destruction of her home. The image troubled me, but at heart I was indifferent to her fate. Lucan's actions had nipped that passion in the bud and stripped from me all but the thinnest veneer of sentiment. I wished things were different, that I could indulge in mercy, that I could wound myself with love or its imitation, that I had time for such games, but that wish was subsumed by the eagerness we feel at the onset of war. The desire to wield power, to destroy, to win—they were the enticements of a more involving game. Yet as I gave the order that would erase Diamante from the maps of the world, I nourished a twinge of regret, I savored it, I stored it away in memory for whatever use I might one day find for it. Though we were flying away from the town, the flash, when it came, was visible as a reflection in the helicopter's plastic canopy. It held for several seconds, considerably less long than the light of Lucan's release, then swiftly faded. Jenay sighed—in satisfaction, I believed. She rested her hand atop mine, and we continued north toward Rome.

⬙

The magnitude of what's happening to our planet troubles all rational people . . . and some of us feel the need to do something a little extra. Take Nancy Kilpatrick, for instance. "We sit with fingernails psychologically bitten to the quick, awaiting nuclear, biological, bacterial, environmental disasters to strike," she says, "and to strike soon. Most of the fiction I've read that deals with such horrors employs the 'big' story—one that that involves groups battling for survival against both other groups and the elements . . . with the odd heroic individual in their midst.

"But I needed to know how a real woman—an average woman, alone—would fare in such an extreme situation, because women have very specific concerns that are rarely addressed in apocalyptic fiction." They are now.

Nancy's title comes follows on from all the other "ages"—the Ice Age, the Industrial Age and so on. "'The Age of Sorrow,'" she says, "is meant to have a double meaning, both marking a global era and a personal passage, as events of cataclysmic proportion would do." Watch out for Nancy's new novel, Hunted, *any time now.*

The Age of Sorrow
Nancy Kilpatrick

Grief had taken hold of her long ago. Long before the cataclysm. Long before everything had disintegrated: the planet; its people; her life. Hope for the future.

She crouched at the top of the hill, turning her head slowly from side to side, seeing only what the UV aviator goggles allowed her to view, scanning 180 degrees of verdant landscape, watching. Always watching. This valley had once been prime farmland, teeming with crops, and quietly nestled in it twin villages alive with quaint houses, one school that catered to the children of the entire population, a church each for the big two branches of Christianity, a synagogue, and a mosque. The two church steeples poked above the foliage, their crosses glinting in the afternoon sun, and she remembered reading what Joseph Campbell had said: you can tell what a culture values by its tallest buildings. She wondered if that applied to the beings who now dwelled in the villages.

There must still be fields for soccer and softball, the hospital, the shops, that the populace had supported, although she hadn't visited the villages in months, and couldn't be certain. Here and there a house was partially visible—she could just make out the pastel clapboard walls, splotches of color on this oh-so-green canvas of life that now flowed down the hills like lava. Over the last few years the plants had grown at an unnatural pace, devouring everything in their wake: the homes, the fields, the people. No, not the people. They had managed anyway. For a while.

Despite it all, she could not view this land so far from the place of her birth as anything but lush, the green vibrant, shades ranging from yellow-tinged to near black. The sun, despite the thick layer of ozone which trapped its rays, managed to give the plants what they needed. They weren't suffering from any "greenhouse effect" but seemed to flourish and propagate. It was just humanity that had fared badly in all this.

She knew she should head back. Even if a freak storm didn't crop up, sunset wasn't far off. And there was plenty to do. Always. The crops she tended religiously that provided her only fresh food needed watering. She should examine that weakness in the fence, figure out the strongest repair possible with the materials she had on hand so that she didn't need to go to either of the villages. There were fruits and vegetables to harvest, cook and put up, which meant gathering wood that had to be gotten out here, where it wasn't safe when darkness set in. Her life had become all work, everything geared towards survival. "Of the fittest," she said aloud for some reason, her voice sounding odd, the words ringing strangely in her ears. It had been so long since she'd heard herself speak.

But inertia had hold of her. She knew she was about mid-cycle, her most fertile time, halfway between periods— scant though they were now. Energy was not especially low during ovulation, just not high, and she felt a lack of focus. That would change within two weeks, when the flow began. But that would be later. Today she just wanted to sit and stare into the infinity of the horizon. "Slouching towards menopause," she had written in her journal. Now,

slouching, lounging, slacking off, literally or figuratively, all of that was a rarity in her life. There was too much to do, all the time, every day, and in the night the never-ending battle with loneliness and despair. And terror.

She pulled the glasses down for a second, hoping the hat brim could protect her eyes, but she could not help a quick glance at the sun, a brilliant orange, heading down the hazy sky and tried to recall its precise color when it had been yellow. She could not. It was as if the sun had always been the color of a pumpkin. As if everything in nature had always been this way. She fixed the glasses back over her eyes and willed herself to stand, to get moving, but her body refused to be pushed. Just a few more minutes. I've got a few minutes to spare, she assured herself.

Suddenly the bells at one of the churches began to ring, just as they did automatically every Sunday morning, afternoon and evening. Then the bells of the other church answered, the two playing back and forth. The sound reverberated around the valley, through her, washing away worries and fear, leaving her mellow, and remembering.

Church bells had rung the morning she and Gary married. A happy sound, full of the promise of a history yet to be lived. I was so young, she thought. So naïve. Now, it seemed as if she had always been her current age, forty. But then, on that day, at twenty, and Gary twenty-one, she had trusted him with her future; had trusted him to not betray her; to not betray them.

The house, the bills, a pregnancy that ended in an abortion because they were too young, he said, and she had agreed, yes, they were too young, with plenty of time ahead. A job that held her interest while she finished law school, then clerking at a prestigious firm until they hired her and she moved up the ranks of corporate law. A job she ultimately detested, now that she was honest with herself on a full-time basis. But back then, she tolerated it all, even the loss of the child she had not birthed. She tolerated it because of Gary, in the name of their love.

A lot of good that did her now. Gary. Her profession. Her childless life, and now it was too late for children. Not chronologically, although forty pushed it, but in all the other ways that made conceiving impossible, especially the circumstances of her life.

The choices we make, she thought grimly, as the last bell tolled. Those roads not taken. One road leads to another and that to another and eventually those choices have taken you down a path of no return. Why hadn't someone told her? Why hadn't her mother said this is how it is before she died? *Decide here, now, and go this way or that; some choices are irreversible.* But her mother was a liberal thinker, an early feminist. Someone who believed possibilities defined life and allowed it to constantly evolve. And her father? She had never gotten a fix on him. And after her parent divorced, he became a ghost. The man whose sperm had helped form her was friendly enough. He bought her things. Paid for her education.

Walked her down the aisle. But if she went blind she couldn't pick him out of a crowd. Not his voice, his scent, his touch.

All the wrong choices, she thought. Me. Gary. My parents. Everybody on the planet. The earth reeked with wrong choices. And now there were just two choices: Live or Die.

Her gloomy reverie broke when she caught movement in the distance. She pulled the goggles down to her neck; the sun had set. The sky had grayed fast, without her noticing. Startled, she jumped to her feet, staring to the west, watching the figure that looked male coming through the trees quickly. She spun in a quick circle and saw movement in most directions. Nearly surrounded, she had to hurry.

She raced down the mound, tearing through the high green towards the compound, a bootlace untying en route. She ripped off her gloves and threw them aside so she could get to the key hanging around her neck and pull the rope over her head as she ran.

Tonight they were moving swiftly and she had just reached the gate when she heard rustling behind her. She didn't dare take the time to look. Her hand trembled as she forced the large key into the huge padlock, yanked it open, pulled it from the bar and got herself inside and the door locked just as the first of them reached the gate.

The stench of rot forced her back. The solar yard light that increased illumination with the darkness allowed her to see this one all too clearly. A face no longer recognizable, living decay. His bloated blue fingers pushed their way through the chain links, reaching out for her.

All around the compound they gathered, aligning their dull eyes, the light of life missing, with the openings of the links. Her stomach lurched and her heart hammered. Three years and she had not gotten used to the sight of them and imagined she never would.

What flesh had not thoroughly corrupted or fallen away was bilious and left her gagging. They made sounds, low, moany noises that reminded her of sick or hurt animals. At one time, when it all began, she had felt sorry for them, imagining they were in pain. But that was early on. Back when she did not, could not believe that they wanted her dead. But now she believed.

She forced herself to turn, commanded herself to not look at any of them. The fence needing repair filled her thoughts, but she knew it could not be breached. Not tonight, not next week. It was just her constant worrying, something to focus on. How she had to be, always alert, never able to rest, the price of survival.

Despite the sounds that filled the air of their groans and shufflings and the squishy noises of flesh no longer alive pressing against other dead flesh or metal or grass underfoot, she managed to walk to the well and with trembling hands began lowering the metal bucket. It dropped down into the water with a splash and although it was too dark now to see to the bottom, through the rope she held she could feel the bucket submerge. She turned the crank to hoist it

up. When the pail reached the top she grabbed it to the ledge, untied it, locked the carbon filter on top and hauled it, water sloshing over the sides, to the vegetable garden, where she moistened one row of plants. Above her the sky had turned slate and no stars shown through the thick cloud cover. *The moon goddess is not making her presence known tonight*, she thought. *Artemis the huntress. Nothing worth hunting anymore.*

The numbers of them had grown until they were two and three deep around the fence in places. Every day she thanked whatever deities still cared about this poor planet for the fact that this disease first rotted the brain of the inflicted, otherwise they would long ago have taken to using tools and breaching her barrier. Tonight their presence seemed to turn the air from warm to hot, or at least *she* felt hot.

A flash memory, the day one of them touched her. Putrid flesh clamping onto her shoulder, cool puffy fingers curling around her, grabbing on, trying to hold her back, trying to absorb her warm life through her T-shirt. Panicked, she broke free and ran as fast as she could, snagging a shovel for protection as she went, racing until the breath burned her lungs and her vision blurred. And still it pursued her until she found safety in an abandoned store, bolting the door, watching it pawing the glass to get at her, unable to think clearly enough to shatter the glass, which told her a lot.

The news had declared this outbreak another super bug, spread by physical contact. Unresponsive to antibiotics. Not to worry, the man on Channel 7 said, a serum was being developed. All would be well. But she had felt its touch through thin fabric, watched its face close up all through the night until the first rays of the sun forced it to take refuge from the impending light which must hurt its rotting skin. By morning she knew that all would not be well. Things would never be right again. After that experience, she had changed.

Fueled by mounting terror, she booked a flight, just wanting to get as far away from the horrors as possible. An article had identified a few spots on the planet as trouble free; the more isolated, the scientist said, the better. He named New Zealand as the safest place on Earth. He was wrong.

Muscles trembling, she hefted another pail of water to the garden. The lettuce looked wilty, so she gave each plant extra liquid, hoping they would perk up. The growing season here extended all year, although last summer the heat had been almost unbearable and much of her crop burned. She lost forty pounds over four months and had been forced to go into the villages and raid gardens, and cupboards for tinned food, and stock up on all the vitamins she could get her hands on. Now she took a handful of those plus the brown seaweed extract she'd been swallowing for the last half decade to detoxify her body of radiation fallout. One good thing about no more humans on the planet: no more politicians dropping bombs on one another.

The garden had been, like so much in the last few years, a learning experience. Come this summer she planned to add a UV filter to the shade over the plants for the hottest part of the day. Thank god the well was artesian and would, theoretically, last forever. Not that she would. And there were no heirs to take her place. Fortunately.

The things outside the gate continued to moan and groan and produce squishy sounds. Sometimes she thought she heard her name, but that couldn't be. They were no longer living beings, not living in the way she was. Flesh and organs and bone decomposing, they moved by instinct, and the instinct the nearly dead seemed to possess directed them towards the living of which she was, to her knowledge, the last in this region. Perhaps in this country. The world. She had no way of knowing.

She finished the watering, sprayed organic pesticide on the plants, and then did a final visual check of the compound. Everything in order. An acre was not too much to manage, and from the front yard she could see every inch of the property but for what lay behind the mound. She had machetted the vines and scrub that grew wildly and regularly mowed the grass with an old hand mower she'd found on one of the farms, flattening everything but the garden. Facing the mound, she walked to her right, stopping two feet from the fence and at her approach the sounds from the cool bodies increased in volume like insects swarming. She could see one side of the back fence. None of them were at that corner, where repairs were needed. She reminded herself that the damage wasn't urgent. Still, knowing that a weakness existed made her nervous. Not nervous enough to go there, in the darkness of night, which would draw attention to that area. And to her. She couldn't do anything to fix it now, and a sudden pain as her ovary struggled to expel an egg into her fallopian tubes turned her away from the yard and towards the house.

On the way she plucked four lettuce leaves, picked a ripe tomato, a yellow pepper, and with the Army knife she always carried in a sheath around her belt she sliced off one small head of a broccoli, all of it going into a basket which she carried in one hand. With the other hand she hefted the last pail of water. Carefully she headed down the two steps and inside, closing and locking the door after her, which drowned out most of the din that unnerved her still, and stood, back resting for a moment against the wooden barrier, happy for contact with even the inanimate.

Finally she pushed herself away, dropped the basket on the table and set the pail by the sink, took off the goggles and her hat and began to roll up her shirt sleeves. As an after-thought she removed her shirt but left the cotton tank top on. Immediately her body temperature lowered.

She crossed the room to the wall under the one window and checked the bank of batteries charged by eight 75 Watt solar panels on the roof. A flip of a switch cranked up the air filtering system from low—where she kept it when she went out—to high. The fully charged batteries meant she could waste a few amps to enjoy a bit of music

as she ate. Something soothing. She flipped through the CDs and found Pachelbel's *Canon*, then changed her mind—too gloomy. Maybe Delibe's *Lakme*. Something lighter, that spoke of hope. Of springtime. Springtime.

As the music played, she scrubbed all of the vegetables thoroughly in the carbon-filtered water. Likely it did nothing much for the pollutants in the air still circling the earth, but then she wasn't certain what to do about them. She pulled a chopping knife from the rack and started on the pepper, gutting it, setting the seeds aside to dry, her mind wandering to a springtime only five years ago. The last one where she had seen Gary alive.

How could life have seemed so ordinary? she wondered. She rinsed and sliced into the tomato, the pungent smell reaching her nostrils, and added it and the pepper to the lettuce she washed and tore into bite-size pieces.

Spring, the weather beautifully mild, the scent of lilac in the air, the scent of hope. She and Gary met for lunch at a small café downtown, near the campus where he taught. She told the receptionist she'd be gone for an hour and a half but when she was seated Gary said he had to get back to the college and could only stay thirty minutes.

They sat on the terrace and ordered—both had salads and café lattes—and she remembered gazing at the young people, semi-stripped for the mild temperature. They all looked so healthy and happy. Nothing like a twenty-year-old body, she thought, although at thirty-five she wasn't in bad shape at all, thanks to a daily jog before work.

She recalled looking over Gary's shoulder as he munched on Caesar salad and seeing her reflection in the restaurant's window: chestnut hair, large dark eyes, an oval face with few signs of wrinkles, nothing that tri-monthly derma-abrasions and a bit of Botox couldn't fix.

She glanced at Gary and saw him not watching her but staring at those same bodies. It was only a fragment of time, and yet in that split second she knew he had been unfaithful.

He felt her look and his handsome face closed around the emotion. "How's your day?" he asked.

She put down her fork. "Who is she?"

"She?" He looked uncomfortable. "You'll have to be more precise than that or—"

"The one you're fucking. What's her name?"

He opened his mouth, his expression guarded, his eyes haughty, but she locked onto him, a human laser, and said, "Don't bother lying. Just tell me." Her voice, remarkably calm to her own ears, must have put him at ease.

"Her name is Eileen."

"A student?"

"First year."

"I suppose she came to discuss a paper or project."

"A project. Not a very good one. I gave her direction."

They could have been talking about the city's plans for revamping the water-front, or a new movie to be seen. Sud-denly, she couldn't bear it, the strain of the last fifteen years. Without a word, she picked up her bag and stood.

"Wait, look—"

But before he could say more she was out of earshot. My life is a facade, she thought. Years and years of ignoring truth. In those moments of that perfect spring day she knew that she had barely loved him when she was twenty and now did not love him at all. At least in the way that mattered between a woman and a man. The most hurtful part was that she knew it was mutual.

She ran for an hour, but she could not have said what streets, or even what district. Her ringtone—nineteen notes of *The Flower Duet*—played again and again until she pulled the cellphone from her purse and tossed it into a trash can, then, when the shoulder bag grew annoying, she pitched it as well.

Sometime later she showed up at the front door, without keys. Darkness had set in. The trees and grass and the other homes on the street looked stunned. And she saw everything as if for the first time.

She rang the bell and he let her in, moving away from the door as she passed him, not wanting a fight, but neither did she. Apparently the rela-tionship was not worth fighting for. She climbed the stairs, suddenly exhausted, and entered their bedroom to find his matching suitcases on the bed, both three-quarters packed.

Slowly she removed her clothes and let them drop to the floor then ran a bath and sank into a hot tub, a glass of Beaujolais in her hand, and fell asleep.

When she woke, the water was cold, tinted with the undrunk wine as if it had been blood that spilled. The house was tomb silent. His suitcases were gone. She found a note on the dresser: something about being sorry, and wishing her a nice life. She had ripped it into tiny pieces and flushed it down the toilet.

She cut up the broccoli raw and added it to the salad. A small bottle of olive oil sat on the floor in the coolest part of the kitchen area and she opened it to add a few drops to the vegetables, then pushed the cork back in. For a moment she stood looking at the salad, then covered the bowl with an elasticized net to keep insects out, turned and walked to the couch that doubled as a bed in this one-room house and fell onto it, exhausted. Always exhausted. Always unable to sleep.

Why was all this coming back to her now? It felt like the disease of memory crept through her mind and heart, hiding, surging to the fore when she least expected it and did not want it.

She glanced around the room helplessly. She had positioned the couch so that from here she could see every corner, and the door. One room. Convenient. Life condensed. Half buried in the earth like a grave, the design geared to keeping the heat down. And a small *Alice Through the Looking Glass* door behind the couch, but it only locked from the other side. The tunnel led through the dirt mound and would bring her 100 feet outside the compound should this house be invaded.

One high-pitched, sharp laugh erupted from her. The idea was absurdity itself. If the compound was invaded, she would have no home. Outside the compound, where could she escape to? She had watched the villagers succumb until none were left uninfected. And if any were whole she had not come across them in the last year. But she had been making less and less trips into the villages because seeing these creatures cowering from the light became too much. Besides, most of the supplies she needed she already had, stored in a small shed just outside the door— canned goods, ammunition for the one rifle stationed next to the couch, and the handgun she carried in a holster around her waist—weapons she had only fired in practice and was not sure she could actually use on these formerly-living humans.

While there was still gas in the pumps and a couple of functioning vehicles left in the villages, she had already brought up many bottles of water, in case the well ran dry. Clothing, shoes, sheets and towels and kitchen equipment. Propane tanks, although she rarely cooked meals anymore. Over time she had learned through books how to use the solar panels. Getting them from the hardware store to the compound had been one thing, hauling them to the roof had been another. And the heavy batteries had tested her physical strength and ingenuity even more. Batteries to store the raw energy, a converter to turn it into something useful which then powered what had become a decreasing need for energy. With no TV broadcasts, no radio, no phones, no

Internet, no contact with the outside world but for a CB radio that she left on but had stopped sending out messages from months ago, she only needed lighting and music to get by. Get by. That's what she was doing, getting by. Barely. "Everything the female survivalist needs," she said aloud, hearing her voice, the sound in the stillness so alien to her ears it brought tears to her eyes.

Why was she alive when others were not? How had this nightmarish existence come upon her? Maybe she really had died and gone to hell and this was it. The Dante book she had read in her youth with the lovely Doré etchings described hell but she knew there were many more than nine levels.

When the bacterial infections began, they rampaged through chronic care facilities, then hospitals in general, schools, workplaces, anywhere and everywhere human beings had physical contact with one another. At the same time, the ozone layer altered sufficiently that the icebergs at the North Pole melted, raising the sea level, turning what had been frozen tundra into almost pastoral terrain. Then the Antarctic ice began breaking off in large chunks and microorganisms trapped in the ice at both poles were released. Scientists learned that some lifeforms could lie in wait for millennia.

Wars became the norm, day to day reality on the news, thousands killed here and there, weaponry of all types employed and the "limited nuclear war" became reality. Suddenly the air was not just polluted with smog but radioactive dust circled with the altered jet streams.

Soil and water turned toxic, and multinationals focused their resources on cleaning out the poisons so that food could still be grown and water drunk, but only by citizens wealthy enough to pay for purification. The masses could not. Brand new immune-system diseases soared.

With enormous loss of life, human society began to disintegrate: garbage piled up; transportation came to a halt; medication ran out; electrical and cellular services died and depending on the season, people froze or burned to death, unless they were preyed upon by other human beings.

Her mind scanned the hellish reality she had witnessed over five short years, descending circle by circle. And all the while humanity tried to adapt. Her heart felt heavy: the naivety, the stupidity, the complacency. The men in power said it would all be alright in the end. But it wasn't alright. It would never be alright again. And just when things couldn't get worse, they did: the new plague spread rapidly, and suddenly the dying could not die.

But by then she was in New Zealand, traveling aimlessly. Nowhere to go. Nothing to do but sit back and watch the apocalypse unfold. *Wait your turn*, she told herself, but her turn had not come.

In truth, New Zealand, and some of the other isolated islands in this region were the last to go. Although this country was not spared the nuclear fallout, they did manage to stem the flow of visitors and immigrants and eventually movement by their own citizens—

nobody went in or out. But by then it was too late. For humanity, for Gary's plea with her to come home to him in that last phone call. Everything was always too late.

She picked up the journal she had been keeping, the latest one, atop a pile of five large books, one per year since she had arrived here, chronicling the deterioration and her own existence. Writing helped keep her sane, even though some days took up barely half a page, filled with mundane details of gardening, eating, defecating. Other entries analyzed the politics, or the science as she understood it—and with all the time in the world and all the books and magazines and newspapers in the library she had learned quite a bit. But the worst entries, the ones that made her cringe, were those where she saw her emotions sprayed on the page as if they were her blood. Tortured by loneliness and despair, she could barely re-read those. Because despite all that she had learned, and all that she understood, as far as she knew, she was the last person alive on the planet. Every attempt with the CB had met with dead air.

"Dante had no idea!" she mumbled, her voice almost an echo in her ears. The circles of hell were infinite.

Suicidal thoughts nearly overwhelmed her more times than she could count, and she did not know yet know why she still lived, unscathed by the new plague, unaltered by the deadly air. But answers, like everything else, were in short supply, and she'd long ago stopped her obsessive reading and wondering about why she seemed immune to what affected others. Diseases that should have killed everyone, if only the others could die.

But they could not die. They hid from daylight and wandered aimlessly at night. No, not aimlessly. They always found their way to her compound. She wondered if they sought her out for a connection to life when they possessed little resembling that. The walking dead, her only companions. And the worst part was, some were not as decayed. Some she recognized still: Joe who used to run the butcher shop; Lucy from the pharmacy; Ned and his wife Sarah who farmed just outside the villages and ran a fruit and vegetable stand . . . The memory of their faces as they had been overlapped with how they were now moved a wave of hysteria up from her gut that caught in her throat and suddenly she found herself sobbing uncontrollably.

This fit lasted only seconds. Her last eruption had been about six months ago.

She picked up the pen and began writing, trying to convey in words the feelings that washed through her like waves in a storm. She could never get over how quickly the illnesses overtook the living. One day she had gone into the chemist's and Lucy had been fine. The next day she had dark circles beneath her eyes and sneezed uncontrollably. The third day Bill, the owner, said she was "Out with a sniffle." The next night Lucy was spotted walking the streets at midnight, her skin mottled, her eyes bearing an opaque sheen.

People tried to talk with her, to help her, but she seemed incapable of speech, only incoherent mutterings and soft moans. And those that she touched came down with the sickness.

Lucy was the first local to go. As the numbers of the undead increased, people packed up their families and fled the villages, as many as could get away. She had no idea where they went, where they *could* go.

She found this house and when the grocery store and the hardware shop were abandoned she began stocking up, building the fence, securing her world. And then they came. Those who were left. Dozens from villages that once had claimed a combined population of 10,000. Every night they swarmed from their homes and headed to hers. A macabre ritual. *Maybe they're as lonely as I am*, she wrote. *I'm half dead in a different way. Maybe it's a strange, symbiotic curse and we need each other. If I cease to survive, will they? If they disappear tomorrow, will I still exist? How Zen*, she wrote. *How perfectly, horribly Zen.*

Suddenly she felt heavy, tired, and her eyes would not stay open. She sank down to a full recline, telling herself that if she fell asleep now she would be up in the middle of the night, but not heeding the warning.

In a dream that she knows to be a dream she walks over fields covered with wildflowers under a yellow sun crossing a blue sky with few clouds. The cool earth beneath her feet, the sweet scent of lilac in the air, a mild and warm breeze blows her skirt and her hair . . . She closes her eyes and feels heat pene-

trate to her bones, warming her, even as she thinks: the sun is too strong!

A sound jolts her and she spins around to see a man coming towards her. He is dressed in blue jeans, a t-shirt and his body is muscular. With hair the color of the sun and eyes that she can see as he nears are blue as the sky, he is as alive as the day. As real as nature that heals and cleanses itself, over time.

Suddenly the man is Gary, and he stops before her and reaches out to cup her chin. His touch is electric. It is as if her body is nothing but electrical current as sparks explode throughout her, sending signals to her brain, her heart, her genitals. She quivers, hungry for this, fearful of it at the same time. Without opening his mouth he says to her "Don't worry! This was meant to be."

How? she wonders. "Are you dead?" she asks.

He smiles and pulls her to him, kissing her full on the lips, and she tastes his familiar tongue inside her mouth, moving, probing. An image flashes through her of dark unwholesomeness. An invasion.

She jerked awake, her body covered with sweat. She sat up abruptly and felt chilly, as if the temperature had plummeted. She grabbed the blanket from the foot of the couch and wrapped it around her shoulders, still shivering.

Disoriented, she looked around the darkened room, lit only by one 15 Watt coiled florescent that she kept lit over the kitchen table to stave off the demons of darkness. But the demons had gotten through, again.

She stood on shaky legs, feeling her cool forehead, and then headed to a cupboard where she kept a first aid bag. She placed the thermometer under her tongue and walked to the one window while she waited, moving the bar that held the thick wooden shutters so she could open them and look out.

Darkness filled the night. And silence. Nothing. Once her eyes adjusted, she scanned the periphery of the fence to the gate, as far as the window would let her see. They had gone, at least from the area within her view.

A full moon hung in the sky as if pasted there on top of the blackness. She squinted at the orb, struggling to see the face that she had seen as a child, but the thickened atmosphere blurred details.

When she pulled out the thermometer and read it under the lamp she saw that her temperature was normal. She did not feel sick. A glance in the mirror by the door showed a too-thin face, haggard, but she had accepted that. She looked weary but bright-eyed. Absently she smoothed back her short hair, running fingers through it like a comb. I'm alright, she thought, feeling both relief and despair that she was not sick. "You're ovulating," she told her image. The serious image looked back at her with an expression that said: So? What does it matter? "Soon you'll get old and die," she said. The image did not reply. Old and die. Would she, *could* she die? Or was her destiny that of the undead, the ones who were sick but unable to get well, unable to die, caught in a balance of the battle of microorganisms that kept them in a terrible stasis. That kept them walking endlessly, feebly,

helplessly, unable to give themselves wholeheartedly to entropy. Weak, mindless, incapable of using tools— "Isn't that what defines us as human?" she challenged her image. But the image, as always, did not long to respond.

Suddenly, in anger, she threw off the blanket, stalked to the couch, grabbed the rifle, and unbolted the door. The night air felt cooler, and the cold wind of a storm snapped at her. Tonight she wanted change. Something would die. One of them. Or her. It didn't matter. This couldn't go on!

Aware of the insanity of her thinking, she would not stop herself. She stormed to the fence and strode along the periphery. Soon she was passing the side of the vegetable garden, the side of the mound then reached the back of the dirt mound that enclosed her house, her prison. Nothing. No one. Where were they? Had they fled in despair? Had an alien ship come down and taken them all away? Did the balance of power finally fall to one side and the life-destroying organisms win and they at long last died? Tonight of all nights she wanted to find out. She wanted to stare into one of those hideous faces, to confront this half-being, to find a way to send it to oblivion. Maybe that was the way to go. Get over her aversion and shoot them in the head, one by one, until there were no more. Then she could walk free! What would it matter if that left her alone? She was alone now, totally. Thoroughly. The world she remembered had receded like a long-ago dream barely recalled.

She passed the weakness in the fence and saw that it had not been breached. Nothing had been breached, just her psyche.

Her quick strides brought her around to the other side of the mound, then back into what she deemed the front yard. Not one of the not-quite-dead. Frustrated, she stepped outside of the glow of the yard light and glared up at the impassive moon. Suddenly she gave in to an impulse of a different sort: snapping her head further back, letting the glow of the other-worldly light freeze her face, she howled like an animal. Wailed over and over into the impending storm until the sounds turned to shrieking. She dropped the rifle. Out of her control, her body staggered around the yard, arms protecting her solar plexus, screaming, sobbing, blind with the impossibleness of despair. She only stopped when she slammed against the fence and crumpled to the ground, her back braced against the chain link, her body curled into a fetal position.

Out of her mind with grief, it took time to realize that something was different. She felt a burning at the back of her neck. The hotness moved along her flesh from side to side and at first she did not know what caused it. But then she did. Cold, so intense it felt hot, comforting, caressing her skin. Behind her, close, she heard breathing. Wet breathing. And while her mind warned her that she should be frightened, at the closeness, the touch, another part of her ached for more. She sat up, pressing her back against the fence. More fingers touched her, caressing her as a lover would, as Gary had. Their foul odor entered her nostrils as flowers. Lilacs. She reached back over her shoulder; flesh met flesh. And as the rain blew from every direction, for the first time in a long time her sorrow evaporated into the wind.

⊠

When a man carelessly steps in front of a speeding garbage truck, that's usually the end of his story. But for Jake Hallman it's just the beginning. He awakens on a metaphorical stretch of the Afterlife called the Golden Road, where the angel Brendan comes to escort him to Heaven. But Jake isn't having any:

Jake becomes one of the rarest and most valuable commodities in the Afterlife: a free soul. Dead people aren't supposed to change—that's a big part of what being "dead" means—but the rules don't seem to apply to Jake. This draws the unwelcome attention of the competing Divine Wills whose domains make up the Afterlife. They see Jake's potential as a threat or, even more worryingly, as an opportunity. Jake teams up with a disgruntled ex-Valkyrie named Freya and hits the Golden Road, the mystic path that links the Heavens and Hells of every mythos, plus a few places even the gods forgot. The unlikely pair undertake a rare quest: to discover if there is any place in the cosmos where a spirit can be truly free

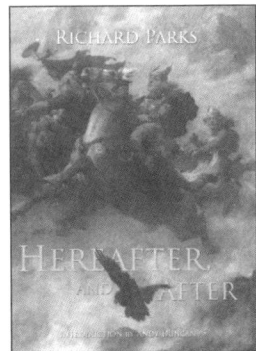

"'Eels' is spun from something that happened a few years back in the Lancashire village where I live," novelist/screenwriter Stephen Gallagher tells us. "The idea fell into a form almost immediately, but if I'd written it then it would have been a simple, EC-type story of the kind that the comics did better. I hoped that if I let it sit for a while then it would grow on that framework to become something more resonant."

Steve's short fiction has earned places in numerous "Year's Best" anthologies, and a "Best Collection" British Fantasy Award. His new novel, a historical macabre set in the world of Victorian theatre, is published next year by Random House's Shaye Areheart Books imprint.

Eels

Stephen Gallagher

He said, "Give me a minute and I'll shut the dog in."

The dog was a little Jack Russell terrier and its owner was Johnny Clifford, whom I saw most days of my working life but barely knew. He was middle aged, shaved infrequently, dressed like a tramp, and was never seen without the same shapeless hat. He owned the big house at the mouth of the quarry where all the lockup garages were.

Back then I rented one of the few lockups that wasn't burned-out or falling down. I used it to store tools and scrap and sometimes as a workshop, if I was on a job that needed one. I'm a plumber.

I could never quite work out how Johnny Clifford made his living. It was always one scheme or another. For a few weeks after any big storm, he'd be a roofer fixing broken slates. In the record summer of '03 he'd been seen selling ice cream. Turning his hand to anything, chasing the money wherever it was.

I reckon he just scraped by. His house was big but he spent nothing on it, or on the battered old Transit that he drove. The only new-looking feature of the place was those two plastic shelters that had appeared around the back of the property. They'd arrived on a truck and gone up in a day, tent-like structures of thick polythene stretched over hoops. They looked like a little space colony in his back yard. The polythene was cloudy, and you couldn't see through it.

He said he had a job for me. So right now, on what felt like the coldest day of the year, I was about to get a peek at whatever new scheme he had going back there in Moonbase Alpha.

Once the Jack Russell was out of the way, I followed Johnny around the back of the house. His dog had never given me any problems apart from the times when I had to chase it out of the garage for trying to pee somewhere. But it would bark ferociously whenever anyone approached the house, and I was happy to see it secured. Dogs change when they're on their own turf.

We went into the first of the plastic shelters.

"Watch your head," Johnny said as he ducked in the entranceway.

It was warmer in here than outside, but not by much. The two domes were linked by a tunnel and I could see into both. Because of the plastic the light was soft and pure, like you'd imagine the light in heaven to be.

My first thought was that he was making wine. There were six big vats like those above-the-ground swimming pools that you get in suburban gardens. You fill them from a hose, and water pressure keeps the sides up. He'd insulated and put covers on them, and they were linked with pipes and filtration units.

He'd done all the assembly himself, but I could see why he needed me because his plumbing skills had their limits. On the ground before one of the vats lay an immersion heater coil, in pieces. I'd no idea what he'd been trying to achieve with it and, by the evidence, neither had he.

He said, "Can you do anything with this? I've been trying to rig up something that'll keep the water at a steady twenty-five degrees."

"What's it for?" I said.

"Never mind what it's for."

At this, I bristled a bit.

"It'll make a difference," I said. "Are we talking average or ambient?"

He looked at me as if I was trying to put one over on him. I actually was bull-shitting, but he couldn't be sure of it. After a few moments he walked over to one of the other vats and drew the canvas back.

I went and stood beside him, and looked into the water.

"Fish?" I said.

"Eels."

Now that he said it, I could see that they didn't move like fish. They rippled. They were all down at the bottom of the tank and were sliding around one another in one seething, living knot. Their sizes varied.

I said, "What are you doing? Breeding them?"

"You can't breed eels," he said. "You buy in the young and then raise them 'til they reach a commercial weight. It's supposed to take about eighteen months, but these aren't thriving. Doesn't matter what I feed them on. It's this winter that's doing it. I've insulated the tanks, but they lose too much heat. The cold stops the elvers from growing."

"Who do you sell them to?"

"Smokehouses. Top class restaurants. They're a delicacy."

He got a net and fished one of them out for me to see. It looked like the devil and fought like one, too.

"They don't *look* very delicate," I said.

"They're tough little buggers, I can tell you that. If I'd known what it took to kill them, I'd have thought twice about taking them on."

He lowered the net into the water and tipped it so that the creature could swim out and rejoin the others. It quickly settled amongst them, a dark sliver of pure muscle flexing its way through the complex maze of its kin.

Johnny told me that he'd picked up all the gear from a would-be eel farmer who'd gone bust. Personally I'd have taken that as a warning sign, but I said nothing. He explained how he bought the live elvers straight from the fishing boats. Eels lived in freshwater but they spawned out at sea, and the young were caught as they swam inland.

"Everything's got to be just right," he said. "The people you're selling to . . . they won't take less than perfect."

He wasn't looking at me as he said it. He was looking down at his eels. His face was set and grim. I got the feeling that "less than perfect" was something that had been dogging him for all of his life.

He left me to it and I got on with the job.

Johnny Clifford had been married once, and for a long time, but his wife had left him about three years before. She'd stuck by him for long enough to earn people's sympathy for it, rather than their disdain. She was a pleasant, practical woman, and Clifford was the village grump who always looked as if he'd choke or cross the street rather than bid you good morning. Most people reckoned her a saint, and weren't scandalised even when it was revealed that her new partner was female. If anyone could drive a woman to that kind of thing, the feeling seemed

to run, then Johnny Clifford was the man.

When she first left the village some joked that, irritated by her patience and good humour, he'd probably done her in and buried her on the moor behind the quarry. But she turned up every few weeks to collect her maintenance money. I'd seen her myself, a couple of times. She arrived in a silver car, driven by a woman who waited in it. She stayed for about an hour and I reckon she was probably making sure that Johnny had at least one decent meal in his month.

I don't believe he actually owned his house. If he did, then he could have sold it and moved into a smaller place and his money worries would have disappeared. I think he inherited the tail-end of a lease when his parents died, and there weren't enough years left on it to have any market value. So there he was, stuck with it—not so much a home, more a gigantic brick albatross. Not worth selling, nor worth investing in. If a window broke, he simply closed up the room and stopped using it.

He'd tried to bargain down my hourly rate, but I'd told him to take it or leave it. I think he knew what I'd say, but he tried it anyway. With that settled, he left me to work on my own.

In the course of the morning I rebuilt the heater unit and replaced the thermostatic control, and then I installed it and gave it a test. This tank, as he'd explained it, was the fingerling tank, for the most critical growing stage in the eels' life cycle. Eels thrive in warm water, which is why you get so many eel farms alongside power stations. They grow quickly in the waste heat from the cooling towers.

Johnny Clifford reappeared when the job was all but done. Most punters make a point of looking in every now and again to see how it's going, maybe offer you a brew, but not Johnny.

He stood there for a while as I put away my tools. I saw him check his watch and then he said, "I suppose you'll want paying."

"I'll drop off a bill when I've worked it out," I said.

"Listen," he said. "I showed you what I've got going, here, but I'd prefer it if you don't broadcast what you've seen. All right?"

"Okay," I said. "Why's that?"

"I don't want everyone to know my business."

"Well, good luck keeping it quiet, around here," I said. Here, where everybody seemed to find out everyone else's secrets before too long.

"I've got my reasons," Johnny Clifford said darkly.

With an hour or two of daylight left I had a couple of things to finish off for customers in the village, small tidy-up jobs. Fitting a vent cowl. Bleeding the air out of a system that I'd installed the week before. By the time I'd done, the light was gone and my working day was over. I picked up a pint of milk from the local Spar store and drove home to my cottage, which stood on the lane heading out towards the town.

The lane was on the other side of the moor from the quarry. From my upstairs window I could just about see Johnny Clifford's chimneys beyond the moor's distant edge. Whereas Johnny's house was huge and a burden to run, mine was tiny, and just turning around in it could be a challenge. Especially with the new bath standing upright in the hallway, waiting to be fitted. I was sprucing the place up, planning to put it on the market in the spring. I'd always promised myself that if I wasn't married by fifty-five, I'd retire early and move up to Scotland while I could still enjoy the walking. I'd scouted an area and had my eye on the shell of a house that I could renovate, but I had to sell this one to raise the capital.

You always need a plan. Something to aim for. In pursuing mine I spent little and I saved everything. Every job took me a little closer to it.

I typed up Johnny Clifford's bill and put it in a brown envelope, ready to drop through his letterbox the next morning.

Over the next couple of weeks, two things happened. The cold weather grew even colder, and I didn't see any sign of my money. Late one afternoon, after taking the battery out of my van to give it an overnight charge, I set out across the moor to seek out Johnny and give him a shake for it.

There hadn't been any snow, but all the grasses had frozen. The sky was grey and the air was clear and it was as if the entire moor had been fossilised with a single breath. I followed the old mill path as far as the quarry's edge; the quarry had been the source of stone for the original houses in the village, and was like a bite out of the side of the moor. From where I stood I could look down onto the roofs of the lockup garages and the back of Johnny Clifford's place.

The lights were on in his eel farm. I could see the vague dark shape of him through the polythene, about his no-longer-secret business. I'd no idea how the news had got out. But even in the post office pension queue they were talking about Johnny Clifford's mad venture in the quarry.

I followed the safety fence down. It was broken in lots of places and I was able to step over it into Johnny Clifford's yard. When I reached the bubble I stopped, and then I banged on the plastic with the flat of my hand. It made a muffled, thundery sound, like a drum. I waited a moment and then opened the door to look inside.

I didn't spot Johnny straight away. He was in the adjoining bubble and I saw him through the linking tunnel, up on a set of steps and stirring something in one of the vats. He was leaning into it like a gondolier, the pole supporting a part of his weight. He looked my way and I assumed he'd seen me, so I started toward him.

The next thing I was aware of was a frenzy of yapping and a sudden, sharp pain in my right thigh as Johnny Clifford's Jack Russell took a running leap at me and nipped my leg. Johnny Clifford looked up in shock and I realised that he hadn't seen me after all. He jumped down off the steps and came toward me, shooing the dog back as he did.

"What do you mean," he said, "just walking in like that on somebody else's property?"

"He's torn my trousers," I said.

He had, too. The dog's teeth had ripped a triangular flap that now hung loose. I rubbed around inside it, easing the sting of the bite and looking for signs of blood.

"It's just a scratch," Johnny said.

"You can get rabies from a scratch."

"Don't be so soft," Johnny said. "Come into the house."

He sat me down in the kitchen and gave me a glass of cheap brandy. It was early for me but, what the hey, I was possibly the first man in the village to get a drink out of Johnny Clifford. The dog got shut into the next room and stood right up close on the other side of the glass door, glowering at me through the frosting.

"Has it broken the skin?" Johnny asked.

"No," I had to admit. "It still hurts, though."

"I expect you'll live," Johnny said, and went over to the mantelpiece. On it stood an old clock with its hands at a quarter to two. He reached in behind it and brought out what I recognised as my own envelope, with a slender wad of folded banknotes poking out of the top.

He'd have counted it already but he counted it again, lips pursed, breathing loudly through his nose.

I kept rubbing the bite. "A word of apology would be nice," I said. The skin hadn't broken but the place was staring to throb, and I could bet that it would bruise.

Johnny looked up from the money, and he didn't seem repentant.

"You swore to me that you wouldn't tell anyone what I'd showed you," he said.

"And I haven't."

"No?"

"No," I said. "And if you're astonished that word still managed to get around the village in spite of that, then you must be a bit simple."

"Certain people could make a lot of trouble for me," Johnny said.

I was starting to get angry now. "And you'll be wanting someone to blame for it if they do," I said. "Well, leave me out of it. Just pay up what you owe me and the next time you think of calling on me for something, don't."

I made a point of re-counting the money for myself once he'd handed it over. Then something happened that I hadn't been expecting at all.

"All right," Johnny said. "I got it wrong. I'm sorry."

And there was more to come.

The cheap brandy went away and a good whisky came out. "See if this helps," he said.

I'd never seen him unwind like this before. He even took the hat off.

I asked him what he was so worried about and his answer could be summed up in two words: animal welfare. He feared being raided by the animal welfare people.

I couldn't understand why. From what I'd seen, he took unusually good care of his stock. I wondered if he was operating without some license that he needed to have, but it wasn't that.

"You keep this to yourself," he said. "Okay?"

He took me into one of the back rooms. It was empty apart from a row of domestic freezers along one wall, all rescued from scrap and no two alike. They were rusting but functional. He opened one of the freezer doors and inside it I saw newspaper-wrapped packages stacked three or four deep on every shelf. They were end-on, like bottles in a wine cellar. Each package was the size of an adult eel.

I didn't get it.

I said, "So?"

Johnny said, "They're alive when I put them in there."

Now I got it.

"Why?" I said.

"The traditional slaughter method is to pack them in dry salt and then eviscerate them. The salt deslimes them and then it's the disembowelling that kills them. Can you imagine that?"

"It sounds barbaric."

"Exactly. I tried it once." He shook his head. "Never again."

I looked at the stiff little corpses in their newspaper shrouds. They made the inside of the cabinet look like one of those Parisian catacombs filled up to the roof with skulls and bones. If it had been a freezer full of meat, I wouldn't have thought anything of it. But meat's already dead when you put it in.

I said, "Is this not just as bad?"

"I hope not," Johnny said. "But who can say? I keep 'em in cold water for a week. Cleans out their intestines and slows them right down. Then I wrap them up and put them in the freezer and it's like they go to sleep."

"Up at the trout farm they use a stunning tank."

"Up at the trout farm they can afford one. She's bleeding me dry. The only thing the judge wouldn't let her do was pack me in salt first."

We went back to the kitchen. Johnny's dog joined us and showed me no hostility now, apart from a growl when I reached for my glass and he thought I was going to pet him.

Johnny elaborated.

"She reckons that taking money from me is the way to guarantee her independence," he said. "I told her, try earning your own, that's how you guarantee your independence. It didn't go down well."

There was more like that, all about his ex and her new relationship, and I have to admit that after a while I started tuning out.

"You know what gets me most?" he said. "Her turning up every month in a fucking Mercedes to collect it."

I shouldn't have walked back across the moor in the dark, but I did. Blame the whisky. There was just about enough spilled light from the village and the lane to keep me on track, but I could easily have stuck my foot in a rabbit hole or missed my way and taken a tumble into the old mill pond. I stopped at one point and looked back; the lights were still on in Johnny's eel farm, making the domes glow like winter beacons. Then I walked on and they were lost from sight.

It wasn't the start of anything. I mean, no blossoming friendship. The next time I saw Johnny the hat was back on and he was his old, morose, eye-contact-avoiding self. But I felt differently toward him. Behind the façade was a man who sought to spare his charges pain and to give them a gentler death than the rules required, even if it meant breaking them. Sometimes the gruffest people are the most sensitive. It's the way they protect themselves.

Although often, of course, you're cutting them slack they don't deserve and they're just bastards.

I was busy that winter. Whenever there's a cold snap, lots of ageing boilers fail and need to be repaired or replaced. I was doing a job for an old dear in the sheltered housing and it needed a valve they don't make any more, and rather than have to replace an entire section of her system I remembered that I had something compatible in my lockup.

When I went to get the part, I saw that there was a silver Mercedes parked outside Johnny Clifford's house with someone inside it.

I'd a rough idea where the valve was, but I had to rummage for it. I'd saved it from an old job for an occasion like this. I save everything. If I don't use it again, I'll eventually weigh it all in and get the scrap value. It won't be much but it'll be something.

I became aware of someone watching me from the open garage doorway. It was the woman from the car.

She was in her forties and what my mother would have called "well turned out". Tailored clothes, powdered skin, hair in a neat professional set. Kind of like a younger version of the Queen, if the Queen had worked in admin for the local council.

She didn't introduce herself. She just indicated the polythene outbuildings behind her and said, "Are those greenhouses?"

"Sort of," I said.

"What's he growing?"

"Tomatoes," I said, and the lie came out easily and without any forethought. I'd nothing against Johnny Clifford's wife, but this woman had annoyed me in an instant and without effort.

"Hardly the weather for it," she said.

"That's why you need a greenhouse."

She looked at me again, with one eyebrow raised. "Do I take it you're a friend of his?"

"Not particularly," I said.

"You don't surprise me. He doesn't exactly strike me as a kind man."

"Actually," I said, "I'm not sure that's true."

She took it no further than that, but shrugged and went back to her car to continue the wait. When I'd finally located the valve and emerged from my garage about fifteen minutes later, the car was gone.

I was watching *Gladiator* for the umpteenth time on DVD when someone rang my doorbell. I don't get evening visitors. If anyone calls by, they're either lost or they want something.

I opened my front door to find a uniformed policeman standing there. My cottage fronts onto the lane itself, so his car was right behind him with his partner inside it. Things have changed and coppers don't look like they used to. The old Boys in Blue now dress like action figures with every available accessory hanging from their flak jackets.

This one said, "Which one of these is Quarry Bank House?"

"None of them. You're coming out of the wrong end of the village."

"But isn't that the quarry right there?"

"Different quarry. There's three."

He looked around with a sense of repressed frustration, as if he'd half-known that they'd gone wrong somewhere but had been hoping not to get it confirmed.

He said, "Anywhere along here we can turn around?"

"Not until you get to the Saab garage," I said. I didn't have a driveway. There was the lay-by where I parked my van, but I wasn't about to move it.

I went to my window and watched the car move off, along with the two police vans that were following right behind. The Saab garage was about half a mile down the lane, and the management had become so pissed-off with people using their forecourt for a turning circle that they'd installed bollards that locked into the ground at night. Something I'd failed to mention.

I picked up the phone and called Johnny Clifford.

"Coppers and vans asking for your place," I told him. "Don't know why. Now you know." Then I hung up.

I watched another twenty minutes of the film but my mind wasn't on it. After the first five minutes, I heard the police convoy going back in the opposite direction. When I went up to my bedroom window and looked across the moor, I was half-expecting to see the police helicopter with its searchlight shining down on Johnny Clifford's house.

Was this the raid that he'd feared? It seemed awfully heavy-handed if it was. When he'd referred to the animal welfare people, I'd imagined a daylight visit from a couple of officials with clipboards and maybe a threat of prosecution to follow. This bunch were going in like the SAS.

It was a cold, wild night, and I'd little inclination to go out. I gave it a while longer, but I couldn't settle. So in the end I caved in and went over to see what was happening.

By then I'd missed most of it. The vans were in the quarry and the car was in front of the house, and there was a lot of flashlight work going on around the back. I could hear Johnny Clifford's dog barking inside. Most of the coppers were just standing around, and one was making a phone call.

I caught the attention of one who was standing alone by the car. He was young, with a thin fringe of a moustache, and he looked too little and fat to be in the police force.

I said, "What's going on?"

True to his training, he didn't give me a straight answer but said, "Would you know anything about this?"

"About what?"

"You see many strangers coming and going?"

"Only you lot."

The one from my doorstep had spotted me, and now came over. He had the air of a much harder customer.

Slapping his gloves together and with his breath feathering in the cold air, he said, "Do you ever have dealings with John Clifford? Do you know how he makes his living?"

"This is supposed to be a drugs raid," I said. "Isn't it? I know how it looks, but those aren't greenhouses. You'll have seen it for yourself, there's no plants growing in there. If anyone's told you different, they've been winding you up."

"Have you seen John Clifford tonight?"

"No." Which was true.

"Or spoken to him?"

I shook my head.

"If he isn't here," I said, "then I've no idea where he is."

I was half-expecting to find him waiting for me when I got home, and I wasn't sure what I'd do with him if I did. But he wasn't there.

It wasn't hard to see who'd made a call to the police. The woman from the Mercedes, I supposed. The "why" of it was a little bit harder to imagine. Maybe she was just anti-drugs. Or maybe she'd seen a chance to destroy Johnny Clifford's source of income and thereby her lover's small measure of independence. Some people are like that. They can only feel at ease with another person if they've absorbed them.

Whatever the reason, it wouldn't work. There was no net result beyond an hour of needless panic.

His dog was still barking when I went by the next morning, though.

The lower half of the kitchen window was a smeary mess of saliva and paw marks. The kitchen door was unlocked when I tried it. Remembering my previous experience with the dog I stood well back as I pushed the door open, but the terrier was desperate and paid me no attention at all. It shot out, started hunkering down while still on the move, and crapped its way to a tottering halt. That should have been funny, but it wasn't.

I went inside and called Johnny Clifford's name. I made a cautious ascent upstairs but he wasn't in his bed. When I came back down, I was uncertain of what to do.

He'd fled at my call, that much was clear. But with the door unlocked and the dog shut in, it was equally clear that he'd intended to return. Why hadn't he?

When I went into the room where all the old freezers were, I found three of them with their doors wide open and all of them shut down. Two of those with open doors had been emptied. The third had been partly cleared. The freezer motors must have laboured on into the night until they'd tripped a fuse and cut the power to all the sockets in the circuit.

The packages must have been thawing for some hours, because they settled and shifted as I walked out of the room. I heard them move.

I started to get an inkling of what might have happened.

I checked the eel farm, but he wasn't in there. The police hadn't disturbed anything. The first confirmation that I was on the right track came when I found Johnny Clifford's hat on the far side of the safety fence. I don't suppose I should have picked it up, but I did. With the hat in my hand, I ascended to join the mill path.

All trace of the mill itself had been erased from the village before I was born, but the name remained in the Mill Field below the moor and the mill path that ran across it. This was the way trodden by weavers a century before. As a boy I'd played by the mill pond, and over the years I'd seen it polluted and spoiled when a local farmer used it as a dump for rubble and sheep carcasses. It was half the size it had once been, and the banks were treacherous because they were nothing but dirt, loose bricks and bones.

That was where I found Johnny Clifford.

The water was a grey, cloudy slush. He'd broken through the ice and it had re-formed over him. He was like something suspended in a paperweight; I could see him lying below the surface, face-down with his arms above his head as if frozen in the act of a butterfly crawl. All around him in the slush hung sheets of half-unfurled newspaper, like snapshots of waking birds.

My guess was that he'd been using the pond as a place to ditch the evidence from his freezers. The soft bank had given way on his second or third trip, pitching him headfirst into the water. I picked my way down to the edge with care.

There was nothing I could do for him. I wondered if he'd suffered, or if he'd even known anything at all after the initial shock of the cold. I wondered if it really was just like "going to sleep".

Then I saw something move under the ice.

Nothing was clear. It was like looking through the opalescent plastic of the farm. The further from the surface an object was, the less detailed it became. But something rose, passed over his body, and sank from view again. It moved slowly. Slowly enough for me to see the shape and length of it and be certain that it was an eel.

Another coiled around his head and then faded off into the murk, just as another rose and slipped between his ankles. Sleek ribbons, moving in slow motion. I watched in fascination as they orbited Johnny Clifford's corpse, sliding around him like a lover's caress.

Different police came. They put canvas screens around the pond and divers hacked through the ice to get him out. They found no eels in there, or

so they said. I wonder if they even looked. Perhaps they should have dug down into the mud.

Anyway, I don't care. I know what I saw.

I've described it to people, and they always make a face and shudder. But I don't think that's right. I don't think it was anything sinister at all. I think it was beautiful, in its way.

And I sometimes wonder what Johnny Clifford would have made of it, if he'd been able to foresee his own end. I doubt that it was like anything he might have envisaged. And I doubt that it was like anything he would have chosen.

But that's probably true for most of us, however our lives may turn out. We can dream our dreams, write the scenarios in our heads. Scenes of valour, scenes of peace, scenes of farewell in the arms of those we love. We die like heroes, like knights, like champions. Our lives count for something, and in death we're always missed. Not for us the ignominious slip, the lonely conclusion.

We can always dream.

But when it finally comes, the chances are that we'll have to settle for something that's less than perfect.

⚅

Rick Hautala has always considered Rod Serling one of his major influences, but since he attended the Twilight Zone conference last year at Ithaca College in upstate New York, he's noticed a subtle change in his writing. "Everything I've written since then seems even more 'inspired' by Serling's work," he says. "Most of my published writings, from my first novel, Moondeath in 1980, to my most recent novel, Unbroken under the pseudonym A. J. Matthews, has aimed to evoke the nostalgic and employ the twist ending, of which Serling was a master. 'Hearing Aid' is a case in point. I might even say it has been 'submitted for your approval.'" And why not.

Hearing Aid
Rick Hautala

"**H**ow's that . . . comfortable?"

"You want to *what?*"

The blood drained in a cold rush from Evan Marshall's face as he sat bolt upright in the chair and stared at Doctor Hunnefield.

Doc raised his bushy, white eyebrows and, looking genuinely confused, shrugged his shoulders and said, "I didn't say . . . What do you think I said?"

Flushed with embarrassment, Evan looked down at the floor as he tried to collect his thoughts. It was a struggle to reconcile what he was *sure* he'd heard Doc say and what he *thought* he had heard. Raising his hand to his right ear, he gingerly touched the hearing aid he was being fitted for. This had to be at least the tenth one they'd tried this morning, and he was getting pretty tired of sticking one small device after another into his ear. They all felt heavy and uncomfortable. While he was sure Doc had asked if the one he was

trying now was comfortable, he had also heard another voice . . . a voice that sounded exactly like Doc's . . . say something else . . . something he didn't really want to think about.

"How does this one feel?" Doc asked, pushing ahead with the fitting as if he *hadn't* muttered under his breath, *If you don't like this one, I'd like to try putting a goddamned bullet in your head.*

Evan tried to focus on the task at hand, but the truth was, he couldn't blame Doc for getting frustrated. Maybe the inside of his ear had a unique shape, and he would *never* find a hearing aid that fit comfortably . . . not unless he had one custom made, and on his pension, he sure as hell couldn't afford *that*.

"Yeah. I . . . I think this might do," Evan said, closing one eye and tilting his head to the right as he wiggled and settled the device deeper into his ear. "It's . . . It doesn't feel too bad."

"It's hardly visible at all," Doc said, leaning close and inspecting it; but even as the words came from his

129

mouth, that other voice said, *So just take the damned thing and get the hell out of here, why don't c'ha?*

Evan stiffened as he studied at Doc for a few seconds and then glanced around the exam room to see if anyone else was in there with them, or if there might be a radio or speaker nearby that he hadn't noticed before.

"Yeah . . . yeah, I can hear much better," Evan said. He wasn't really sure if he could hear better or not. It almost didn't matter. He was ready to say anything just to get this whole exam over. He was too wound up to try to figure out if his hearing was any better or worse. "It's good . . . really good."

"Excellent. I'm glad we finally found one for yah," Doc said even as that other voice whispered, *Now get your sorry ass out of here before I smack you upside the head!*

Evan felt wobbly on his legs as he stood up. His right hand was still adjusting the hearing aid, but it was about as good as it was going to get.

"See how it works for a day or two, then come back for an adjustment if you think you need one." That's what Doc said, but Evan also heard him say, *I'd rather you eat shit and die.*

Evan had no doubt his face was as pale as parchment as he walked out of the exam room and into the reception area. An assortment of patients was waiting to see Doc. Evan knew he'd taken longer than he should have for the fitting, but for what he was paying, he was determined to make sure it was *exactly* what he needed. Every sound in the reception room—the hum of the air

conditioner, the scuffing of feet on the floor, the creaking of chairs as people shifted their weight—seemed exaggerated, almost painfully loud, but nobody spoke until a young mother admonished her child, who looked like he was about to tear a page from a magazine.

"Oh, now, Sweetie. You shouldn't do that," she said in a high, sweet voice, but at the same instant, another identical voice said, *Put that down, yah little brat, or I'll spank your ass 'till it's raw.*

Evan glanced at the little boy. The kid didn't have to say anything to his mother for Evan to be able to read *his* thoughts. It might take a while . . . maybe years, but Evan could see that the kid was going to get back at her.

"Do you need to make a follow up appointment?" Doc's receptionist, Ethel, asked from her desk behind a sliding glass window. Evan also heard her say, *Please, Lord, don't make me have to deal with you* ever *again.*

Evan hesitated for a second. His finger was still pressing the hearing air deeper into his ear, and both voices were a bit muffled, sounding like his head was packed with cotton. Then he shook his head *no* and went out the door as fast as he could before anyone could say anything else to him.

On the street, though, it was even worse. People passing by were engaged in conversations, but every fragment of conversation Evan overheard, there was a dual voice saying something else. It was impossible for him to distinguish what people were really saying from what they were thinking, but their

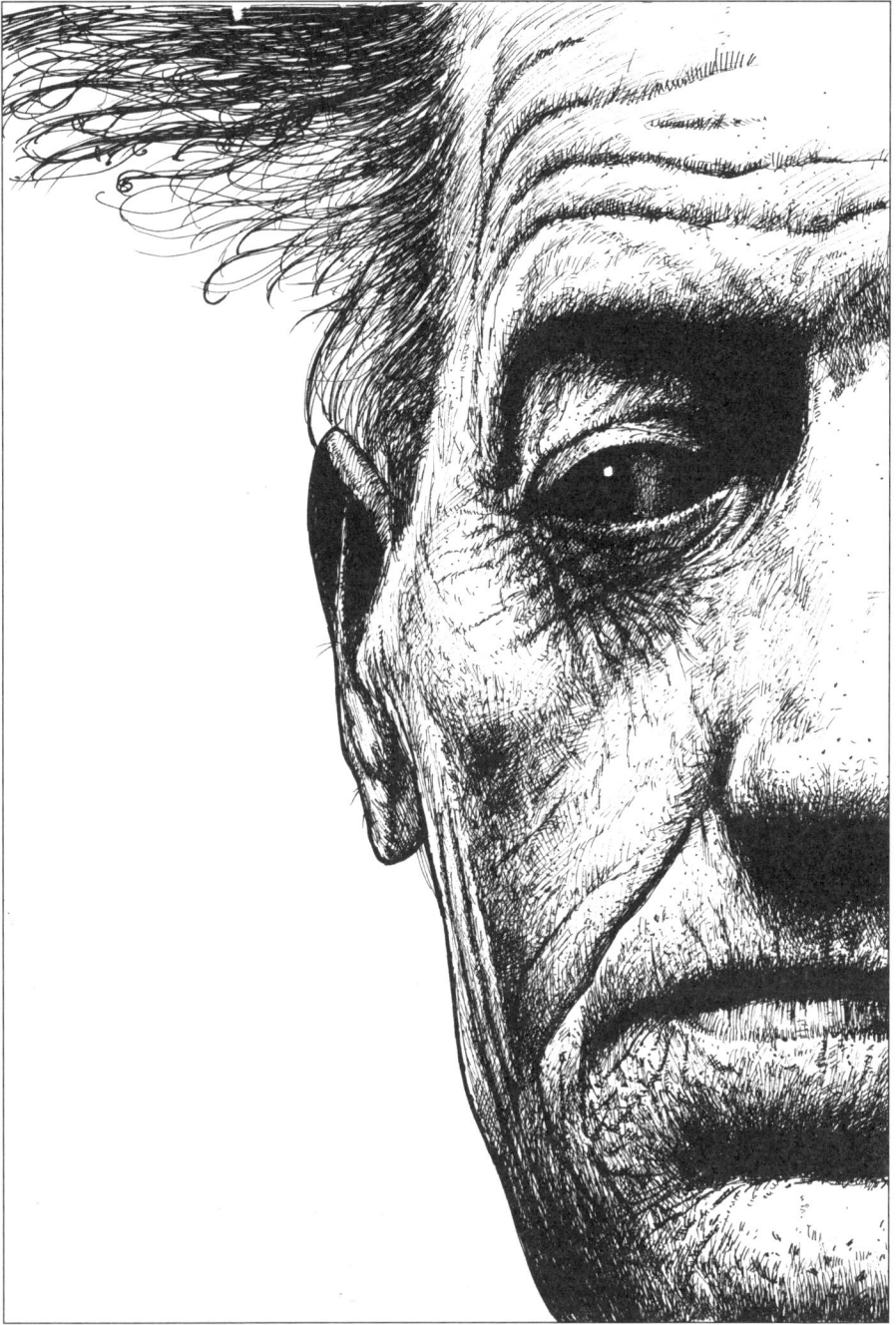

thoughts were so clear, Evan could hear them swelling all around him.

What's happening? he wondered. *Is this hearing aid . . . special?*

He froze mid-step when the thought hit him. It was crazy . . . impossible, but as impossible as it seemed, something . . . something had definitely happened . . . *was* still happening.

A man was following behind him, perhaps a little too close, and he bumped into Evan, almost knocking him off balance when Evan slowed his pace. The man—middle-aged and more than a little overweight—was quick to say, "Sorry 'bout that," but simultaneously Evan heard the man also say, *Watch where the fuck you're goin', asshole!*

As the man continued down the sidewalk, Evan stepped back and huddled against the brick wall of a storefront, shivering as the cacophony of voices rose around him. He realized it wouldn't be long before they drove him crazy . . . if he wasn't crazy already. If his new hearing aid actually made it possible to hear what people were thinking when they spoke, how could he believe anything anyone said to him ever again? As bad as it was to be losing his hearing at his age, it would be much worse to have to live like *this.*

A couple walked by. When Evan overheard the man telling the woman how much he wanted to do something special for her birthday tomorrow, he also heard the man mumble something about how he'd much rather be sleeping with her sister instead of her. Both voices were so clear Evan was confused

as to what the man had said and what he had been thinking. He gaped at the woman as she walked away and, judging by the rounded swelling of her hips and her slim waist, Evan found himself thinking he wouldn't mind sleeping with her.

At that instant, the woman turned and glanced over her shoulder at him, a faint smile twitching her lips. Evan gasped and covered his mouth with both hands, suddenly afraid that he had said that out loud, not thought it.

Did she hear me, or can she hear my thoughts . . . ?

She didn't have to say anything for Evan to know that she was thinking, *What a cute little old man.*

A chorus of voices, both real and imagined, suddenly filled his head as he watched the woman and her companion walk away. Other people—men and women walking alone or in couples or groups—walked by, their voices and thoughts rising higher and higher. Unable to handle the onslaught, Evan sagged against the brick wall until his knees buckled, and he sank slowly to the ground. He was barely aware that he was sitting in a pile of litter the wind had swept against the wall. Something cold and wet began to soak into the seat of his pants, but he ignored it as he watched in horror as people . . . too many people with too much to say and too much to think . . . passed by. Most of them scarcely paid him any attention at all, but every now and then, someone would say or think—*oh that poor homeless man . . .* or *fucking alcoholic—serves him right . . .* or *what is he, a retard?*

"I can't live like this . . . I can't live like this," Evan muttered, but even as he spoke, he also heard his own voice say, *I'm going to kill myself if this doesn't stop.*

The voices kept rising higher and higher in swells that crashed against him like storm-tossed waves.

"If we're late for the movie, we'll just get a ticket for the late show."

If you didn't have to spend half an hour fooling with your makeup, we'd have made the cheaper showing.

"I'm sorry I missed the meeting. I told him I'd be there as soon as I could."

If I show up at all, I'll bring a nine millimeter with me and blow his fucking head off!

"Oh, great. Just what we need. Another parking ticket."

You're lucky I don't roll it into a cone and shove it up your ass.

"What a surprise, you meeting me after work."

Jesus, you'd think he never heard of deodorant.

"I can't take it," Evan said . . . or thought . . . he could no longer distinguish his own thoughts from what he said out loud any better than what the people around him were thinking or saying.

"It's this damned hearing aid."

His hand went to his right ear, but when he tried to pry his fingertip under the edge so he could pop it out, his finger slid across the smooth plastic apparatus, and his fingernail jabbed his ear lobe.

What the hell?

He pulled his hand away and saw the smear of blood on his fingertip. Frantic, now, he started clawing at the hearing aid, trying to dislodge it, but no matter what he did, it seemed to push the hearing aid deeper and deeper into his ear canal.

Is that what's happening? . . . It won't let me take it out? . . . It wants me to hear all of this so I'll go crazy?

Using the wall for support, he got up slowly, his knees creaking loudly. As the blood rushed from his head to his legs, a dark wave of dizziness swept over him. White spots of light weaved across his vision, and it took several seconds for him to get his balance. His pulse was racing so fast his neck and wrists hurt. He knew he should go back to Doc Hunnefield's office right now and have him take this infernal thing out of his ear . . . if he could . . . if it wasn't already too late.

Maybe the hearing aid had a mind of its own, or maybe Doc had planted this thing in his ear on purpose to drive him mad. Maybe the device was melting into his flesh, filling every available space of his ear canal and sending out tiny hooks that were so small he couldn't even feel them as they burrowed into his flesh and cartilage . . . and now they wouldn't let go.

Evan groaned as he staggered forward onto the sidewalk and started pushing and shoving his way through the crowd. Voices and thoughts screamed all around him, wavering up and down the scale until they sounded more like wailing sirens than voices or thoughts.

Crazy asshole!

Watch where you're going!
Get out of the way, you old drunk!
I wanna smoke what he's *smoking.*
Are you off your meds or something?

Evan was so confused he didn't remember the way back to Doc's office. The crowd on the sidewalk was pressing in around on him, sweeping him up and carrying him along in whatever direction it wanted to take him. And all the while the voices and thoughts rose louder and louder, sounding increasingly shrill.

"I have to get away from this!" Evan screamed—or thought—as he glanced to the left and saw the almost deserted street. Waving his arms wildly to help him keep his balance, he lurched into the street, moving his arms like a swimmer who was drowning. Behind him, a young man driving a sports car saw him and laid on his horn. The sudden blast filled the air, but Evan didn't hear it above the voices and thoughts that filled the street. There was a loud skidding sound as the sports car driver slammed on his brakes, but it was too late. Before he could stop it, the car slammed into Evan from behind hard enough to catapult him into the air. For a moment or two, Evan had a dizzying sensation of flying, but then he hit the pavement—hard. His face scraped across the asphalt a good ten or twelve feet, leaving a long, red smear on the street.

The driver jammed his car into park and hopped out, leaving the engine running. He was sure he was about to faint because he knew—but couldn't yet accept—the terrible truth. An old man

had walked out onto the street from between two parked cars. It had all happened too fast for him to have a chance to react.

"Jesus, didn't he hear my horn?" the driver asked as he stared in shock at the crowd that was gathering. Someone must have had the presence of mind to call 9-1-1 because from far off in the distance there came the rising wail of a siren.

"Why didn't he hear me?" the driver asked no one in particular as he looked around until—finally—he was able to bring himself to look down at the old man lying in a crumpled heap, facedown on the pavement. There were no signs of life. No rise and fall of his back as he breathed. And the flow of blood from his head wound was spreading like dark ink across the pavement.

And then the driver noticed something. He saw the hearing aid sticking out of the old man's ear. It was tiny and flesh-colored, barely visible, but in his bewilderment, he focused on it as if it had some significance.

"I blasted the horn," the driver said. "He should have heard me . . . "

As he was saying this, he reached out and took the hearing aid from the dead man's ear. He was surprised by how light it felt in his hand, almost weightless. As more and more people gathered around and as the wailing siren came ever closer, the driver was barely aware that he was fiddling with the hearing aid, rolling it between his thumb and forefinger, until his thumb inadvertently flicked the back of the device, and the small covering for the battery compartment slipped open. Looking down, he saw that there was no battery in the device.

"He forgot to put the battery in," the driver said. His voice was low and flat with shock. He couldn't begin to imagine how much trouble he was in. "No wonder he didn't hear the horn. He didn't have a goddamned battery in his hearing aid."

As he clutched the hearing aid in his right hand and looked around, no one said a word until—finally—one man standing near the front of the crowd said, "Okay, people. Let's back up and give the medics a chance to check him out."

At that same instant, it seemed to the driver who was still holding the hearing aid that he also heard an identical voice say, *Man, your ass is gonna fry for this!* ☒

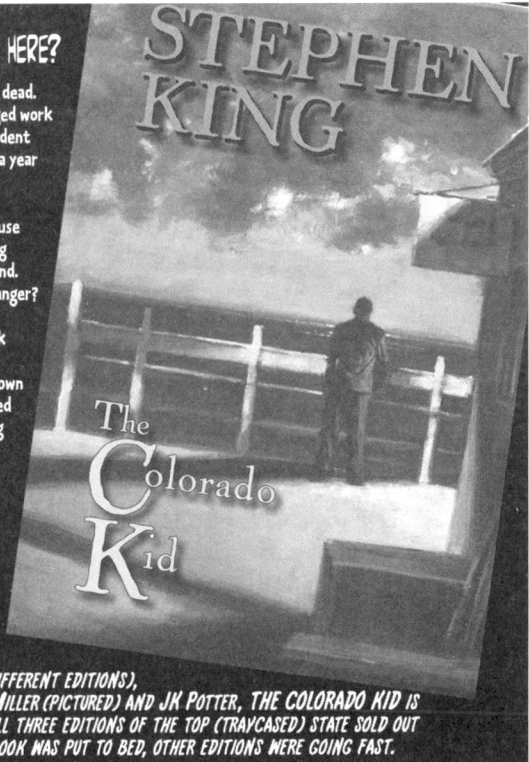

The small 'what if?' idea for this new story from Stephen Volk was a jokey throwaway in conversation, he tells us. But for some reason it grew in his mind, and then grew on the page into much more than he thought it was. "I suppose it's about the expectations and demands we make of our entertainment," he writes. "It's about art and real life. It's about desensitization and trauma. And movies."

A previous contributor to Postscripts, *last year Stephen published his first collection of short stories,* Dark Corners *(Gray Friar Press) and more recently his novella "Certain Faces" appeared in the anthology* Choices *(Pendragon Press). However, he is best known for film and television screenplays, including* Gothic, Shockers, Octane *and the notoriously traumatizing BBC Hallowe'en Night* Ghostwatch. *Over the last three years he has been working as creator and lead writer of the hugely successful, award-winning ITV drama series* Afterlife, *and his new science fiction movie* Telepathy *is slated to go into production later this year.*

Who Dies Best

Stephen Volk

I watched my mother die again today. The movie was playing at the new Odeon near Kingsmead Square. It was the usual multiplex set-up; minimum-wage kids with iridescent acne dispensing tickets with a concentration that implied the task was at the very penumbra of their intellectual capabilities. Various stains discoloured the carpet even though it had only been up and going a matter of weeks. Occasional constellations of scattered popcorn seemed almost like wilfully applied decoration. There was a level of noise in the lobby because there was a level of young people, and if they weren't talking to each other, in line, they were talking into their mobile phones. What they find to talk about that's so important, so all-consuming, I have no idea.

I was told it was showing in Screen Three. "Enjoy the movie." I said "Thank you."

As I climbed the stairs I passed posters of coming attractions: a gun-toting Tom Cruise prequel to the end of the world, something about dinosaurs, and a feel-good rom-com which looked anything but.

Upstairs was deserted. Almost inaudible muzak sounded like Michael Bolton trapped in the wainscoting. I walked to the illuminated number three.

I entered the semi-dark and sat in row K, about half way back, half way along. I was early so I was the only one there. It didn't matter to me. The group experience was a matter of immense indifference to me. What mattered was the picture quality, and the sound system. I'm no purist, but if you want to see a feature film I believe you should see it in the manner the director intended.

I'd seen this film thirty-three times now, almost following it round its distribution circuit like a stalker. I wondered if I was becoming one of those people who say they've seen *The Sound of Music* a hundred and twenty times, or *Star Wars* five hundred times. One of those movie nerds. I told myself I didn't have the obsession, the compulsion, the excitement you relate to that kind of avid fan. I wasn't like them at all. But I didn't feel that seeing it this time would be my last, either: though I wanted it to be. Desperately, if I were honest about it. I wanted to see the movie but I didn't want to see it, if that makes any sense.

If it was a kind of addiction, it didn't operate like an addiction. It wasn't like I wanted to capture the feeling I had last time. I wanted it to be different. I longed for it to be different. When the opening shot came up and the movie began with that plaintive honky-tonk piano, and I waited yet again for the scene where my mother was killed, I was desperate that, for once, I would feel something.

Anything.

They step quickly through the door. They stand side by side, the three of them. The man in the flat cap, who now has the tip of his pistol barrel buried in the thick, hairy neck of the uniformed guard. The man in the white hat with the black band, set at a jaunty angle. The girl with the blood-red

beret, who whips a Derringer out of her puce handbag.

The clerk looks up, startled through his round glasses.

"We're the Clyde Barrow gang," barked the man in the jaunty hat. "We rob banks."

He smiled as he cocked his gun.

The clerk raised his hands.

One day, someone who had known Mum bumped into me in Sainsbury's. They brightened and seemed eager to talk to me and said "She was really good in it. You must be ever so proud of her." I took the compliment and said some pleasantries and moved on. I know it should have lifted my spirits a bit, but I can't say it did.

My mother had been one of those millions affected by the collapse of the pension industry. Do you remember Black November? With company after company going to the wall, many people suddenly realised that the hard earned cash they had paid into personal pension funds all their lives had evaporated. It simply didn't exist. Not only did they have little to live on themselves for their ripe old age, they had nothing to pass on to their children either. That was where the studios stepped in. And the politicians, of course, were hardly minded to stop them. In fact they rushed the legislation through without touching the sides.

In that climate of total financial panic came the offer of a substantial lump sum, free of inheritance tax, in return for supplying one's services, on a one-off basis, to the motion picture industry.

Your financial worries and those of your dependants could be over at a stroke. All that was required was that you'd be a "featured player" in a scene that required an act of death by violence. Basically, instead of agreeing to supply your body to medical science, you'd be offering it to be disposed of in a manner prescribed by the film company that contracted you. For a substantial pay cheque you would go, not with a whimper, but with a splash, or a splatter, or in a hail of bullets. You could be a marine cut down at Iwo Jima, or Jack the Ripper's fifth victim in some Whitechapel alley, or savaged in a gladiatorial ring, or third stormtrooper on the left in a galaxy far away. You could be a heavy gunned down in a fire fight by James Bond. You could be road kill in a car chase, barely glimpsed through a windscreen. You could be shoved off a tall building followed by a quip by Bruce Willis. The opportunities were endless. The possibilities were limited only by the film-makers' imaginations.

What was the alternative? Seeing out the end of your days in a cash-strapped NHS dive with doctors that didn't care and probably didn't even know what was wrong with you?

No contest. Dying in a movie beat dying in real life, any day.

A year ago, Mum hurt her head in a fall. It wasn't evident at first but one night she had difficulty getting out of the bath: no sensation in her limbs at all. When we got her to the hospital the doctors detected that she had been haemorrhaging inside the skull for some time. The explanation was the most stupid thing, almost comical. She'd been standing on the bed in the spare room (my sister's old room) bouncing up and down to dust the lampshade—this a woman of seventy-two—and had fallen off, knocking her head and of course, typically, didn't tell anybody at the time. The consultant gave the impression that a brain operation wasn't uncommon any more, was almost passé, but as I said to my sister, "You can't tell me that anything to do with the brain is passé."

After that Mum quickly lost her spark. She recovered but she was put on pills. When your parents get beyond a certain age, it's disarming to see how quickly fragility sets in. Physical fragility, that is, even if they are fortunate enough to hang onto all their marbles. She didn't want to go out for Sunday lunches the way we always had when Dad was alive. She seemed afraid of the outside world. Unable to cope. She suffered from awful sleeplessness, telling me she'd gone weeks lying wide awake thinking she would go mad but she didn't want to go to the doctor for fear she might go back to the Heath. She said she'd rather die than go back to that place. She'd had horrible nightmares after her skull was opened up and the anaesthetic was still sloshing around her system. She thought sometimes she was on a cruise liner and all the doctors were waiters, or on a film set, or that she'd been abducted. Possibly she had dreams that were much worse than that, but she didn't tell me. Only that she'd wake in the middle of the night in Intensive Care and hear all the old people moaning and weeping.

Six months later we learned that she was full of cancer and it was inoperable, and all I could think was of her saying she never wanted to go back to that place.

Screech of brakes. The headlights stop inches from the chalk-striped navy suit. The brown and white shoes do a shuffle. He spins. His unbuttoned jacket splays, fans like a skirt, there's a glimpse of a starched cuff.

"Get out of the car! Get out of the car!"

The old woman in the driving seat doesn't move. She's too terrified to move. Her mouth opens and closes a few times. Her hands are glued to the wheel.

He looks over his shoulder. The alarm is ringing in the bank. He looks back at the woman and yanks open the door of the Model-T. He looks down at the splint on her leg and raises his pistol against her face, only six inches from her parchment-coloured skin. All sound vanishes into the black hole of an explosion. The bullet pops a small hole under her cheekbone and my mother's entire face puckers in and a tooth flies out of her mouth, hitting the inside of the windshield with a painterly trail of blood.

Mum handed me a leaflet. Sometimes they came in the junk mail, sometimes you got cold calls from some centre in India asking if you were interested. As it happened, she'd picked it up in her doctor's surgery. It included a form to fill in and send off to the UK Film Council to see if you were eligible.

She asked my opinion. I answered truthfully that I didn't have any.

She said "You know I'm doing this for you and Rom."

I said "Do it for yourself, Mum, if you want to do it. Don't think about us. We're all right."

When I told my kids about it, they said, "Nan in a film? Brilliant."

My sister didn't say much. She didn't express any strong reservations, as I recall, though later she behaved as though she had done. I suppose the results of our actions come out in different ways, and even though we're siblings we've never particularly understood each other. Anyway, there was no great debate about it.

We just put her name down with the casting agency, helped her fill in the form, and waited.

Mum went and got her hair done. When I saw her next, I swear the colour had come back to her cheeks.

It was what they called the "chicken shot." The term came from Sam Peckinpah's film *Pat Garrett and Billy the Kid*, in which live chickens were used in a scene in which they were required to get their heads shot off. It was deemed as quite outrageous at the time.

Old people were way down the pecking order, of course. They were assigned to bystander roles rather than big deaths. The most gory or eye-popping trailer moments usually went to others: healthy-looking individuals with terminal diseases, mostly. Still, Mum could expect to go out in a "blaze of glory," to coin the phrase beloved of the tabloids. "Blaze of glory films" had long since replaced "snuff movies" and "video nasties" as the *bete noir* of the media.

The obvious fact of the matter is that every generation requires, and reinvents, a new level of realism in films. In the thirties it was enough for James Cagney to stagger interminably and collapse on the cathedral steps. In the fifties a dab of tomato ketchup at the base of the arrow in Jeff Chandler's arm seemed adequate enough for believability. By the sixties acts of violence began to be depicted in confrontational, socially-conscious detail. By the machine-gunning and zombie-strewn nineties we were well accustomed to death porn as the lifeblood of summer blockbusters, and by the noughts of the new century audiences had become keen-eyed, astute and aesthetically discerning. With political beheadings on the internet and CCTV car crash footage and happy stabbings to download, nobody bought the glibness of Max Factor and a bit of pyrotechnics any more. It wasn't enough for stunt doubles to fall off buildings onto cardboard boxes, we had to see their faces hit the pavement. We had to see the life ebb out of their shattered bodies. It wasn't enough for a serial killer to squeeze Kensington Gore though a fake knife any more— we had to see him hacksaw that Kitchen Devil right through the jugular, we had

to see that blob of arterial goo hit the lens, we had to see the blade cut through sinew and muscle as the maw of the throat-wound widened, and see the flickering non-expectation in the victim's eyes as the final four inches of breath stammered from both ends of his, or her, freshly-slit oesophagus.

That's entertainment.

And, if truth be told, it always was. Think about it. Tyburn Tree. Ancient Rome. Surely the idea of faking violence was a mere aberration during the prurient Twentieth Century: the much larger arc of civilisation showed that real, actual death had a much more permanent role in keeping us amused than mere "pretend." You could argue, we were simply going back to our roots.

"**G**et out of the car! *GET OUT OF THE CAR!*"

My mother looks up and into the black button hole at the end of the gun barrel which is pointing at her face. The side-lighting makes her hair look whiter than usual. For the very first time, looking at that close-up, I notice three lines, wrinkles pointing up to one side of my mother's mouth. Three each side. There is a surprising symmetry to that. Why three? It is almost as if someone had put them there.

The air punctures her skin and the far side of her head vomits blood like shit coming out of the back end of a cow, cascading over the warm leather of the passenger seat. She doesn't react as though slapped on the cheek, but whatever keeps her jaw up goes slack.

His rough hands grab her by the lapels.

He lifts her out. There is a little sucky-sticky sound because her hair and little shards of broken bone stick to the seat-back, and the pull makes her head wiggle, then her head flops as if she has nothing in her neck at all to support it.

Having extracted her from the driver's seat, he lets go of her, and her body, that lump, falls upon the tarmac, awkwardly, twisted, one shoulder spiking up, one knee offering itself outwards, foot and ankle having no restraint, or shame.

Low angle shot. Camera level with the ground.

One eye fucked, one still flickering. Chest still heaving like broken bellows. NOT DEAD YET. The human being in extremis, when all else is stripped away, this flesh, this bone, if nothing else, gulping a breath, even one breath, anything to cling on to life. Even when the brains are shot out. Even when half the head is missing. Even when everything that ever represented or was my mother is gone, destroyed, spirit, mind, the body screams, Life. Life.

One eye bats its closing lid. Her empty cheek sucks in like a popped balloon, then huffs out again. Hiss, huff. Hiss, huff. She is still alive, lying there in the steady flow of urine and blood, at his feet.

A t the casting call, they were very good with her. The Second Assistant Director sat down and discussed everything in full. I thought at the time he had a lot of patience with an old biddy, but then he probably had to deal with people like Mum all the time. After that she was required to have a medical examination, and produce the state-ment her GP had given her that said she was in good mental health. There was a lot of emphasis put on that. They had to make sure all the legalities were watertight. They were especially attentive that Mum understood what was being asked of her, since they had her sign an Equity/SAG "D&D" waiver that she did not consider the work "demeaning or distressing." (It was the producer's responsibility to ensure that there was "no undue suffering" involved.) If there was a problem with the paperwork, they could be had up for homicide, technically. The studios did not employ extremely expensive lawyers for nothing.

Still, they were very nice to her and treated her well and offered her breakfast (she toyed with a Danish pastry out of politeness) and called her Mrs Genn, which pleased her. She said it was respectful to her generation and you don't hear that enough these days.

We were given copies of the script, which had blue pink and yellow pages. It was a remake of *Bonnie and Clyde* starring two young American marquee names I didn't know from Adam. The Second AD read the scene to us and described how it would be done. My mother nodded obediently. People often did not fully take in what was told to them on these occasions, so you were advised to bring along a friend or relative. "Do you have any questions, Hugo?" the Second AD asked me at the end of the conversation. I said no, thanks, I thought he'd covered everything.

Then we met and shook hands with the Co-ordinator. Stunt men had adapted: they no longer risked life and limb in burning buildings or falling out of planes. Instead they designed cinematic deaths for others. Real, actual deaths.

The AD smiled and said that "unless anything untoward occurred," she had the part. Mum was like an excited schoolgirl. As I drove her home—the traffic was a pig because they'd shut the M4 to film a suicide for a Sandra Bullock movie—she started asking what dress she should wear. I was fiddling with my Sat Nav searching for an alternative route, saying "Don't worry about that, Mum. They have costume people to do that."

She looked worried at that and bit her lower lip. "Will they make me look nice, though?"

I said "Of course they will. On films they make everyone look nice. It's their job."

It didn't stop her fretting and she starting thinking out loud about what she had at the dry cleaner's. I wondered if everyone took their death scene so seriously.

In America prisoners who'd waited through fifteen years of appeals on death row had been known to "take the option" and volunteer to be cannon fodder in war films, much the same way as black regiments provided cannon fodder in actual wars. I know of only one instance of a terminally ill actor in a major role: Nelson John Verso in *Leniency*, a film about death by injection, which earned him a posthumous

Best Supporting Actor nomination at the Golden Globes. But such star billing was seen as stunt casting, and actors did not like to be upstaged by such hype. The "walking dead," as they were sometimes uncharitably known, were mostly bit part players in the drama—as indeed they were in life. Last year, Universal chose to shoot the Jake Gyllenhall epic *Rwanda Beat* in Africa because they could get easy access to available featured players for the slaughter scenes in the kind of numbers impossible to find elsewhere in the world. They were there because life was, quite literally, cheap.

It was surprising how incredibly quickly audiences got used to the new level of realism. As with the advent of CGI special effects which immediately overshadowed and out-dated the bluescreen FX of the past, it took barely one thick-necked, bare-knuckled summer of action movies before we all happily accepted "post mortem participation" as the norm.

And it has to be said that, as a result, old-style sequences from bygone eras do look decidedly stagy and unconvincing, now. It was like Technicolor replacing black and white. Method acting replacing John Wayne. The artificiality was glaringly apparent.

For instance, only the other week on TV I saw that old seventies film *Don't Look Now* starring Julie Christie and Donald Sutherland. That opening scene where Sutherland plunges into the garden pool to rescue the already-drowned body of his young son is so embarrassingly fake by today's standards. It's obvious that the little boy isn't really dead. He's just a living child actor with his eyes closed and very wet. Today, it's amazingly hard to think how anyone watched it then and didn't find it laughably bad. On the other hand last year's remake where they used the terminally ill boy from the Maudsley was so much better. You knew he wasn't breathing as he lay under the lichen-green surface of the pool, and you knew he was dead when his father was on the lawn on his knees trying to give him the kiss of life, and of course it made it so much better.

They sent a car to pick her up. My sister went with her. Per the contract we'd signed, Mum required a chaperone. Just after lunchtime my sister phoned up and said it was fine, it had all gone according to plan. Her mobile signal broke up a little bit but I said she was OK, she was coming through loud and clear. She said they'd got what they wanted in the can, so that was good. The director was busy lining up the next shot but the younger guy we'd met at the casting session told Romily the shot was terrific. I asked if he'd said any more than that, but she said no, he'd moved away and she didn't like to bother him. I said "Fair enough." I said I'd talk to her more that evening because my meal was getting cold. She said there was no point really, there was nothing more to tell. And anyway she was going out.

Part of the deal is the family and close friends are treated to a private screening of the finished film. We gathered in one of those small Soho viewing theatres off Berwick Street, down some narrow stairs, somewhere you imagine a movie mogul sitting in a camelhair coat with a big cigar in his mouth. It wasn't the same as going to your local flea pit, that's for certain.

Afterwards we were given sandwiches and wine and filter coffee and the two women from the PR Company were particularly friendly. They'd put a big vase of white lilies on the table and I thought that was particularly thoughtful of them.

I don't know what I was expecting. I suppose I had a touch of trepidation about seeing it, but the scene went by in such a flash I felt I hadn't seen it at all. It was almost like someone had covered the lens for twenty-five seconds. Or maybe I'd done that myself, internally, in my head.

I felt strange. As if none of it had happened. And on the way home I had the urge to keep driving the car past Junction 17 and keep going to Mum's place, to see her, but of course I knew she wasn't there. I suppose you could say my heart was working and my brain wasn't.

We got in late and I was tired from driving so I didn't watch any TV and went straight to bed. The children thought it was a really exciting day, though, and couldn't get to sleep. They couldn't wait to tell their friends in school in the morning. They loved their Nan but they loved her more now she was famous.

It wasn't long, days, before I realised I needed to see *The Notorious Barrow Gang* again. Alone.

As soon as it was released, I went to the cinema and watched two showings in succession, and did the same thing the day after. By now I'd absorbed the plot-line. I had no difficulty with that. It was the scene that was important. But again the feeling it produced in me could only be described as a kind of hollow blankness.

The need to see it again surfaced once more after I had to deal with removing the contents of my mother's bungalow. The minute the house clearance van had left, I sped to the multiplex off the A460 and bought a ticket. The viewing had no more effect than had the previous ones, and it set a pattern for the future.

The evening after her funeral I found myself making an excuse to my wife that I wanted to go for a walk, but in fact I drove to an art house cinema ten miles away, and watched the film again.

Again, I felt nothing.

It became this sordid, illicit activity: private, introspective and strangely onanistic in its self-absorption. Even though it had no emotional effect on me, I was compelled to do it, at least once a day and sometimes as many as four times in one sitting. I even made excuses at work when I saw there was a matinee screening and I thought if I rushed I could make it. Even with my heart pounding from the stress and deception I sat blank and unblinking in the dark, waiting for the dull bludgeon of some kind of pain to hit, some kind of grief, but it never did.

Everyone knows why you go to the movies. They make you laugh, scream, cry—all those reasons.

But when my Mum was dying, I was numb.

When my Mum was dying, I was watching but I wasn't seeing.

When my Mum was dying, I was dead too.

I watched my mother die again today.

The weeks go by and I'm slightly terrified of when they might pull it from general release, but I suppose sooner or later it will be put out on DVD. I wonder if I can wait that long and I wonder what I'll do if I can't.

I'm standing in line and there is only one person in front of me. She has russet brown shoulder-length hair like my sister and I get a whiff of shampoo. I like the shade of aubergine of her cardigan. She moves away to the Ben & Jerry's counter and I buy a ticket and the machine pokes out its tongue. I'm not usually aware of the audience and I'm not really aware of her.

In Cinema One, under squinting house lights, "Air in C Minor" by J.S. Bach seeps incongruously. A couple of sniggering hoodies in the front row have their excessive trainers up on the chair backs in front of them.

My index finger runs round the inner circle of the beverage holder in the arm-rest, clockwise then anti-clockwise. Other than that I'm motionless. Anaesthetised.

I'm wearing my business suit and haven't shaved. Nobody sees you in the dark. I'm not here to be seen, I'm here to do the seeing.

It begins as it always begins.

*H*iss, huff. Hiss, huff. She is still alive, lying there in the steady flow of urine and blood, at his feet.

Clyde Barrow looks down at my mother, his waistcoat buttons all done up. He doesn't do it as an afterthought, or for expediency. It was as if his gun is doing it and he is just going along with the decision.

Her eye is still alive. Her lungs are still groping to drag some air through that wreckage which is her half a head. Her brain-dead eyeball swivels in its socket. It doesn't plead silently to die: it screams silently to live.

One, two bullets stab into the polkadot dress. Some inner or outer gust makes one side of it puff out like bagpipes. One arm swivels and flaps. The liver-spotted head, what was left of it, pancakes, the jaw twisting to an inconceivable angle. An elbow juts. Fingers prop the hand. The crepey skin of an old woman's forearm sags like sail cloth. The third and fourth bullets spit into her ribs, simply burying themselves in a bag of meat, pock-marking the asphalt under her—and she moves no more.

She did not jiggle in balletic slow motion, as might be wanted of her in the choreography of previous era. Instead she was crushed by a resolute dullness. And, if you ever doubted it I can tell you, there is a tangible moment when you know the person you love

is gone, and what you're looking at is a corpse and it may still look like her but it isn't her, and suddenly, absolutely clearly, you're in no doubt about that: there's nothing there. And you feel crushed by the dullness too, and you wonder what is it left her body if not the soul? And if you don't believe in the soul what are you looking at? Just—stuff.

In the background of the shot of my dead mother lying like a sprawled mannequin in the dirt, Clyde Barrow with a flash of his two-tone shoes jumps into the car she had been driving, slams the door and drives away, wrenching up the gears. As the Model-T disappears into the out-of-focus Kansas haze, the other members of his gang, the flat-capped kiddo and brother Buck, who had been hopping from foot to foot outside the Wells Fargo bank, hastily pile inside. His gangster's moll, Bonnie Parker, played by somebody well-known from a daytime medical soap, jumps onto the running board, her blond hair trailing like a golden goodbye.

*T*he experience isn't any different this time. I don't expect it to be, any more.

My eyes stay fixed on the screen until the last of the white-on-black end titles levitate and the scarlet curtains close. I keep my eyes resting there and I'm not distracted by the peripheral sight of members of the audience sloping off towards the exits. I always like to be the first to arrive and the last to leave, don't ask me why.

The lights come up, and I'm about to stand up and move along the row to leave when I notice the girl with russet-coloured hair sitting in one of the seats along my row. We are the last two people in the theatre, and I know immediately I can't get out that way unless I pass her, so I sink back into my chair trying to regain some kind of anonymity. But I've noticed in that single glance, without particularly trying to notice, that she has tears running — no, streaming—down her cheeks. And that is why she hasn't stood up, I realise. The reason is that she is rummaging in her handbag for a tissue. And I realise

I'm looking over at her again, this time with an air of puzzlement.

Which is when she notices me, or half-notices me. Not quite looking up, not quite hiding her face, embarrassed by her own emotion. I don't think she sees anything in the blankness of me, but perhaps she thinks she does. Needing to apologise.

"I know it's stupid," she says, still looking for a tissue. "It's only a movie."

⬚

Damian Veers enjoys a rich, comfortable existence. Using only his own restless mind, Damian visits distant worlds, seducing dream-women of every sort; when he wishes, he leaps casually back and forth through his own rich memories, replaying little portions of a gigantic existence that may never end. This is the fate of every intelligent species. Minds grow to a point where thought is more real than reality, and the simplest daydreams are more compelling than any starship.

Then a strange woman moves into the house next door to Damian's: Dot James, physical and plainspoken. She seems immune to the addictive kinds of genius that every other person embraces. Damian is astonished and intrigued. Somehow, Dot and Damian's pasts are linked, and it's only a matter of time until his intellect figures out this amazing puzzle . . . But if the mind has no limits, how can you trust what your mind tells you?

In an alternate history dominated by Imperial China, the forces of the Dragon Throne control most of the Earth, and now turn their attentions to the heavens. In the tradition of its great fifteenth century admiral, Zheng He, the Chinese Empire constructs a massive Treasure Fleet. But unlike the dragon boats which coursed across terrestrial seas, the ships of this new armada are ceramic and steel, fuelled by nuclear reactors. Rather than sailing to open new trade routes to foreign shores, this new fleet sails interplanetary gulfs, to the red planet fourth from the sun, in search of mineral wealth and territorial claims.

T.M. Wright is nearly certain ("though by no means positive") that "Rainy Day People" is a story about love and hate and electronics, about becoming lost within our toys—about becoming our toys. "I'm as enamored of my computers (my wife, the lovely Roxane, and I own four or five) as anyone," T.M. continues, "but when I rise in the early morning, alone, before the sun, sit down with my double shot of espresso, orange juice, raspberry Danish and banana (to keep my faulty heart rhythm from becoming troublesome) in one hand and scour the Internet on my Sony laptop with the other, I have to ask myself if the damned thing (the laptop) possesses me— if that four or five-pound package of nifty, high-tech electronics has overwhelmed and now defines my expectations, my outlooks, my love life, my existential self . . . "

Who knows? But it's possible (though by no means certain) that these questions may have dictated, in some small way, the words the good Mr. Wright used, their arrangement and direction (on and within the same Sony laptop) when he wrote "Rainy Day People" . . . "early one morning," he says, almost wistfully, "long, long ago (as the lifespan of laptop computers is judged)."

Rainy Day People
T.M. Wright

I love my laptop.
This thing that glows in the dark.

12:43 PM

It is possible for beings to appear out of the rain that are *created from* the rain. Remember that.

12:58 PM

He said:
I don't believe I've seen such beings, although I admit I've seen something I can't explain. But there's much I can't explain, of course—gravity, for instance, and electricity, and why, according to experts, the universe is expanding instead of falling in on itself.
I telephoned Fred and told him what

I'd seen and he told me I was tired or hungry or hallucinating. I told him I wasn't; he said okay, and that was that. Fred's never believed me about much of anything, anyway, so to hell with him.
Ronnie was asleep at the time, and when she woke, I told her what I'd told Fred and she said, "Christ, that's creepy! Are you sure?" I said yes, I was sure, then hesitated and added, "Maybe I'm not so sure, really. But I saw *something*."
She nodded in her agreeable way and asked if I'd like some lunch.
"Yeah," I said. "Macaroni and cheese?"
"It's bad for you," she said. "Full of fat and cholesterol. You'll die young."
I shrugged; "Just like Alexander the Great. That'd be all right."

148

2:14 PM

Odd, that need. Or desire. So fatalistic. *If it's going to happen, anyway, shit— why not just let it happen now instead of later.*

He said, "I'm your friend. You can talk to me."

3:30 PM

It's been raining on and off here for weeks. I like the rain. I like it a lot, in fact, and so does Ronnie. It's comforting, on several levels. But, after a while, too much rain is too *damned much* rain and I've found myself peering at the sky for signs of a break in the overcast. This afternoon, however, there is no break, although, thankfully, no rain either.

Ronnie just came in and asked, "Where'd you tell me you saw those . . . "—she looked suddenly perplexed—". . . those *things*?"

"Out the back window," I said, and inclined my head to the south. "Near the woods."

"Oh," she said. "That's where I looked." She cocked her head, appeared confused, said, "Creepy," again, then, after a moment, flashed her beautiful and wonderfully appealing *I'm-horny-as-a-goat* smile: "Wanna fuck?"

"Of course I wanna fuck," I said, and smiled back. "Just give me a minute, okay?"

"Okay," she said. "I'll be you-know-where, Josh."

"And I'll be there with bells on," I said.

5:21 PM

Such magic in all that glows in the dark. We don't know everything about magic and that's why it's magic. Maybe everything we don't know *everything* about is magic.

Maybe if we don't know *all that we can know* about a thing, we don't know *anything* about it.

Maybe *everything* is magic.

Gravity, electricity. Rain.

8:30 PM

It is constant and unnerving, now. I think I hate it.

Ronnie said, "This rain is incredible. Do you think it's ever going to stop?"

I sighed. "Of course it is. It stopped this afternoon, remember?"

"I mean for good, Josh?"

"For good? Well, that would be unfortunate, don't you think?"

"No."

"If it stopped for good, where would the flowers come from?"

"Oh, crap, Josh, they'd come from my goddamned ass, I don't know! Can't you at least . . . play along with me!"

I think the almost-constant rain is making her cranky.

10:45 PM

Odd what he said. All the odd things he said. All his odd behaviors.

And now what?

This thing that glows in the dark?

The dark.

The rain.

11:02 PM

Went to the back window, looked out, toward the woods, saw nothing, not even the woods.

Ronnie came up beside me. "Shit," she said.

"Too dark. Too rainy," I said.

"Oh hell, Josh," she said, "you didn't see anything out there and we both know it. I'm going to bed."

And that's where she went. To her bed. *Our* bed.

And left me to the things I imagine.

5:30 AM

Couldn't sleep because of the rain. That's a first. All my life, a good hard rain has lulled me to sleep. Now it conspires to keep me awake.

Ronnie has no trouble sleeping. She sleeps so soundly I sometimes half believe she's dead (and, earlier, I actually put my hand on her chest to be certain she was breathing).

I wish we had a dog. It would be good company, now that it's just me and the laptop. And the rain. The omnipresent rain. The tortuous rain. The unforgiving rain. (What other adjectives can I come up with? Me—the king of adjectives! But I'm stumped. If we had a dog, I'd ask *him*.)

6:12 AM

I can not describe what I saw minutes ago.

They—these beings—are as opaque as ice.

They smile and grimace at the same time.

They look *at* me and look *away* at the same time.

I'm shutting this off.

I'm shutting this off.

9:02 AM

Josh is asleep. At least he's trying to sleep. He told me what he saw and I have to believe him, I know I have to believe him, but I went to the window too and I didn't see anything at all, only the rain. No "ice," like he said. It's too warm for ice.

He speaks to me and I believe it's real.

He lays his hands on me while I sleep, and I believe it's real.

He comes to me and I believe it's real. Belief is enough, isn't it?

Isn't it?

2:33 PM

Note to myself: I've mentioned that these beings (*Things, creatures, entities*) smile, but that seems unlikely because I don't believe they have *faces*.

4:20 PM

Ronnie's upset because I threatened to change the Windows password. She called me "a putz," a word I hadn't heard from her before, then asked what I was hiding. "Nothing," I said, and she said, predictably, "Well then, why would you want to change the fucking password?"

I think this constant, unrelenting rain is wearing us down.

We came here for a reason, she said. To ease the tension, I think. Who knows for sure? But what does it matter? Why "ease the tension" if there's *reason* for it? And isn't there *always* reason for it? If it exists, isn't there always reason for it? If animosity exists and discord exists, isn't there *always* reason for it?

Let such things exist.

Let discord and animosity create whatever they create: whatever grows from them is natural, after all.

5:30 PM

She sleeps as soundly as a still day in winter. Minutes ago, I put my hand on her chest again. Felt for a heartbeat.

7:25 PM

I went out, into the rain, out to those woods, stood where those things stood, looked back at the house—saw only the house, the windows, Ronnie looking at me from the bedroom. I raised my hand a little, a kind of wave. She did nothing.

So frigid out there, in that cold, cold rain. It will change to snow, I think—the season's right for it. Then we'll be in trouble.

I believe I saw footprints in the wet earth at the front of the woods. They could have been my own footprints, of course, though that's doubtful: these footprints (if that's what they were) lay parallel to the edge of the woods. They could have been made by anything. They could have been made by deer, raccoon, foxes. Then the endless rain made them look provocative.

I didn't go *into* the woods, of course.

9:47 PM

Ronnie said, "Josh, I saw them. Those things out there."

I said, "When?" and she hemmed and hawed and I could tell she was lying.

"Why are you lying to me?" I said.

"I didn't want you to feel like you were alone," she said. "I lied out of love for you."

It's the first time she's mentioned love in months, I think. I don't know how I feel about it. The word slides too easily from her mouth, as if it's merely convenient.

Perhaps because *I* am merely convenient.

I said, "Do you know that I feel for your heartbeat while you sleep, Ronnie?" and she only smiled.

I'm sick of noting the time.

If I do not note it, then perhaps it will cease to exist.

It's early morning. Still raining hard. I'm having coffee—*Jamaican Me Crazy*; good stuff. I just brewed it. And I'm careful, of course, not to spill it on the laptop. I sip the coffee while holding the cup over the floor in front of the laptop because I tend to be clumsy about things like drinking full cups of scalding coffee. Sometimes, the coffee even squirrels its way out of my mouth.

We've been here a week.

At least a week.

It could be longer.

3:45 AM

Better to note the time, I think. It adds parameters to this . . . thing, this odd experience. Parameters? Reality? Same thing—same function. The laptop's clock says **3:45.23**. That's good. Good, tight parameters.

Ronnie's asleep. She sleeps so damned much, now! I want to wake her, want her to sit here with me and wait for first light, want to see if she really sees what *I* see. How could she not?

5:22.42 AM

Some light, now. Not enough. It's so weak it might as well be darkness.

Can't see much. I can hardly see even the rain because it's so thick and fast. No wind.

Ronnie's still asleep. It's not like her. She always wakes very early. 5:00 AM. An hour earlier than I, usually. 5:00 AM, always. Even earlier. Makes eggs and toast for herself. Makes them later for me—wakes me up with them, puts the plate under my nose, says, "Good eggs, Josh."

The laptop feels warm against my thighs.

I love it. My laptop. This thing that glows in the dark.

I look out this window, at that wall of rain and near-dark, and I think, *It will always rain like this because it has been raining for an eternity.*

I love Ronnie. I believe I love her much more than I knew. I need her, too.

I want her to wake.

I wish to heaven she would wake.

6:01.21 AM

I see you there! I see you! No smile, and no frown or grimace.

I see you! I see you, dammit!

They speak, I'm sure of it.

I speak and so *they* speak.

6:10.12 AM

She's awake, at last! Bustling about the kitchen behind me. She turned the light on. I told her, "Turn it off!"

She turned it off, said, "I can't see to cook."

I said, "Cook later."

"Shit on you!" she said.

"Sure," I said.

"Shit on you twice!" she said.

"I saw them again, Ronnie!" I said.

She said nothing. I turned my head, looked at her; I could hardly see her, as if she were no more than a pale shadow in the dark. I said to her, "You're spooky like that. Turn the light on."

"Shit on you three times," she said, and I know she smiled a little, though I couldn't see it.

She turned the light on.

The rain went away. I could only

hear it. I hear it always. I've heard it forever.

She was smiling.

She has a smile as clear as sunlight.

I said, "I love you more than I ever realized, Ronnie."

"It sounds like you're confessing a revelation," she said.

"Of course," I said. "Yes. I am."

"Thanks," she said. "Thanks," she repeated. "I'll make us eggs and toast."

"Yes, thank you," I said. "I'm very hungry."

8:43

"Do not go to bed with anger or wake with anger," I said.

Ronnie said, "Who wrote that?" because a book lay open on the table in front of me.

"I don't know. Not this guy." I nodded at the book. "Someone else. I don't remember who."

"It's good advice," she said, and yawned. "I like it."

"Why so sleepy?" I said.

She shook her head. "I'm not sleepy. Just yawning." She nodded at my empty plate. "Good eggs, huh? I did something different with them. Did you notice?"

"Yeah," I said. "They were great."

"You didn't notice," she said, collected my plate and silverware from the table, took them to the sink, looked out the window and said, "I feel like Noah's wife."

"You're not Noah's wife," I said. "You're *no one's* wife." I smiled.

She looked at me, smiled back, though it seemed to be as much a frown as a smile. "Do tell," she said, and ran some water on my plate.

12:00

I have seen them clearly. Or, perhaps, as clearly as they'll allow. They're like mannequins made of mist. I can't explain them to Ronnie, and I won't try. I've given up telling her anything about them, or about anything important, for that matter.

I know she won't listen.

She never listens.

She never hears me, no matter how loudly I speak.

She's asleep again.

She sleeps almost constantly now. I check her breathing every five minutes, put my hand on her chest and check her breathing. Put my ear close to her mouth and check her breathing.

The rain is constant.

Breathing is constant.

My laptop glows in the dark.

1:00

It's an approximate time. I have stopped caring about good and tight parameters.

The mannequins made of mist spoke to me not long ago. Who knows what they said. They drew closer to the window, closer to me through the rain, and they spoke to me. What I assume were their mouths moved abundantly, but I heard nothing. Only the hard and constant rain.

1:00

Ronnie woke at last, said, "I had such a good nap, Josh. It's so restful here. Thank you for bringing me," then she added that I might need a nap too. I assured her I didn't. "I may never sleep again," I said.

She said, after giving me a peck on the cheek, "Uh huh, and someday the dead will rise and sing Christmas carols in fulsome voice."

I smiled. I thought it was an unusual remark for her, even interesting. I said to her, "Jesus, that was stupid."

2:00

She's sleeping again.

I don't know what to do about all of this.

I woke Ronnie; I said, "I'm sorry," and she said, without opening her eyes, "For what?"

"For my insensitive remark."

"It's all right," she said, and opened her eyes a little. "It's still raining."

"Yes," I said.

"Christ!" she said. "Christ, the rain!"

"Yes," I said. "The rain."

She closed her eyes.

I can do nothing but write and stare out the window while she sleeps. I can hear her, now, snoring in her soft and appealing way. So odd that I would hear it above the endless drone of the rain.

It wasn't *her*. Good Lord, it was them. The mannequins. Talking.

They were in this room with me, I'm certain of it. They weren't at the window. I'd have seen them; I always see them. And I see them *always* at the window.

If I had turned away from it, the window, when I thought I was hearing only Ronnie, I would have seen them here. In the room with me. Here. In the room.

I've sponged up their leavings. Moisture on the linoleum.

I am not frightened.

I believe in them, so I can't be frightened. I *know* them, so I am not frightened of them.

The laptop is warm, comforting on my thighs.

Ronnie wakes. I hear her. She wakes. And then appears.

"Hello," she says. "Hello, Josh," she says. "What a good nap I had. What a wonderful place this is to nap. Thank you for bringing me here."

We made love wildly and urgently. It's Tuesday, 3:45 PM.

Moments ago, Ronnie said, "That was remarkable. Josh, that was remarkable."

"I agree," I said, and patted her ass. We're in the kitchen. She's making coffee, I believe. A drink of some kind.

She's still naked. She knows I like it—that continuation of her nakedness after lovemaking. Her *reveal.* Her realization of my purposes and need. My revelation, and hers too.

3:46 PM

She read over my shoulder what I wrote here, some of it. She tapped the screen (I don't like that; leaves marks), said, "You're not *very* odd, Josh, but you're *somewhat* odd." She cocked her head; a coquettish gesture, said, "My 'reveal'?"

I said, "Ronnie, I heard them."

"Heard them?" she said. "Oh yes." She formed quotes with her fingers. It's a gesture I despise from anyone, even her, even when she's naked, when all gestures are appealing. It's posturing and false. "'*Them!*'" she said and grinned.

"Don't grin," I said. "Please."

She stopped grinning, looked confused, a little anxious, too, I think. Why not?

I said, "I believe in them. I believe in them."

"No need to repeat yourself," she said. "My hearing's perfect."

"Nothing's perfect," I said.

She grinned. It was a nervous grin. Obviously nervous.

She said, "A little bit, just a little bit, Josh, you're scaring me. Like maybe you're going to do something strange to me while I'm asleep."

I cocked my head. "Huh? Huh?" I grinned. "I already have," I said, and laughed a little, which elicited a laugh from her, and when we stopped laughing, I said, "If I were going to do anything *strange* to you, my love, it wouldn't be while you were *sleeping.*" I smiled.

She didn't.

"Joke," I said.

"I believe you," she said.

4:25 PM

Of *course* the constant hard rain produces creatures such as these—the creatures I've seen beyond the window. Rain is the offspring of lakes, rivers and oceans, after all, and those are places of life, places teeming with life.

So it's no great mental task to believe that the rain can produce, from itself, *within* itself, *of* itself, creatures such as I have seen here, at this house.

4:49

She read aloud, over my shoulder, one of my phrases above: "Rain is the offspring of lakes, rivers, oceans, after all . . . " was as far as she got before I slammed the laptop shut and shouted, "Dammit, Ronnie, dammit, goddammit!" then wheeled around on my stool and watched her back quickly, quickly away from me.

"Shit, I'm sorry!" she said, and disappeared into the bedroom.

Which is where she is now.

Snoring softly and appealingly.

————

I apologized to her, of course. I needed to. They told me to. And she was very understanding, said it was "all right," said the rain was making us both "contentious and irrational."

"I'm not being irrational, just contentious," I said in an offhand way, so she'd think I was joking, and she said, "I need to sleep again," so I said, "Okay, sleep," and she left the room.

7:23.14

Here I am, on this spot, this tall stool, at my window, and happy about it, even happy about the hard and constant rain because of the gifts it has produced.

Oh, and she appeared not long ago, very sleepy, wiped her eyes, yawned, said, "Oh, Josh, yes, by the way, I've seen them too. Honestly. I believe you now, I really do, and I'm sorry for doubting," then wandered back into the bedroom. I hollered after her, "Thank you, my love!" and got, moments later, what was, of course, an affirmation, a "Yes."

We go back a long, long way.

High school sweethearts, you know. Proms and hops and so forth. Dated at soda shops. Watched movies that we really didn't *watch* (wink, wink). How many relationships have been spawned by just such scenarios? The world doesn't spin because of such scenarios, of course, but such scenarios do spin the world.

I love her as much as I can love anything, anyone, and that's an enormous amount. More than I can hold in both hands.

They told me, "Love her deeply, Josh, love her very, very deeply," and I said, "I do, and have," and they nodded and smiled and said, "Yes, we know."

She's in the bedroom, now.

I have no idea what she's doing in there.

I'll go and find out.

I'll go and see.

9:02.23 PM

Darker than hate in that bedroom. No light. The rain's done it at last—destroyed the light. I should have known, but didn't.

I said in that darkness, "Ronnie?"

"Josh?" she said.

"I'm here, Ronnie. Are you afraid?"

"Yes," she said.

"Why?" I said.

"I think you know why," she said.

"I do, yes," I said.

"Can you leave now, Josh?"

"Yes," I said, "I can leave," and I did.

10:19 PM

The laptop's working on batteries only. It's no good on batteries. Never has been. Lasts maybe two hours, tops. What kind of shit is that?

I'll write quickly, type quickly, get lots said.

The rain has not stopped.

And they, whom the rain has produced for me, are pushing against the window *en masse* and grinning, mumbling: odd, they were so articulate not long ago, an hour ago, two hours ago, or three.

Interesting, almost ironic, that the laptop keeps the time beautifully when the lights are gone.

Oh, she said, *Ronnie* said, moments ago, "You shouldn't use it on batteries, Josh. Those batteries are shitty."

"I know," I said.

I like it when she says "shitty." It's a feminine thing—that word.

I said, "Are you still afraid, Ronnie?"

"Yes, I am. I'm going to leave, I need to leave," she said.

"No," I said.

She said nothing. She went back into the bedroom. I heard her packing. Hard to believe she can do that in the pitch dark?

4:15.21 AM

And so she's gone. How can I deal with that? How can I deal with her absence? We've been together since high school. We went to parties together, the Senior Prom, you know. We played "Find The Mule" in the backseat of my father's Dodge.

But she's gone.

And that's a very critical thing.

Like the condition of my laptop's batteries.

A very critical thing.

4:22:12 AM

I watched her go. The mannequins

watched with me. And they kept silence, except for what they said:

Such as:

"Enough of her already."

And:

"That's the end, possibly."

"That's the end of her, possibly."

And:

"Grieve as much as you deem appropriate, Josh."

And:

"As much as you deem appropriate, grieve, now, Josh."

"Yes," I said, "I will."

6:19:22 PM

Odd, yes, how time is wrapped up in static moments that don't represent *time* at all. The moment, for instance, in which a quick inhale is taken. We feel or hear or experience, within us, only that breath, in that static moment of the breath, so it's *apart* from the flow of time. Whether it's the first breath or the last, it is only one breath out of literally millions in the flow of time, the flow of a life.

If I were to construct an analogy, it would be this: time is wrapped up in static moments that don't represent *time* at all, in the *same way* that skin and blood and flesh is wrapped up in microscopic cells that, singularly, have next-to-nothing to do with skin and blood and flesh.

If you think about it, as I do, you will agree.

I love my laptop.

This thing that glows in the dark.

I love it.

Still raining. Very, very hard, now. As if an ocean is draining. I know of it though I can't hear or see it because, at last, I can't hear or see anything. I feel the comforting warmth of my laptop against my thighs, and I feel my fingertips on the keyboard, the little guide bumps on the "F" and "J," which are so important for blind typists and touch typists, or blind touch typists.

Of course.

And *their* touch, as well, is comforting, even warm, surprisingly warm, considering what it's composed of, the small moments of the life-giving rain, the life-creating rain, the rain that is life.

Where do I go now? From here?

Where?

And why?

And why?

I'm the first to admit that I don't have his critical sense, his intelligence, or his lyricism, and his perverse philoso-phies have always annoyed and eluded me.

And now, *he* doesn't have any of that, either.

I can't be happy about it. I want to be happy about it, but it's not possible.

You'd think I'd have adjusted after so long.

My God, we went to proms together, and movies, too, and we played "Find the Mule" in the back of his father's Dodge. So how could I be happy now?

I can't.

I'm not.

I'm as sad and confused as a new puppy blindly searching for its mother's teat.

I have his laptop. It's a strange parting gift for our years of loss and gain and heartache. This thing that glows in the dark.

It *will* rain again. It must rain again. And then he'll *be*, once more, once more, and I'll *see* him, and *hear* him— singing Christmas carols in fulsome voice. ⬚

Max Gorshen lives in a dark, hot apartment in a medium-size, though unnamed, north American city with someone he refers to only as "the other [man]," who, Max tell us, lives in the apartment's "long, dim hallway." Max and "the other [man]" never seem to encounter each other in the apartment (although Max sees "the other [man]" mingling with and bedeviling "the interlopers and trespassers" on the city streets below the window Max sits at while he writes the novella), though they talk to one another through letters and brief notes: neither man is certain the other man really exists. Both of these characters live with "Langley," a very talkative and apparently highly intelligent African gray parrot. Something else exists in the big apartment, too, and all three first-person narrators (Max, the other [man], and Langley) lead

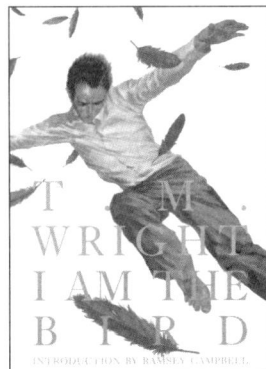

As the following story eloquently proves, Thomas Tessier is a man of few words...but they all count. "This tale passed me on the road one day, more or less as described," he says. "But I think I got a little bit of it."

Tom's new novel, Wicked Things, *will be published by Leisure Books this summer.*

If You See Me, Say Hello

Thomas Tessier

Ted was on his way back into town, less than a mile from home, when he saw the car coming in the opposite lane. An orange Mini Cooper. It was actually called Rally Orange and it wasn't a stock color. You had to special order it. Her car, her color, she'd waited months for it to come in. A car he expected never to see again. The traffic was steady, the road wide at that point. It was early in the afternoon on a Friday in February, in an unusually mild winter.

Impossible to think it could be her. But the Mini drew closer and he saw the same racing stripe, and then the long blonde hair. No, it can't be. She sailed past, her eyes on the traffic ahead, not looking for him or his nondescript Accord. Yes, no doubt at all. In his rearview mirror, the clincher: the Pennsylvania license plate.

Ted's heart pounded and he was breathing through his mouth as he hit the horn, then the button to lower the window. He stuck his arm out and waved, but he knew it was too late then. Too many cars had passed. He couldn't do a U-turn in this traffic. Then he was in a line at a red light. He could turn

left, turn around somewhere up that street, head back and try to catch up with her, but he knew it was hopeless, he'd be guessing which way she went. She would soon reach both a major intersection and the highway. Ted pulled into a bank parking lot and sat for a moment, breathing deeply, trying to calm down.

It had been a little over a year since she decided that her life was going in a different direction and that he wasn't going to be in it any longer. She never gave him a good reason. It wasn't someone else. They were just not right together, at least not right enough for her. So she left him and moved back to the Philadelphia area, where she had family and old friends.

But now, here she was, and they'd just missed each other. He had been out driving for an hour or so, nothing important. The only reason she would have driven hundreds of miles to Connecticut was to see him. Why hadn't she called first or sent him an email? And why hadn't she waited at the apartment building for him to return? Ted tried to consider all the possibilities, but none of them made much sense.

160

He'd seen her, she was there, she was real for a moment. But now she was gone again, and he was still lost.

He thought about the direction she was heading. He put his car in gear and started to drive. He decided to swing by the ice cream stand, the state park and a couple of other places in the area that they used to visit. Maybe she was driving around there too, killing time, before going back to the apartment building to see if he had returned home. Maybe he would spot her. If not, perhaps he would get back to his place—their place, really—and find her there, in the parking lot, in her orange Mini, waiting for him.

Jen accelerated and pulled into the flow of traffic on I-95. She had spent a couple of hours there, but she'd allowed for it, and she would be in Boston in time for the evening reception at the comic book convention. So many things seemed to get better for her after she left Connecticut—the talented people she'd met at Blue Terror Comics, the way she walked into the job and was doing so well at it, seeming to understand everything at once. She didn't feel bad about any of it. She had grown up a great deal in the space of a year.

But sometimes she felt bad about Ted. This visit was for him. She hadn't been growing up with Ted, not enough,

and maybe that was why they couldn't last. But at the same time, maybe she wouldn't have grown up at all without him, and that was why she felt she still owed him something and would always miss him. For her, he'd been both necessary and impossible.

She drove past Swirlee's, the ice cream stand, but of course it was closed until April. She swung through the state park on the edge of town, where they'd had picnics and necked passionately, but where the trees were now bare and the parking lots empty. She sat in her car outside the apartment building where she had spent so many delightful hours, and felt a sense of a loss that was still beyond her control.

She felt lonely and sad today. There were moments, now and then, when Ted still felt like a real presence in her life.

They'd found him on his sofa, fully dressed but with his shoes off, looking as if he had simply stretched out to take a nap. That was about six months after she'd left.

The autopsy found no apparent cause of death and therefore ruled it was the result of natural causes. As if to say, his heart just stopped. But she knew better. Nobody dies of natural causes at the age of 33.

I'll always love you.

Traffic on I-95 opened up. Jen hit the gas.

◪

Christopher Fowler tells us that this story is ninety per cent true. "It began when I went to my old school pal Simon's wedding to be his best man," he says. "I wrote out my wedding speech while I was attending the annual British Fantasy Society convention, and somehow the two events became conflated in my mind, mixed in with a third event I once attended called 'Harbour Frights', a festival of horror films that took place somewhere on the Southwest coast. Quite why the story has the outcome that it has is a mystery to me, and I find that fact alone very disturbing. But it is said that we never know why we fall in love, and such a tenet may well hold true for those we choose to hurt. Chalk this one up to the cruel forces that render us powerless but ultimately govern us all." Indeed. Read on.

The Luxury Of Harm
Christopher Fowler

When I was eleven, I was warned to stay away from a new classmate with freckles and an insolent tie, so naturally we became inseparable partners in disruption, reducing our educators to tears of frustration.

For the next eight years our friendship proved mystifying to all. Simon horrified our teachers by illegally racing his Easy Rider motorbike across the football field. We took the deputy headmaster's car to pieces, laying it out in the school car park as neatly as a stemmed Airfix kit. We produced a libellous school magazine with jokes filched from TV programmes, and created radio shows mocking everyone we knew. When you find yourself bullied, it's best to team up with someone frightening. Simon perverted me from learning, and I made his soul appear salvageable whenever he superglued the school cat or made prank phone calls. I fretted that we would get into trouble, and he worked out how we could burn down the school without being caught.

Boys never tire of bad behaviour. Through the principles of economics and the theory of gravity, the Wars of the Roses and Shakespeare's symbolism, we cut open golfballs and tied pupils up in the elastic, carved rocketships into desks and forged each others' parental signatures on sick notes.

During puberty, Simon bought a mean leather jacket. I opted for an orange nylon polo-neck shirt with velcro fastenings. He looked like James Dean. I looked like Simon Dee. In order to meet girls, we signed up for the school opera. Simon met a blue-eyed blonde backstage while I appeared as a dancing villager in a shrill, offkey production of "The Bartered Bride". We double dated. I got the blonde's best friend, who had legs like a bentwood chair and a complexion like woodchip wallpaper, but her father owned a sweetshop so we got free chocolate. I rang Simon's girlfriends for him because he was inarticulate, and hung around his house so much that his mother thought I'd been orphaned. Our friendship survived because he gave me visibility, confidence and a filtered charisma that reached me like secondary smoking. He stopped me from believing there was no-one else in the world who understood me. And there he remained in my mind and heart, comfortable and constant, throughout the years, like Peter Pan's shadow, ready to be reattached if ever I needed it, long after his wasteful, tragic death.

But before that end came, we shared a special moment. By the time this happened, we had gone our separate ways; he became the conformist, with a country home and family, and I turned into the strange one, living alone in town. Recontacting Simon, I persuaded him to come to a horror convention with me, in a tiny Somerset town called Silburton, where the narrow streets were steeped in mist that settled across the river estuary, and fishing boats lay on their sides in the mud like discarded toys. The place reeked of dead fish, tar and rotting shells, and the locals were so taciturn it seemed that conversation had been bred out of them.

The hotel, a modern brick block that looked like a caravan site outhouse, had no record of our booking, and was full because of the convention. In search of a guest-house, we found a Bed & Breakfast place down beside the river ramps and lugged bags up three flights through narrow corridors, watched by the landlady in case we scratched her Indian-restaurant wallpaper. The beds felt wet and smelled of seaweed.

By the time we returned to the convention hotel, the opening night party was in full swing. A yellow-furred alien was hovering uncertainly in the reception area, struggling to hold a pint mug in his rubber claws, and a pair of local Goth girls clung to the counter, continually looking around as though they were afraid that their parents might wander in and spot them, raising their arms to point and scream like characters from *Invasion Of The Body Snatchers*.

Every year the convention had a theme, and this year it was "Murderers on Page and Screen", so there were a few Hannibal Lectors standing around, including a grinning lad with the top of his head sawn off. The bar staff took turns to stare at him through the serving hatch.

"Is this really what you do for fun?" Simon asked me, amazed that I could take pleasure from hanging out with guys dressed as Jason and Freddie, films no-one even watched anymore. "Who comes to these things?"

"Book people, lonely people," I said simply, gesturing at the filling room. "Give it a chance," I told him. "There's no attitude here, and it gets to be fun around midnight, when everyone's drunk. Come on, you said your life was very straight. This is something new."

Simon looked unsure; he hardly ever read, so the dealer rooms, the panels and the literary conversation held no interest for him. He talked about his kids a lot, which was boring. I wanted him to be the kid I'd admired at school. He could relate to drinking, though, and relaxed after a couple of powerful local beers that swirled like dark sandstorms in their glasses. Simon could drink for England. "So," he asked, "are they all writers looking for tips?"

"In a way. Take this year's theme. We're intrigued by motivation, method, character development. How do you create a realistic murderer? Who would make a good victim?" I tried to think of a way of involving Simon in my world. "Take the pair of us, for example. I'm on my home turf here. People know me. If I went missing, there would be questions asked. For once, you're the outsider. You were once the tough guy, the bike riding loner nobody knew, and you're unknown here. That would make you the perfect victim."

"Why?" Simon wasn't the sort to let something beat him. His interest was piqued, and he wanted to understand.

"Because taking you out would require an act of bravery, and would be a show of strength. Killers seek notoriety to cover their inadequacies. But they also enjoy the remorse of loss."

Simon snorted. "How the hell does that work?"

"There's a strange pleasure to be taken in melancholy matters, don't you think? A kind of tainted sweetness. Look at the Goths and their fascination with death and decay."

"Okay, that's the victim sorted, so who's the killer?"

"Look around. Who would you choose?"

Simon scoped out the bar area. "Not the Jason or Freddy look-alikes. They're geeks who would pass out at the sight of a paper cut. They'd be happy to watch, but they wouldn't act."

"Good, keep going."

"And the Goths couldn't kill, even though they're professional mourners. They look tough but play gentle."

"Excellent."

"But him, over there." He tapped his forefinger against the palm of his hand, indicating behind him. "He looks like he's here to buy books about guys who murder their mothers. It wouldn't be such a big step to committing a murder."

"Yeah, we get a few of those at conventions. They sit in the front row at the Q&As, and are always the first to raise their hands with a question. There's one guy, a retired doctor, who even gives me the creeps. Over there." I pointed out the cadaverous Mr Henry, with his greasy comb-over and skin like the pages of a book left in the sun. He never missed a convention, even though he wasn't a writer or publisher, or even a reader. "He once told me he owns one of the country's largest collections of car crash photographs, and collects pictures of skin diseases."

"That's gross. I knew there would be freaks here."

"Relax, he's too obvious. If there's one trick to serial killer stories, it's making sure that the murderer is never someone you suspect. Have you noticed there are some very cute girls hanging around the bar?"

"You're right about that," Simon

grudgingly admitted, watching two of them over the top of his glass.

"You should go and make their acquaintance," I suggested. "I'll just be here talking weird books with old friends, or the other way around."

I got into a long discussion/argument about the merits of *Psycho 2* and *3*, about Thomas M. Disch and William Hope Hodgson and what makes a good story, and lost all track of the time. I only checked my watch when the waiter started pulling shutters over the bar. Bidding farewell to my fellow conventioneers, I staggered off through the damp river air toward the guest house.

Somehow I managed to overshoot the path, and ended up on the seaweed-slick ramp to the harbour. The only sounds were the lapping of the water and the tinging of masts. The tide was coming in, and the boats were being raised from their graves like reanimating corpses. Drunk and happy and suddenly tired, I sat down on the wet brown sand and allowed the sea-mist to slowly reveal its secrets. It formed a visible circle around me, like the kind of fog in a video game that always stays the same distance no matter how hard you run. A discarded shovel someone had used to dig for lugworms stood propped against the harbour wall. Orange nylon fishing nets, covered with stinking algae, were strung out like sirens' shawls.

And through the mist I gradually discerned a slender figure, its head lolling slightly to one side, one arm lower than the other, like the skeleton in Aurora's "Forgotten Prisoner" model kit, the one that features on the cover of the *Seventh Pan Book of Horror Stories*. It was standing so still that it seemed more like the unearthed figurehead of a boat than a man.

There was a strong smell of ozone and rotting fish. The figure raised a ragged, dripping sleeve to its skull, rubbing skin to bone. It seemed as though it had ascended from the black bed of the sea.

"I fell off the fucking dock and tore my jacket. I am so incredibly slaughtered," said Simon, before tipping over and landing on his back in the sand with a thump.

The next morning, screaming seagulls hovered so close to my bedroom window that I could see inside their mouths. Shafts of ocean sunlight bounced through the window, punching holes in my brain. My tongue tasted of old duvet. I needed air.

I knocked on Simon's door, but there was no answer. Breakfast had finished, and the landlady had gone. The Easy Rider motorbike still stood in the car park behind the guest house.

The tide was out and the mist had blown away, leaving the foreshore covered in silvery razor-clams and arabesques of green weed. On the stone walkway above the harbour, an elderly lady in a teacosy hat marched past with a shopping bag. There was no-one else about. The gulls shrieked and wheeled.

Carefully, I walked across the beach to the spot where Simon had fallen, and knelt down. It took a moment to locate the exact place. Rubbing gently at a patch of soft sand, I revealed his sand-filled mouth, his blocked nostrils, one open shell-scratched eye that stared bloodily up into the sky. I rose and stood hard on his face, rocking back and forth until I had forced his head deeper into the beach. I carefully covered him over with more sand, smoothing it flat and adding some curlicues of seaweed and a couple of cockle shells for effect. Finally I threw the shovel I had used on his neck as far as I could into the stagnant water of the harbour.

As I headed back to the convention hotel, ready to deliver my lecture on "Random Death: The Luxury Of Harm", a heartbreaking happiness descended upon me. I knew that there would be plenty of time to savour the full delicious loss of my old friend in the days, the months, the years to come.

Teenagers Maddy and Rogan Tierney are cousins, two among dozens living in a tumbledown family enclave outside New York. Secretly, or not so secretly, the pair are lovers, and if this weren't bad enough, they are also drawn to the stage, to music, reviving a Tierney tradition of artistic involvement long since abandoned for more practical, worldly pursuits. Parents and siblings radiate disapproval. But encouraged by their mysterious Aunt Kate, and by a magically animated toy theatre hidden in a forgotten attic room, Rogan and Maddy become involved in a school production of *Twelfth Night*. Their own lives eerily echoing the play's concerns with twinning and disguise, they are destined for brief apotheosis and lasting heartbreak, in a narrative of stark emotional power and potent nostalgic richness. Elegant and fraught as only Elizabeth Hand's novellas can be, *Illyria* is a superb tale of illicit devotion and the fleeting potentials of childhood, one of the finest stories of the year.

In the near future, as eco-disaster and political repression take their devastating toll on the human race, the past seems like an ideal destination, quieter, more hopeful, *known*. In response, a few individuals develop an ability to travel in time: first, simply to cast their consciousnesses back, passively sharing the experiences and sensations of people and creatures long dead; then, actively to usurp the bodies of our ancestors, and, ultimately, to venture into history physically, standing in their own right on the streets of Elizabethan London or Pompeii. But human nature being what it is, madness, jealousy, and fear accompany the time travellers wherever they go. . . Highly imaginative and powerfully bleak, *Where or When* is Steven Utley's mosaic vision of time travel as a crucible of the human soul. Visit ancient cities or modern battlefields, and you begin to understand history and yourself; whether liberating or imprisoning, satirical or hopeful, the resulting insights are cogent indeed.

Allen Ashley is the author of one novel, two short story collections and a collection of non-fiction. In 2006 he received the British Fantasy Society's "Best Anthology" award for his editorship of The Elastic Book Of Numbers *. . . the success of which prompted him to take up the editor's gavel once more with* Subtle Edens, *due from Elastic in 2008. Allen got the idea for "D-Leb" on the tube train heading towards the office one morning. "You could probably have guessed that," he adds somewhat laconically. "In the best British SF traditions, there's always a touch of reality and a hint of wish fulfilment in my stories. I'll say no more." A wise decision.*

D-Leb

Allen Ashley

As my personal life continues to splutter like damp blue touch paper, I keep thinking back to Oliver and wishing things had worked out with him. Of course, he was typically commitment-phobic but, to my knowledge, he was always faithful. And he had the excuse that we were both in our early twenties so why the need to settle down or "get glued" as he charmingly put it? I could have saved myself a stack of false dawns if I'd persevered. He cast my need for proximity as possessiveness; my desire as desperation. Twelve years on from our first meeting and five years since we split, he remains the high water mark of a feeble tide. If only I'd known.

I was thinking about Oliver purely because from my cramped position by the tube carriage doors all I could see clearly was an advert for some men's health supplement and the guy's face was vaguely similar. I'd bought a copy of *Heat* on my way in. Standing on the grey platform, I flicked through the contents and was annoyed to notice several of the pages were either blank or unprinted. It was too late to go back for an exchange. The station started filling up. The indicator board froze on the "next train one minute" announcement. By the time it actually arrived, the vehicle was seriously over capacity. A one-metre surge of desperate commuters at least got me aboard for the half-hour hell ride to Kings Cross Sans Pancreas, where I could gratefully change lines. And if that suit with the laptop and the half-folded *FT* poked me in the tits once more I swear I'll take my stiletto and rupture his cruciates.

If I could lift my foot. If I could breathe enough regurgitated air to oxygenate my flabby muscles sufficiently.

Why had we stopped again? There had been no trains ahead of ours within ten minutes so what could possibly be the hold-up down the line?

Looking askance over my left shoulder, I could see that the tunnel wall with its trunks of wiring was no longer visible, which meant we were close to one of the innumerable sidings and access tunnels which were attached to the main tube lines like barnacles to a cetacean. An old boyfriend had once conjectured a story in which a computer glitch causes points failure and all the trains are re-routed down these dead ends. *Passenger Peril*, he called it. I think it even got published somewhere.

The boyfriend was Oliver. Why was I suddenly obsessing? For the first eighteen months after we split, I was still hurting. An Internet trawl through the Electoral Register and a carefully worded plea on *Friends Reunited* had yielded zilch. Let it go, girl.

But then he'd started his own web site a couple of years back, just after his first (and so far only) novel hit the shops. I logged on to look . . . but resisted contacting him. Let him go, Claire! Read the book again if you want to, but otherwise . . .

Let us move. Please. I'm already sweaty and late.

Technically, I was in charge at the office this morning. Joyce was at a midweek media awareness conference in Leicester and Nasreen was due to escort our major patron, the Earl of Tetchley, through a meet and greet at the Park Lane Hilton. I'd held down better jobs in my life but this was the first place I'd ever worked in which the top three posts down the chain of command were all filled by women. That ought to be worth something. A twenty-five per cent pay rise or a huge

hike in my tax-free clothing allowance would be worth even more.

I decided to let a few items rest easy in my Inbox and make myself available for the junior members of staff. They might need a gee-up or a comforting big sisterly walk through a complex procedure.

In truth, it was remarkably quiet for the first couple of hours. Darren and Andrew—our recently appointed trainees—seemed to be diligently absorbed at their monitors but I could detect a faint susurrus every time I wandered away. They were probably just gossiping football tittle-tattle like the majority of males below the age of ninety. I couldn't see them sticking it here more than six months.

Janie had the company TV running in the rest room. The smell from her herbal infusion tea reminded me of past diets and health kicks. These days it was caffeine all the way on a regular two-hourly schedule.

"Is there a big news story?" I asked.

"Nah, I was just catching a bit of *Celebrity Airship*, except it's stopped transmitting."

"The first series was all right," I responded. "I used to go to school with Annie Clarke."

"She shoulda won it. What's she doing now?"

"I don't know, actually. I'll have to call her some time."

I'd let Janie wrong-foot me and felt I couldn't now boss her back to the empty desk.

The day ticked over. At half past twelve, Nasreen returned with her green jade earrings mysteriously steamed over and her usually immaculate black hair sticking out like she'd had a fight with a crow.

"Bloody English nobility!" she blurted out. "Useless toffee-nosed toff. Wants to be our president but can't get off his fat white arse to attend any functions."

"Needs a bit of the Indian work ethic," I told her.

"Absolutely. My grandparents kept grafting into their seventies. I tell you, Claire, come the revolution, that Tetchley prick will be the first up against the wall."

"Right on, sister," I smiled.

Q: So how does it feel to have one of the most instantly recognisable faces on the planet?

A: It's not something I'm entirely comfortable about but I've learnt to live with it.

Q: Do you find there are other unexpected benefits from being so well known?

A: I suppose I have a certain amount of influence. How much is open to conjecture. Politicians come calling from time to time wanting to get me "on board" or "singing from the same hymn sheet" or some such jargon. I don't want to be allied to some party line, especially when it inevitably all goes tits up. But if there's a cause I believe in, my attitude's different. If I can, for example, get people behind an irrigation project in Central Africa just by pledging my own support, that's a fair use of celebrity status, I'd say.

Q: Any regrets?

A: Bundles. I'd love to be spontaneous and inconspicuous again. It would be nice to just pop out to the local café for a cappuccino without the need for bodyguards or minders or people "setting it up". I mean, how much setting up should it take just to put some beans in the grinder and heat the milk up?

Cancellations crowded the tubes beyond their usual sweaty capacity. I couldn't force my way to the exit door and had to wait a couple of stops and make a different connection. This had me coming in to Finsbury Park on the Victoria Line. Just as we reached the station, the tunnels merged and the Piccadilly train briefly curved towards us with its cargo of commuters like a subterranean apparition, then veered smoothly onto its own platform. Somehow I manoeuvred my way on to a vacant blue seat with red armrest. The guy opposite was poring over the *Evening Standard* which sported the headline, "Why is the government on holiday?" Lucky sods! I didn't have any leave available for a couple of months yet.

I didn't recognise the newsreader on TV and I had the sound down anyway. Without any captions. Oliver would have accused me of practising my lip-reading skills and I would have smiled. The accusations grew much worse prior to the break-up. Occasionally I logged onto his web site . . . just to check that he was still OK. There was rarely anything of any import happening.

I was on a tube train one day and they did that typical thing of giving you 30 seconds warning that they'd decided for no acceptable reason to terminate the service at Wood Green. So we all shuffled onto the platform and the driver closed the doors. But there was one passenger in the next to last carriage who had failed to heed the call and we all chuckled in a nervously macabre fashion as he was shunted off into the dark sidings. Of course, eventually, he would have been released by the negligent driver from the mysterious staff only tunnel. It brightened up the journey home no end for the rest of us.

I was leafing through old copies of *Grazia* and *Prima* wondering if I could bear to send the dreams of designer lifestyles and diet couture to the recycling bin. I was failing to eat properly most evenings and sometimes it made me a little light-headed. It was certainly cheaper than binge drinking with the girls from my old office.

My stomach hurt, anyway. I could feel my period coming on. I bet Britney and Angelina didn't suffer like me.

The tube was unusually roomy this morning as if the government had declared a public holiday but forgotten to tell me. Maybe it had been announced during the ad break punctuating *Tynesiders* or *Celebrity Airship*. I thought I spied my old friend Annie Clarke beyond the double plated glass at the end of the adjoining carriage. I couldn't be certain—her face was half-covered by an unseasonal woollen shawl as if she'd recently crossed the Gap from Gucci chic to Islamic haute couture. She didn't look up and I was left with a five per cent doubt.

Nasreen and Joyce were busy at their desks but the junior staff members were gathered in the rest room. Janie was manipulating the TV remote like she was a Playstation hotshot. Had we given up charitable fund raising and simply become a social club?

"Here comes the news again," Darren muttered.

The screen held only the latest BBC logo, not even a studio shot.

"Westminster sources have ruled out foul play in the recent celebrity disappearances and people are urged to get on with their regular lives. A minister has insisted that we should simply carry on as normal."

"Why's there no newsreader?" I asked.

"That's the whole point," Janie answered. "No one wants to be seen. No one wants to be famous."

"They're all vanishing," Darren added.

"You're having a laugh," I told them as they channel flicked again. "And why won't they send the Home Secretary or someone to make a statement?"

I left them to their conspiracy theorising and made myself a much-needed coffee. It wasn't the best drink of the week but it was the timeliest.

My period was kicking in with a vengeance and I had that low, dull ache I associated with the left ovary. Sinister sister. My vision was getting just a tiny bit blurry, too. The headache couldn't be too far behind despite the best efforts of copious reinforcements from Planet Paracetamol and Mount Nurofen.

Nasreen was waiting for me as I stepped gingerly out of the washroom. Surely I hadn't been *that* long?

"We're sending everybody home, Claire," she informed me.

"Is there some sort of national emergency, Nas?"

"Not exactly. This disappearing celebrity business has got everybody right shitted up, though. Can't stand them but can't live without them in the charity business."

"We'll cope."

"I'm not sure we will, Claire. People don't dig in their pocket for spare change or use a swipe card because they feel sorry for a starving African child or some AIDS victim on life support—they do it because Sir Bob or Her Ladyship does it and they want to ape their lifestyle—"

I wasn't entirely convinced by her logic but the prospect of snuggling up under a duvet with a couple of slabs of Galaxy chocolate and a hot water bottle was suddenly a mere hour away and no sick leave allowance to use up. Count me *out*.

When I got home, I bedded down on the sofa, strategically placed between television and computer screens. I had never got around to having the whole electronic caboodle in one package so now I suffered double eyestrain to go along with the dull ache in my legs and the throbbing in my womb.

If I'd expected the country to have already descended into apocalyptic meltdown, I was disappointed. The news stories were cannily read off-camera or by on the spot reporters who appeared only briefly in the shots. A little of the Blitz spirit still survived, it seemed, along with some Churchillian chicanery. No one was offering a holistic view, everything was disparate: a sneering little item about a drug-addicted pop star missing yet another festival gig; concern is growing for a raft of Hollywood "A" Listers, the so-called "Ocean's Fifteen", believed lost or stranded on exotic location; or the tongue in cheek amusement of, "If senior government ministers are still on holiday and the country is running itself quite adequately, should we bar them at customs upon their return?"

The Internet was no more helpful. The long arms of Microsoft / Google / AOL and the other usual suspects and linked limbs across the ether had imposed a Soviet style clampdown on the possible "real" stories. Out of habit, I had Oliver's home page up and some of his links to other fantasists and conspiracy nutters were still active.

At last I found *WIES*. Short for *Warhol In Extremis Syndrome*. The gist of this seemed to be a sudden limitation imposed upon celebrity—but how? by whom?—which meant that if you'd already had your proverbial fifteen minutes then your time was quite literally up.

Don't you always find that these end of the world freaks concoct the most ridiculous theories and yet somehow there's a tiny irritating nugget that tempts you into believing them?

I went back to Oliver's web page but the welcome had changed to, "This site is being discontinued. Please remove it from your address book." He'd probably defaulted on the payment. Clearly the market for science fiction stories was being squeezed by true-life technological advances and WWW wild rumours dot com.

I couldn't take any more painkillers for at least another hour so sleep was the only curative action. I was tempted to pop a couple more. After all, I'm quite a big girl; not some "size zero" bimbo. Surely I could stand a higher dosage?

The Day of Judgement might have to wait until I'd bled a whole lot drier.

Q: You had a full five years at the very top of your profession. You had all the success you'd craved since you were a child. You had accrued all the trappings and benefits concomitant with fame: wealth, influence, access. Any car you wanted, any building or food you required, any woman who took your fancy, any stimulants or sedatives to keep your mood cool and on task. You could walk into any shop or restaurant in the Western Hemisphere and have a gaggle of obsequious staff instantly attend to your every whim. Yet you gave it up. Why?

A: That's just it, everything was all too easy. I was getting bored with the facility of my life. And it was all so unreal. I was a product. I was a snivelling little creature behind a gigantic, powerful public mask. It wasn't me everyone was celebrating and clamouring over, it was a dream. And not even my dream, anymore.

Q: Some would say that what followed, when you abandoned the dream, constituted a nightmare.

A: I went through . . . some changes. A personality breakdown of sorts. It was important for me to withdraw from the public gaze for a while. In therapy speak: I went to some strange places during this journey.

Q: We're not adding any visuals to this piece but I have to say how different you look now to the abiding poster image that adorned so many student walls.

A: I'm keeping a much lower profile nowadays. It's the only way to survive.

"**Y**ou again!" he sneered. "What do you want?"

"I was just a bit worried about you, Oliver, that's all."

"Well, after five years apart, I'm no different. I'm even living in the same poky flat. You've changed, though. Fuller figured."

"You mean I'm fat."

"No, not at all. Curvier, sexier . . . you always were sexy, of course . . . but, hey, Claire, we've put all that baggage behind us."

"Can I come in? I need to change my tampon."

"My new girlfriend wouldn't like it, Claire."

"You haven't got a new girlfriend. I've read your web log for the past hundred weeks. Come on!"

I pushed past him, desperate for the bathroom. A few minutes later, a scene of domestic destruction greeted me in the living room.

"What are you doing, Olly? Why are you destroying all your books?"

"Don't you know what's been happening? Everybody remotely famous is dying or disappearing. I've got to go incognito."

I took a deep breath, surveyed the wreckage again, finally stated, "Oliver, I don't want to stride back into your life and puncture your balloon like some evil harpy, but you're not actually that famous."

"I can't take the risk, Claire. Nice mixed metaphor, by the way. And you should be worried, too."

"Me? Why on earth?"

"That spot you did on *Blue Peter* when you were eleven. It's always on the box in some *I Heart TV Cock-ups* type show. BBC3 had it on the other night."

"I'm totally different now. I was a little madam then but nowadays I just want to keep a low profile. We're neither us in danger from this . . . whatever this celeb killing plague is."

"Then why did you come all the way over here on a rescue mission?" He had me there. The boyish smile signalled his small victory. He continued, "Who knows what's happening? Divine judgement? Some government or terrorist inspired form of biological warfare? An anti-fame virus? It's already sent the currency and shares market through the trapdoor. Property values are plummeting. All my savings have been wiped out. But that's not the worst of it."

"OK," I muttered, "go on: what is the worst of it?"

"Well, suppose this disease is retroactive."

"Meaning?"

"Suppose it works backwards, into the past. No Shakespeare, no Dickens, no Queen Victoria."

"No Hitler, Stalin or Pol Pot. Doesn't sound such a bad idea."

"But history is what shapes us, Claire. It's the bedrock of our whole civilisation."

It was good to see him animated again, and not simply with anger over some minuscule domestic tiff. I hadn't filled the gap; he hadn't filled the gap. We could still . . .

"But nobody knows who tamed fire or invented the wheel," I told him, "so just how much do we stand to lose?"

"You're right—up to a point. But so much progress has been initiated by individuals. Thomas Jefferson, Emmeline Pankhurst, various Ancient Greeks, James Logie Baird, Robert Louis Stevenson."

"Who?"

"Steam trains. Liverpool to Manchester."

I had a sudden thought, a half-crazy

memory. Or maybe a clear route out of the killing maze.

"Olly," I whispered, "I've just developed a theory."

I could feel our whole society just about keeping things together but teetering on the brink. No one needed celebrities and stars for anything of productive value—the factories and schools could still operate, the buses run and the shops open their usual hours. After a few cold turkey days with literally nothing worth watching on the TV, perhaps we'd all start relating better to each other in a face to face way.

The few channels still running were thin on news. The announcements came from off-screen voices lightly disguised by vocoder effects. Did anyone honestly expect the populace to take such cyber bulletins seriously?

A recorded message at my office announced that we were "on hiatus". Displaying a foolhardiness I hadn't shown since my teenage years, I took the tube into town anyway. The big department stores had armed guards. A looting spree was surely imminent. I phoned Oliver and told him to bring the plan forward. The reception was really crappy.

A shrewish woman in a hoodie gave me a lingering look and asked, "Dun I know you?"

I suspected it was the prequel to a mugging. "Nah, sister, I ain't nobody," I answered, heading for the stone steps and then the stalled escalator. I ran down it, ignoring the wobbly leg feeling when the gaps became uneven. Fortunately, she didn't pursue me.

Even my friendly local Turkish shopkeeper was acting nervous. I bought double quantities of a few essentials. He gave me my change hurriedly, pressed the button that activated the metal shutters as I exited the store.

One of the TV stations was broadcasting only old black and white films with Humphrey Bogart, John Wayne, Ava Gardner and their ilk. Too long dead to be affected by this . . . virus, syndrome, decimation, removal, plague or whatever it was.

So we lose all our celebrities? Big deal. They're just leeches and parasites and over-inflated, hyped-up egotists, all of them.

The old Soviet Union had survived pretty well without such abundance of luminaries: Stalin, Yuri Gagarin . . . uh, that was your lot.

But were we also losing a sense of direction, our aspirations and dreams, even if they only amounted to a shallow desire for fame and fortune?

Plucked from obscurity into instant stardom.

Culled by an unknown hand as Britain descended overnight into a grey gulag of scared non-entities.

"You're late," was his greeting.

For a moment, I had the worst sense of deja vu. And why not? We were re-activating a dormant, close to extinct relationship. The old behaviour patterns and petty squabbles were all likely to re-ignite into pyroclastic flow.

"I'm not cut out for this Mulder and Scully business," I muttered. "Can't we get somebody else to save the world?"

"Just get this safety jacket on," he ordered. It was bright orange and didn't flatter either my figure or complexion.

"What about ID?" I asked.

"Sorted. The hackers and spooks have still preserved their secret identities. So I printed some stuff off the Internet and got it laminated this morning. Let's move."

I was sure his confidence was all bluster. I'd seen him go full speed ahead before like the captain of the *Titanic*. Then I'd watched him crash and splinter into emotional pieces. I didn't relish the prospect of sinking into the icy waters with him. SOS should be SYS— Save Your Self. Or "Sauve Qui Peut", as the French have it.

The nocturnal travellers were as self-contained and reticent as ever. Nobody wanted to be looked at lately; nobody wanted to be recognised. My throat was unbearably dry and I wished I'd thought to bring a bottle of water. We were laughably under-prepared.

The supervisor at Wood Green underground station spent so long poring over our security passes that I was certain Oliver's handiwork had been rumbled.

"Where's Obafemi and Chantelle?" the boss asked eventually.

Ollie executed a cool shrug. "We just go where we're told. We did Hammersmith last night."

"All right. Cupboard's open for anything you need. No slacking."

I wanted to say we haven't even started so quit the discipline, but I held my tongue. Ollie fetched gloves, bin bags, brushes, a bucket and two slightly manky mouth and nose masks. Like using someone else's discarded tissues . . .

"Are you sure the power's off?" I said for the third time.

"It's safe, Claire. Promise."

It was hard, physical work clearing the tracks of accumulated litter beneath the emergency lighting. I'd never complain about a tough day of meetings and phone calls ever again. Despite all the precautions, the dirt and grime gagged the back of my throat and collected under my inappropriately long fingernails. The soot accumulating on my face and itching my tied-back hair made me feel like an over-aged Victorian chimney sweep.

At the second toilet break, Oliver whispered, "I think I've found what we're looking for. But I don't quite understand it."

"What? Where?"

"Down the sidings, like you said. Give me a minute then follow me."

I can see you but I can't touch you.

You're there and yet somehow not there.

No longer fully here.

Carriage after stacked carriage of the

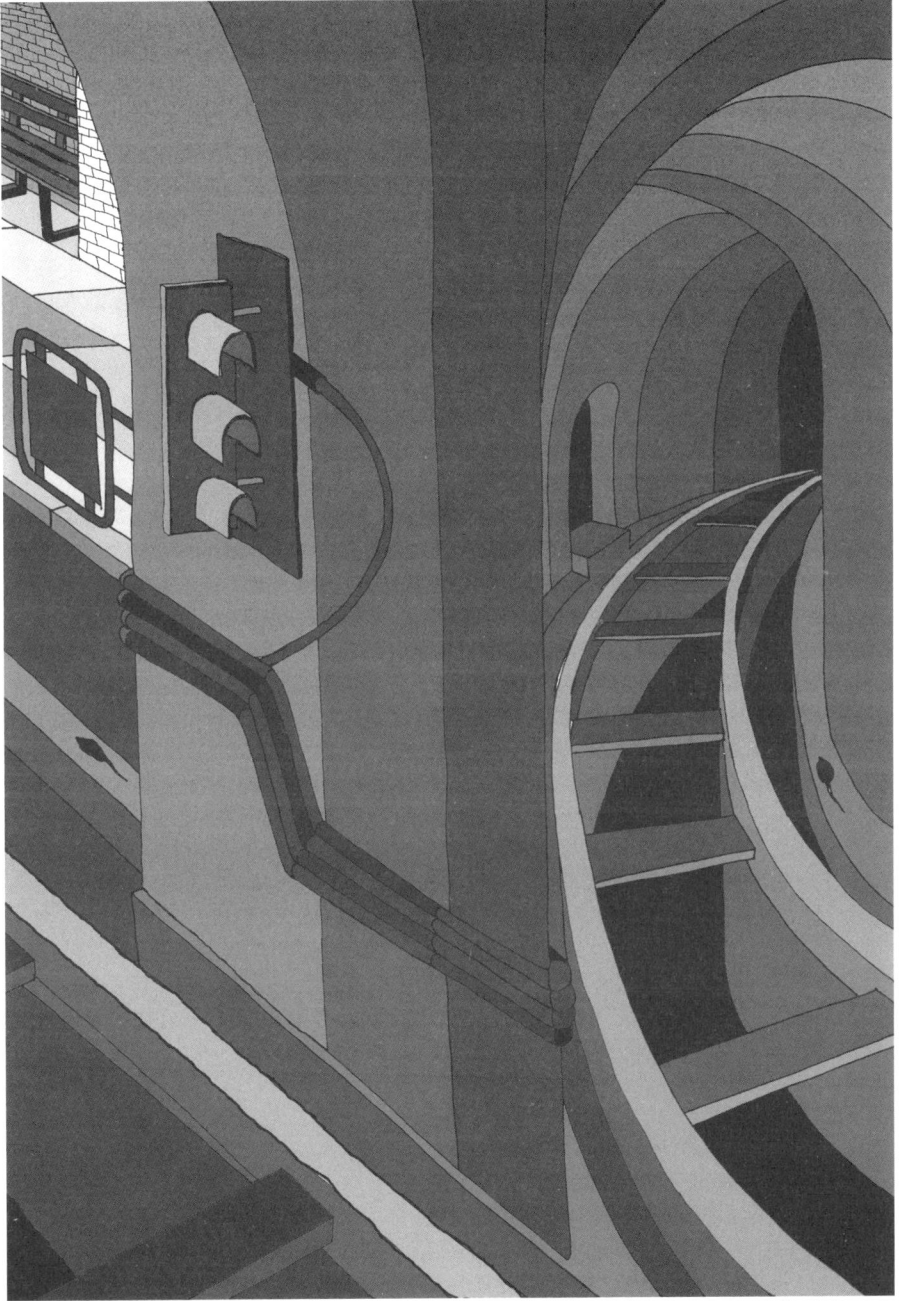

recently famous and more recently disappeared. Actors, politicians, pop stars, athletes and footballers, media-faced captains of industry. All trapped together with no apparent rhyme or reason. Like a subterranean *Sergeant Pepper* sleeve.

And here before me: Annie Clarke; the guy from the toothpaste ad; someone who plays for Chelsea; that topless bimbo who made a million after shagging the washed-up singer on *Love Island*; and also... Nasreen? How did she get taken? How long does the recognition thermometer register its crucial setting?

We're all at risk. I told you so. Oliver talking again.

I can see them but can they see me? Their shocked, vacant faces suggest not. When I reach my hand forward I pass right through both the window glass and human flesh. They are apparitions. Or they are out of kilter with this reality. Oliver again with his theories of parallel worlds and his early manuscript which posited travel between them.

No wonder he's worried.

I can still see you. And you. And all you others. But I can't touch you. And I can't help you.

It's eating me up.

You're no longer fully here.

I can't bring you back.

It may be all I can do to prevent my non-celebrity soul joining you in this limbo.

This hell.

Nothing works any more.

Not the telephones, not the traffic lights, not the holes in the wall. I feel I may yet need some cash to smooth over a few transitions and transactions, although money is only a promise to pay the bearer upon demand. We're moving not into a cash-less society but a cash-free society. Wealth has become a fatal encumbrance. Society itself is crumbling, dissipating.

The Internet still functions occasionally. The American soldiers may be on their way to liberate us... although both their president and deputy commander in chief have gone mysteriously AWOL. My Wi-Fi connection now defaults to a server calling itself "The Radical Nobodies". Better be careful, boys, word gets around...

There's a guy has stationed himself atop a nearby tower block with some sort of rifle. He's challenging everybody who walks by to identify themselves. But either response is dangerous, potentially fatal...

Oliver is desperately trying to post some theories on the Web before the whole thing crashes. Before he disappears, too.

We're all so media literate nowadays. Our knowledge is remarkably wide and yet scandalously shallow. We know names, faces, and remember one trivial fact about each personality. We attach equal importance to all those we casually recognise.

There are more famous people alive today than have existed throughout the whole of human history. We recognise every character from *Eastenders* and contestant off *Big Brother* but know not the philosophers and philanthropists of yesteryear.

I never wanted fame of any sort. That disastrous appearance on *Blue Peter* as a child prodigy has been an albatross for the rest of my non-entity life.

Some religions have it that Humankind's purpose is to list all the names of God. We have spent most of our history simply shouting our own names and "qualities" at the tops of our voices.

Look at me. Recognise me. Celebrate me.

It's dark and cold now. There's no light or gas for the boiler. The batteries on these laptops won't last much longer. We're sitting wrapped in blankets and safety jackets against the cold of the universe. Soon I will stop tapping and reach out to touch Ollie's hand, to know he's there, to feel him, until one of us is taken . . .

When we came staggering out of the tube station, the maintenance crew had vanished and the steel trellis gates were pulled together but, fortunately, not fastened.

Even more of the world has vanished overnight. So much more of our influence, our habitation, our *conquest* has disappeared since . . . Was it just a

week or so ago I was worried about Lord Edgar not turning up to lead the fund raising for our charity.

Oliver is fond of saying, "Charity begins at home." He always was a selfish git.

Look at me.

Look, don't touch.

Don't look any more.

Forget all you knew me for.

No face, no name, no number.

We're holding out here. Just. We have provisions, bottled water, First Aid kits and rudimentary weapons. I'm low on a few necessities such as Nurofen and sanitary towels. I'm dreading my next period.

Claire. There is no Claire. It's an assumed name to protect my true identity. If you knew my real name, you might remember me. And we can't allow that to happen.

Oliver, also, is a nom de plume. Nasreen, Joyce, Janie, Darren, Andrew, even Annie Clarke and the Earl of Tetchley—all fictitious monikers to muddy our trail, to cloak and disguise, keep us out of the *slime* light for a little bit longer.

If you see me on what's left of the street, don't say hello, don't even acknowledge me. Look away. Recognition is fatal.

Celebrity is death.

🔀

P. D. Cacek's "Call Waiting" is not only dedicated to Charles Grant—who died in 2006—but also inspired by him. "When I heard of his death," she tells us, "I called his widow, Kathy Ptacek, to offer whatever sympathy I could . . . and heard Charlie's voice on the answering machine. I couldn't leave a message. Instead I wrote this story. Thanks, Charlie."

The winner of both a Bram Stoker and World Fantasy Award, P.D. "Trish" Cacek has penned over two hundred short stories (according to a fan who did the research) and has appeared in numerous anthologies, including 999 *and* Night Visions 12. *Her newest collection,* Sympathy for the Dead, *will be out in time for Hallowe'en. Trish is currently working on her fifth novel,* Visitation Rites, *inspired, in part, by the haunted house in Fort Washington, PA where she now resides. When not writing, she can often be found with a group of costumed story-tellers called* The Patient Creatures *(www.creatureseast.com). You can visit her web-site at www.pdcacek.com*

Call Waiting
P.D. Cacek

All he had to do was finish cleaning up. That was it, just finish. Not an insurmountable task to be sure, but somehow things kept getting in the way.

There were clients to see, arrangements to be made, friends to avoid whenever possible, meetings to attend . . . and long hours to put in behind his desk when it wasn't necessary.

Those friends he couldn't evade offered to help, but he, in some fit of male pride, declined each and every one with what he hoped sounded like genuine sincerity. He appreciated it, but it was just something he had to do. They understood, of course, because they were friends, so they didn't push except to remind him that they were here if he needed them. All he had to do was call.

He promised he would—*cross my heart and hope to kiss a duck*—but it was only cleaning up, after all; shouldn't take more than a day or two at most.

Yet here it was almost three weeks later. He'd started, certainly, and now all he had to do was finish. Just finish.

Best laid plans and all that.

Jonas deposited his briefcase and tie on the dining table that had become his home office because of its proximity to the *important things* in the apartment and walked the four paces to the liquor cabinet. The liquor cabinet was one of the "important things"; the cell phone charger, sitting on top of the cabinet, was the other. Or maybe it was the *most* important thing, God knows he'd become hopelessly dependent on the thing. It'd become habit that even before his work-wearied mind pondered the age-old question of "scotch vs bourbon vs gin," he'd unclipped the tiny clamshell phone from its holder on his belt and set it into its recharger with the tenderness of a new father tucking in his only child.

180

Ena teased him about it, calling it his lifeline recharger each and every time the electronic first bars of Beethoven's *Fifth* echoed through the apartment.

"What would you ever do without it?"

"I'd have to use your phone," he'd tease back and shudder dramatically.

The landline phone—the *real* one—was hers, the cell his.

And never the twain did meet.

With the cell resting comfortably, Jonas reached for the closest bottle and nodded. Scotch. Fine. Great. Straight up. It would do.

He poured a shot and swallowed it down with only a minor grimace and quick gulp of air at the end. Usually it'd be a double shot, with just enough water or soda to cut some of the smokiness, that he'd nurse through dinner. He didn't drink much during the week.

But dinners had devolved from shopped for and planned-out menus to whatever microwavable Epicurean delight a blind snatch-and-grab into the freezer produced. Meals that came prepackaged in their own disposable plates weren't meant to be lingered over.

And it was Friday night after all.

Jonas helped himself to a second, then a third which he carried to the kitchen before finishing. Some things were easier to finish than others. Liquor was easy. Cleaning up, on the other hand . . .

"Right."

While that night's entrée of Salisbury steak, glazed baby carrots and macaroni-and-cheese took its 8-minute ride on the microwave carousel, Jonas wandered back into the living room. Slipping off his suit coat, he hung it over the back of one of the dining room chairs—a life-long habit he seemed incapable of breaking even now—and stopped.

Night had filled the rest of the apartment with shadows while his back was turned. There were more than enough lamps scattered about, efficiently placed for either mood or reading; all he needed to do was take a few steps, turn them on. He'd done that a lot over the past few weeks, chasing away the dark, but suddenly it seemed like too great an effort.

He didn't mind the darkness, unlike Ena, her of the bright smiles and shining eyes. At the first hint of dusk—whether in her office or at home—she'd scurry around like a chipmunk after seeds, turning on one light after another as if she owned shares in a hydroelectric company.

"I have too many things to do that need light."

Yet despite her best effort, the dark always won.

Jonas turned from the shadows and walked back to the liquor cabinet. Another drink couldn't hurt, he decided, but instead of the scotch bottle, he watched with some amazement as his hand closed around the cell phone and punched in a number.

Her number.

"Hi . . . and in case you're wondering, yes . . . this is a recording. Therefore I'm either away doing something exceptionally brilliant or being perverse and screening the call. Either way, take a chance and leave a message . . . you might get lucky."

—beep—

Just hearing Ena's voice made him smile.

"Hi . . . just me. Wanted to—God, nothing much, I guess. Just wanted to tell you . . . that I had a crappy day at work. So what else is new, right? But—" He took a deep breath. "—I guess it's getting better. Little by little and . . . I think it's going to be okay. Yeah. I do. Oh, and I wanted to tell you that I'm going to finish cleaning up. Really. Promise. Miss you."

Jonas waited a moment, in case something *"exceptionally brilliant"* came to mind, then closed the phone and set it back into the charger. There was still the hint of a smile when the microwave dinged the announcement his dinner was ready.

Weekends were for sleeping in— lounging in bed, buried beneath the covers in a semi-conscious state until hunger or the call of nature required becoming vertical and somewhat functional—and Jonas loved that.

Had.

Past tense.

Recently, and despite numerous attempts at over-the-counter medications and liberal doses of self-prescribed, bottled-and-bond "sleep aids," his bed had become a place to get out of as quickly as possible. More often than not he'd find himself at the window, coffee cup in hand, watching the western horizon fill with ghosts.

Ena was the morning lark.

The window fogged under his sigh and one more ghost was added to the landscape.

Dammit, it was too early and his head ached and his tongue felt three times too large for the confines of his mouth and it was Saturday, for Christ's sake, and . . . and . . .

And he had nothing to look forward to but cleaning up.

Because he promised her—said it out loud and couldn't take it back.

Another sigh and the ghosts were obliterated.

"Some people just don't know when to keep their mouths shut."

It took a full pot of coffee—black to start, then cut with milk when his stomach started to complain—and almost half a bottle of aspirin, but by noon Jonas had filled three black plastic bags and two large boxes. The bags would go to charity, the boxes into storage.

There were some things he didn't want to get rid of, couldn't get rid of. Not now, not yet. Maybe later, but she'd forgive him.

Jonas was filling a third box, sitting crossed-legged in front of the linen closet, when he found the small carton of photos he'd hidden behind a stack of towels. It was like finding buried treasure. No, it was better than that . . . it was finding a part of his life he'd forgotten he'd lost.

They were snapshots, some in color, some in black-and-white, but all humble protests against digital technology. And all of them were of Ena. The rejects, the ones—unlike those sent to friends and family, or stuffed into albums—she hated because she thought they made her look fat or ugly or dull. These were the photos she'd threatened him with great and unmentionable physical harm if he 1) didn't tear them into a million bits, and 2) burn those bits to ash.

But he only promised to get rid of them . . . and he did . . . by hiding them behind the towels, because destroying them wasn't an option. They were part of her, part of them . . .

Even if some of them did make her look fat.

Hunched over the carton, the "*cleaning up*" put on hold for a moment, Jonas riffled through the photos as carefully as a small boy examining the wings of a butterfly; smiling more often than not.

Then finally laughing.

The picture showed Ena in hip-waders, covered in mud and glaring. Her fiery-bright hair, tarnished and tangled, was half hidden beneath an equally mud-speckled hat; and she'd stuck out her tongue. At the camera. At him. For having brought her to the slippery banks of a trout river in the first place.

It was his fault. He'd made the fishing trip sound exciting and romantic, because it was. To him.

Jonas pulled the cell phone—his life-line—off his belt and punched in the number without taking his eyes off the photo.

". . . *message . . . you might get lucky.*"

—*beep*—

"You'll never guess what I found. Remember when you fell in the mud? I kept saying you'd hooked onto a log . . . you should have listened to me. No, that's not what I wanted to say. I wanted to tell you I'm sorry I talked you into going. I know you must have hated every minute of it—" He ran his thumb across the front of the picture. "—but you never said a word. I was selfish, I'm so sorry . . . and I'm sorry about not throwing these pictures away, but I can't, you know that. I—"

—*beep*—

Jonas hardly closed the cell when *Beethoven's Fifth* filled the hallway. The name on the caller ID screen made him take another breath before answering.

"Hey—how goes the cleaning?"

"Loving every minute of it."

"Really?"

"Really. And you can tell that wife of yours she owes me an apology. I am *not* going through the place with a leaf-blower." Jonas glanced down the hall toward the bedroom. "At least, not yet."

Andrew, his life-long friend and temporary guardian angel, chuckled through the phone.

"I'll bring over the weed-whacker. But you made a start."

Jonas put Ena's picture back in the box. "I made a start."

"Great."

A pause followed. Jonas couldn't think of anything to say that wouldn't sound forced, so he just waited. Andrew finally cleared his throat.

"That's really great, knew you could do it. Come to dinner tonight as a well deserved reward. That's the real reason I called, by the way . . . even if you hadn't started."

Sure it is. Jonas put the carton back behind the towels. "Thanks, but I've had dinner at your place five times in the last three weeks."

"Six," Andrew corrected, "but who's counting?"

"Well, then. I appreciate it, but . . . "

"No buts allowed. Nina's currently making her world famous lasagna and you know what that means."

Jonas scooted backwards across the narrow hallway until his spine met the opposite wall, then slowly stretched the kinks out of his legs. Pins-and-needles tickled the underside of his left foot.

"Leftovers?"

"A *lot* of leftovers. You remember the last time she made it? I was bringing lasagna sandwiches to work for a week."

Jonas remembered Ena laughing about it when he told her.

"So get her a smaller pan."

"What? And miss out on all those wonderful leftovers? Are you mad, man?" His friend honestly sounded terrified at the thought. "Then it's settled. I'll tell Nina you're coming . . . and that you're going to eat like a horse, right?"

"Okay."

"Great! Come around six."

"Can I bring anything?"

"Besides a ravenous appetite? You can bring wine. Red."

"Will do. Andrew . . . Tell Nina thanks."

"You can tell her yourself when you get here. Six, but come early and I'll give you a tour of the backyard . . . finally finished the barbecue pit. Hint, hint."

"Hint, taken. Cleaning up here, boss."

Jonas called Ena a moment later to tell her about the invitation, Andrew's reluctance to do without leftovers, and how lucky he was to have friends who cared enough to badger him.

He called three more times.

Once while he was picking out the wine—it reminded him of the time she'd surprised him at work with a wine-and-cheese-and bread picnic basket—then when he got back from dinner, and once again before he went to bed.

They were just calls, nothing important, no real reason behind them other than to hear her voice.

But that was enough.

—beep—

"Would you believe it? I'm almost finished. Ta-dah! Did the living room and bathroom—*ugh*—and hall closets, both of them . . . you'd be proud of me. Only have the bedroom left and—"

Jonas shifted the cell to one side and used the coffee mug to stifle the yawn. The combination of physical labor plus the wonderfully heavy and wine-laden lasagna dinner had conspired against him. He woke to a blue sky and the sound of church bells. The birds were well into their mid-morning repertoire when he finally made it to the shower.

"Sorry," he apologized, "just got up and haven't had enough coffee to keep the engine lit. Where was I . . . oh, yeah. So, as I was saying, I only have the bedroom to do but I don't think it'll be that bad now. You wouldn't recognize me, I've become a regular cleaning fool!"

He laughed and ignored the —*beep*— when it sounded.

"And I'm thinking about repainting, how's *that* for being motivated, huh? Nothing flamboyant . . . probably gray, light gray."

Pausing, he listened to the white-noise static and watched the morning sun brighten the apartment. Light gray walls would look nice.

"I didn't throw everything away— you never were much of a pack rat— but I didn't keep much. Just a couple of things . . . mementos, you know. Small things that won't get in the way. I promise. Ena . . . I wish things had been different. It's not fair, but . . . since when is life fair, right?"

Snapping the phone shut, Jonas tossed it onto the dining room table and finished the coffee before heading for the bedroom. He'd need his hands free to fill the boxes and bags that were already laid out in front of the doublewide closet; and it wasn't as if he hadn't gotten through most of the really hard stuff already.

Still . . .

Jonas leaned against the doorframe, looking at the room they'd shared for far too short a time. The small personal things were already gone—her hair brush, jewelry box, perfume bottles, the porcelain roses she collected then complained about being nothing but dust

catchers—all carefully packed and put away because it'd been too hard to look at them.

But there were still the memories, still the faintest scent of her in the room. Jonas closed his eyes and breathed her in and for a moment, only a moment, pretended she was there— stretched out in the rumple of sheets and the Sunday paper, frowning at that week's crossword puzzle she'd balanced on one upraised knee.

He opened his eyes to the rumpled sheets and scattered papers and empty bed, and tucked the memory away . . . just another *small thing, a memento* he'd keep forever.

The answering machine blinked "*8 New Messages*" at him from the nightstand on her side of the bed.

Jonas exhaled slowly as he walked over to it. His finger paused over the *Delete* button before he reached over and hit *Play*. Ena's voice filled the room.

"Hi . . . and in case you're wondering, yes . . . this is a recording. Therefore I'm either away doing something exceptionally brilliant or being perverse and screening the call. Either way, take a chance and leave a message . . . you might get lucky."

—*beep*—

"I love you, Ena, I always will. Just wanted to tell you one more time."

Jonas deleted the messages he'd left and her recorded greeting. It was harder than standing at her grave and packing away everything she loved, but he'd made her a promise.

"Good-bye, baby." ⌘

"Being a bit of an anorak myself when it comes to these things," says Peter Atkins, "I'd like to apologise to those readers who may notice or care that, in the 1970s of this story, Patti Smith's Horses *apparently predated Roxy Music's first record. It didn't of course, but I couldn't resist the thematic relevance of the particular Smith song that Michael references." Atkins is the author of two novels, one story collection, and a bunch of horror movies. "Between the Cold Moon and the Earth" was originally written for the October 2006 tour of* The Rolling Darkness Revue, *a multi-media collective he founded with his friends and fellow-authors Glen Hirshberg and Dennis Etchison.*

Between The Cold Moon And The Earth

Peter Atkins

They only brushed his cheek for a second or two, but her lips were fucking *freezing*.

"Christ, Carol," he said. "Do you want my coat?"

She laughed. "What for?" she asked.

"Because it's one in the morning," he said. "And you're cold."

"It's summer," she pointed out, which was undeniably true but wasn't really the issue. "Are you going to walk me home then?"

Michael had left the others about forty minutes earlier. Kirk had apparently copped off with the girl from Woolworth's that they'd met inside the pub so Michael and Terry had tactfully peeled away before the bus stop and started walking the long way home around Sefton Park. He could've split a taxi fare with Terry but, given that they were still in the middle of their ongoing argument about the relative merits of T.Rex and Pink Floyd and that it was still a good six months before they'd find Roxy Music to agree on, they'd parted by unspoken consent and Michael had opted to cut across the park alone.

Carol had been standing on the path beside the huge park's large boating lake. He'd practically shit himself when he first saw the shadowed figure there, assuming the worst—a midnight skinhead parked on watch ready to whistle his mates out of hiding to give this handy glam-rock faggot a good kicking—but Carol had been doing nothing more threatening than staring out at the center of the lake and the motionless full moon reflected there.

"Alright, Michael," she'd said, before he'd quite recognized her in the moonlight, and had kissed his cheek lightly in further greeting before he'd spoken her name. Now, he fell into step beside her and they began to walk the long slow curve around the lake.

187

"God, Carol. Where've you been?" he asked. "Nobody's seen you for months."

It was true. Her mum had re-married just before last Christmas and they'd moved. Not far away, still in the same city, but far enough for sixteen-year-olds to lose touch.

"I went to America," Carol said.

Michael turned his head to see if she was kidding. "You went to *America*?" he said. "What d'you mean, you went to America? When? Who with?"

Her eyes narrowed for a moment as if she were re-checking her facts or her memory. "I think it was America," she said.

"You *think* it was America?"

"It might have been an imaginary America," she said, her voice a little impatient. "Do you want to hear the fucking story or not?"

Oh. Michael didn't smile nor attempt to kiss her, but he felt like doing both. Telling stories—real, imagined, or some happy collision of the two—had been one of the bonds between them, one of the things he'd loved about her. Not the only thing of course. It's not like he hadn't shared Kirk and Terry's enthusiastic affection for her astonishingly perfect breasts and for the teasingly challenging way she had about her that managed to suggest two things simultaneously: that, were circumstances to somehow become magically right, she might, you know, actually *do it* with you; and that you were probably and permanently incapable of ever conjuring such circumstances. But her stories, and her delight

in telling them, were what he'd loved most and what, he now realized, he'd most missed. So yes, he said, he wanted to hear the story.

There was some quick confusion about whether she'd got there by plane or by ship—Carol had never been a big fan of preamble—but apparently what mattered was that, after a few days, she found herself in a roadside diner with a bunch of people she hardly knew.

They were on a road trip and had stopped for lunch in this back-of-beyond and unpretentious diner—a place which, while perfectly clean and respectable, looked like it hadn't been painted or refurbished since about 1952. They were in a booth, eating pie and drinking coffee. Her companions were about her age—but could, you know, *drive* and everything. Turned out boys in America could be just as fucking rude as in Liverpool. One of them—Tommy, she thought his name was—was giving shit to the waitress. Hoisting his empty coffee mug, he was leaning out of the booth and looking pointedly down the length of the room.

"Yo! Still need a refill here!" he shouted to the counter.

Carol stood up and, announcing she was going to the ladies' room, slid her way out of the booth. Halfway down the room, she crossed paths with the waitress, who was hurrying toward their booth with a coffee pot. The woman's name tag said *Cindi*, a spelling Carol had never seen before and hoped could possibly be short for Cinderella because that'd be, you know, great. Carol spoke softly to her, nodding back towards Tommy, who was impatiently shaking his empty coffee mug in the air.

"Don't mind him, love," Carol said. "He's a bit of a prick, but I'll make sure he leaves a nice tip."

Cindi, who was harried-looking and appeared to be at least thirty, gave her a quick smile of gratitude. "Little girls' room's out back, sweetheart," she said.

Carol exited the main building of the diner and saw that a separate structure, little more than a shack really, housed the bathrooms. She started across the graveled parking lot, surrounded by scrub-grass that was discolored and overgrown, looking down the all-but-deserted country road—the type of road, she'd been informed by her new friends, which was known as a two-lane blacktop. The diner and its shithouse annex were the only buildings for as far as her eye could see, apart from a hulking grain silo a hundred yards or so down the road. As Carol looked in that desolate direction, a cloud drifted over the sun, dimming the summer daylight and shifting the atmosphere into a kind of pre-storm dreariness. Carol shivered and wondered, not without a certain pleasure in the mystery, just where the hell she was.

Done peeing and alone in the bathroom, Carol washed her hands and splashed her face at the pretty crappy single sink that was all the place had to offer. The sound of the ancient cistern laboriously and noisily re-filling after her flush played in the background. Carol turned off the tap and looked for a moment at her reflection in the pitted and stained mirror above the sink. As the cistern finally creaked and whistled to a halt, the mirror suddenly cracked noisily across its width as if it was just too tired to keep trying.

"Fuckin' 'ell!" said Carol, because it had made her jump and because she didn't like the newly mis-matched halves of her reflected face. She turned around, ready to walk out of the bathroom, and discovered she was no longer alone.

A little girl—what, six, seven years old?—was standing, silent and perfectly still, outside one of the stall doors, looking up at her. Oddly, the little girl was holding the palm of one hand over her right eye.

"Oh shit," said Carol, remembering that she'd just said *fucking hell* in front of a kid. "I didn't know you were . . ." She paused, smiled, started over. "Hello, pet. D'you live around here?"

The little girl just kept looking at her.

"What's your name?" Carol asked her, still smiling but still getting no response. Registering the hand-over-the-eye thing, she tried a new tack. "Oh," she said. "Are we playing a game and nobody told me the rules? Alright then, here we go."

Raising her hand, Carol covered her own right eye with her palm. The little girl remained still and silent. Carol lowered her hand from her face. "Peek-a-boo," she said.

Finally, the little girl smiled shyly and lowered her own hand. She had no right eye at all, just a smooth indented bank of flesh.

Carol was really good. She hardly jumped at all and her gasp was as short-lived as could reasonably be expected.

The little girl's voice was very matter-of-fact. "Momma lost my eye-patch," she said.

"Oh. That's a shame," said Carol, trying to keep her own voice as equally everyday.

"She's gonna get me another one. When she goes to town."

"Oh, well, that's good. Will she get a nice color? Do you have a favorite color?"

The little girl shrugged. "What are you, retarded?" she said. "It's an eye-patch. Who cares what color it is?"

Carol didn't know whether to laugh or slap her.

"You can go now, if you like," said the little girl. "I have to make water."

"Oh. Alright. Sure. Well, look after yourself," Carol said and, raising her hand in a slightly awkward wave of farewell, headed for the exit door. The little girl called after her.

"You take care in those woods now, Carol", she said.

"I hadn't told her my name," said Carol.

"Well, that was weird," Michael said.

Carol smiled, pleased. "*That* wasn't weird," she said. "It *got* weird. Later. After I got lost in the woods."

"You got lost in the woods?"

Carol nodded.

"Why'd they let you go wandering off on your own?"

"Who?"

"Your new American friends. The people you were in the café with."

"Ha. Café. *Diner*, stupid. We were in America."

"Whatever. How could they let you get lost?"

"Oh, yeah." She thought for a second, looking out to their side at the boating lake and its ghost moon. "Well, p'raps they weren't there to begin with. Doesn't matter. Listen."

Turned out Carol *did* get lost in the woods. Quite deep in the woods, actually. Heart of the forest, Hansel and Gretel shit, where the sunlight, through the thickening trees, was dappled and spotty and where the reassuring blue sky of what was left of the afternoon could be glimpsed only occasionally through the increasingly oppressive canopy of high leafy branches.

Carol was tramping her way among the trees and the undergrowth on the mossy and leaf-strewn ground when she heard the sound for the first time. Faint and plaintive and too distant to be truly identifiable, it was nevertheless suggestive of something, something that Carol couldn't quite put her finger on yet. Only when it came again, a few moments later, did she place it. It was the sound of a lonely ship's horn in a midnight ocean, melancholy and eerie. Not quite as eerie, though, as the fact that once the horn had sounded this second time, all the other sounds stopped, all the other sounds that Carol hadn't even been consciously aware of until they disappeared: birdsong; the footsteps of unseen animals moving through the woods; the sigh of the breeze as it whistled through the branches.

The only sounds now were those she made herself: the rustle and sway of the living branches she was pushing her way through and the crackle and snap of the dead ones she was breaking beneath her. Carol began to wonder if moving on in the same direction she'd been going was that great of an idea. She turned around and started heading back and, within a few yards, stepping out from between two particularly close trees, she found herself in a small grove-like clearing that she didn't remember passing through earlier.

There was a downed and decaying tree-trunk lying in the leafy undergrowth that momentarily and ridiculously put Carol in mind of a park bench. But she really wasn't in the mood to sit and relax and it wasn't like there was, you know, a boating lake to look at the moon in or anything. So she kept moving, across the clearing, past the downed trunk, and stopped only when the voice spoke from behind her.

"What's your rush, sweetheart?"

Carol turned back. Sitting perched on the bench-like trunk was a sailor. He was dressed in a square-neck deck-shirt and bell-bottomed pants and Carol might have taken a moment to wonder if sailors still dressed like that if she hadn't been too busy being surprised just to see him at all. He was sitting in profile to her, one leg on the ground, the other arched up on the trunk and he didn't turn to face her fully, perhaps because he was concentrating on rolling a cigarette.

"Ready-mades are easier," the sailor said. "But I like the ritual—opening the paper, laying in the tobacco, rolling it up. Know what I mean?"

"I don't smoke," said Carol, which wasn't strictly true, but who the fuck was he to deserve the truth.

"You chew?" he asked.

"Chew what?"

"Tobacco"

"Eugh. No."

The sailor chanted something rhythmic in response, like he was singing her a song but knew his limitations when it came to carrying a tune:

"Down in Nagasaki,
Where the fellas chew tobaccy
And the women wicky-wacky-woo."

Carol stared at him. Confused. Not necessarily nervous. Not yet. She gestured out at the woods. "Where'd you come from?" she said.

"Dahlonega, Georgia. Little town northeast of Atlanta. Foot of the Appalachians."

That wasn't what she'd meant and she started to tell him so, but he interrupted.

"Ever been to Nagasaki, honeybun?"

"No."

"How about Shanghai?"

The Sailor was still sitting in profile to her. Talking to her, but staring straight ahead into the woods and beyond. He didn't wait for a reply. "Docked there once," he said. "Didn't get shore-leave. Fellas who did told me I missed something, boy. Said there were whores there could practically tie themselves in knots. Real limber. Mmm. A man likes that. Likes 'em limber."

Carol was very careful not to say anything at all. Not to move. Not to breathe.

"Clean, too," said the sailor. "That's important to me. Well, who knows? Maybe I'll get back there one of these days. 'Course, once they get a good look at me, I might have to pay extra." He turned finally to face her. "Whaddaya think?"

Half of his face was bone-pale and bloated, as if it had drowned years ago and been underwater ever since. His hair hung dank like seaweed and something pearl-like glinted in the moist dripping blackness of what used to be an eye-socket.

"Jesus Christ!" Carol said, frozen in shock, watching helplessly as the sailor put his cigarette in his half-ruined mouth, lit it, and inhaled.

"Calling on the Lord for salvation," he said. "Good for you. Might help." Smoke oozed out from the pulpy white flesh that barely clung to the bone beneath his dead face. "Might not."

He rose to his feet and grinned at her. "Useta chase pigs through the Georgia pines, sweet thing," he said, flinging his cigarette aside. "Let's see if you're faster than them little squealers."

And then he came for her.

"I was a lot faster, though," said Carol. "But it still took me ten minutes to lose him."

"Fuck, Carol," said Michael. "That wasn't funny."

"I didn't say it was funny. I said it was weird. Remember?"

Michael turned to look at her and she tilted her face to look up at his, dark eyes glinting, adorably proud of herself. They'd walked nearly a full circuit of the lake now, neither of them even thinking to branch off in the direction of the park's northern gate and the way home.

"Well, it was weird alright," Michael said. "Creepy ghost sailor. Pretty good."

"Yeah," she said. "Turns out there was a ship went down there in the Second World War. All hands lost."

"Went down in the woods. That was a good trick."

"It wasn't the *woods*. Didn't I tell you that? It was the beach. That's where it all happened."

"Was it Redondo?"

"The fuck's *Redondo*?" she said, genuinely puzzled.

"It's a beach. In America. I've heard of it. It's on that Patti Smith album."

"Oh, yeah. No. This wasn't in America. It was in Cornwall." She thought about it for a moment. "Yeah. Had to be Cornwall because of the rock pool."

"You didn't say anything about a rock pool."

"I haven't *told* you yet," she said, exasperated. "God, you're rubbish."

Michael laughed, even though something else had just hit him. He was walking on a moonlit night alone with a beautiful girl and it apparently wasn't occurring to him to try anything. He hadn't even put his arm around her, for Christ's sake. Terry and Kirk would give him such shit for this when he told them. He wondered for the first time if that was something Carol knew, if that was what had always been behind her stories, why she found them, why she told them, like some instinctive Scheherazade keeping would-be lovers at bay with narrative strategies. He felt something forming in him, a kind of sadness that he couldn't name and didn't understand.

"Is everything alright, Carol?" he asked, though he couldn't say why.

"Well, it is *now*," she said, deaf to the half-born subtext in his question. "I got away. I escaped. But that spoils the story, dickhead. You've got to hear what *happened* first."

The park was silver-gray in the light from the moon. He wondered what time it was. "The rock pool," he said.

"Exactly," she said, pleased that he was paying attention.

She hadn't seen it at first. Had kept moving along the deserted beach until the sandy shore gave way to rocky cave-strewn outcrops from the cliffs above the coastline. It was only when she clambered over an algae- and sea-weed-coated rock wall that she found it. Orphaned from the sea and held within a natural basin formation, the pool was placid and still and ringed by several large boulders about its rim. It was about twenty feet across and looked to be fairly deep.

On one of the boulders, laid out as if waiting for their owner, were some items of clothing. A dress, a pair of stockings, some underwear. Carol looked from them out to the cool inviting water of the pool. A head broke surface as she looked, and a woman started swimming toward the rock where her clothes were. Catching sight of Carol, she stopped and trod water, looking at her suspiciously. "What are you doing?" she said. "Are you spying?" She was older than Carol, about her mum's age maybe, a good-looking thirty-five.

"No, I'm not," Carol said. "Why would I be spying?"

"You might be one of them," the woman said.

"One of who?"

The woman narrowed her eyes and looked at Carol appraisingly. "You know who," she said.

"No, I don't," Carol said. "And I'm not one of anybody. I was with some friends. We went to France. Just got back. The boat's down there on the beach."

"They've all got stories," the woman said. "That's how they get you."

"Who?! Stop talking shit, willya? I . . . " Carol bit her tongue.

For the first time, the woman smiled. "Are you moderating your language for me?" she said. "That's adorable."

Carol felt strangely flustered. Was this woman *flirting* with her?

"I understand," the woman said, still smiling, still staring straight into Carol's eyes. "I'm an older lady and you want to be polite. But, you know, I'm not really *that* much older." She stepped out of the pool and stood there right in front of Carol, glistening wet and naked. "See what I mean?" she said.

Carol felt funny. She swallowed. The woman kept her eyes fixed on Carol as she stepped very close to her. "I'm going to tell you a secret," she said, and leaned forward to whisper the secret in Carol's ear. "I'm real limber for my age."

Carol jumped back as the woman's voice began a familiar rhythmic chant.

"Down in Nagasaki,
Where the fellas chew tobaccy,
And the women wicky-wacky-woo."

Carol tried to run but the woman had already grabbed her by the throat. "What's your rush, sweetheart?" she said, and her voice was different now, guttural and amused. "Party's just getting started."

Carol was struggling in the choking grip. She tried to swing a fist at the woman's head but her punch was effortlessly blocked by the woman's other arm.

"Your eyes are so pretty," the woman said. "I'm going to have them for earrings."

Her mouth opened inhumanly wide. Her tongue flicked out with reptile speed. It was long and black and forked.

"**B**ut like I said," said Carol, "I escaped."

"How?" said Michael, expecting another previously unmentioned element to be brought into play, like a knife or a gun or a really sharp stick or a last-minute rescue from her Francophile friends from the recently-invented boat. But Carol had a different ending in mind.

"I walked into the moon," she said.

Michael looked up to the night sky.

"No," said Carol. "Not that moon. This one."

She was pointing out towards the center of the utterly calm lake and the perfect moon reflected there. Looking at it with her, neither of them walking now, Michael felt the cold of the night as if for the first time. He waited in silence, afraid to speak, afraid to give voice to his questions, afraid that they would be answered.

She told another story then, the last, he knew, that his sweet lost friend would ever tell him, the tale of how the other moon had many ways into and out of this world: through placid lakes on summer evenings; through city streets on rain-slicked nights; from out of the ocean depths for the eyes of lonely night-watch sailors.

And when she was done, when Michael could no longer pretend not to know in whose company he truly was, she turned to him and smiled a heartbreaking smile of farewell.

She looked beautiful in monochrome, in the subtle tones of the moon that had claimed her for its own. Not drained of color, but richly re-imagined, painted in shades of silver, gray, and black, and delicate lunar blue. She looked almost liquid, as if, were Michael to reach out a hand and even try to touch her, she might ripple into strange expansions of herself.

"Thanks, Michael," she said. "I can make it home from here."

Michael didn't say anything. Didn't know what he could possibly find to say that the tears in his young eyes weren't already saying. The beautiful dead girl pointed a silver finger beyond him, in the direction of his life. "Go on," she said kindly. "Don't look back."

And he didn't look back, not even when he heard the impossible footsteps on the water, not even when he heard the shadow moon sigh in welcome, and the quiet lapping of the lake water as if something had slipped effortlessly beneath it.

He'd later hear the alternative versions, of course—the stories of how, one moonlit night, Carol had walked out of the third-floor window of her step-father's house and the vile rumors as to why—but he would prefer, for all his days, to believe the story that the lost girl herself had chosen to tell him.

He continued home through the park, not even breaking step as his fingers sought and found the numb spot on his cheek, the frozen place where her cold lips had blessed him, waiting for her frostbite kiss to bloom in tomorrow's mirror.

Ӡ

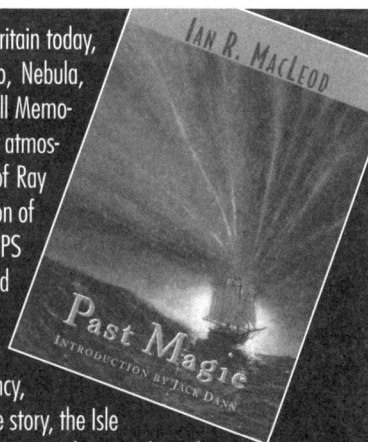

"Summer's Lease" grew out of an ongoing project of Chaz Brenchley's which seems to do all its evolution in his favourite pub—as good a place as any (and better than most) for any kind of evolution to take place. "We were in there," Chaz explains, "when m'friend Sean O'Brien said, 'What we should do, Chaz, we should write ghost stories and read them to people at Christmas.' So we did. We were in there when m'friend John said, 'We should publish those stories, with live CD recordings of the readings.' So we did. We were in there when Sean said, 'We should do another set of readings at midsummer.' So we did. And this is my story written for the occasion." [For more information about the Phantoms project, see Chaz's website, www.chazbrenchley.co.uk]

Chaz's most recent book is River of the World, *the sequel to* Bridge of Dreams; *these form a fantasy sequence set in an alternate Ottoman Istanbul. He's currently working on two separate projects set in Taiwan, as well as numerous other books and stories.*

Summer's Lease
Chaz Brenchley

When I talk about it, looking back, I call it my Brideshead summer, but that's an act of cowardice. I have this whole riff that I can do, poor boy playing with the aristocracy, and it's as superficial as the bloom of youth. In truth, it was Juliet's summer from the start, given to her, a gift I could never afford; in truth it's hers still, and always will be, a gift I can never reclaim.

Sometimes, when I talk about it now, I never mention her at all; but her grip is still on my heart, light as a breeze, quiet as a brook, implacable as sunshine. Somewhere deep inside me, it's always summer now.

End of term, summer vac, summer in the city: what's that for? All my friends would be going away. I'd go away myself, I needed to.

"Good," Toby said at length, his own length where he lay sprawled in defiance of collegiate orders, doubly defiant, half-naked on the hallowed college lawn. "You can come to us."

"Can't. I need a job. I'll go down to Cornwall and pick potatoes . . . "

". . . And break your back, be bored out of your skull, let your friends go hang? You will not. You'll come to Brockwood. You don't have to idle like the rest of us; it's farming country and we know everyone, you can do all the work you want. Say yes, and then I'll tell you why you should. Come on, buy a pig in a poke."

He always did that, slipping in something extra to sweeten the deal. It was the generosity of inheritance, like a slap in the face, a reminder that he never truly had to bargain. It stung every time, and he knew it, which was why he did it, every time; and I still bought it, every time. "All right," I said, "I'll come. But I will need a job."

"Good man." He rolled onto his back and smiled up at me, golden youth bare-chested and alluring and knowing it, knowing it all. "And your door-prize is, Juliet will be around."

That stopped me, in the sense that a bullet in the chest will stop a man. I sank down onto the grass beside him, slow and silent; and of course the college porter chose that as his cue to come across, to remind me bluntly that the lawns were sacrosanct, and to request Mr Rochester kindly to respect the Dean's ruling that shirts at least must be worn within the quads of College.

J uliet.

She came with warnings added, but only the first time; Toby never said anything twice, he wouldn't see the point.

The first time, mid-term, he said, "My cousin's coming up for the weekend. I want you to come out and play, she'll like you."

"Uh. Is there any point in saying I've got an essay?"

"None at all. I want you."

"Well, I know that, but it's a hopeless passion, Tobes, I've told you . . . "

His hand on my shoulder slipped casually, stiflingly into a chokehold. "I want you for *her*," he said, "lover," he said, which was the one thing I had never been to him, the one way in which I'd managed to say no. Just the once, all it took; he didn't need telling twice.

"Friday, six o'clock, at the Memorial," he said. "Don't be late. We'll go somewhere. You dress up nicely, because she won't. Oh, and treat her kindly, Rook."

"Of course," I said. "Why wouldn't I?"

He smiled. "Of course. But—well, she's had a hard time, and she could use a little tenderness. I'm too ruthless for her."

It was still him she was coming to see. That was Toby; he might batter you bloody, but you still came back for more.

"What's happened?"

"Oh, family stuff. It's hers to tell, if she wants to. Mostly, I just want to see her smile."

"I don't do jokes, Tobe."

"No. It's all right, you won't need to." And that time his own smile was pure evil, and it made my heart falter. He had something in mind, and he wasn't saying what; and as he said and a s I knew already, he was utterly and unthinkingly ruthless with his friends.

F riday, six o'clock. I'm never late.

Toby was, as a matter of course. I knew that, and I was still on time; and there was someone else already there, sitting on the steps of the Memorial. *You dress up nicely,* he'd said—which for me meant my one suit, heavy linen in charcoal grey, over a new black T-shirt that hadn't had the chance to fade—

because she won't, he'd said. I saw bare feet in cheap sandals, under ragged jeans, under something long and loose and chintzy that could only have come from a charity shop, under one of those faces that do challenge and vulnerability both at once.

Everything about her said 'poor little rich girl', with emphasis. I thought it was designed that way. Even the way she moved, languidly graceful as she got to her feet, generations of ballet class and finishing school behind her; even the biology of her, bones and skin and a deep-down physical frailty.

"You're Rook," she said. "Toby described the suit to me. In detail." And then she laughed, and slipped her arm through mine, and said, "Let's get a drink. Or two."

"Um, aren't we waiting . . . ?"

"For him? No. He'll be late."

"Well, yes, but—"

"Seriously late, I mean. He's been held up. He said to start without him, he'll catch us when he can. Oh, and your money's no good tonight, by the way."

"Oh, no, wait . . . "

"Toby's orders," she said.

"Well, but Toby's not here yet."

"No, but his credit card is. That's all we need."

So there were drinks and more drinks, gin all the way from one cocktail bar to the next. She had that glint in her eye that made a challenge of it. I wasn't worried. I'd drunk with heroes, oar-pulling prop-forward giants

among men; I could keep up with a slip of a girl.

Then there was the restaurant, and gin martinis while we looked at the menu, and there I might have fallen behind if she hadn't got serious over the wine-list. She ordered a bottle of something I couldn't pronounce, which apparently had to be drunk in due solemnity. What with that slow lap, and the food, and getting to eat most of hers as well as my own, I caught a breath of second wind.

It was round about then that I finally realised, Toby wasn't going to catch us up tonight. We'd blazed a trail bright enough for three wise men to follow, and there'd been no sign of him, no word.

No surprise, then, when I took Juliet home—later, much later—and there was still no Toby.

Until next morning, when he washed in late, while I was fumbling in the kitchen with the intricacies of kettle and tap and gas.

"Matches?" I said vaguely.

"Here. Where's Jules?"

"In bed, being sick."

His gaze moved ostentatiously to the uninhabited sleeping-bag laid out ready on the sofa, and from there to my bathrobe, and his eyebrows twitched.

"Rook, my son, I am proud of you. Pleased and proud. And a little bit jealous, of course."

"What? Toby, she's your cousin. And a girl."

"Even so. Neither of those is actually

illegal. I'd better go and have a word with her."

"Uh, let me check first . . . "

"It's all right, Rook boy. I've ferried bowls of Juliet's upchucking to the toilet before now. I'm the one who taught her how to drink. Though to be honest, I thought I'd made a better job of it."

"Uh, Toby, you do realise, if I'd known she was that drunk . . . "

"You wouldn't have laid a grubby hand on her? I know, Rook. I do know."

He ran lightly upstairs, and I heard my own door close firmly against me. A murmur of voices carried down to the kitchen, maddeningly indistinct; I drank coffee, black, and waited.

After too long, there were steps on the stairs, Toby coming down; he said, "You fit for a walk?"

"Well, but what about—?" My eyes moved upwards.

"There are times, my lad, when a girl tires of throwing up under a boy's anxious gaze, and would quite like the chance to throw up on her own; and perhaps drag her poor abused body into the shower, to wash away certain sour and musky odours, and clean her teeth, and generally present a sweeter fresher body to that same boy, when he returns from a short walk with his friend, her cousin and watchdog, as it were . . . "

We went down to the canal, a favourite Saturday-morning haunt of ours for post-match analysis; and I said, "You've never set me up with a girl before. Not like that. Why her?" Unless the proper question was, *why me?*

"I thought you'd be good for her. Good for each other, the pair of you, but—look, did she tell you about her brother?"

"Yes, she did." Even through the haze, I remembered that much. "He died, from anorexia . . . ?"

"Well, with complications. Technically pneumonia, in the end; one of those hospital infections. That was two years ago. And I bet she didn't tell you this, that she had a half-hearted go at her own eating disorders after, but hey, she's half a Rochester; the girl's got an appetite. She's skinny as a very skinny thing—well, you'll know that—but she won't die of it. What she needs, though, she needs something solid, a rock to cling to. That's not you, don't get me wrong, I'm not signing your life away here. I just thought you'd be a good step up. A happy evening with a sensible guy, and her choice for whatever follows. You get me?"

"Yes, Toby, I get you."

"You don't resent me?"

"No," I said, running all of last night in review and discovering that what he'd said hadn't discredited a moment of it, "I don't resent you."

"Good. Nor I you, although you have laid my childhood sweetheart. Shall we go back, then, see if she does? Or see how she's doing, anyway. That's not a hangover she's nursing. More likely she ate a dodgy oyster."

"We didn't eat oysters."

"Whatever. Trust me, sweets, I've drunk with you and I've drunk with her; you couldn't do that to that girl and stay conscious yourself. She's got a bug."

Back at the house, we found Juliet pale but interested, up and about in my bathrobe; and we spent the rest of that slow Saturday as a cozy threesome, us two boys making great palaver of nursing her. That night I offered to sleep on the sofa, but she was having none of it; so we nestled and talked and slept in awkward jags all out of time with each other, and she was ill again the following morning before she left for home, which somehow made me feel better, because that meant it definitely wasn't the booze.

That was six weeks ago, and I hadn't heard from her since, bar one scrawled postcard from Venice. I already knew she was abroad, because I'd phoned a couple of times—just to be sure she was all right, not sick, not fainting in coils—and I only got her parents. The first time, they said she'd gone to Brussels for a few days with friends of the family; so I gave it a week and tried again. By then she was in Bayreuth. They thought she would benefit from an extended stay overseas, so she was travelling on with an old schoolfriend.

I listened to that cut-glass accent describing a cut-glass life, and briefly I thought we'd timeslipped back to the 'thirties. When did people last go to the Continent for a rest-cure? She'd only had a virus. It really was a different world I was fringeing here, and Toby was drawing me right into the heart of it.

We went by train, because it amused him not to keep a car at college. "No taxis," he said, "and it's a five-mile walk from the station," but he was lying to me. We got off at this bone-bare platform in broad flat country, and there was a Land Rover parked in the lane waiting for us, and Juliet was sitting on the roof.

Toby held a hand up to her, and she slid gracefully down. Kissing cousins, they kissed each other chastely on the cheeks; and then she turned to me, and twined her arms around my neck, her body a couple of times around mine like a snake—well, no, but that was how it felt, sinuous and all-enveloping, too intimate for open skies and someone watching. And then she kissed me, and it needed a different word, maybe a whole different language; and I felt a cold yearning ache in me, deep in the bones of me, that passed from me to her and we clung to each other, shuddering under its moment.

After a while, uncounted time, Toby's slow voice said, "You have got rooms, guys. Your choice of views and wallpapers, just one short drive away. I'll get in the back here, look, this is me riding with the luggage; soon as you're ready, now . . . "

Juliet drove with one hand on my leg all the way, which was—well, exhilarating, distracting, a little disconcerting. She talked, too, bright and high and happy. She'd changed her hair and got herself a tan; I thought she'd put on weight a little, too. She looked fantastic: contented, fit, ready for anything. I mentioned all these things except the weight, winning myself extra smiles, a squeeze of the thigh, all the attention she could spare. Even with the memory of our weekend together stoked up into smoky life again, I wasn't sure that I merited quite so much full-on passionate attachment. I suppose I didn't feel I'd done enough, to deserve this; I was outclassed, outgunned, out of my depth and drowning.

And, yes, loving it, with all a young man's nervous urgency, all his readiness to risk, all his restless seeking.

B rockwood must have been a simple farmhouse once, but it had grown with the family fortunes: a Georgian wing, a Victorian makeover, grandeur on a human scale. There were a tractor and a Range Rover and a TR7 side by side in the yard; there were dogs, of course, running to meet us, barking; there was a woman in the doorway, waiting.

Juliet didn't park, so much as slew heedlessly to a halt. She left the keys in the ignition, left Toby in the back, seized my hand and towed me over.

"Aunt Ginny, this is Rook . . . "

"So I'd gathered." She was tall, Toby's mother, iron in her hair and perhaps a little in her spine. A firm handshake, a glance up and down, a reserved smile: "Welcome to Brockwood. I'm not sure which room Juliet's put you in, but—"

"He's in Morris," Juliet interrupted.

"Just opposite me, Rook. Come on, I'll show you."

"Um, I'd better help Toby with the bags—"

"He's a big strong boy, he can manage. Come *on* . . . "

"What my niece is trying to say, Rook, is that she thinks I might like a minute or two alone with my son. And she's quite right, of course. Go on, you two trot along. I'll send Toby up shortly. With your bags."

I didn't think Juliet was trying to say any such thing, and nor did Mrs Rochester. There were currents and eddies between these people that I could barely read and couldn't hope to understand. One thing was clear to me already, though: I was a tool here, if not a weapon, and I was suddenly unsure whether it was Toby who had brought me after all.

U p a staircase, down a corridor, through a door into what was clearly a guest bedroom; and they called it Morris because of the wallpaper, clearly, and I was rather disconcertingly certain that it was original. Oh, my.

Not that Juliet gave me long to admire, or to worry. Just long enough to look; then she had my hand and was pulling it, and the rest of me, out of that room and into another. This clearly wasn't a guest room at all, it was very much lived-in; there were photos on the dresser, hangings on the walls, candles in every corner. An incense-burner, smoking already, lending a spicy perfume to the air. And a bed, a double bed, old and undoubtedly creaky.

I said, "Juliet . . . "

"Oh, God. Don't look so trapped, Rook. I thought you liked me?"

"You thought I liked you. Right . . . " Somehow my hands were on her hips and she was leaning into me, and there was some shift of air in that room that wasn't stirring the joss-smoke at all but made all the hairs on my arms stand up at the electric chill of its touch.

She said, "Listen, do you know why I have a room here? Why I have carte blanche, come and go, whenever?"

She was their cousin, it was a big house; that was obviously a wrong answer, one of many, so I just said no.

"When, when Kit died, I kind of fell apart. Dropped out of uni, got myself in a mess or two, the whole thing. People thought I'd be better here. And I am, more or less. I still have my bad times, but he doesn't haunt me here, the way he did at home. So I get to stay, and I'm welcome, but . . . Well, they watch me. All the time. Even Toby, he's got his eye on his favourite cousin. They just want to see me happy, but it's really oppressive. So . . . "

"So you thought you'd show them what they want to see."

"Only if you're up for it, Rook. I'm not asking you to marry me. Just—be with me, for the summer. That's all. And it is true, I do want to move on. But I need help. I need you, not just to do it, but to make them realise . . . "

A cheaper girl, a meaner girl would have had her hands under my T-shirt by then, wheedling by touch. Juliet was

very still, and somehow all the more urgent. I was all the more breathless as I tried to measure the confidence against the need, the arrogance against the self-exposure, the casual morality against the utter desperation. I said, "That weekend you came up, that was . . . ?"

"That was Toby," she said, "trying to matchmake for me, setting me up with his flat-mate. And that was me, looking for a break, and finding it. Finding you. And that was you . . . ?"

Oh yes, that was me, and I hadn't changed. I said, "What do you want me to do?"

She shrugged against me, a little movement that was somehow more erotic than a club full of lap-dancers. "Be happy," she said. "I'll help. Don't pretend, don't act up. We don't need to. This is real enough for anyone."

And then she curled an arm around my neck, pulled my head down and kissed me, not for any audience, only for ourselves.

Sounds of Toby on the stairs, and the door was open. I went to lift my head, to pull away, but she wouldn't let me. All I caught was a flash of movement in the dressing-table mirror. Juliet had draped a scarf over it, so there was barely any glass visible: just enough to show a hint of dark, a hint of shape, there and gone.

Her fingers were cold on my neck; I felt her gasp, where my hands lay against her ribs.

Then there was a great shadow in the

doorway, and that was Toby festooned with luggage, and for sure Juliet had meant for him to catch us. I couldn't keep up with this girl, what was real and what was show; except that her body was very real in my arms there, and there was a shudder in her that she wasn't faking at all. I rubbed her back and turned to face him, and he said, "Shall I dump your things here, Rook, or are we maintaining a decent pretence?"

No answer to that, so I didn't offer one; I just took my own bag from him, and carried it across the passage to my own room. On the way I glanced at lights and skylights and tried to judge angles, what source Toby had eclipsed at the head of the stairs to cause that swift shadow on the mirror, but I couldn't work it out.

Juliet followed me in. She looked pale suddenly, really strained; I said, "Are you sure you're up to this?"

"I'm not up to anything," she muttered, and right then I believed her, as she sat down abruptly on the bed. Too much fussing is impertinent; I did ostentatious unpacking for a few minutes, then went to sit with her.

When Toby looked in twenty minutes later, we were lying awkwardly, wonderfully tight on that single bed together, and I was cradling her where she was curled up small against my belly.

I t was a complex game she was playing, conspiracies within conspiracies. The fiction of separate bedrooms was meant to be blown apart, and duly was; there's

nothing like sharing a shower in a house with not enough bathrooms, to give yourselves away.

"You do realise," Toby said that first morning, when the three of us were alone in the big farmhouse kitchen, "that my mum is going to tell your mum that you came down to breakfast rubbing each other's hair dry and smelling of the same shampoo? As it were?"

Juliet made a little shrug of uncaring. "She should just be glad I'm eating breakfast." My breakfast, largely, picking mushrooms off my plate.

"You're not eating much. Sure you don't fancy one of my famous bacon sarnies? You had one yesterday..."

"Oh, for God's sake, Tobes! What do you want, blood? A girl can't do everything..."

And she stormed out, leaving Toby and me staring at each other, and I had no idea whether this was just the effect she was playing for, or how it might help her campaign. After a moment, he said, "Well, she has been eating better, since she got back. Just, not today."

"Is that my fault?" I asked, wondering if I sounded as defensive as he did.

"Nah. Well, I don't know, but I'd rather see her picking with you than stuffing her face on her own. She's a cat, she'll eat when she's hungry."

"Should I go after her?"

"She's a cat. She'll come back when she wants company."

He made bacon sandwiches and another round of coffee, and we talked about her dead brother and how close they'd been, how there was an

unbridgeable gulf between Juliet then and Juliet now, how she simply had to start again; and she walked into the middle of that conversation, and either genuinely misunderstood the sudden silence or else she pretended to, and I couldn't work that out either. But she pulled a face and apologised swiftly and sweetly to the pair of us; and then she sat on my knee and fought us both for the crunchy bacon rinds, which showed well enough willing, I thought.

A house that big, a family with that much money, I'd have expected a swimming-pool. Turned out they didn't need one. There was a pond, freshened by a stream, down between the farmland and the woods. It must have been a fish-stew once, to keep the house in carp; there were still fish, Toby said, that took a nibble sometimes if you floated. It wasn't much for Olympic training, maybe, but for an idle summer's afternoon with friends, with drinks in a cooler and sun on wet skin, for splashing about and diving for trinkets lost in the muddy bottom, it couldn't be bettered.

For girlfriends, however complicated, lying sprawled on the grass beside me, again it couldn't be bettered.

"Rook," she said.

"Mmm?"

"How d'you get to be called Rook?"

"I'm a bird of ill omen," I murmured, "and you lie within the shadow of my wing."

"Move your arm, then, I'm working on a tan. But seriously?"

"He's a north-country lad," Toby said, "and they do that kind of thing up there. It's his mother's maiden name, isn't that right?"

"Grandmother's. My mum had no brothers, and they wanted to keep it in the family."

There was one of those silences that say you found a tripwire, and I didn't quite know what. After a moment she rolled over, which took her just that little arm's-reach away from me, and said, "So how did you two meet, anyway?"

"First year, first term," I said. "He tried to pick me up."

"No, did you?"

"Damn right I did," Toby said comfortably. "Who wouldn't? You're not the only one with an eye for a fine body and a good head."

"No, but I won." She chanted a little song of victory, that had him lobbing ice-cubes at her. Allegedly at her. Most of them hit me.

I slung a couple back without caring, and said, "So has he always been gay, then? And have you always known?"

"Oh, he's not *gay*. Gay implies some degree of discrimination, or preference, or something. He'd shag anything that moved, when we were younger. It's polymorphous perversity, that's what it is."

"Well, you'd know," he said. "Must run in the family."

That invoked another of those nuclear silences, only this one was a nuclear winter. And then she was gone again, swift and sudden, and Toby was cursing himself in a dull monotone.

"I don't understand."

"No. You shouldn't, so don't ask. Other people's families can't bear too much probing. Just remember to kick me, any time I start to get clever. And— go after her, this time, yeah? She won't come back without, and she can't go blundering around all tearful in a bikini. You go and do your good thing, and tell her I'm off to hang myself from shame."

"Hasn't she had too much death already?"

"Yes, of course. You're right. See? I told you, kick me. Just tell her I'm truly sorry, and she'll find me doing penance in the thistle-bed. If she wants to find me. Don't suppose she will."

I found her in the woods, barefoot and heedless, all scratches and nettle-stings and distress. She wouldn't talk, or couldn't, but she clung to me. I didn't understand her upset, but it was utterly genuine and she was utterly needful.

I coaxed her back to the pond only because her clothes were there. Toby wasn't, which was relief to both of us. She slipped into the water to wash; when she came out again, I had a towel waiting for her, and, "D'you want to tell me what that was about?"

"No."

"No, I figured. Toby neither. He's feeling pretty guilty."

"He should."

She didn't want to talk about Toby, didn't want to talk at all. I just sat behind her and worked the towel until she sighed and settled back against me; then I lost the towel and hugged her skin on skin, my cheek against her hair.

It was one of those utterly still moments on an utterly still afternoon, where you hold your breath waiting for the world to stir again, something to happen. I gazed out over the mirror-glass surface of the pool—and saw what disturbed that surface, a curious fuzziness like a breath of wind just breaking up the tension. It wasn't a fish, and there was no wind, but a moment later Juliet and I both shivered in harmony.

She said, "It's getting chilly. Let's go in."

The unadulterated sun was on my back, and her body was leeching heat from mine; the chill was all in her head. Even so, I didn't argue. We dressed scrappily and headed for the house, leaving everything else for Toby to gather up as extra penance, as and when.

Juliet didn't eat much at dinner. When her uncle quizzed her about it, at least she didn't flare back; she just shook her head and said she wasn't hungry, wasn't feeling grand, thought she'd go to bed.

"Too much sun, perhaps?" her aunt conjectured, after she'd gone.

"Oh, come on, Mum, she's only just back from Italy..."

"Thank you, Toby, I was trying not to remember that all the other options are worse."

"Not necessarily." Mr Rochester looked at me, and I thought he was thinking *too much Rook*, that it might have been me who'd upset her. Which only goes to prove how I'm not telepathic, because he went on to say that he'd fixed for me to work for his neighbour down the valley, as I'd asked; and I was expected first thing the next morning, so perhaps I should consider an early night myself?

I've never come closer to a man saying *go on, fool, go follow my daughter up to bed.*

So I did that, sidling into her twilit room, and she peeped over the duvet at me in a kind of mute startlement.

"Work tomorrow," I told her. "I've been sent to bed. I can sleep in the other bed if you're really not feeling well, I just—"

"I'm really not feeling well," she said, "but don't go."

"You sure? You don't need to convince them of anything now, they've got that message."

She was already sliding over to make room. "Maybe I need to convince you," she said. "Light some candles and close the door. There's a bottle of brandy in the dresser; if you drink that, it'll make me feel better."

"How's that?"

"Osmosis."

What it is, the brain fools itself so easily, or it lets the body persuade it. You shiver, so you think you must be cold. Pins and needles is all about the circulation. Something stabs through you and your girlfriend both, two for the price of one, and it must have been

a static charge from somewhere. Of course it must. What else?

If you doze off with candles burning, in a room all hung with silks, you're an idiot. If you wake up and all the candles have gone out, you're a lucky idiot, guiltily grateful that she's still asleep and thank God it's an old house, plenty of drafts saved up for emergencies, and never think about how the flames weren't guttering at all before.

What was hard was slithering away from her at five in the morning, trying not to wake her. And failing, feeling her arm reach after me, hearing her voice hoarse and choked with sleep: "Where are you going?"

"Work. You know that. How are you feeling?"

She grunted, burrowed down into the warmth that I was leaving, and pulled the duvet over her head. Which I suppose was an answer, of sorts.

Berryfields was a mixed farm, dairy and arable: hard hot work, but nothing I wasn't used to. Sunshine and sweat, stretching muscles that had been pretty much dormant through term-time; country food and lemonade to keep me going, and the promise of pay at the end of the week; I was happy.

Come knocking-off time, walking up the valley with my T-shirt slung over my shoulder and the sun like a living weight pressing at my back, I came round a hedgerow and she was suddenly there, sitting on a gate weaving wild flowers into a wreath. Waiting for me.

"Hey." I lifted her down, and she weighed nothing in my hands. She kissed me, and crowned me; and stroked my bare ribs and said, "Sticky. Fancy a swim?"

"More than anything," which wasn't quite true, but true enough. "How are you, though, how was your day?"

She snorted. "Day, what day? I didn't get up till twelve."

"All right for some. How was your lie-in, then?"

"Rotten. I felt lousy all morning. Even my dreams were bad. Better now, though."

"Good. But—don't you think you should see a doctor, maybe?"

"No."

"I'm just wondering if you're anaemic or something, something they could fix, and then you wouldn't need—"

"Rook, I went through all the tests in the world when I was ill, after Kit died. There's nothing wrong with me."

"That was two years ago."

"And I've had two years of people watching me like hawks, trying to fatten me up, taking blood every time I sneeze, wanting to seal me in bubblewrap and put me back in the box. So don't start, all right?"

"No, but seriously, Jules. If you're ill like this all the time . . . "

"I'm not, though. I've been fine. Seriously. I've just had a couple of bugs or something, when you've been around. Or maybe it's you, maybe I'm allergic."

"Maybe you are. Maybe this is a rash coming up on your arm here, look, when I do this. I thought it was just goosebumps, but . . . "

"That? That's hackles. Over-protective boyfriends raise 'em. Be warned."

That set the pattern for the next weeks. Some mornings Juliet would surface as I woke, sweaty and clinging and incoherent; some mornings she'd just be a mound under the covers. Either way, all the working day and every day, I had her on my mind. I was anxious, obsessed, intrigued, entranced, excited—I suppose I was in love. I couldn't swear that it was mutual, she was scarily opaque to me; but she would come down to meet me most days after second milking, and I'd wash off the muck of the day in the swimming-hole, and we'd spend the evening and the too-brief night together.

And she would sleep badly and feel worse, all through that night; and she'd stay in bed till midday and recover just a little less than yesterday, and she was pale and frail and not eating well, and I wasn't the only one who worried.

Old house, not enough bathrooms; I came out of the shower one morning, in jeans and nothing, rubbing my hair dry, to find Toby's mother waiting demurely in dressing-gown and nightie. Country folk rise early, but I think this was deliberate; she smiled and said good morning, and then, "How's Juliet?"

"Asleep," I said. "Um, if you want me to, you know, give her space, you need to talk to her . . . "

"Actually, I think I need to talk to you. Finish dressing, and I'll see you downstairs."

"I have to be down the hill in twenty minutes..."

"I'll phone David Raglan. If his cows can't wait, he can bring them in himself." And then she was into the bathroom and closing the door very politely in my face.

I didn't need to worry on my own account; she only wanted to talk about Juliet. And her dead brother.

"Kit was a charmer, but he was very possessive of his little sister. Especially once he fell ill. I almost feel that he died to spite us, to keep his hold on her. She had just started to assert some independence, to find her own friends and her own life in college, but she threw all that away to be at his bedside while he was ill. And once he was dead, there was no question of her letting him go. Or vice versa. In my day, we'd have said she had a breakdown. These days they have better words for it, but she was ill, and we were all afraid that she'd follow him. Or that she wanted to.

"She did recover, though, or she seemed to. She's even been talking about going back to university next year. And now this: I don't want to call it a relapse, but I don't have another word for it. And I do want her to see a doctor, and I want to bring her parents back from the Bahamas, and I think your good offices might help, because I can't achieve either of those without her

consent. Brockwood is her sanctuary, and I won't poison that, but she does need help, Rook."

I nodded. "No argument here. But I don't see what I can do?"

"She's not stupid. She knows what she needs, she just needs someone now to press her to it. I think you'd be surprised, what influence you can have. Her first serious boyfriend..."

"You're kidding!"

"No. Kit monopolised her, before university. She was just starting to find her feet when he fell ill; and since he died, she's had a couple of flings, but nothing that lasted. Nothing that had the chance to last, she got scared and ran home again each time."

Something in the way she said that struck me as insincere. I said, "Got scared, or got ill?"

"Well, yes. When she went home, she went to bed. The doctors couldn't find anything wrong and we thought it was just a reaction, but..."

But she was doing it again now, except that she hadn't run away from me. Maybe she just had nowhere left to run. Or else she was stubbornly holding on to the very thing that was making her ill...

"Do you want me to go?" I asked.

"No. I want you to use your influence, to help her stop fighting what she needs."

"But if it's something in her head, that has her throwing up every time she has a date..." I put it crudely, only to avoid Mrs Rochester hearing what I really didn't want to say, *every time she has sex.*

"Then either we can chase all her dates away and condemn her to a life alone, or we can try to sort it out. Which would you prefer? Talk to her, Rook. No work today, she needs you more than those cows do."

Maybe so, but she didn't need to hear anything I had to tell her. She knew it all already; she could see it all stretched out before her, from the GP to the psychiatrist to the hospital, the same route her brother had gone. With the same end always in view.

I let her sleep, and just went walking. Eventually Toby found me, down by the swimming-hole, and I met him with a question.

"Do you believe in ghosts?"

"Whoo." He sat down, quite abruptly. "Are you making a metaphor?"

"Could be, if you want me to. If that makes it easier. What I am doing, I'm seeing a pattern. Juliet didn't use to have boyfriends, she had Kit instead. And then that changed, she got away from him, and he didn't like that. It made him ill. In his head, obviously, but that's the trouble with heads, what goes on in there can work its way right through the body. So he got really sick, and she came back to him—but then he couldn't get well again, he couldn't switch it off. I'm not saying he died to spite her, or even to keep her, but that's what happened. He did die—and I bet she was there, wasn't she?"

"Yes. Yes, she was. We all were, but she sent the rest of us out, even the par-

ents, so they could be together, just the two of them at the end."

"Figures. That's the way he always wanted it, after all. And I think he's been in possession ever since, I think he haunts her. Oh, metaphorically, if you like," though that really wasn't what I meant at all. "Maybe she feels guilty, maybe she blames herself; maybe seeing other boys just sends her back to Kit every time, and he punishes her. Only in her head, if that's the way you want it—but that's the trouble with heads, right?"

Toby was hunching up against me, staring at his feet, and this was the last thing I wanted to be doing but I did it anyway. All of this only made sense if one other thing was true. I said, "You never did sleep with her, did you?"

"No," he said slowly. "No, I never did."

"Right. So that crack about polymorphous perversity . . . "

"She just—oh, come on, Rook, she just meant I sleep around a lot. Not with her, I never—oh, and not with him either, if that's what . . . "

"Uh-huh. And what did you mean, when you flung it back at her?" She'd run away then, too, but now I was tracking her. I had Freud in one hand and a ghost in the other, and actually I thought it was a double handful, one single tangled mess.

His lips tightened, and he turned away again. "You'd have to ask Juliet about that."

"Yes. Yes, I suppose I will."

"Christ, Rook. Be careful . . . "

I wanted to do that, but I didn't know how. It was too late for treading lightly. The whole house felt very still, as I went inside; even so, just walking upstairs was like walking into a wall of wind, almost impossibly hard. Was that in my head? Maybe so, but I didn't believe it.

At first I thought her door was locked, except that she never locked it. It needed my shoulder and all my weight, all my summer's muscle to force it open. And then of course it gave all in a rush, and I barely saved myself from sprawling on the carpet.

Juliet didn't wake up, despite that slapstick entrance. Her face looked grey and pinched against the pillow, like a fairytale gone bad. I reached out to touch her cheek and felt the familiar shudder, saw it bite into her dreaming. Once I used to think that was the electricity between us; now I thought it had another name.

Her eyes opened and she half-smiled at me, through the grog of sleep and sickness. "Rook . . . Shouldn't you be working?"

"Day off," though I thought this was the end of it, no more the cowherd for me. "Listen, can you sit up a bit? Here, I'll help . . . "

I built her a nest of pillows and settled her into it, marvelling at how frail she was in my hands, how little flesh she had to hold her up against the world's malevolence. How much I wanted to stay with her, to lend her what strength I could, as much as she'd allow.

"What's this about, then?"

"I want to tell you a story," I said.

"Won't take long. I just want to see if it makes sense to you. It's about a boy who dies, but he still doesn't want to go away. His sister doesn't want him to, either. So he stays around. Maybe he's waiting for her to join him; maybe he'd like to hurry that along. But the thing is, he can't get at her directly. It's like magnets, maybe, like poles repel. I think the two of them really were very alike. Anyway, he needs a catalyst, a vector, he has to come at her piggy-back, through other people. Which means her boyfriends, necessarily, it has to be someone close. I suppose he's a sort of incubus by proxy. For sure he has the same effect, he drains all the energy out of her.

"What I can't work out," I said, "is whether she knows this or not. And if she does, whether she's clinging to her boyfriend anyway because letting him go would be an unbearable defeat, or whether she just wants to follow her brother. Whether she's defying him or surrendering to him, I suppose. What do you think, which would it be?"

She just looked at me, her eyes huge and black in the dim light.

"Oh," I said, "and one other thing. The only way this story makes sense is if the brother and sister had been doing something that nobody wants to talk about. People keep saying how close they were; and if the ghost can only come at her through boyfriends, because they get that close, then that's how close he needs to be, because that's how close he used to be. It's polymorphous perversity, these kids just never grew up. They didn't grow out of their childhood games; and he died because he couldn't let them go, and now he won't let her go and she's still haunted, and . . . I'm sorry, sweetheart, is this making any sense to you at all?"

She was crying, almost silently, which was answer enough. I loathed myself, but I hadn't dared stop until I'd laid it all out; and now I didn't dare touch her, for fear of what would then be touching her through me.

And there was one thing more that I had to do, and that was worst, and hardest. I said, "This is all that's left, hon: I have to go away. I don't care about any of that, what you got up to with Kit or what he made you do or however it worked out, it's over and it doesn't matter; but I can't stay without hurting you, and that does matter. It's gone too far already; it goes much further and I'll be killing you, and I won't do that. I don't believe you want it, and I don't think there's anything we can do to stop it. You're haunted, or I am, and neither of us knows how to exorcise him. He's only here when I touch you. And then he sucks you dry.

"Think of all that as a metaphor if you want to, it's still true, and we still don't have the cure. I love you, I'm going to leave you, and I'm not going to kiss you goodbye, you can't afford it. Be kind now, don't make this any harder."

She'd stopped crying, I think because it took too much out of her, and she had so little left. She looked at me, and her mouth worked, and she said, "I don't want to be alone."

Which was an answer to pretty much all the questions I'd asked. I nodded, and sketched a meaningless little wave, and left her. I was out of there in an hour, and home by evening.

Toby moved out during the summer, and I had to find a new flatmate. We stayed in touch, though; even as a metaphor, the story was too strong to resist. When we saw each other, I asked about Juliet and he talked about psychiatrists, treatments, therapies. He always said that she was better, stronger, doing fine. On her own, he always added, when I asked.

It's been a while now, but I'd be willing to bet that nothing's changed. She'll be strong, she'll be coping. She'll be alone. ☒

Connie Willis doesn't believe in ghosts. Not a jot. Not one iota. "I don't believe in unearthly moans or drifting white shapes or rattling chains," she says, adamantly. "I don't believe you can hear Katherine Howard's screams at Hampton Court or catch glimpses of a suicide on the stairs or speak to your dead loved one through the voice of a medium at a séance. I don't buy any of it.

"And that's because I know for a fact they exist. We are haunted every single day of our lives and everywhere we go. As Don Marquis's archie said:

> you want to know whether I believe in ghosts
> of course I do not believe in them
> if you had known as many of them as I have
> you would not believe in them either.

"Exactly," says Connie. "They're much too real to be reduced to white sheets and double-exposed photographs and chilling shrieks. And anyway, it isn't seeing or hearing them that terrifies us. It's that we don't, that we can't. Poor murdered Katherine is silent, like all the dead. They cannot speak. Their mouths are stopped forever, and it is that fact that haunts us: that no matter how frantically they signal to us, we don't see it, that no matter how urgent the message they need to send us is, they cannot make themselves heard . . . "

Turn the light up a little . . . I think I can hear something—

Distress Call
Connie Willis

Caroline was not in the room. Amy could hear her crying somewhere down the hall. Her crying sounded louder, as though some other, all-pervading sound had suddenly ceased. "The engines have stopped," Amy thought. "We are dead in the water. Something has happened," she thought. "Something terrible."

She had gone to get Caroline, to get her out of this house, and Caroline had run from her, sobbing in terror. Had run from Amy, her own mother. She had found Caroline with the women, clinging onto their gray drifting skirts. They had dressed her like themselves.

"When did they do that?" Amy thought frightenedly. "I have let things go too far."

She had said firmly, so they wouldn't know how frightened she was, "Get your things together, Caroline. We are going home."

"No!" Caroline had screamed, hiding behind their skirts. "I'm afraid. You'll hurt me again."

"Hurt you?" Amy said, bewildered and then furious. "*Hurt* you? Who has been telling you that, that I would hurt you?" She reached angrily into the protective circle of the women for Caroline's hand. "What have you been telling her?" she demanded.

Debra stepped forward, graceful as a ghost in the drifting gray, and smiled at Amy. "She wanted to know why she got so sick at the picnic," she had said.

Amy had had to hold her hands stiffly against her body to keep from slapping Debra. "What did you tell her?" she had said, and Caroline had shot past her, out the door and down the hall to the parlor.

Caroline had hidden under the big seance table in the parlor. Amy had gotten down on her knees and crawled toward her, but Caroline had backed away from her until she was almost hidden by the massive legs of the carved chair.

Amy had crawled out from under the table so she would not frighten her, and squatted back on her heels, her arms extended to the six-year-old. Caroline stayed huddled behind the chair. "Come here, Caroline," she had whispered, horrified that she should be reduced to having to say such a thing, "I won't hurt you, honey."

Caroline shook her head, the tears still wet on her face. "You'll poison me again," she whispered. Amy could hardly hear her.

"Poison?" Amy whispered. Caroline in her arms and dying, and then Jim, carrying her across the park to the house, she running after him, her heart pounding, running here because the police station was on the other side of the park and she was afraid Caroline would die before Jim got her there. Jim carrying her here, to this house, which was so much closer. To these people. Thinking hysterically as Ismay took Caroline's limp body from Jim's arms, "We should not have brought her here."

"Somebody poisoned you," Amy said, and knew it was true. She was so shocked that for a long minute she was not able to say anything. She crossed her hands on her breast as if she had been wounded there and whispered, so quietly some one standing behind her could not have heard her, her lips moving in almost silent prayer, "I would never hurt you, Caroline. I love you."

The sound of Caroline's crying was louder again, as though someone had opened a door. "I must go find Caroline," she said aloud, and tried to keep that brave thought in her mind as she went out the open door toward the sound of the crying. But before she had come to the room where they had Caroline, she was saying over and over, like a prayer, "Something terrible has happened, something terrible has happened."

She stopped, standing in the open door, and looked back toward the parlor. The lamps in the hall wavered like candles and then steadied, dimmer than before. The hall was icy. "I should go back for my coat," Amy thought. "It will be cold on deck." And then the other thought, even colder, "I mustn't go in there. Something terrible has happened in the parlor."

Ismay had taken her into the parlor to wait while the doctor saw Caroline. Amy had been standing at the foot of the wide stairs, clutching the newel post, trying not to think, "She's going to die," for fear she would know it was true.

"Don't give up hope," one of the gray-haired women had said, patting Amy's clenched hands as she went up the stairs with a blanket. She was dressed in the floating gray all the women, even the young one, wore. They had clustered like spectres around Caroline's limp body, and Amy had thought, "It's some kind of cult. I shouldn't have brought her here." But the young one—Debra, Jim had called her—had gone immediately for the doctor. Debra had led the doctor up the stairs past Amy, saying, "The little girl collapsed in the park. They were having a picnic. Her father brought her here," and she had sounded so normal, in spite of the drifting ghost's dress, that Amy had begun to hope again.

"Hope persists, doesn't it?" someone said behind her. "Even with the most blatant evidence to the contrary."

"What do you mean?" Amy stammered. This was the man Jim had called Ismay. Debra and Ismay. How had he known their names?

"Did you know," he said, "it was nearly an hour before the passengers on the *Titanic* knew that she was sinking? Then they looked down at the lights still shining underneath the water on the lower decks and said, 'How pretty! Do you think perhaps we should get into a lifeboat?'"

Amy was very frightened at what this talk of sinking ships might mean, and she half-started up the stairs, but his

hand closed over hers on the banister, and he said, "They won't let you up there. The doctor's still with her. And your husband." He moved his hand to her arm and led her into the parlor.

"Caroline's dead," she thought numbly, and looked unseeingly at the parlor.

"The body is like a ship. It does not die all at once. It is struck by death, the fatal iceberg brushing past, but it does not sink for several hours. And all that time, the passengers wander the decks, sending out S.O.S.'s to rescue ships that never come. Have you ever seen a ghost?"

"There were survivors on the *Titanic*," Amy said, her heart pounding so hard it hurt. "Help came."

"Ah, yes," Ismay said. "The *Carpathia* steamed boldly up at four in the morning. Captain Rostron stumbled about among the icebergs for nearly an hour, thinking he was in the wrong place. He was too late. She was already gone."

"No," Amy said, and she knew from the panicked sound of her heart that this conversation was not about sinking ships at all. "They weren't too late for the lifeboats."

"A few first-class passengers," Ismay said, as if the survivors did not matter. "Did you know that all the children in steerage drowned?"

Amy did not hear him. She had turned away from him and was looking at the parlor. "What?" she said blankly.

"I said, the *Californian* was only ten miles away. She thought their flares were fireworks."

"What?" she said again, and tried to get past him, but he was behind her, between her and the door, and she could not get out. "What is this place?" she said, and could not hear her voice above the sound of her heart.

Amy stood in the doorway, looking back to the parlor. "I must go back there," she thought clearly. "Something terrible has happened in the parlor."

"Mama!" Caroline said, and Amy turned and looked in through the open door.

The women stood motionless around the little girl, their hands reaching out awkwardly to comfort her, Debra kneeling at her feet. "They should be getting her lifebelt on," Amy thought. "They must get her up to the boat deck." Caroline held out her arms in joy toward Amy.

Amy said, "We're going home now, Caroline." But before she finished saying it, one of the women said, not interrupting but instead superimposing her words over Amy's so that Amy could not hear her own voice, "Your mother's gone, darling. She can't hurt you now."

"She is not gone," Caroline said. The three women looked up at the little girl and then anxiously at one another.

"You miss her, of course, but she's happy now. You must forget all the bad things and think of that," Debra said, patting Caroline's hand. Caroline yanked her hand away impatiently.

"Do you think we should give her a sedative?" said the woman who had

spoken first. "Ismay said she might be difficult at first."

"Caroline," Amy said loudly. "Come here."

"No," said Debra, and at first Amy thought she was answering her, but she didn't reach out to restrain Caroline, and her voice sounded as it had when she was playing ghost at the seance, "perhaps she does see her mother."

A shudder, like the sudden settling of a ship, went through the women.

"Caroline?" Debra asked carefully. "Where is your mother?"

"Right there," Caroline said, and pointed at Amy.

The women turned and looked at the doorway. "Perhaps she does see something," Debra said. "I think we should tell Ismay," and she went out the door past Amy and down the hall to the parlor.

"Oh, something terrible has happened in the parlor," Amy thought, "and Ismay has done it."

The parlor was the room she had seen from the park. Handing Caroline her glass of milk, she had looked at the heavy gray drapes in the windows and wondered what the gaudy Victorian house was like inside. She had imagined it like this room, rich woods and faded carpet, but the room they had hurried Caroline into upstairs was barren, a folding cot, gray walls, and she had thought again, "The house has been taken over by some kind of cult."

Near the windows was a large round table with chairs around it and candles burning in a candelabra in the center. One of the chairs was more massive than the others and heavily carved. "The captain's table," she thought, thinking of the *Titanic*, "and the captain sits in that chair."

She had turned away from Ismay, and in turning, seen what was behind her, dimly white in the darkness of the room. An iceberg. A catafalque. A bier. "I have seen it too late," Amy thought, and tried to get past Ismay, but he was at the door.

"The *Titanic* went down very fast," he said. "A little under two-and-a-half hours. People usually take longer. Ghosts have been seen for years afterwards, although it is my experience that they go down in a matter of hours."

"What is this place?" Amy said. "Who are you?"

"I am a man who sees ghosts, a spiritualist," Ismay said, and Amy nearly fainted with relief.

"You hold your seances in here," she said, relieved out of all proportion to his words. "You sit in this chair and call the ghosts," she said giddily, sitting down in the carved chair. "Come to us from the other side and all that. Have you ever had a ghost from the *Titanic*? "

"No," he said, coming around to face her. "Every ghost is his own *Titanic.*"

He made her uneasy. She stood up and looked out the window. Across the park she could see the police station, and she was overcome by the same wild relief. The police within signaling distance and the doctor upstairs, and all the ghostly ladies only harmless table-turners who wanted to talk to their dead

husbands. In this room Ismay would make the windows blow open and the candles go out, he would cause ghosts to hover above the catafalque, their hands folded peacefully across their breasts, and what, what had she been afraid of?

"I had a progenitor on the *Titanic*," he said. "Rather a cad actually. He made it off in one of the first boats. Did you know that the *Titanic* was the first ship to use the international distress signal? And the *Californian*, only ten miles away, would have been the first to receive it, an historic occasion, but the wireless operator had already gone to bed when the first messages went out."

"The *Carpathia* heard," Amy said, and walked past him and out the door, to go to where Caroline was already getting better. "Captain Rostron came."

"There were ice reports all day," Ismay said, "but the *Titanic* ignored them."

Amy leaned against the wall after Debra passed, pressing her hands to her breast as though she had been wounded. "I must find Jim," she thought. "He will see she gets in one of the boats."

She had a very hard time with the stairs. They seemed to slant forward, and it took all her concentrated thought to climb them and she could not think how she would make Jim hear her, how she would convince him to save Caroline. Even the hall listed toward her, so that she struggled toward Debra's room as up a steep hill. When she came to the closed door, she had to stand a minute before she had the strength to put her hand on the doorknob. When she did, she thought the door must be locked. Then she looked down at her hand. She dropped it to her side, as if it had been injured.

Debra opened the door, leaning her graceful body against it. "Don't worry," she said.

"You can't just leave her in there," Jim said. "What about the police?"

"Why would the police come unless someone went to get them? We don't have any phones. The outside doors are locked. Who would go get them?"

"Caroline."

Amy came into the room.

Debra shook her head. "She's only six years old, and it isn't as if she saw anything. We told her her mother died in her sleep."

"No," Amy said. "That isn't true. I was murdered."

"I'd feel safer if Ismay had taken care of her, too. She might have seen something afterwards."

"She did," Debra said, and watched the color drain from Jim's face. "She thought she saw her mother this morning." She hesitated cruelly again. "Ismay has decided to have a seance," she said. She waited to see the effect on him and then said, "What are you afraid of? She's dead. She can't do anything to you." She went out the door.

"You poisoned her," Amy said to Jim. "She wasn't sick. She was poisoned. You planned the picnic. It was a trick to bring us here, to Debra, whose name you knew before. To bring us here so Ismay could murder me."

Jim was watching the door, the color slowly coming back into his face. He took a plastic prescription bottle out of his shirt pocket and rolled it in his hand. Amy thought of him standing in the park, looking first at the police station and then at the house with the gray curtains, measuring the distances and whistling, waiting for Caroline to drink her milk.

"I will not let you kill her," Amy said. "I am going to save Caroline." She tried to take the poison out of his hand.

Jim put the bottle back in his shirt pocket and opened the door.

She had gone to the seance because Caroline was better and she could not be frightened by anything, even Jim's unwillingness to leave. The windows had banged open and the curtains had drifted in, flickering the candles. Amy thought, "He is doing something under the table." She looked steadily through the candles' flame at him.

"Come to us, oh spirit," Ismay said. He was sitting next to the big carved chair, but not in it. "We call you. Come to us."

It was Debra, projected somehow above the bier though she had not let go of Amy's hand. Debra made up with greasepaint and dressed in flowing white. She hovered there, her hands crossed on her breast, and then drifted toward the table.

"Welcome, spirit," Ismay said.

"What message do you bring us from beyond?"

"It is very peaceful," the ghost of Debra said.

Ismay slid his hand under the table. The stars were very bright, glittering off the ice. The ship hung like a jewel against the dark sky, its lights too low in the water. "He is doing something," Amy thought. "Something to frighten me." She tried to fight it, watching the phony ghost of Debra drift to the table. The candles guttered and went out as she passed. She drifted down into the carved chair. "I bring you word from your loved ones," she said, her hands resting on the carved arms. "They are at peace."

The stern of the ship began to rise into the air. There was a terrible sound as everything began to fall: the breaking glass of the chandeliers, the tinny vibrations of the piano as it slid down the boat deck, the people screaming as they struggled to hang onto the railings. The lights went out, flickered like candles, and went out again. The stern rose higher.

"No!" Amy blurted, standing up, still holding Jim's and Debra's hands.

Ismay did something under the table and the lights came on. The ghost of Debra disappeared. They were all looking at her.

"I heard . . . everything started to fall . . . the ship . . . we have to save them." She was very frightened.

"Some see the dead," Ismay said. "Some hear them. You should have been on the *Californian*. They didn't hear anything until the next morning."

He waved the others out of the room. He was still seated at the table. The candles had relit themselves.

"Did you know that when the *Titanic* went down, she created a great whirlpool, so that all the people who were too close to her were pulled down, too?" he said, and she had bolted past him out the door, running to find Caroline, who had sobbed and run from her.

Jim left the door open and she hurried after him, but at the head of the stairs she stopped, too frightened to go down, afraid that the parlor would already be underwater. "I must hurry. I must save Caroline," she thought. "Before all the boats are away," and she went down the slanting stairs.

They were at the table in the parlor. "Come to us, Amy," Ismay said. "We call you. Can you hear us?"

"I hear you," Amy said clearly. "You murdered me."

Ismay was not looking at her. He was watching the carved chair, and there was someone in it. "I am happy here," the ghost of Amy said. Debra made up with greasepaint, sitting with her hands easily on the carved arms. "I wish you were here with me, darling Caroline."

"No!" Amy screamed, and tried to get across the table to the image of herself, but the floor was tilting so that she could hardly stand. "Don't listen to her," Amy sobbed, "Run! Run!"

Ismay turned to Caroline. "Would you like to see your mother, dear?" he said, and Amy flung herself upon him, beating against his chest. "Murderer! Murderer!"

"We'll go see her now," he said, and he moved from the table, holding Caroline's hand.

"Nuh-oh!" Amy shouted in a hiccup of despair and swung her arm against him with a force that should have knocked him against the table, spilling the candles into pools of wax. The candles burned steadily in the still air.

"Help, police! Murder!" she screamed, scrabbling at the window latches that would not open, hammering her hands against the windows that would not break. They could not hear her. They could not see her. Not even Ismay. She dropped her hands to her sides as if they were injured.

Ismay said, "The shipbuilder knew immediately, but the captain had to be told, and even then he didn't believe it."

She turned from the window. He was not looking at her, but the words had been intended for her. "You can see me," she said.

"Oh, yes, I can see you," he said, and stepped back from the bier. They had washed off the blood. They had pulled a sheet up to her breast and crossed her hands over it to hide the wound. Of course they could not see her, wandering the halls, shouting over their voices to be heard. Of course they could not hear her. She was here, had been here all along, with her useless hands crossed over her silent breast. Of course she could not open the door.

"I cannot save Caroline," she thought, and looked for her among the women, but they were all gone. "They have put her in the boats after all," she thought.

Ismay stood by the seance table, watching her. "We are on the ice," he said, smiling a little.

"Murderer," Amy said.

"I can't hear you, you know," Ismay said. "I can tell what you are saying sometimes by watching you. The word 'murderer' comes through quite clearly. But my dear, you do not make a sound."

She looked down at her body, at her still face that would not make any sound again.

"The dead do make a sound," Ismay said. "Like a ship going down. S.O.S. S.O.S."

Amy looked up.

"Oh, my dear, I see you hope even yet. Isn't the human soul a stubborn thing? S.O.S. Save our ship. Imagine tapping out such a message when the ship cannot be saved. The *Titanic* was dead the moment she struck the iceberg, as you were the moment after I discovered you at your prayers. But it takes some time to go down. And till the very last the wireless operator stays at his post, tapping out messages no one will hear."

There was something there, hidden in what he had said, something about Caroline.

"It is apparently a real sound, dying cells releasing their stored energy, although *I* prefer to think of it as dying cells letting go of their last hope. It's down in the subsonic range, so its uses are limited. The lovely Debra and a few hidden speakers are far more practical in the long run. But it's useful at seances, although its effect is not usually as theatrical as it was on you."

He had reached under the table. The forward funnel toppled into the water, spraying sparks. There was a deafening crash as it fell, and then the sound of screams. The ship hung against the sky, nearly on end, for a long minute, then settled back at the stern and began to slide, slowly at first, then gaining speed, into the water.

She must not let him do this to her. There was something before, about her being at her prayers when he killed her. He thought she was kneeling under the table to pray, but she wasn't. She was looking for Caroline.

He turned the sound off. "The range is, as I said, very limited, and the wireless operator on the *Californian* shuts down at midnight, fifteen minutes before the first call."

"The *Carpathia*," Amy said.

"Ah, yes," Ismay said. "The *Carpathia*. It's true I've had the police at my door several times, but they stumbled about in the front hall among the icebergs of apology and foolish explanation for an hour or so and then went away, thinking they were in the wrong place. By then, there was not even any wreckage for them to find."

"Caroline," Amy said.

"You think I would be so foolish as to let her lead the police in here? No, she will be in no position to lead them anywhere," Ismay said, misunderstanding.

Amy thought, "I must not let him distract me." There was something about Caroline. Something important. He had killed her at her prayers. At

her prayers. "Why did you kill me?" she said, making an effort to form her words clearly so he could read them.

"For the most prosaic of reasons," he said. "Your husband paid me to. It seems he wants the lovely Debra. Did you think I was vain enough to murder you for trying to find out my tricks? Snooping about under my seance table like a child looking for clues?"

"He did not see Caroline under the table," she thought. "He does not know she saw me murdered." But that meant something, and she did not know what.

"He has paid me for Caroline, too," he said, and waited for her face.

"I won't let you," Amy said.

"You won't?" he said. "My dear, you still will not give up hope, will you? I could use your body as an altar on which to murder your beloved Caroline, and you could not lift a finger to stop me."

He had been standing by the seance table. Now she saw that he was leaning casually against the door. "The end is very near. I would like to stay and watch, but I must go find Caroline. Don't worry," he said. "I will find her. All the lifeboats are away." He shut the door.

"He did not see her hiding under the table when he murdered me," Amy thought, and now the other thought followed easily, mercilessly, "She is hiding there now."

"I must lock the door," she thought, and she waded toward it across the listing room. The lock was already under water, and she had to reach down to get to it, but when her hand closed on it, she saw that it was not the lock at all. It was her own stiff hand she touched. She had not moved at all.

"The end must be very near," she thought, "because I have no hope left at all. S.O.S.," she cried out pitifully, "S.O.S."

She stood very straight by her body, not touching it, and at first the slight list was not apparent, but after a long time, she put her hands out as if to brace herself, and her hands passed through and into her body's hands, and she foundered.

Caroline let the policemen in. They had a search warrant. Caroline said clearly and without a trace of tears, "They killed my mommy," and led them to the body.

"Yes," the captain said, pulling the sheet up over Amy's face. "I know."

"We have had a tragedy here, I'm afraid," Ismay said coming into the room. "The little girl's mother. . ."

"Was murdered," the captain said. "While she knelt by this table. With her hands crossed on her breast." Caroline silent behind the chair, watching. Amy's lips moving as if in prayer. The sudden explosion of blood from behind her hands, and Caroline backing against the wall, the tears knocked out of her. "Murdered by you," the captain said.

"You cannot possibly know that," Ismay said.

Jim ran in. He sank to his knees by Caroline and clutched her to him. "Oh, my Caroline, they've murdered her!" he sobbed. Caroline wriggled free and went and put her hand in the captain's.

"It's no use," Ismay said. "It would seem these gentlemen have received a message."

"Caroline!" Jim said, moving threateningly toward her. "What did you tell them?"

"Caroline didn't tell them anything," Ismay said. He reached under Jim's jacket into his shirt pocket and took out the medicine bottle. He handed it to Caroline. "You have been rescued," he said to her. "All the first class children were, except for little Lorraine Allison, only six years old. But your name isn't Lorraine. It's Caroline." He looked up at the captain. "And yours, I suppose, is Captain Rostron."

"Who sent a message?" Jim said hysterically. "How?"

"I don't know," Ismay said calmly. "I doubt if even these fine policemen know, in spite of their search warrant and their familiarity with the facts of the crime. But I will wager I know what the message was," he said, watching the captain's face. " 'Come at once. We have struck a berg.' "

₪

Joe Hill asks us to express his thanks to former servicemen Brian, Weston, and Mike, who reviewed "Thumbprint" for accuracy in all things military. "Any errors of fact are my responsibility alone," he adds. "Thanks are also due to my friend and former military brat Shane Leonard; his structural knowledge of the thriller form was handy in helping me sharpen the last draft.

"Some of the events I describe taking place at Abu Ghraib prison did in fact occur. Most are fictional. However, even the fictional events have a basis in reported incidents. It should be noted that hundreds of soldiers have served at the prison in the desert with honor and decency."

Thumbprint
Joe Hill

The first thumbprint came in the mail.

Mal was eight months back from Abu Ghraib, where she had done things she regretted. She had returned to Hammett, New York, just in time to bury her father. He died ten hours before her plane touched down in the States, which was maybe all for the best. After the things she had done, she was not sure she could've looked him in the eye. Although a part of her had wanted to talk to him about it, and to see in his face how he judged her. Without him, there was no one to hear her story, no one whose judgment mattered.

The old man had served, too, in Vietnam, as a medic. Her father had saved lives, jumped from a helicopter and dragged kids out of the paddy grass, under heavy fire. He called them kids, although he had only been 25 himself at the time. He had been awarded a Purple Heart and a Silver Star.

They hadn't been offering Mal any medals when they sent her on her way. At least she had not been identifiable in any of the photographs of Abu Ghraib—just her boots in that one shot Graner took, with the men piled naked on top of each other, a pyramid of stacked ass and hanging sac. If Graner had just tilted the camera up a little, Mal would have been headed home a lot sooner, only it would have been in handcuffs.

She got back her old job at the Milky Way, keeping bar, and moved into her father's house. It was all he had to leave her, that and the car. The old man's ranch was set three hundred yards from Hatchet Hill Road, backed against the town woods. In the fall, Mal ran in the forest, wearing a full ruck, three miles through the evergreens.

She kept the M4A1 in the downstairs bedroom, broke it down and put it together every morning, a job she could complete by the count of twelve. When she was done, she put the components back in their case with the bay-

225

onet, cradling them neatly in their foam cutouts—you didn't attach the bayonet unless you were about to be overrun. Her M4 had come back to the US with a civilian contractor, who brought it with him on his company's private jet. He had been an interrogator for hire—there had been a lot of them at Abu Ghraib in the final months before the arrests—and he said it was the least he could do, that she had earned it for services rendered, a statement which left her cold.

Come one night in November, Mal walked out of the Milky Way with John Petty, the other bartender, and they found Glen Kardon passed out in the front seat of his Saturn. The driver's side door was open and Glen's butt was in the air, his legs hanging out of the car, feet twisted in the gravel, as if he had just been clubbed to death from behind.

Without thinking, she told Petty to keep an eye out, and then Mal straddled Glen's hips and dug out his wallet. She helped herself to a hundred and twenty dollars cash, dropped the wallet back on the passenger side seat. Petty hissed at her to hurry the fuck up, while Mal wiggled the wedding ring off Glen's finger.

"His wedding ring?" Petty asked, when they were in her car together. Mal gave him half the money for being her lookout, but kept the ring for herself. "Jesus, you're a demented bitch."

Petty put his hand between her legs and ground his thumb hard into the crotch of her black jeans while she drove. She let him do that for a while,

his other hand groping her breast. Then she elbowed him off her.

"That's enough," she said.

"No it isn't."

She reached into his jeans, ran her hand down his hard-on, then took his balls and began to apply pressure until he let out a little moan, not entirely of pleasure.

"It's plenty," she said. She pulled her hand out of his pants. "You want more than that, you'll have to wake up your wife. Give her a thrill."

Mal let him out of the car in front of his home, and peeled away, tires throwing gravel at him.

Back at her father's house, she sat on the kitchen counter, looking at the wedding ring in the cup of her palm. A simple gold band, scuffed and scratched, all the shine dulled out of it. She wondered why she had taken it.

Mal knew Glen Kardon, Glen and his wife Helen both. The three of them were the same age, had all gone to school together. Glen had a magician at his tenth birthday party, who had escaped from handcuffs and a straightjacket as his final trick. Years later, Mal would become well acquainted with another escape artist who managed to slip out of a pair of handcuffs, a Ba'athist. Both of his thumbs had been broken, making it possible to squeeze out of the cuffs. It was easy to do, if you could bend your thumb in any direction—all you had to do was ignore the pain.

And Helen had been Mal's lab partner in sixth grade biology. Helen took notes in her delicate cursive, using different colored inks to brighten up their reports, while Mal sliced things open. Mal liked the scalpel, the way the skin popped apart at the slightest touch of the blade to show what was hidden behind it. She had an instinct for it, always somehow knew just where to put the cut.

Mal shook the wedding ring in one hand for a while and finally dropped it down the sink. She didn't know what to do with it, wasn't sure where to fence it. Had no use for it, really.

When she went down to the mailbox the next morning, she found an oil bill, a real estate flyer, and a plain white envelope. Inside the envelope was a crisp sheet of typing paper, neatly folded, blank except for a single thumbprint in black ink. The print was a clean impression, and among the whorls and lines was a scar, like a fishhook. There was nothing on the envelope: no stamp, no addresses, no mark of any kind. The postman had not left it.

In her first glance she knew it was a threat and that whoever had put the envelope in her mailbox might still be watching. Mal felt her vulnerability in the sick clench of her insides, and had to struggle against the conditioned impulse to get low and find cover. She looked to either side but saw only the trees, their branches waving in the cold swirl of a light breeze. There was no traffic along the road and no sign of life anywhere.

The whole long walk back to the house, she was aware of a weakness in her legs. She didn't look at the thumbprint again but carried it inside and left it with the other mail on the kitchen counter. She let her shaky legs carry her on into her father's bedroom; her bedroom now. The M4 was in its case in the closet but her father's .45 automatic was even closer—she slept with it under the pillow—and it didn't need to be assembled. Mal slid the action back to pump a bullet in the chamber. She got her field glasses from her ruck.

Mal climbed the carpeted stairs to the second floor, and opened the door into her old bedroom under the eaves. She hadn't been in there since coming home and the air had a musty, stale quality. A tatty poster of Alan Jackson was stuck up on the inverted slant of the roof. Her dolls—the blue corduroy bear, the pig with the queer silver button eyes which gave him a look of blindness—were set neatly in the shelves of a bookcase without books.

Her bed was made, but when she went close, she was surprised to find the shape of a body pressed into it, the pillow dented in the outline of someone's head. The idea occurred that whoever had left the thumbprint had been inside the house while she was out, and took a nap up here. Mal didn't slow down, but stepped straight up onto the mattress, unlocked the window over it, shoved it open, and climbed through.

In another minute she was sitting on the roof, holding the binoculars to her eyes with one hand, the gun in the other. The asbestos shingles had been warming all day in the sun and provided a pleasant ambient heat beneath her. From where she sat on the roof, she could see in every direction.

She remained there for most of an hour, scanning the trees, following the passage of cars along Hatchet Hill Road. Finally she knew she was looking for someone who wasn't there anymore. She hung the binoculars from her neck and leaned back on the hot shingles and closed her eyes. It had been cold down in the driveway, but up on the roof, on the lee side of the house, out of the wind, she was comfortable, a lizard on a rock.

When Mal swung her body back into the bedroom, she sat for a while on the sill, holding the gun in both hands and considering the impression of a human body on her blankets and pillow. She picked up the pillow and pressed her face into it. Very faintly, she could smell a trace of her father, his cheap corner store cigars, the waxy tang of that shit he put in his hair, same stuff Reagan had used. The thought that he had sometimes been up here, dozing in her bed, gave her a little chill. She wished she was still the kind of person who could hug a pillow and weep over what she had lost. But in truth, maybe she had never been that kind of person.

When she was back in the kitchen, Mal looked once more at the thumbprint on the plain white sheet of paper. Against all logic or sense, it seemed somehow familiar to her. She didn't like that.

He had been brought in with a broken tibia, the Iraqi everyone called The Professor, but a few hours after they put him in a cast, he was judged well enough to sit for an interrogation. In the early morning, before sunrise, Corporal Plough came to get him.

Mal was working in block 1A then and went with Carmody to collect The Professor. He was in a cell with eight other men: sinewy, unshaved Arabs, most of them dressed in fruit-of-the-loom jockey shorts and nothing else. Some others, who had been uncooperative with CI, had been given pink, flowered panties to wear. The panties fit more snugly than the jockies, which were all extra-large and baggy. The prisoners skulked in the gloom of their stone chamber, giving Mal looks so feverish and hollow-eyed, they appeared deranged. Glancing in at them, Mal didn't know whether to laugh or flinch.

"Walk away from the bars, women," she said in her clumsy Arabic. "Walk away. She crooked her finger at The Professor. "You. Come to here."

He hopped forward, one hand on the wall to steady himself. He wore a hospital johnnie, and his left leg was in a cast from ankle to knee. Carmody had brought a pair of aluminum crutches for him. Mal and Carmody were coming to the end of a twelve-hour shift, in a week of twelve-hour shifts. Escorting the prisoner to CI with Corporal Plough would be their last job of the night. Mal was twitchy from all the Vivarin in her system, so much she could hardly stand still. When she looked at lamps, she saw rays of hard-edged, rainbow-shot light emanating from them, as if she were peering through crystal.

The night before, a patrol had surprised some men planting an IED in the red, hollowed-out carcass of a German Shepherd, on the side of the road back to Baghdad. The bombers scattered, yelling, from the spotlights on the Hummers and a contingent of men went after them.

An engineer named Leeds stayed behind to have a look at the bomb inside the dog. He was three steps from the animal when a cell phone went off inside the dog's bowels, three bars of "Oops, I Did It Again." The dog ruptured in a belch of flame, and with a heavy thud that people standing thirty feet away could feel in the marrow of their bones. Leeds dropped to his knees, holding his face, smoke coming out from under his gloves. The first soldier to get to him said his face peeled off like a cheap black rubber mask that had been stuck to the sinew beneath with rubber cement.

Not long after, the patrol grabbed The Professor—so named because of his horn-rimmed glasses and because he insisted he was a teacher—two blocks from the site of the explosion. He broke his leg jumping off a high berm, running away after the soldiers fired over his head and ordered him to halt.

Now The Professor lurched along on the crutches, Mal and Carmody flanking him and Plough walking behind. They made their way out of 1A and into the pre-dawn morning. The Professor paused, beyond the doors, to take a breath. That was when Plough kicked the left crutch out from under his arm.

The Professor went straight down and forward with a cry, his johnnie flapping open to show the soft paleness of his ass. Carmody reached to help him back up. Plough said leave him.

"Sir?" Carmody asked. Carmody was just nineteen. He had been over as long as Mal, but his skin was oily and white, as if he had never been out of his chemical suit.

"Did you see him swing that crutch at me?" Plough asked Mal.

Mal did not reply, but watched to see what would happen next. She had spent the last two hours bouncing on her heels, chewing her fingernails down to the skin, too wired to stop moving. Now, though, she felt stillness spreading through her, like a drop of ink in water, calming her restless hands, her nervous legs.

Plough bent over and pulled the string at the back of the johnnie, unknotting it so it fell off The Professor's shoulders and down to his wrists. His ass was spotted with dark moles and relatively hairless. His sac was drawn tight to his perineum. The Professor glanced up over his shoulder, his eyes too large in his face, and spoke rapidly in Arab.

"What's he saying?" Plough asked. "I don't speak sand nigger."

"He said don't," Mal said, translating automatically. "He says he hasn't done anything. He was picked up by accident."

Plough kicked away the other crutch. "Get those."

Carmody picked up the crutches.

Plough put his boot in The Professor's fleshy ass and shoved.

"Get going. Tell him get going."

A pair of MPs walked past, turned their heads to look at The Professor as they went by. He was trying to cover his crotch with one hand, but Plough kicked him in the ass again and he had to start crawling. His crawl was awkward stuff, what with his left leg sticking out straight in its cast and the bare foot dragging in the dirt. One of the MPs laughed, and then they moved away into the night.

The Professor struggled to pull his johnnie up onto his shoulders as he crawled, but Plough stepped on it and it tore away.

"Leave it. Tell him leave it and hurry up."

Mal told him. The prisoner couldn't look at her. He looked at Carmody instead, and began pleading with him, asking for something to wear and saying his leg hurt while Carmody stared down at him, eyes bulging, as if he were choking on something. Mal wasn't surprised The Professor was addressing Carmody instead of her. Part of it was a cultural thing. The Arabs couldn't cope with being humiliated in front of a woman. But also, Carmody had something about him that signified to others, even the enemy, that he was approachable. In spite of the 9mm strapped to his outer thigh, he gave an impression of stumbling, unthreatening cluelessness. In the barracks, he blushed when other guys were ogling centerfolds; he often could be seen praying during heavy mortar attacks.

The prisoner had stopped crawling once more. Mal poked the barrel of her M4 in The Professor's ass to get him going again and the Iraqi jerked, gave a shrill sort of sob. Mal didn't mean to laugh, but there was something funny about the convulsive clench of his buttcheeks, something that sent a rush of blood to her head. Her blood was racy and strange with Vivarin, and watching the prisoner's ass bunch up like that was the most hilarious thing she had seen in weeks.

The Professor crawled past wire fence, along the edge of the road. Plough told Mal to ask him where his friends were now, his friends who blew up the American GI. He said if The Professor would tell about his friends, he could have his crutches and his johnnie back.

The prisoner said he didn't know anything about the IED. He said he ran because other men were running and soldiers were shooting. He said he was a teacher of literature, that he had a little girl. He said he had taken his twelve year old to Disneyland Paris once.

"He's fucking with us," Plough said. "What's a professor of literature doing out at two AM in the worst part of town? Your queer fuck Bin-Laden friends blew the face right off an American GI, a good man, a man with a pregnant wife back home. Where do your friends—Mal, make him understand he's going to tell us where his friends are hiding. Let him know it would be better to tell us now, before we get where we're going. Let him know this is the easy part of his day. CI wants this motherfucker good and soft before we get him there."

Mal nodded, her ears buzzing. She told The Professor he didn't have a daughter, because he was a known homosexual. She asked him if he liked the barrel of her gun in his ass, if it excited him. She said, "Where is the house of your partners who make the dogs into bombs? Where do your homosexual friends go after murdering Americans with their trick dogs? Tell me if you don't want the gun in the hole of your ass."

"I swear by the life of my little girl I don't know who those other men were. Please. My child is named Alaya. She is ten years old. There was a picture of her in my pants. Where are my pants? I will show you."

She stepped on his hand, and felt the bones compress unnaturally under her heel. He shrieked.

"Tell," she said. "Tell."

"I can't."

A steely clashing sound caught Mal's attention. Carmody had dropped the crutches. He looked green, and his hands were hooked into claws, raised almost-but-not-quite to cover his ears.

"You okay?" she asked.

"He's lying," Carmody said. Carmody's Arab was not as good as hers, but not bad. "He said his daughter was twelve the first time."

She stared at Carmody and he stared back, and while they were looking at each other, there came a high, keening whistle, like air being let out of some giant balloon . . . a sound that made Mal's racy blood feel as if it were fizzing with oxygen, made her feel carbonated inside. She flipped her M4 around to hold it by the barrel in both hands, and when the mortar struck—out beyond the perimeter, but still hitting hard enough to cause the earth to shake underfoot—she drove the butt of the gun straight down into The Professor's broken leg, clubbing at it as if she were trying to drive a stake into the ground. Over the shattering thunder of the exploding mortar, not even Mal could hear him screaming.

M al pushed herself hard on her Friday morning run, out in the woods, driving herself up Hatchet Hill, reaching ground so steep she was really climbing, not running. She kept going, until she was short of breath and the sky seemed to spin, as if it were the roof of a carousel.

When she finally paused, she felt faint. The wind breathed in her face, chilling her sweat, a curiously pleasant sensation. Even the feeling of light-headedness, of being close to exhaustion and collapse, was somehow satisfying to her.

The army had her for four years before Mal left to become a part of the reserves. On her second day of basic training, she had done push-ups until she was sick, then was so weak she collapsed in it. She wept in front of others, something she could now hardly bear to remember.

Eventually, she learned to like the feeling that came right before collapse: the way the sky got big, and sounds grew far away and tinny, and all the colors seemed to sharpen to an hallucinatory brightness. There was an intensity of sensation, when you were on the edge of what you could handle, when you were physically tested and made to fight for each breath, that was somehow exhilarating.

At the top of the hill, Mal slipped the stainless steel canteen out of her ruck, her father's old camping canteen, and filled her mouth with ice water. The canteen flashed, a silver mirror in the late morning sun. She poured water into her face, wiped her eyes with the hem of her T-Shirt, put the canteen away, and ran on, ran for home.

She let herself in through the front door, didn't notice the envelope until she stepped on it and heard the crunch of paper underfoot. She stared down at it, her mind blank for one dangerous moment, trying to think who would've come up to the house to slide a bill under the door when they could just leave it in the mailbox. But it wasn't a bill and she knew it.

Mal was framed in the door, the outline of a soldier painted into a neat rectangle, like the human silhouette targets they shot at on the range. She made no sudden moves, however. If someone meant to shoot her, they would have done it—there had been plenty of time—and if she was being watched, Mal wanted to show she wasn't afraid.

She crouched, picked up the envelope. The flap was not sealed. She tapped out the sheet of paper inside and unfolded it. Another thumbprint, this one a fat black oval, like a flattened spoon. There was no fishhook shaped

scar on this thumb. This was a different thumb entirely. In some ways, that was more unsettling to her than anything.

No—the most unsettling thing was that this time he had slipped his message under her door, while last time he had left it a hundred yards down the road, in the mailbox. It was maybe his way of saying he could get as close to her as he wanted.

Mal thought police, but discarded the idea. She had been a cop herself, in the army, knew how cops thought. Leaving a couple thumbprints on unsigned sheets of paper wasn't a crime. It was maybe a prank, and you couldn't waste manpower investigating a prank. She felt now, as she had when she saw the first thumbprint, that these messages were not the perverse joke of some local snotnose, but a malicious promise, a warning to be on guard. But it was an irrational feeling, unsupported by any evidence. It was soldier knowledge, not cop knowledge.

Besides, when you called the cops, you never knew what you were going to get. There were cops like her out there. People like that you didn't want getting too interested in you.

She balled up the thumbprint, took it onto the porch. Mal cast her gaze around, scanning the bare trees, the straw-colored weeds at the edge of the woods. She stood there for close to a minute. Even the trees were perfectly still, no wind to tease their branches into motion, as if the whole world were in a state of suspension, waiting to see what would happen next, only nothing happened next.

She left the balled up paper on the porch railing, went back inside, and got the M4 from the closet. Mal sat on the bedroom floor, assembling and disassembling it, three times, twelve seconds each time. Then she set the parts back in the case with the bayonet and slid it under her father's bed.

Two hours later, Mal ducked down behind the bar at the Milky Way to rack clean glasses. They were fresh from the dishwasher and so hot they burned her fingertips. When she stood up with the empty tray, Glen Kardon was on the other side of the counter, staring at her with red-rimmed, watering eyes. He looked in a kind of stupor, his face puffy, his comb-over disheveled, as if he had just stumbled out of bed.

"I need to talk to you about something," he said. "I was trying to think if there was some way I could get my wedding ring back. Any way at all."

All the blood seemed to rush from Mal's brain, as if she had stood up too quickly. She lost some of the feeling in her hands, too, and for a moment her palms were overcome with a cool, almost painful tingling.

She wondered why he hadn't arrived with cops, if he meant to give her some kind of chance to settle the matter without the involvement of the police. She wanted to say something to him, but there were no words for this. She could not remember the last time she had felt so helpless, had been caught so exposed, in such indefensible terrain.

Glen went on: "My wife spent the morning crying about it. I heard her in the bedroom, but when I tried to go in and talk to her, the door was locked. She wouldn't let me in. She tried to play it off like she was all right, talking to me through the door. She told me to go to work, don't worry. It was her father's wedding ring, you know. He died three months before we got married. I guess that sounds a little, what do you call it, Oedipal. Like in marrying me she was marrying daddy. Oedipal isn't right, but you know what I'm saying. She loved that old man."

Mal nodded.

"If they only took the money, I'm not sure I even would've told Helen. Not after I got so drunk. I drink too much. Helen wrote me a note, a few months ago, about how much I've been drinking. She wanted to know if it was because I was unhappy with her. It would be easier if she was the kind of woman who'd just scream at me. But I got drunk like that, and the wedding ring she gave me that used to belong to her daddy is gone, and all she did was hug me and say thank God they didn't hurt me."

Mal said, "I'm sorry." She was about to say she would give it all back, ring and money both, and go with him to the police if he wanted—then caught herself. He had said "they": "if they only took the money" and "they didn't hurt me." Not "you."

Glen reached inside his coat and took out a white business envelope, stuffed fat. "I been sick to my stomach all day at work, thinking about it. Then

I thought I could put up a note here in the bar. You know, like one of these fliers you see for a lost dog. Only for my lost ring. The guys who robbed me must be customers here. What else would they have been doing down in that lot, that hour of the night? So next time they're in, they'll see my note."

She stared. It took a few moments for what he had said to register. When it did—when she understood he had no idea she was guilty of anything—she was surprised to feel an odd twinge of something like disappointment.

"Electra," she said.

"Huh?"

"A love thing between father and daughter," Mal said. "Is an Electra complex. What's in the envelope?"

He blinked. Now he was the one who needed some processing time. Hardly anyone knew or remembered that Mal had been to college, on Uncle Sam's dime. She had learned Arabic there, and psychology too, although in the end she had wound up back here behind the bar of the Milky Way without a degree. The plan had been to collect her last few credits after she got back from Iraq, but sometime during her tour she had ceased to give a fuck about the plan.

At last Glen came mentally unstuck and replied: "Money. Five hundred dollars. I want you to hold onto it for me."

"Explain."

"I was thinking what to say in my note. I figure I should offer a cash reward for the ring. But whoever stole the ring isn't ever going to come up to me and admit it. Even if I promise not

to prosecute, they wouldn't believe me. So I figured out what I need is a middleman. This is where you come in. So the note would say, bring Mallory Grennan the ring, and she'll give you the reward money, no questions asked. It'll say they can trust you not to tell me or the police who they are. People know you, I think most folks around here will believe that." He pushed the envelope at her.

"Forget it, Glen. No one is bringing that ring back."

"Let's see. Maybe they were drunk, too, when they took it. Maybe they feel remorse."

She laughed.

He grinned, awkwardly. His ears were pink. "It's possible."

She looked at him a moment longer, then put the envelope under the counter. "Okay. Let's write your note. I can copy it on the fax machine. We'll stick it up around the bar, and after a week, when no one brings you your ring, I'll give you your money back and a beer on the house."

"Maybe just a ginger ale," Glen said.

Glen had to go, but Mal promised she'd hang a few flyers in the parking lot. She had just finished taping them up to the street lamps when she spotted a sheet of paper, folded into thirds and stuck under the windshield wiper of her father's car.

The thumbprint on this one was delicate and slender, an almost perfect oval, feminine in some way, while the first two had been squarish and blunt.

Three thumbs, each of them different from the others.

She pitched it at a wire garbage can attached to a telephone pole, hit the three-pointer, got out of there.

The 82nd had finally arrived at Abu Ghraib, to provide force protection, and to try and nail the fuckers who were mortaring the prison every night. Early in the fall, they began conducting raids in the town around the prison. The first week of operations, they had so many patrols out, and so many raids going, they needed back-up, so General Karpinski assigned squads of MPs to accompany them. Corporal Plough put in for the job, and when he was accepted, told Mal and Carmody they were coming with him.

Mal was glad. She wanted away from the prison, the dark corridors of 1A and 1B, with their smell of old wet rock, urine, flopsweat. She wanted away from the tent cities that held the general prison population, the crowds pressed against the chain-links, who pleaded with her as she walked along the perimeter, black flies crawling on their faces. She wanted to be in a Hummer with open sides, night air rushing in over her. Destination: any-fucking-where else on the planet.

In the hour before dawn, the platoon they had been tacked onto hit a private home, set back in a grove of palms, with a white stucco wall around the yard, and a wrought-iron gate across the drive. The house was stucco too, and had a swimming pool out back, a patio and grill, wouldn't have looked out of place in southern California. Delta Team drove their Hummer right through the gate, which went down with a hard iron bang, hinges shearing out of the wall with a spray of plaster.

That was all Mal saw of the raid. She was behind the wheel of a two-and-a-half ton troop transport for carrying prisoners. No Hummer for her, and no action either. Carmody had another truck. She listened for gunfire, but there was none, the residents giving up without a struggle.

When the house was secure, Corporal Plough left them, said he wanted to size up the situation. What he wanted to do was get his picture taken, chewing on a stogie and holding his gun, with his boot on the neck of a hog-tied insurgent. She heard over the walkie-talkie that they had grabbed one of the Fedayeen Saddam, a Ba'athist lieutenant, and had found weapons, files, personnel information. There was a lot of cornepone whoop-ass on the radio. Everyone in the 82nd looked like Eminem—blue eyes, pale blonde hair in a crewcut—and talked like one of the Duke boys.

Just after sunup, when the shadows were leaning long away from the buildings on the east side of the street, they brought the Fedayeen out and left him on the narrow sidewalk with Plough. The insurgent's wife was still inside the building, soldiers watching her while she packed a bag.

The Fedayeen was a big Arab with hooded eyes and a three-day shadow on his chin, and he wasn't saying anything except, "Fuck you," in American. In the basement, Delta Team had found racked AK-47s, and a table covered in maps, marked all over with symbols, numbers, Arabic letters. They discovered a folder of photographs, featuring US soldiers in the act of establishing check-points, rolling barbed wire across different roads. There was also a picture in the folder of George Bush, Sr., smiling a little foggily, posing with Steven Seagal.

Plough was worried the pictures showed places and people the insurgents planned to strike. He had already been on the radio a couple times, back to base, talking with CI about it in a strained, excited voice. He was especially upset about Steven Seagal. Everyone in Plough's unit had been made to watch *Above the Law* at least once, and Plough claimed to have seen it more than a hundred times. After they brought the prisoner out, he stood over the Fedayeen, yelling at him, and sometimes swatting him upside the head with Seagal's rolled-up picture. The Fedayeen said, "More fuck you."

Mal leaned against the driver's side door of her truck for a while, wondering when Plough would quit hollering and swatting the prisoner. She had a Vivarin hang-over and her head hurt. Eventually she decided he wouldn't be done yelling until it was time to load up and go, and that might not be for another hour.

She left Plough yelling, walked over the flattened gate and up to the house. She let herself into the cool of the kitchen. Red tile floor, high ceilings, lots of windows so the place was filled with sunlight. Fresh bananas in a glass bowl. Where did they get fresh bananas? She helped herself to one, and ate it on the toilet, the cleanest toilet she had sat on in a year.

She came back out of the house and started down to the road again. On the way there, she put her fingers in her mouth, and sucked on them. She hadn't brushed her teeth in a week, and her breath had a human stink on it.

When she returned to the street, Plough had stopped sweating the prisoner long enough to catch his breath. The Ba'athist looked up at him from under his heavy-lidded eyes. He snorted and said, "Is talk. Is boring. You are no one. I say fuck you still no one."

Mal sank to one knee in front of him and said in Arab, "Smell that? That is the cunt of your wife. I fuck her myself like a lesbian and she said it was better than your cock."

The Ba'athist tried to lunge at her from his knees, making a sound down in his chest, a strangled growl of rage, but Plough caught him across the chin with the stock of his M4. The sound of the Ba'athist's jaw snapping was as loud as a gunshot.

He lay on his side, twisted into a fetal ball. Mal remained crouched beside him.

"Your jaw is broken," Mal said. "Tell me about the photographs of the US soldiers, and I will bring a no-more-hurt pill."

It was half an hour before she went to get him the painkillers, and by then he had told her when the pictures had been taken, coughed up the name of the photographer.

Mal was leaning into the back of her truck, digging in the first aid kit, when Carmody's shadow joined hers at the rear bumper.

"Did you really do it?" Carmody asked her. The sweat on him glowed with an ill sheen in the noonday light.

"The wife?"

"What? Fuck no. Obviously."

"Oh," Carmody said, and swallowed convulsively. "Someone said—" he began, then his voice trailed off.

"What did someone say?"

He glanced across the road, at two soldiers from the 82nd, standing by their Hummer. "One of the guys who was in the building said you marched right in and bent her over. Face-down on the bed."

She looked over at Vaughn and Henrichon, holding their M-16s and struggling to contain their laughter. She flipped them the bird.

"Jesus, Carmody. Don't you know when you're being fucked with?"

His head was down. He stared at his own scarecrow shadow, tilting into the back of the truck.

"No," he said.

Two weeks later, Carmody and Mal were in the back of a different truck, with that same Arab, the Ba'athist, who was being transferred from Abu Ghraib to a smaller prison facility in Baghdad. The prisoner had his head in a steel contraption, to clamp his jaw in place, but he was still able to open his mouth wide enough to hawk a mouthful of spit into Mal's face.

Mal was wiping it away when Carmody got up and grabbed the Fedayeen by the front of his shirt and heaved him out of the back of the truck, into the dirt road. The truck was doing thirty miles an hour at the time, and was part of a convoy that included two reporters from MSNBC.

The prisoner survived, although most of his face was flayed off on the gravel, his jaw rebroken, his hands smashed. Carmody said he leaped out on his own, trying to escape, but no one believed him, and three weeks later Carmody was sent home.

The funny thing was that the insurgent really did escape, a week after that, during another transfer. He was in handcuffs, but with his thumbs broken he was able to slip his hands right out of them. When the MPs stepped out of their Hummer at a checkpoint, to talk porno with some friends, the prisoner dropped out of the back of the transport. It was night. He simply walked into the desert, and, as the stories go, was never seen again.

The band took the stage Friday evening, and didn't come offstage until Saturday morning. Twenty minutes after one, Mal bolted the door behind the last customer. She started helping Candice wipe down tables, but she had been on since before lunch, and Bill Rodier said go home already.

Mal had her jacket on and was headed out when John Petty poked her in the shoulder with something.

"Mal," he said. "This is yours, right? Your name on it."

She turned. Petty was at the cash register, holding a fat envelope toward her. She took.

"That the money Glen gave you, to swap for his wedding ring?" Petty turned his shoulder to her, shifting his attention back to the register. He pulled out stacks of bills, rubber-banded them, and lined them up on the bar. "That's something. Taking his money and fucking him all over again. You think I plop down five hundred bucks, you'd fuck me just as nice?"

As he spoke he put his hand back in the register. Mal reached under his elbow and slammed the drawer on his fingers. He squealed. The drawer began to slide open again on its own, but before he could get his mashed fingers out, Mal slammed it once more. He lifted one foot off the floor and did a comic little jig.

"Ohfuckgoddamyouuglydyke," he said.

"Hey," said Bill Rodier, coming toward the bar. He carried a trash barrel in one hand. "Hey."

She let Petty get his hand out of the drawer. He stumbled clumsily away from her, struck the bar with his hip, and wheeled to face her, clutching the mauled hand to his chest.

"You crazy bitch. I think you broke my fingers."

"Jesus, Mal," Bill said, looking over the bar at Petty's hand. His fat fingers had a purple line of bruise across them. Bill turned his questioning gaze back her way. "I don't know what the hell

John said, but you can't do that to people."

"You'd be surprised what you can do to people," she told him.

Outside it was drizzling and cold. She was all the way to her car before she felt a weight in one hand, and realized she was still clutching the envelope full of cash.

Mal held it in her hand, against the inside of her thigh, the whole drive back. She didn't put on the radio, just drove, and listened to the rain tapping on the glass. She had been in the desert for two years and she had seen it rain just twice, although there was often a moist fog in the morning, a mist that smelled of eggs, of brimstone.

When she enlisted, she had hoped for war. She did not see the point of joining if you were not going to get to fight. The risk to her life did not trouble her. It was an incentive. You received a two hundred dollar bonus for every month you spent in the combat zone, and a part of her had relished that her own life was valued so cheap. Mal would not have expected more.

But it did not occur to her, when she first learned she was going to Iraq, that they paid you that money for more than just the risk to your own life. It wasn't just a question of what could happen to you, but also a matter of what you might be asked to do to others. For her two-hundred dollar bonus, she had left naked and bound men in stress positions for hours, and told a nineteen-year-old girl that she would be gang-raped if she did not supply information about her boyfriend. Two hundred dollars a month was what it cost to make a torturer out of her. She felt now that she had been crazy there, that the Vivarin, the ephedra, the lack of sleep, the constant scream-and-thump of the mortars, had made her into someone who was mentally ill, a bad dream version of herself. Then Mal felt the weight of the envelope against her thigh, Glen Kardon's pay-off, and remembered taking his ring, and it came to her that she was having herself on, pretending she had been someone different in Iraq. Who she had been then and who she was now were the same person. She had taken the prison home with her. She lived in it still.

Mal let herself in the house, soaked and cold, holding the envelope. She found herself standing in front of the kitchen counter with Glen's money. She could sell him back his own ring for five hundred dollars, if she wanted, and it was more than she would get from any pawnshop. She had done worse, for less cash. She stuck her hand down the drain, felt along the wet smoothness of the trap, until her fingertips found the ring.

Mal hooked her ring finger through it, pulled her hand back out. She turned her wrist this way and that, considering how the ring looked on her crooked, blunt finger. *With this I do thee wed.* She didn't know what she'd do with Glen Kardon's five hundred dollars if she swapped it for his ring. It wasn't money she needed. She didn't need his ring

either. She couldn't say what it was she needed, but the idea of it was close, a word on the tip of her tongue, maddeningly out of reach.

She made her way to the bathroom, turned on the shower, and let the steam gather while she undressed. Slipping off her black blouse, she noticed she still had the envelope in one hand, Glen's ring on the finger of the other. She tossed the money next to the bathroom sink, left the ring on.

She glanced at the ring sometimes while she was in the shower. She tried to imagine being married to Glen Kardon, pictured him stretched out on her father's bed in boxers and a T-shirt, waiting for her to come out of the bathroom, his stomach aflutter with the anticipation of some late night, connubial action. She snorted at the thought. It was as absurd as trying to imagine what her life would've been like if she had become an astronaut.

The washer and dryer were in the bathroom with her. She dug through the Maytag until she found her Curt Schilling T-Shirt and a fresh pair of Hanes. She slipped back into the darkened bedroom, toweling her hair, and glanced at herself in the dresser mirror, only she couldn't see her face, because a white sheet of paper had been stuck into the top of the frame, and it covered the place where her face belonged. A black thumbprint had been inked in the center. Around the edges of the sheet of paper, she could see reflected in the mirror a man stretched out on the bed, just as she had pictured Glen Kardon stretched out and waiting for her, only in her head Glen hadn't been wearing gray-and-black fatigues.

She lunged to her side, going for the kitchen door. But Carmody was already moving, launching himself at her, driving his boot into her right knee. The leg twisted in a way it wasn't meant to go, and she felt her ACL pop behind her knee. Carmody was right behind her by then and he got a handful of her hair. As she went down, he drove her forward and smashed her head into the side of the dresser.

A black spoke of pain lanced down into her skull, a nailgun fired straight into the brain. She was down and flailing and he kicked her in the head. That lick didn't hurt so much, but took the life out of her, as if she were no more than an appliance, and he had jerked the power cord out of the wall.

When he rolled her onto her stomach and twisted her arms behind her back, she had no strength in her to resist. He had the heavy-duty plastic ties, the flex-cuffs they used on the prisoners in Iraq sometimes. He sat on her ass and squeezed her ankles together and put the flexicuffs on them too, tightening until it hurt, and then some. Black flashes were still firing behind her eyes, but the fireworks were smaller, and exploding less frequently now. She was coming back to herself, slowly. Breathe. Wait.

When her vision cleared she found Carmody sitting above her, on the edge of her father's bed. He had lost weight and he hadn't any to lose. His eyes peeked out, too bright at the bottom of deep hollows, moonlight reflected in the water at the bottom of a long well. In his lap was a bag, like an old fashioned doctor's case, the leather pebbled and handsome.

"I observed you while you were running this morning," he began, without preamble. Using the word *observed*, like he would in a report on enemy troop movements. "Who were you signaling when you were up on the hill?"

"Carmody," Mal said. "What are you talking about, Carmody? What is this?"

"You're staying in shape. You're still a soldier. I tried to follow you, but you outran me on the hill this morning. When you were on the crest, I saw you flashing a light. Two long flashes, one short, two long. You signaled someone. Tell me who."

At first she didn't know what he was talking about; then she did. Her canteen. Her canteen had flashed in the sunlight when she tipped it up to drink. She opened her mouth to reply, but before she could, he lowered himself to one knee beside her. Carmody unbuckled his bag and dumped the contents onto the floor. He had a collection of tools: a pair of heavy-duty shears, a taser, a hammer, a hacksaw, a portable vise. Mixed in with the tools were five or six human thumbs.

Some of the thumbs were thick and blunt and male, and some were white and slender and female, and some were too shriveled and darkened with rot to provide much of any clues about the person they had belonged to. Each thumb ended in a lump of bone and sinew. The inside of the bag had a smell, a sickly-sweet, almost floral stink of corruption.

Carmody selected the heavy-duty shears.

"You went up the hill and signaled someone this morning. And tonight you came back with a lot of money. I looked in the envelope while you were in the shower. So you signaled for a meeting and at the meeting you were paid for intel. Who did you meet? CIA?"

"I went to work. At the bar. You know where I work. You followed me there."

"Five hundred dollars. Is that supposed to be tips?"

She didn't have a reply. She couldn't think. She was looking at the thumbs mixed in with his mess of tools.

He followed her gaze, prodded a blackened and shriveled thumb with the blade of the shears. The only identifiable feature remaining on the thumb was a twisted, silvery, fishhook scar.

"Plough," Carmody said. "He had helicopters doing flyovers of my house. They'd fly over once or twice a day. They used different kinds of helicopters on different days to try and keep me from putting two and two together. But I knew what they were up to. I started watching them from the kitchen with my field glasses, and one day I saw Plough at the controls of a radio station traffic copter. I didn't even know he knew how to pilot a bird until then. He was wearing a black helmet and sunglasses, but I still recognized him."

As Carmody spoke, Mal remembered Corporal Plough trying to open a bottle of Red Stripe with the blade of his bayonet, and the knife slipping, catching him across the thumb, Plough sucking on it and saying around his thumb, *motherfuck, someone open this for me.*

"No, Carmody. It wasn't him. It was just someone who looked like him. If he could fly a helicopter, they would've had him piloting Apaches over there."

"Plough admitted it. Not at first. At first he lied. But eventually he told me everything, that he was in the helicopter, that they had been keeping me under surveillance ever since I came home." Carmody moved the tip of the shears to point at another thumb, shriveled and brown, with the texture and appearance of a dried mushroom. "This was his wife. She admitted it too. They were putting dope in my water to make me sluggish and stupid. Sometimes I'd be driving home, and I'd forget what my own house looked like. I'd spend twenty minutes cruising around my development, before I realized I had gone by my place twice."

He paused, moved the tip of the shears to a fresher thumb, a woman's, the nail painted red. "She followed me into a supermarket in Poughkeepsie. This was while I was on my way north, to see you. To see if you had been compromised. This woman in the supermarket, she followed me aisle to aisle, always whispering on her cell phone. Pretending not to look at me. Then, later, I went into a Chinese place, and noticed her parked across the street, still on the phone. She was the toughest to get solid information out of. I almost thought I was wrong about her. She told me she was a first-grade teacher. She told me she didn't even know my name and that she wasn't following me. I almost believed her. She had a photo in her purse, of her sitting on the grass with a bunch of little kids. But it was tricked up. They used Photoshop to stick her in that picture. I even got her to admit it in the end."

"Plough told you he could fly helicopters so you wouldn't hurt him anymore. The first-grade teacher told you the photo was faked to make you stop. People will tell you anything if you hurt them badly enough. You're having some kind of break with reality, Carmody. You don't know what's true anymore."

"You would say that. You're part of it. Part of the plan to make me crazy, make me kill myself. I thought the thumbprints would startle you into making contact with your handler and they did. You went straight to the hills, to send him a signal. To let him know I was close. But where's your back-up now?"

"I don't have back-up. I don't have a handler."

"We were friends, Mal. You got me through the worst parts of being over there, when I thought I was going crazy. I hate that I have to do this to you. But I need to know who you were signaling. And you're going to tell. Who did you signal, Mal?"

"No one," she said, trying to squirm away from him on her belly.

He grabbed her hair, and wrapped it around his fist, to keep her from going anywhere. She felt a tearing along her scalp. He pinned her with a knee in her back. She went still, head turned, right cheek mashed against the knubbly rug on the floor.

"I didn't know you were married. I didn't notice the ring until just tonight. Is he coming home? Is he part of it? Tell me." Tapping the ring on her finger with the blade of the shears.

Mal's face was turned so she was staring under the bed at the case with her M4 and bayonet in it. She had left the clasps undone.

Carmody clubbed her in the back of the head, at the base of the skull, with the handles of the shears. The world snapped out of focus, went to a soft blur, and then slowly her vision cleared and details regained their sharpness, until at last she was seeing the case under the bed again, not a foot away from her, the silver clasps hanging loose.

"Tell me, Mal. Tell me the truth now."

In Iraq, the Fedayeen had escaped the handcuffs after his thumbs were broken. Cuffs wouldn't hold a person whose thumb could move in any direction . . . or someone who didn't have a thumb at all.

Mal felt herself growing calm. Her panic was like static on a radio, and she had just found the volume, was slowly dialing it down. He would not begin with the shears, of course, but would work his way up to them. He meant to beat her first. At least. She drew a long, surprisingly steady breath. Mal felt almost as if she were back on Hatchet

Hill, climbing with all the will and strength she had in her, for the cold, open blue of the sky.

"I'm not married," she said. "I stole this wedding ring off a drunk. I was just wearing it because I like it."

He laughed: a bitter, ugly sound. "That isn't even a good lie."

And another breath, filling her chest with air, expanding her lungs to their limit. He was about to start hurting her.

He would force her to talk, to give him information, to tell him what he wanted to hear. She was ready. She was not afraid of being pushed to the edge of what could be endured. She had a high tolerance for pain, and her bayonet was in arm's reach, if only she had an arm to reach.

"It's the truth," she said, and with that, PFC Mallory Grennan began her confession. ☒

Coming Soon In Postscripts

Coming up in our next few issues: the mysteries of alien communication open up in the shocking, revelatory "Blackbird", by Robert Reed; a doctor tends to the ultimate tyrant in "The King's Physician", a mesmerizing political fable by Richard Paul Russo; Scott Edelman brilliantly reveals the true anatomy of zombie plagues in "Almost the Last Story by Almost the Last Man"; Patrick O'Leary's "The Cane" confronts the magus of speculative fiction in his own magical territory; ghosts walk a transformed metropolis in "The City Without Sleep", Sarah Monette's superb novelette of the supernatural; and Jeff VanderMeer recounts astonishing legends of Old Polynesia in "Island Tales". Add new stories by Brian Aldiss, Steve Aylett, Marly Youmans, Christopher Fowler, Paul Di Filippo, Rhys Hughes, and Adam Roberts, as well as contributions from the brightest new names in SF, Fantasy, and Horror, and *Postscripts* is looking at a glorious 2007—and beyond . . .

COMING IN 2007
FROM SUBTERRANEAN PRESS...

KAGE BAKER	STEPHEN KING
RAY BRADBURY	JOE R. LANSDALE
DAVID BRIN	BRIAN LUMLEY
POPPY Z. BRITE	GEORGE R. R. MARTIN
ORSON SCOTT CARD	JOHN SCALZI
CHARLES DE LINT	ROBERT SILVERBERG
NEIL GAIMAN	CONNIE WILLIS

According to its author, Paul Jessup, "Mud Skin" is a story of many things, one of many layers. "On one hand it is about family," he writes, "and about the strange power struggles that exist between parents and children. On the other hand it is about the abuse of religion to control people, about the problems that arise when you reject responsibility for your actions, and about how people oppress one another and attempt to enslave one another to their ideals. It could be seen as a reflection of the American psyche and the struggles of our own mental history and troubled mythology."

Paul (http://pauljessup.kapo.ws) has been published in the Journals of Experimental Fiction, Jacob's Ladder *anthology and several online journals. He has fiction upcoming in* Electric Velocipede *and* Farrago's Wainscot *and we're delighted to report that we have bought more of his delightful tales for future issues of* Postscripts. *Always busy, he is working on a novella and the indie fantasy rag* GrendelSong. *In 2000 he received the Virginia Perryman award for excellence in short fiction from Kent State University . . . where, as it happens, our editor spent an enjoyable but decidedly strange three weeks in the summer of 1969. But, as they say, that really* is *another story.*

Mud Skin

Paul Jessup

Ma planted her gods in the garden, planted them down deep into the troubled soul of earth. She wanted to see what would grow there with the gods as seeds, wanted to see what roots would gobble up the ground, what flowers would search for sunlight. When she was done she packed it in and spread her own blood across the moist soil.

She heard them whisper in the shadows of the garden.

Everything will be better now, she thought. Gods are nothing but trouble anyway. This last batch of them caused her all sorts of misfortune and mischief, just for their own personal pleasure. Greedy lot, she thought. Selfish lot.

All gods should be buried and be done with.

Ma went into her kitchen and wiped the greasy mud from her hands over the top of her sink. She watched the black stuff ooze on down into the bucket below, clumping and glopping together. She thought of molding this discarded earth, thought of turning it into something she would like.

Not a god, not this time. No, she would make a son maybe. Or a daughter. Someone to keep her and Pa company on the cold days, or to help with the gardens on the warm days. Pa wouldn't mind—he's been thinking the same thing, she knew.

Pa was in the walls of the house, crawling around and looking for spare spirits that might be chained and help out with some chores. He was good at catching a sprite or two, and they would give at least a good day's labor before expiring.

She heard him rattle around for a bit, and then saw his toothless skull emerge out from a hole in the ceiling. His beard roped around and down like brown moss, his eyes wild and filled with glee. "Ma!" he called out, "I caught one! One of them little facks. Right here, I got him good. Rohee, heehaw!"

Down came a sack from the ceiling, wriggling and lively as it smacked against the ground. The old man shimmied himself right behind, moving with a speed and a grace well beyond his age. "This one's a good one, too. We can milk him for magic while he works. Get out the aether pump! Let's get going!"

Ma sighed. He was always this excited at the start of a new project. Almost a tire just being around him, watching him move and dance about, singing and laughing. She wished somedays he would just act his age and settle down for a bit. Live out the last few years calm like, relaxed.

Ma waddled into the backroom and pulled out the pump, and dragged it back to him. Heavy bastard, it was. If they weren't fresh out of spirit slaves she would have one of them do it. Oh well. It didn't take long to hook the tubes and pumps up to the ellefolk and get it working.

He was a curious little bastard. With skin the color of warm bread and eyes the color of milk. She was so hungry these days she just wanted to eat him. She refrained for a bit, and instead waited as the pump did its thing, and

they got a few more gallons of magic to last them through the winter.

When the machine was off and the ellefolk lay slumped on the ground half awake, she turned to Pa and looked him dead on into his ancient eyes. "I'm going to use some of that magic to make us a kin. Out of that mud over there. It's god mud, so it should work."

Pa shook his head. "I see, I see. So you buried them then, eh? Makes sense. They are useless anyhow. Why did you even build them in the first place?"

Ma shrugged and started forming the slick mud into a little body. She clumped together arms and legs, and then a little head, the excess oozing between her fingers. "Just felt spiritual, is all. Sometimes a girl feels the need for gods."

Pa nodded. "Hope that's all out of your system then."

Ma smiled.

"For now at least, for now."

She packed in some of the mud, finishing up her project. She pushed the tips of her fingers into the head, tracing eyes and a mouth and some hair. Behind her she heard the ellefolk twitch and moan in uneasy sleep against the floorboards.

It doesn't take much magic to make something come to life. Just a drop or two, a few of the right incantations, and Ma could make anything. She's made plants and flowers, gods and demons. She's made dancing children no more than an inch or two high, she's made giants and unicorns and all sorts of mystical manifestations.

Of course getting the magic is the trick. You have to get it from a source—be it from a fae or from a dream well. In a dream well, you got it easy. Most of them are never ending. But if you can't get a dream well, you've got to hunt yourself down one of the ellefolk.

She was lucky cause she married someone who excelled at that sort of thing. And the ellefolk made good cheap labor as well. A winning situation no matter how you cut it. Even though the farm was small, an extra hand was always needed.

The little boy still contained traces of mud on his skin, still had bits of earth under his nails and behind his eyes. Overall, though, he looked as normal and as human as they came. Ma placed him at about eight years old. Pa thought something more like ten or twelve. They called him Vadie, and showed him how to do the chores.

He didn't talk very much, but he could listen and think and lift heavy things. Every so often Ma would have to go and teach him a thing or two, show him what most of us take for granted. Some days he would have his skin slip off, or an arm tumble down and Ma would have to pack some new mud, use up some new magic just to keep him together for a little while longer.

Ma loved cleaning up his mudtracks across the house, and loved the sound of his voice in his bedroom playing at all hours. Pa took kind to him, and loved the extra hand in catching the ellefolk as they crawled through the walls and burrowed underground, trying to escape them.

Sometimes at night Ma would hear Vadie in the garden. She would look out the window and see him talking to the plants, whispering to them, rubbing his fingers along the edge of their leaves. She wondered if he was just playing pretend, or if he heard them talk back to him.

At these moments she wondered what kind of magic he was made from. She wondered if it were unstable magic, breaking away at his mind and body. He had no soul, that she knew, yet she felt like he should have one. Maybe that's why he did crazy stuff, Ma thought, because he didn't have a soul. She vowed to get him one. Get him one someday soon.

One of the ellefolk could live without it. They didn't need a soul anyway, not nohow. And it would go to a good home, to a good little clay doll in need of one. Then they would be a whole family.

When she ran the idea past Pa he thought she was crazy. "That boy don't need a soul," he said, "He's just a clay thing, is all. Just god dirt in the shape of a boy. That magic may make him seem real—but he's nothing. Just nothing. Best not to work against the natural order of things."

She knew he was right, deep down inside. But still, his oddities bothered her. She wanted him to be a normal boy, someone they could be proud to show the neighbors or the folks in town. Not some strange soul-less freak that didn't even know proper manners.

Ma decided to see who the boy was talking to at night. She snuck behind, and listened quietly from the shadows in the door frame. He could not sense her—he had no soul to sense with—so he kept on whispering and talking and paying her no mind.

She saw him kneeling in that mud, caressing the flowers. She heard his meek clay voice whispering the names of the gods she had buried there. Is he praying, she thought, praying to those damned creatures? She leaned closer and listened harder.

He was asking for help. He was asking them to destroy him, to let him leave this prison of clay he was trapped in. She held her breath, tears in her eyes. She did not want to believe her ears. He loved being with them, he had to. He was all she had.

She stomped out into the moonlight, her round body like a grey stone. "Vadie, lad. What you doing out here?"

Vadie turned and looked at her. His face was darker, dirtier. Mud face in that moonlight. He had been crying, and it washed the makeshift skin away into mudpuddles beneath him. "Nothing, Ma. Nothing. Just talking to the plants. The ellefolk say they like it."

Ma stared hard at him. She hated him for praying to those little selfish bastards. She hated herself for planting them rather than destroying them. She hated the ellefolk for helping him in his time of crisis.

"Forget what they tell you. They are a lying folk, not a true word ever passed their lips. Come inside. I'll make you a snack before bed."

He looked up at her, his eyes like her fingerprints in mud. "Ok," he said.

She watched him walk back to their house, making sure he went inside. When she was sure he was out of earshot, she leaned over to the dirt and put her ear to the ground. The ground whispered, talking to her. Sending her promises she could not trust.

"You better leave him alone," she muttered to the earth, "If you know what's best for you."

The next day all the ellefolk were gone. Ma and Pa searched the house looking for where they could have gone. They weren't anywhere—not even hiding in the walls or anything like that. When they asked Vadie what happened he just smiled and pointed at the trees.

He stopped talking after that moment, and they didn't know why. They kept trying to get him to say anything, to tell them why he pointed at the trees, but nothing. Nothing would be spoken.

Ma started to think that Vadie was the one who set the ellefolk free. She insinuated such from time to time, but he would not talk. And Pa couldn't find any other ellefolk. Not in the house, not in the barn, not in the forest outside. It was like they all up and left without warning, leaving the world empty of their kin.

She caught Vadie outside again, talking to the plants. She stomped over, the mud and the rain drenching her clothes in colors of grey and brown in the moon shadows. She picked his clay body up, it slick beneath her fingers. She could see a strange glint in his eye as the whispering from below began to echo through the trees around her.

He smiled a smile made of fingerprints.

"Stop talking to those gods. You hear me? They are nothing but a curse on us, on all of us. I shoulda killed them long ago. I shoulda unmade them."

He looked up at her, the rain making the clay skin of his face lopsided. "Why did you make them in the first place? Why you give them power over us? And then just bury them? You think the power you gave them goes away just because they in the ground? Things grow in the ground. I know. I am ground. I am dirt. They talk through me, I talk through them. We grow."

Ma dropped him, his body splashing against the plants. She couldn't tell his body from the mud anymore. She wanted to smack some sense into him but held back due to the love she once held. She heard movement above her, like the leaves were alive and breathing.

"We all growing now. All us earthy spirits. We grow and grow. Grow so big you can't hold us in anymore."

And she saw him, saw him pull the mud from the ground and pack it onto his body. Made him grow bigger, wider, taller. She trapped her breath into her lungs. She wondered if she had any magic back in the house she could use. If Pa could catch another ellefolk they could drain for power.

She took a step back. The trees above her moved, alive with faces and eyes peering out from behind the thin fingers of branches and leaves. "The ellefolk," she said in a half whisper, "Are you messing with those demons? I warned you. They are full of lies. They will corrupt you and destroy us. Everything they touch decays."

He pulled more mud onto his body. "They helped me see what you and Pa are. Nothing but leeches. Nothing but people who build but without responsibility to what they create. You made me. But you use me as a tool. You made those gods, and you discarded them like old toys. How many others have you built and left without you? Without your love or life that sustains them?"

She could not speak. She had no magic, no way of holding him in. He was tall now, much taller than her. She wanted to run, but was frozen in her spot. She heard the ellefolk laughing at her from the trees.

"Go back in the house Ma. Go upstairs, get into bed with Pa. Sleep, rest well for tonight. Tomorrow, you work for me."

He towered over her, his head crowned by the moon. She took one look at him, at the ellefolk as they crawled through the trees, and ran inside. She did not look to see if he followed. She did not want him to follow. She hoped that she would never ever see him again.

The next day Ma and Pa where chained to each other by the neck. Their house was infested with ellefolk, the bodies crawling across wall and ceiling and floor, their eyes peeking out from behind cupboards and paintings. Pa's blood was boiling, but he said no word. They had gotten themselves in this trouble, he was certain they'd be getting out.

Vadie had taken root in the kitchen, making it his own personal office and sanctuary. Daily he grew, packing himself with mud and using borrowed magic from the ellefolk to keep himself together. There he would sit with his counsel of ellefolk and the gods he had dug up from the garden, discussing treachery in the lying tongue of magical creatures.

All over the walls were maps decorated with orange and black knives. All over the floors were ivy and tree roots, breaking up the floor boards and crawling over the furniture. Ma was forced to make him food and tend to the garden he had claimed as his own. Pa was forced to pray to the gods and wait on the ellefolk every second, giving all his strength to those he had drained of their very life essence.

At night Ma and Pa planned and plotted. They used a language they invented. It had no words, and talked using a combination of finger movements and rapping on the floor. They wanted to keep their conversations secret, keep them safe from prying eyes and ears.

They hated their servitude. And each day their hatred for their own son grew and grew. It was easy to hate him—the way he beat and burned them. He wasn't even a real boy—he was just some soulless mound of clay, sculpted to look human.

And now he didn't even look human. He towered in size, his packed mud skin sliding from his body with each movement. Twigs and leaves poked out from his shoulders and knees. When he talked you could see a nest of insects hiding in his throat and in his intestines.

He had transformed himself into a mockery of humanity, and that made it all the easier for his creators to want to destroy him.

Ma crept down to the kitchen. All around her slept the ellefolk, their bodies on the ceiling and floors, curled up into nooks and under the table. At the foot of the kitchen table she saw Vadie asleep, sitting up. His clay eyes closed thumbprints. Pa crept behind her, dragging the aether pump slowly behind them, trying not to make a sound.

Each time they went past an ellefolk, Pa hooked up the pump and nozzles of the aether vacuum as silently as he could and turned the machine on, sucking magic out of each and every one of them. He did it carefully, so as not to wake the others.

Ma saw the clay gods, all arranged behind Vadie in a chaos of vines. They were cause of all the trouble. They fed Vadie lies, gave him promises they could not keep. She walked up, her fingers wrapping around a clay neck. Pa leaned behind, ready and eager for what was to happen.

A smash and the ground was covered in broken clay. Pa clapped his hands together and did a little jig, barely containing his joy. She picked up another and another, smearing the ground with god debris. Around her the ellefolk awoke, angry and drained of all their power.

Pa still did his jig, and Ma finished off the last of the gods, their whispers and promises dying out with each break of clay body. The ellefolk buzzed around them as Vadie woke up, looking at the ground in horror.

"What have you done? What have you foolish mortals done?"

Ma scoffed. "Something I should've done a long time ago. You best unchain us now and let us go free, or we'll destroy you as well."

Rage stung in the eyes of Vadie. "You have no power over me. You cannot unmake me. Nobody can! I am cursed to walk this world. Cursed to grow with the deep earth. You two get back to your room, now. And I will deal with you in the morning."

Ma laughed. "Oh, I can unmake you. I can take you from this world in a second. See all these powerless crea-tures? We've sucked them dry. Ain't nothing you can do about it either. Best just to own up and let us control you again."

Vadie glanced around the room. He saw the aether pump glowing with stolen magical power. Around them the weary ellefolk crawled back into wall and nook, exhausted and trying to hide. They had no magic to speak of, and didn't want to become slaves yet again. "Just destroy me. Destroy me. I am sick of living. Sick of not having a soul. Just do it already."

Ma grinned as Pa shook his toothless head. Pa opened up the back of the aether pump and pulled out some magic. It glowed liquid blue, moving along his fist like a living thing. "No, no. Not that easy my boy. Not after all the damage you done. Not that easy at all."

Vadie backed up against the wall. He looked towards the ellefolk, a pleading looking in his eyes. "You have to lend me your strength," he said to them, "We can stop them—stop them forever and do what we planned! We can destroy all the humans! Never have to worry again about being ensorcelled and drained of our own life."

They moved towards him, but they were too worn and frail to be able to do anything. Vadie screamed and smashed the dishes. He picked up a chair and threw it at Ma, hitting her square in the chest. She hit the ground with a cough, her ribs bruised but otherwise unharmed.

The magic was thrown on Vadie's face. He clutched his skin, the blue crawling over the caked mud and twigs. He thrashed about, trashing the table with his big stone fists. Moonlight sprung from the holes he'd punctured in the walls, coating the ellefolk with an eerie blue. "First," Ma said, "Your going to do is get small. Real small. None of this big giant shit."

She chanted under her breath, a low and murmuring chant. It sounded like the hum of butterfly wings in her lips, trapped and never able to escape. He shrunk as she chanted, getting smaller and smaller and smaller. Soon he was boy sized again. Helpless sized. She stopped her words mid chant. "And now, you're going to be trapped in that form. No more growing for you, boy."

The chant changed to a song, long and high. Like a bird being shot as it sang. Ma's arms danced in the air, the moonshadows stretching out far past their length as the ellefolk screamed and crawled up the walls. The blue of the magic danced on his form, creating seals that would keep him in that shape forever.

Pa laughed and spun around, spraying magic across the walls as Ma chanted. This time the chant was loud and booming, and her voice was that of a man. The walls shrunk and grew, the light spinning in circles. All along the skin of the ellefolk and Vadie imprinted mystical seals, cages of supernatural power.

Ma snorted when she was done and stood up. Her ribs still hurt some, but she could ignore it when she had to. The pain would be gone in a day or two, so not much damage there. Pa laughed and patted the side of the aether pump. "Ma," he said, "I think we're going to be stocked up on magic for quite a long time."

She smiled and nodded. "And we'll have enough servants to keep for at least a year. Don't any of you be getting wise ideas, not now or soon. You seen what happens when you get us mad. Just do as we say."

The ellefolk crawled and tried to flee, but they were trapped in the house, enchanted. Ma and Pa smiled. It was going to be a good year. A good year after all. Pa walked over to Vadie, pulling a key from the table. Pa unlocked his and Ma's chains and then stood over Vadie, the chain dangling to the ground from his fist.

He snapped it around Vadie's neck. Vadie looked up, his face remorseful and full of fright. He whimpered as Pa beat him with the rest of the chain. The moon glinted off of Pa's eyes, making them look like lit holes in his skull. "You best listen to us boy. You have a lot of work to do."

He dragged the body up the stairs. Ma walked behind, looking at the ellefolk as she walked upstairs. Everything was right again, she thought. Everything makes sense once more.

Tim Lebbon lives in South Wales with his wife and two children. He has won two British Fantasy Awards, a Bram Stoker Award, a Shocker and a Tombstone Award, and has been a finalist for International Horror Guild and World Fantasy Awards. His novella White *is soon to be a major Hollywood movie, and several more novels and novellas are currently under development in the USA and the UK. Future publications include* Dawn, *two more fantasy novels, and two contemporary fantasy novels in collaboration with Christopher Golden, all for Bantam Spectra, as well as the novelization of the movie* 30 Days of Night *for Pocket Books. There are also more books due from Cemetery Dance, Night Shade and Necessary Evil Press, among others.*

Discovering Ghosts
Tim Lebbon

Worse than actually seeing a ghost is waiting for one to arrive. I can't remember where I heard or read that, but it's the sort of wisdom that sinks into your subconscious until the time comes when you need it, or when it can perhaps save your life. And when it *does* resurface, you spend a long time trying to work out whether there's actually any wisdom to it at all.

Waiting for one to arrive is painful, yes. But perhaps seeing a ghost is more to do with awareness than anything else. Putting things together. Understanding signs and sighs, inhaling shadows and sensing what you think they have to say. Because some shadows dance, and there's always doubt about whether or not the dance is in the dark, or merely an imperfection on the surface of the eyes.

The ghosts are always at the periphery; the eternal dilemma is, edge of sensation, or edge of understanding? After a long time considering this question, I'm starting to believe I really know the answer.

She died too young. I have no doubts about that. She had a whole lot more to give and live, and the cancer stole it away.

That makes me angry. And every time something happens in my life that I want to tell her about, she's not there, and that makes me angrier. By taking from her the cancer took from me as well; she lost her life, and I lost a big part of mine. Maybe that's selfish, but grief can sometimes be a very selfish thing.

Though I'm starting to think I can cheat it.

She hasn't gone as far as I thought.

We were walking in the woods when she told me, and the shadows were starting to dance.

"I've got cancer," she said.

I stopped, unable to walk on. Unable to *move*. If I did go forward I'd be allowing this horror to continue. Moving on was accepting, and I could not accept this, *would* not. "No," I whispered, barely managing even that.

"Yes," she said, and she smiled. It was a sad smile, but as ever it lit her up. "Where is it? Can they treat it? Are they sure?"

"In my breast. And I'm going for my first test tomorrow."

"Then maybe it's something else!" I said. Desperate even then, because I knew what her answer would be.

"I'm not stupid," she said. "I was a nurse long enough to know."

"Maybe it's nothing." I was clutching at straws that were all short, and trying not to cry.

She closed her eyes and lifted her face to the sun speckling in between the leaves. "I love it in here," she said. "Feels like home. Remember that letter I sent you?"

I nod. It had been a vivid expression of love for nature, poetic and moving. "So *did* you write it?" I asked. "Or was it a poem from a book?"

"I can't tell you that *now*," she said, and I realised how right she was. Revealing something that had been her secret for so many years—ever since I moved to live in the country—would be like settling things. And right then I didn't want her to settle anything, because everything had to go on.

———

I look for signs because I think we all do, believer or not. I had no time for God when I was younger, and have less now. But facing her body in the chapel of rest on the day she died—the first dead body I have ever seen—I'm reaching for something to hold onto.

I speak to her and touch her, startled by the coldness. It's unreal. She lies before me, looking more peaceful and free of pain than she has for weeks, and it's a cheat because she's not really here at all. I kiss her forehead and think of the bastard growths behind her eyes; they stole her sight, which meant that she could not read any more, and books were always one of her greatest loves. I have the last novel she managed to finish at home. I'll read it one day. Maybe.

"You can rest now," I say. "No more worries, no more pain." The strip-light above me flickers, just once. "Was that you?" I ask, smiling. "If it was do it again, I dare you." The light remains level, no flickers. Of course not. Discovering ghosts can never be that easy.

I have a very bad memory, and that terrifies me. There are so many good times that I just can't recall any more, and perhaps never will, and does that mean those times are lost forever? If I can't remember them—the smiles, the laughs, the shared moments—do they really matter now, and did they ever? Some say you're the sum of all you've experienced, but if you can hardly remember most of the good times do they affect you that much? I have to believe they do.

I recall the bad times well enough.

I remember her going quickly blind as secondaries behind her eyes put pressure on her optic nerves. I remember her spending more and more time in bed, popping aspirin to fight the growing pain in her hips and spine. Days later she would be on morphine.

I remember her lying in her bed and telling me she was dying, and those increasingly detailed conversations about the smallest of things which marked her fading weeks, days and hours.

She would tell me how she got up in the morning and made her way to the kitchen on her own to make a cup of tea. She walked past the pain, she said, because tea was so therapeutic, and it was always a cuppa and a cigarette that she craved upon waking. She would pull on her dressing gown, careful of the tube that was feeding her steady doses of morphine so that she didn't scream and cry and rage every single moment of the day. The door was always open and none of the furniture was moved, and she knew the bungalow so well that she could shuffle out to the kitchen by running one hand along the wall and feeling her way. *I see shapes*, she said, *and shades, but no detail.* She'd boil the kettle and pour the water into the cup that had been left ready for her, and she'd dip one finger in so that she knew when the cup was full. The first time she did this she burnt her finger. *Doesn't matter*, she said, *I've got nine more.*

That was the moment I realised we were facing a terrible countdown. *Nine fingers left*, I thought, *then eight, then seven . . . and when she's burnt them all making herself a five a.m. cup of tea, does she go back to the beginning and start again?*

Or will it all be over by then?

Each morning was a victory, and when someone bought her a device which sat on the lip of a cup and beeped when it was full, her fingers were saved. I was deliriously happy upon hearing that, because for a moment I thought the countdown had been halted.

So I remember the bad things, but of all the good things that went before there's very little. I can't recall one single conversation we had on our last holiday together. The barge floating away when we failed to tie it up properly, yes. Walking into Worcester for a bag of fish and chips. But I can't recollect a single word she said from that one glorious week.

What's rich and fresh is the memory of her pain and death. I'm not sure I can live with only that forever.

Details, all these details. When details are all you have, they take on such importance. She once talked to me for a long time about the way the small table next to her bed had to be arranged. Glass of squash here, tin of fruit jellies there, the small talking watch I'd bought her just so, and she reached out to show me how used to the arrangement she had become. She knocked over the drink, and the talking watch buzzed and clicked when it got wet.

She'd only been blind for a couple of weeks.

"I'll get used to it," she said, and I cried silently because I knew she never would. The countdown was always there, ticking away the life that should have lasted for so much longer.

Seven days after she died I hear her in the woods.

I am walking on my own, trying to remember times we spent in here together, listening to the rustle of old dead leaves underfoot and enjoying the spring signs of new buds forming on trees and bushes. *I've got cancer*, is all I remember her saying. I cross the brook and climb the short, steep hill to the ridge, sit on the fallen oak where we've sat and eaten a picnic so many times before, and those three words are all I can hear.

I sit for a while, unable to eat or cry. It's as I'm going back down the hill that I hear her voice in the distance. I'm not sure what she says, whether s he is singing or shouting, or even if she is happy or sad. I stop and hold my breath, letting it out slowly so that my thumping heart doesn't smother my hearing. Birds still sing in the canopy as though they have the woods to themselves. A squirrel darts up a tree and shivers a branch. I'm desperate to move closer to where her voice originated, but it seemed to come from everywhere.

Even though it's warm, a chill runs through me. She could be *anywhere*; moving away or coming close, and I cannot tell which. I *might* have heard her, but I have no idea what I'm looking for, or what I may see.

I stand that way for ten minutes. I don't hear her again. But I think back to the flickering strip light, and there in the woods is the first time I believe she is making her way back to me.

I took her to hospital for treatments, a dozen long journeys from home to Cheltenham General that have now all melded into one in my memory. It was a nice hospital, modern and clean and staffed with caring, wonderful people. I hated it. The first few trips she walked in on her own, holding my arm and keeping her head up, proud and determined and dignified as ever. We had to walk through the chemo-therapy waiting room to get to Radio-therapy, and I looked at all those poor dying people and felt a sick sense of relief that she appeared much better than them. It was selfish and uncaring, perhaps, but at the end of the day there are loved ones, and everyone else. It's the loved ones for whom you always wish the best.

I sat and read the paper to her some-times, and other times we just chatted.

On later visits I had to push her in in a wheelchair, and I saw other people looking at her and knew what they were thinking.

Seventeen days after she died I see her in the supermarket. I am there for my first proper shop since her death, and halfway round I'm in one of the chilled aisles looking at yoghurts when I see her at the end, browsing a selection of cheeses. She looks just like she always did before she was ill, and there's that familiar expression of vague dismay at such a wide selection. I don't see what she's wearing—I can't take that much in—but I blink slowly, and when I open my eyes again she's gone.

"Someone else," I say.

"Sorry?" A shop assistant hears me and thinks I'm asking for help.

"It's okay," I say. "I just saw someone else, that's all."

He nods, smiles awkwardly and moves away.

I hurry along the aisle, passing butter which I need, and sliced ham, and fruit smoothies that offer protection against various forms of cancer. At the cheese rack I pause and pick up a square of mature Cheddar. She loved that. Then I move on, swinging around into the next aisle and searching for her again.

She's not there, of course. There's not even anyone who looks like her. I frown and move on, but now I've lost any shred of enthusiasm I had for shopping. I gather food without really considering what I'm buying: frozen pizza, chips, ice cream, a bag of prawns when I don't even particularly like prawns. I'm just passing time now, and I look at everyone around me in case they suddenly change.

I glance behind more and more. Just like in the woods when I heard her voice, I have no idea exactly where she is. *And if she touches me on the shoulder, I think, or that woman in front of me turns*

around and smiles, and it's her...? I hurry along the final racks of CDs and DVDs and stand at the head of the central aisle, looking the length of the shop. I see two dozen people I don't know, and I wonder if any of them has bumped into her yet.

Trolley full, I approach the till farthest from the entrance and exit. I vaguely know the checkout girl from my village, and we pass the time of day as she clicks stuff through and I pack. I don't know her well enough to talk about my bereavement, and I anger myself by feeling annoyed that she isn't aware.

As I'm packing chilled meats I shiver and look up. I see her walking from the store. She looks around. We don't lock gazes—not quite—but she glances my way, seems not to recognise me, and I see a heartbreaking confusion in her expression.

She doesn't know where she is.

I run. The girl on the till calls me back, but she's not too concerned because I've left all my shopping with her. I ignore a couple of outstretched hands from other shop workers, dodge an old guy wheeling a trolley with wonky wheels, and when I reach the exit I skid to a halt.

The car park is a riot of colour, sound and movement. She's nowhere to be seen. She can't have gone far so I start looking in cars, but after the third angry stare I realise what I'm doing.

I go to sit on a bench and lean forward, holding my head in my hands. The tears come easily and I let them. I'm not embarrassed.

Nobody comes to help.

One time on our way to the hospital she said something that shocked me to the core.

I was driving through the forest, and as we climbed a hill and edged around a sharp bend a church appeared before us. It was beautiful, as churches go; I'd always regarded them as follies to faith, but that didn't mean I couldn't appreciate them as stunning examples of old architecture. I glanced at the church and the well-tended graveyard surrounding it, and she said, "You never realise how much someone loves you, or how much you love them, until a time like this."

"You *know* I love you," I said, shocked and a little upset. *Didn't* she know?

"Of course I do," she said, smiling. "But we all take it for granted. Now, here, I know it for sure."

She was speaking quite slowly by then, the morphine and anti-sickness drugs combining to make her speech slurred and difficult. But she concentrated hard to say this, and for a while she sounded like her old self again.

I glanced in my rear view mirror at the church standing there like some silent, patient hunter awaiting another victim to bury within its grounds. She wanted to be cremated. I smiled. *You won't get her.*

Later that same day, on the way home from the treatment and passing the church again, she told me I was a good man. I'm pretty sure no one had ever said that to me before.

I still feel both proud and sad when I think about that, and I hope one day she will tell me again.

Six weeks after she died she holds my hand while I'm crying in bed.

I've been remembering the moment when it all came clear and she stated what was happening. I knew anyway, of course; I'd know for some time. But I was sitting beside her as she lay in her sick bed, and she said "I'm dying," and it all hit home. She would never visit my house again, sit in my kitchen drinking tea, stand outside to smoke or lean from the window if it was raining. She would never *see* me again, not properly. Only in her mind's eye. "I'm dying," she said, "and I never thought I'd go like this."

I never told her, but I'd never thought that either. I'd *dreaded* it. And I'm thinking about that, lying on my bed listening to the next door neighbour's kids playing in their back garden, hearing cars passing on the nearby main road, people chatting in the street, somebody laughing, and don't they give a *damn*? Can't they acknowledge my grief and give me some peace?

But that's so selfish of me. Grief is very personal, and you can't know it unless you go through it yourself. It's a devious beast too, and no matter how much you *think* you understand, it'll always surprise you. It runs roughshod through your emotions like a wild dog. Sometimes it will let you think you're free of its bite, but then something—a look, a smell, the call of a bird or a note inside a book cover—will give it teeth once more.

Beside me on the bed lies the last book she read. I have just finished it.

The sun streams in my bedroom window, casting zebra patterns through the blinds. I can see the sky from where I'm lying, speckled with cheery, fluffy white clouds. It's pretty damn beautiful, and I know she'd love this weather if she were still alive. She hated the heat and blazing sun, and a cool spring day such as this was much more to her liking.

I close my eyes and feel the tears come, and I welcome them. Sometimes I think I haven't cried nearly enough. Everyone handles it differently, I'm told, but there's a lot of guilt in me. As time passes I'm coming to realise that it's unreasonable guilt, because I have no doubts at all about the complete love that I had—and still have—for her, and which she felt for me. She told me, after all.

Shadows dance across my closed eyes, and I think there must be a breeze moving the blinds.

My eyes burn, I sigh, and then she holds my hand.

Breath catches in my throat. I squeeze, and she squeezes back. I smile and the pressure increases again, and then finally I look.

Perhaps it's the sunlight refracted through my tears, but I'm sure I see the outline of a figure in light as it walks from the room.

———

A sense of humour is one of the hardiest attributes a person can have. She had plenty. Even dying—lying in her bed while that fucking cancer ate her away—she was ready to smile, and she laughed as much there as she ever had before.

Right at the beginning, just after she went blind and the pain from the secondaries in her ribs, spine and hips really started to kick in, the doctors put her on morphine. They tried tablets initially but soon moved on to a morphine driver, a device that gave constant doses of the stuff every twenty minutes or so. For those first few days she was hallucinating liberally.

I walked in the bedroom one morning and she burst out laughing, pointing at me with one hand while the other held the pain in her hip. "You look like Quasimodo!" she said.

"Thanks a million," I said, mock-disgruntled, but her laughter was genuine and infectious, and for a few moments I was completely happy. I didn't forget what was happening—I don't think that ever happened, not even when I was asleep—but there were times when a laugh or a smile could force it to the background.

The great thing was, most of the time she knew she was hallucinating. She didn't go strange with all the drugs they were pumping into her, but she did feel their effects, and doing so consciously meant that others could enjoy some of their side-effects too.

She saw a beautiful painting on her ceiling, a Michelangelo-like image of a huge foot cut off at the ankle. She pointed it out to me. "Amazing," she said. "Even though I know it's not there, I can still see it." I waved my hand in the air above her bed and she shook her head, laughed again, and said, "Nope, still there!"

There were many other visions. Dog's heads sprouting from the walls, bunting hanging above her bed, windows where there were no windows offering views that did not exist. I always asked her the details of these visions, fascinated by where they had come from and what had inspired them.

There were also some troubling hallucinations, and these mostly involved images of things that could be real. She woke up one morning certain that there were hundreds of newspapers strewn across the bedroom floor, and another time the bathroom was piled ceiling-high with dirty washing. She became upset and concerned, because she thought the rest of us weren't managing very well. We told her there was nothing there.

She saw dust and spiders' webs, peeling wallpaper and people wearing funny masks which she said sometimes didn't seem very funny at all. But the humorous visions mostly outweighed the bad ones.

One of the more disturbing hallucinations—for me I think, more than for her—was when she saw her dead mother standing in the bedroom doorway, listening intently as the nurse explained about some new drug they wanted to try. When she told me about this, she seemed very at ease with what she'd seen.

"And she stood just like she used to, shadows shifting around her, head to one side and lips pursed as she listened to the nurse. She had on one of her old smocks. She had a cigarette in her hand, but she never took a puff." She laughed. "That's the only part of it that didn't ring true."

Later that evening, sitting on my own with a bottle of wine and some unidentifiable trash on TV, I thought to myself, *She'll die tonight. She's seen her mother, dead these last fifteen years, and she'll die tonight.* I hoped she didn't. I wasn't quite sure what it would mean if she did, and that scared me a little.

I saw her the next morning, alive, and she proceeded to tell me about the limb she'd seen lying beside her on the bed. "It had a great big tattoo of a panther and its fingernails were long and grubby." I joked about midnight grave robbing and we laughed, but only a little. By then she needed help to get out of bed.

Strange, but we never talked that much about death. I wish we'd talked more. I never asked her if she was scared. And although she always put on a brave face, I believe now that was for me more than her. She didn't want to upset *me*. She didn't want *me* to be afraid.

She must have been frightened, and I'm a bastard for never asking. It's one of my greatest regrets; we only had a little time, and mostly we talked about inconsequentialities. Maybe if I had asked and we'd talked about it, I could have said something to give her some comfort. But it's too late now. She's died through that fear and out the other side to whatever may be there.

Sometimes I think there's nothing there at all, and that terrifies me because she can't just be gone.

Three months after she died, she told me everything was all right.

"Everything's all right," she says, and I turn around, certain that she will be there. She isn't—not yet—but I can still hear the final echoes of her voice.

I'm leaning on a farm gate, staring across a field and trying to remember all the good things. They still won't come to me. All I see is her in bed, all I hear is her steadily weakening voice as the disease takes hold and the drugs bleed away her strength.

"But I want you back," I say. "I miss you, and none of this is fair."

"Everything's all right," she says again, and it's like déjà vu—I want this to last forever. I see the dancing shadows across the field, and realise that I'm crying.

I say no more, afraid that if I ask a question I won't like the answer, or there will be no answer at all.

Everything's all right, I heard her say. How can that be? How can anything be all right ever again?

I walk home over the railway bridge and into the village, and I'm still stretching for memories. She walked this way once and something happened to her, something that made us laugh,

but I can't for the life of me recall what that was.

The closer I get to home, the more I convince myself that she is nearer than ever. Her ghost is coming to me, making itself known now and then in preparation for its true arrival.

I open my back door and expect to see her in the kitchen, but she isn't there. Neither is she in the living room, nor the dining room. There are photos of course, but looking at them makes her seem further away than ever.

I sit with one of her old books in my lap and a glass of whiskey in my hand, and as the alcohol take hold I start to cry again. It's been three months, and sometimes she feels like little more than a sad memory of someone I used to know. Other times—real times, like now—there's the blackest hole of loss at the centre of me, swallowing my thoughts and ideas and sucking away at my soul. I'm hopeless and helpless in its influence, and one day I know I'll just fade away.

Everything's all right, she said.

I pour another whiskey.

"I'm waiting for you," I say. I look from the window, hold out my hand and invite her in.

The night she died still feels like yesterday.

Two ambulance men pushed her from the bungalow in a wheelchair. Her head was lolling, her eyes virtually closed, and she groaned in pain. Her morphine doses were as high as they could be, and she'd spent the afternoon and early evening vomiting thick, putrid fluids, black and green. I burst into tears as they took her over the threshold, and my blurred vision made the shadows shift around her. At the time I was still fooling myself that she would return, but I think I knew deep down that she'd never be back.

"They'll see what they can do," her nurse said to me, holding my hand as I cried. "They'll work on her all night, find out what's causing this sudden turn, help her if they can. But if they can't they'll send her home to die." The nurse knew as well.

I went to the hospital and sat beside her on the ward. She was almost comatose, saying nothing, groaning and uttering an occasional mumble. At one point she reached out, eyes wide and panicked, and when I held her hands she pulled my hand to her lips and kissed it. That seemed to calm her. I had no idea what terrible nightmare she was having, but I hoped she was no longer scared.

Still fooling myself, still blind to the truth and denying the inevitable, I left her to go home for the night. I hugged and kissed her, and even through her delirium she managed to mutter "Bye . . . love you."

She died at three o'clock the following morning, just four hours after being taken into hospital. The phone rang and I sat up in bed, and there's only one reason for the phone to ring at that time of night. I answered and a voice said "She's gone". I sat there for a while, looking around the darkened bedroom and afraid to open the door and go

downstairs. Afraid of the whole new world out there.

Eventually I made it down into the kitchen—still not crying, still not really *knowing*—and stepped outside for a cigarette. The first thing I saw in the clear night sky was a single shining star, and I thought, *There she is*. Stupid, really.

Later that day, back in her house, back in her room, the paraphernalia of her illness looked so worn out and useless. The pill tray sat in the drawer beside her bed, that day's section forever full. There was a half-empty glass of water from which a straw had tipped out, speckling droplets across the tray. The speaking watch was silent. A hundred things belonged to someone no longer there, and it struck me with a sudden sense of hopelessness that the details had been for everyone else as well. Spending half an hour discussing the placement of a glass of juice was not just her way of getting past every hour, it was ours. Now that she was gone such details meant nothing. Her dying had kept us busy, and now I had a dreadful sense of the future being a vast, empty place.

Beside the tray on the small bedside table lay her CD player. She'd been listening to spoken word books since she'd gone blind, enjoying them, and we had chatted about each one at length. There was a disc still in the player, and when I turned it on I found it paused half way through. It didn't matter; I knew she'd read that book before.

Seven months after she died her ghost finally comes to me. It's completely unexpected, and strangely unremarkable. I'm sitting in my office at home, staring through the patio doors at the bird table, and then she is sitting in the easy chair before me, smiling her cheery smile and with me again.

And the memories flood back in. I open my mind and revel in them, relieved that I can at last think back to before that walk in the woods when she'd first told me about the cancer. Good times, fine times, they are personal and wonderful, and they make me laugh and cry. I go to write them down but then I realise that's not necessary; they're back, and I'll remember them forever.

I've known for a while that even some of the bad memories have their positive aspects. I think she did her very best to make them that way for everyone left behind.

The *really* bad memories are still there, of course, and they always will be. But they're soon outnumbered.

She never really came back. I never heard her, or saw her, or felt her squeeze my hand. Sometimes I wish I had, but she's with me now as much as she ever can be again. She's a vibrant memory, a sense of her carved from my grief like the most beautiful statue hacked, chipped and filed from a lump of innocuous marble. I can talk to her once again and tell her my news; I know when she'd be pleased. I can ask her advice; she doesn't reply, but I always know what she *would* have said. She's not a wandering soul, but the wondering of my own soul, more real than any wraith could be.

And like the Michelangelo foot on the ceiling above her bed, even though she's not really here I am always happy to see her. ⬧

ROBERT KOENIG · THE MERMAIDS

An isolated, struggling fishing village, inward-looking and increasingly dependent on the outside world for its survival.

And then at dawn, one early-summer morning, the fifteen-year-old Sarah Carr witnesses a group of mermaids—immediately that small, suspicious world is divided between those of its inhabitants desperate to regard this sighting as their salvation, as something to be advertised and exploited; and those who understand only too well the ridicule, pity and contempt this might equally swiftly bring down upon them.

For those few tumultuous, alarming days a natural balance is irretrievably lost, and the whole village, with the girl immovable and unflinching at its centre, struggles to regain that balance and to ensure that that which might secure and safeguard its future—the sighting of the mythical creatures themselves—does not now, ultimately, lead to its destruction from within.

The roots of this tale lie in a newspaper report that James Cooper stumbled upon which described the physical horror of the condition known as foetus in fetu. "I knew this in itself wasn't enough to drive a narrative," James tells us, "but I quickly realised it could be the perfect hook on which to hang a more involving story that dealt with the trauma such a condition might evoke in the parents. I wanted to explore the nuances of a relationship in crisis, triggered by the memory of a lost son, told from the point of view of a man struggling to come to terms with his new life. It's a pretty dark story that I hope will resonate long after the final paragraph has been read."

James lives in Nottinghamshire with his wife and son. His first novel, The Midway, is due soon from Crowswing Books. He has sold stories to many anthologies and magazines, including Cemetery Dance, Black Static, Hub, All Hallows, Red Scream, Midnight Street, Not One of Us, Cold Flesh and When Graveyards Yawn. His debut short story collection You Are The Fly: Tales of Redemption & Distress will be published later this year by Humdrumming Books. You can visit his website at www.jamescooper.org.uk.

In Fetu
James Cooper

From the moment my son came into the world, it was clear to everyone that something wasn't right. My wife, Kate, had to be cut in order to get him out and she was almost unconscious from the pain; she was being attended to, in blissful ignorance, by a senior nurse. For me, though, the horror was unavoidable. My son, whom I'd watched develop on the hospital monitor from a grainy black and white dot to something recognisably human, had come out all wrong, bearing a distended belly that cast a shadow over his face, as though God already regretted what he'd done. When I saw him for the first time, the proportions just didn't make any sense. His belly was the size of a football, and I could see that the midwife and the junior doctor were both as worried as I

was and had absolutely no idea what to do.

My son was weighed and I could see the electronic digits veering towards a number that couldn't possibly be right; I heard myself say: *14lbs? That's normal, right?* before one glance at the midwife confirmed what I already knew. This was monstrously wrong, and yet there was nothing I felt qualified to do. Even the medical staff seemed uncertain how to proceed.

I watched the child wriggle in the arms of the nurse and felt an overwhelming relief that at least he didn't appear to be in any pain. In every other respect, he seemed fine; his features were normal, his limbs, his eyes. He was perfect. It was just the bloated stomach that we all knew held some terrible truth.

265

I felt physically sick just looking at it, knowing that it differentiated my son in the worst possible way, but felt drawn to watch the glacial heaving as the boy tried to draw in a breath. I looked on helplessly as the nurse washed away the blood and felt my body go numb in the harsh light. I watched the thin membrane around his gut bulge outwards from some obscure internal pressure and was reminded of Kate's abdomen dilating in exactly the same way several weeks before. I raised a hand to my mouth, horrified, unable to process what was happening to my son, only aware that I had just seen the imprint of a perfectly-formed foot pressed up against the fragile window of his skin.

We named the child Peter after his grandfather, though we had few opportunities to call him by name. He spent the first few weeks in intensive care and we were only allowed to see him under close supervision, one of the nurses (Julie, I think—a pretty thing, very life-affirming) in discreet attendance at all times.

After several weeks of sustained testing, the consultant, Dr Hubbard, sat Kate and me down in his office and offered us a cup of tea.

He explained that Peter suffered with a rare abnormality known as *foetus in fetu*, which involves a foetus getting trapped inside its twin. It continues to survive as a parasite, often past birth, by forming an umbilical cord that leeches its twin's blood supply, until it grows so large it becomes harmful to the host.

At this point, Dr Hubbard paused and drew a bead of sweat from his brow. I remember that Kate and I had reached for each other's hand, but I have no recollection of what I was feeling as Dr Hubbard imparted the news. Strange, that; we had been waiting so long to be given some answers that, when they finally arrived, it just felt like another part of someone else's nightmare. It didn't feel relevant to me at all. Not this colourful horror story that Dr Hubbard had disclosed. How on earth could something so . . . *improbable* have any bearing on the reality we had forged for ourselves? Even the language Hubbard had used was absurd: *host*; *parasite*. Wasn't this the vocabulary of 1950s pulp magazines?

Apparently not. Dr Hubbard went on to explain that *foetus in fetu* was such a rare condition there were only 91 reported cases in the world. It happens very early in a twin pregnancy, he told us, when one foetus wraps around and envelops the other. The dominant foetus grows while the foetus that would have been its twin finds any way it can to survive. Usually, the parasitic foetus has no brain or internal organs, though they usually form underdeveloped features such as limbs, hair, nails and teeth.

At this point the doctor leant back in his chair and waited to gauge our response. What he was expecting I have no idea, but it seemed natural to me at this stage to simply play along, as though this was a rather fanciful episode of *Quincey* or *ER*, to which Kate and I had tuned in by mistake.

"Is it fatal?" I asked. I felt like giggling and I felt nauseous, and I knew if I carried this on I would be sick.

"We can perform an operation," Dr Hubbard said, smiling. "We can remove the foetus and Peter will be as good as new."

I deflated then and felt consumed by the terror I'd been trying so hard to resist. My hands were shaking and, somewhere in the distance, I could hear Kate crying, whispering Peter's name.

I tried to think clearly, but it was impossible, and I felt Dr Hubbard reach across the desk for my hand.

I let him take it and began to weep, trying to dislodge images of nails and teeth.

The operation went well and Peter was allowed home some eight weeks after the day he was born. He'd been given a clean bill of health by Dr Hubbard and, though he sported an appalling scar the length of his belly, he had adjusted well to life in his new home, though I know Kate and I occasionally found ourselves thinking about the unremembered shadow of his twin.

We tried to discuss what had happened over the last few months, but we found it increasingly difficult to negotiate the wreckage left in the wake of the birth. Our feelings couldn't be easily isolated, let alone expressed, and so we side-stepped the issue until we felt better equipped to explore them, though I think both of us sensed that, if it happened at all, it would never fully address the darkness we had shared.

I found myself wondering what Peter's twin might have been like, and I know Kate did the same, but we were unable to articulate anything other than the most banal sentiments, which in the blur of learning to be a parent was easily overlooked. Besides which, whenever my thoughts turned to the twin, I automatically pictured that protruding foot in my son's stomach and imagined baby teeth biting into skin.

As difficult as it was for me, I know it was even harder for Kate. She blamed herself, I think, for not being able to adequately protect her boys, for providing such a "hostile environment" in which to grow (another one of those gloriously insensitive phrases Dr Hubbard had uttered without even a thought).

I had worked hard at trying to ease her through the worst of it, but much of what I said had been in vain. I think I lacked conviction, because a part of me, a tiny, *dreadful* part of me, often wondered what more she could have done.

In more lucid moments I knew how dangerous this kind of thinking could be, but in the witching hour the mind has a habit of illuminating our darkest fear, and I would often wake up feeling cold and ashamed, punishing myself for wanting to be free.

To try and help the situation I suggested Kate visit a therapist, just to talk a few things out, but she seemed mortified that I'd even brought it up. Enough doctors, she said. We need to focus on becoming a family, just the three of us.

I tried to picture the twin, just as I did every time I thought of my son, and realised that Kate had made a mistake; at some unmarked point I could barely even define, we had become a family of four. The ghost of the other hovering just out of sight. Waiting for us to remember his name.

Peter continued to thrive, feeding well, sleeping intermittently and bonding easily with both Kate and me, despite the fact that we seemed to be growing further apart. If the baby picked up on our coldness, it certainly didn't show any signs of it, and was soon gurgling and laughing as a matter of course, bringing enough pleasure into our lives to keep us from having to contend with anything else. We were so preoccupied with Peter that any coolness that may have arisen between Kate and me was easily dismissed. After all, we could be forgiven for finding it difficult to come to terms with how our lives had changed; there were only 182 other people in the world who had a true idea of what we'd had to endure.

When Peter was asleep though, usually late at night, the chill that seeped into the house was not so easily ignored. Kate withdrew into a stillness that was almost obscene, where it became less and less easy to reach her, and I found myself leaving the house at ludicrous hours of the night to avoid sharing a room with the woman I loved.

One evening, after a particularly draining day at work, I came home to find Peter asleep in his crib and Kate hunched over a plant that she'd posi-

tioned in a darkened corner of the room. She was watering it and stroking the petals, muttering something under her breath. As I approached, she turned around and looked surprised to see me, as though my presence was an unexpected intrusion. She wedged herself between me and the plant.

I reached down for a kiss and felt like I was stealing a tiny part of her away.

"How's Peter been?" I asked, resting my bag on the floor.

"No trouble," she said, smiling. "A perfect angel."

We stood there for a moment, frozen by how awkward we'd become, and when I heard the plaintive ticking of the clock, I wondered how long it would be before the patchwork life we'd fashioned for ourselves crumbled apart, thread by resentful thread.

"I bought this today," she said, standing to one side, clearly shocked by how uncomfortable we had begun to feel in other's company. "It's called a *Linnaea borealis* and when I saw it I felt instantly at peace."

"Not like you to go shopping for plants," I said lightly, leaning in for a closer look.

The plant had a long green stem that split into a fork at the top. Dangling from the tip of each of the forked stems was a pink flower, the two heads bent over and pointing towards the earth, as though they were sorry for something they'd done. It was a hybrid, the likes of which I hadn't seen before, but just looking at it I could feel my hands and face grow numb. There was an aluminium tag wrapped around the stalk and I unfolded it and turned it to the light.

Linnaea borealis, it read. And directly underneath: *Twinflower. Classified as nationally scarce.*

It was hard to measure the deterioration in our relationship because we were both too preoccupied with other things. I was busy at work and Kate had her hands full with Peter, who now only slept if he could feel the warmth of his mother through the sheets.

Neither of us could account for why we were allowing ourselves to fall further and further apart, it simply became a natural consequence of how we chose to live, and I couldn't help wondering where on earth we would all end up. There were no late-night arguments, no violent altercations in the street, no accusations hurled across the hall. We just stopped talking, which was perhaps the hardest part of the process to accept. Had we blacked each other's eyes and bruised each other's ribs, we would have had something tangible to show for our pain. But this was different, more insidious, like a cancer we couldn't stop, and it was only a matter of time until something inside us died.

Although Kate treasured Peter and was a perfect mother in every possible regard, she had started to pay less attention to her own hygiene. She washed infrequently, which was utterly out of character, and the natural sweep of her hair had become a mess. I offered to brush it for her one evening, just because it looked so desperately neglected, but she declined without even looking me in the eye, claiming she had too much to do.

She shuffled from the room, clutching Peter to her breast, muttering those dreadful baby syllables, the echoes of which I was starting to hear in every room of the house. I tried not to be unduly affected by it, but the truth was, Kate spoke more to the damn baby than she did to me, whispering to it, coddling it, developing that all-important maternal bond in a language I was never destined to know.

She was brilliant with him, fine-tuning her skills as a parent with each passing day, and while she might have been guilty of neglecting certain aspects of her own daily routine, she was mindful of Peter's every random whim, to the point where I began to wonder if she might be protecting him too much. I could understand her concern, given the circumstances, but she wasn't allowing the poor little bugger to find its way in the world. What was it that Ferber guy had said? Let a baby cry itself to sleep? I couldn't recall an occasion where Peter had cried for more than *five* seconds before Kate had swept him into her arms.

I knew why she was doing it; of course I did. I just wasn't sure it was the healthy thing to do. When I tried to raise the issue, she just smiled and showed me how tired and confused she'd become.

"Do you want him to be unhappy?" she asked.

"Of course not. I just think he should learn to understand that we aren't always going to be there."

The tired smile again. "That isn't true," she said. "*I'll* always be there. How can anything come between a mother and her son?"

It hadn't escaped my notice that I had been all but eliminated from Kate's scenario, whether she had intended it or not, and I found myself bristling with an anger that had been repressed for too long.

"Kate, you have to step back and take a look at yourself. It's not healthy, sweetheart. Everything's falling apart."

It was at that moment that Peter began to cry and I placed a hand on Kate's trembling arm.

"Leave him," I said. "Let him feel what it's like to be alone."

She looked at me then, her green eyes dilating, and whatever connection we still had binding us to the present, I felt it crumble beneath the weight of the past.

She walked past me without uttering another word and within seconds the crying had stopped. I wanted to scream, but found that I didn't have the energy for it, so I moved to the couch and lay down. I tried not to think of Kate's hand warming the belly of my son.

There was a distinct chill between us after that, where the silences grew fatter and the nights became cold and black. I felt like I was living alongside my own family in a house I barely recognised any more, sneaking glances at my son as he reclined in his mother's arms, her warm breath soothing him to sleep.

It was during this cold spell that I began to wonder how we could ever realistically survive. I no longer knew what to expect when I arrived home from work and it was abundantly clear that, as far as Kate was concerned, I was nothing more than a poor choice she had once made in a previous life.

And then I discovered the photo, wedged behind the carriage clock on the mantelpiece like an unpaid bill. When I first pulled it out, I thought it was just another baby photo, one of hundreds we had taken to document the arrival of our son. But when I looked closer, I felt that all too familiar chill that had come to mark many of the darker moments I had experienced since Peter's birth.

The photograph was of the very room in which I stood, though it looked tidier in every respect, as though Kate had made a special effort before taking the snap. In the foreground was the sofa, and perched on the brown leather, like something from a fashion shoot, were two identically dressed babies, wearing blue jump-suits that didn't quite fit. Their eyes stared flatly into the lens of the camera, with no knowledge of the obscenity that was being captured on the film. One of the babies was clearly Peter, his fat cheeks still puffy with sleep, but I had no idea who the other child might be. I was appalled by how much he looked like Peter, though I had no doubt his parents would be sickened when they discov-

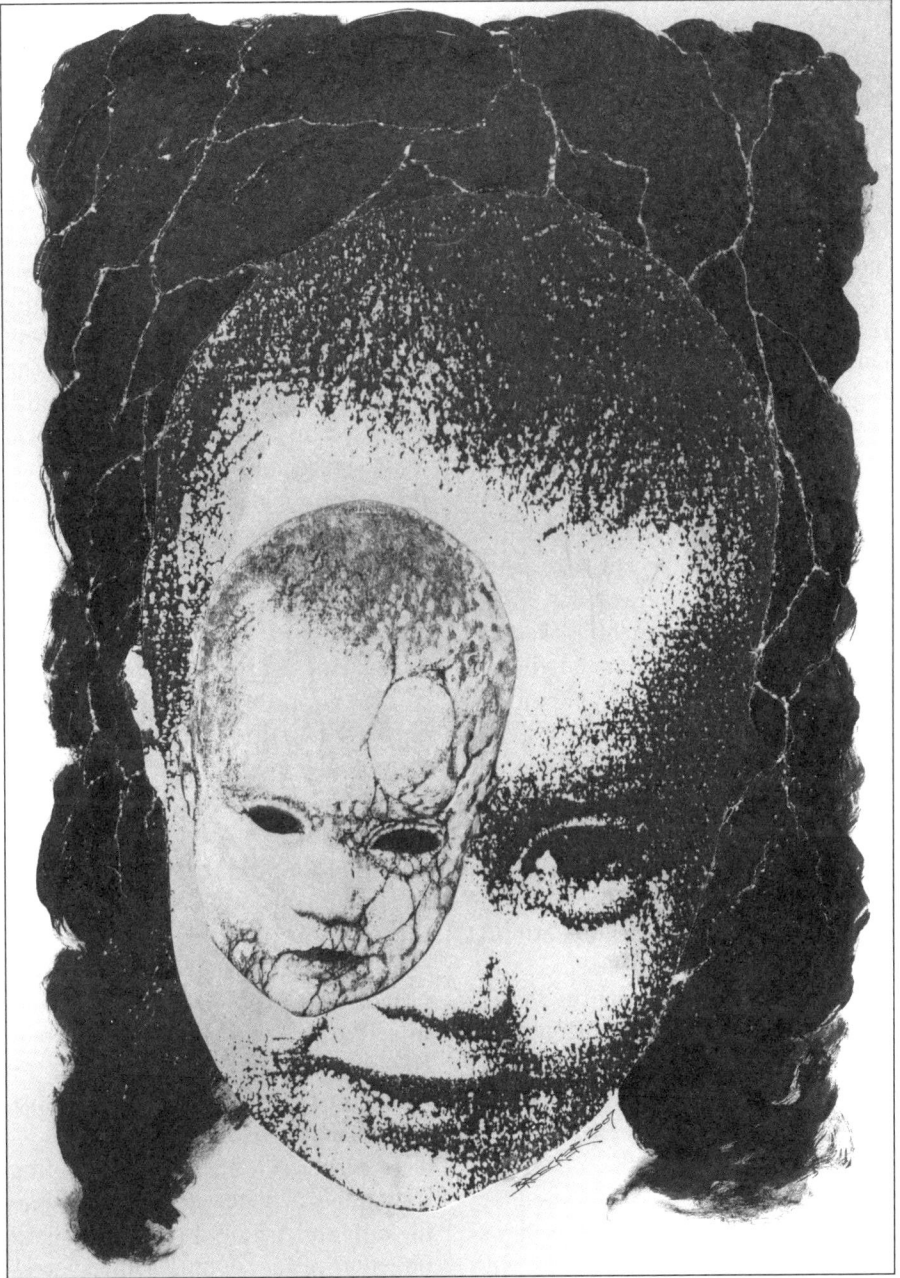

ered the tasteless games Kate had forced him to play. The poor little mite even had Peter's indulgent smile, as though he had been caught daydreaming about something no one but he could understand. It was only when I looked at the image more closely, staring into those steely blue eyes, that I realised just how troubled things had become. Kate hadn't used a real baby in the photograph; she had used a doll, dressing the thing up so that it looked like a perfect mirror image of our son.

I stared hard, wondering how I could possibly have been fooled by that first glance, and had to accept that, wherever she had found the damn thing, there was no denying that it looked like a real kid. Hadn't we commented on it often enough in the past, how companies passed off increasingly realistic plastic babies as a Christmas diversion for young girls? Hadn't we laughed at how terrifyingly *real* they were? Hadn't we laughed and pretended not to care as we secretly imagined, like everyone else, how perversely such a product might be used?

I felt sick to my stomach and let the photograph fall to the floor, determined not to be made a fool of again. Whatever wire was misfiring in Kate's head, it had gone far enough. She needed to be confronted with the truth.

I ran up the stairs and heard her whispering to Peter in his crib. It was too much; my hands felt waxy with sweat. I would find the doll and force her to look it in the eye.

If the doll was still in the house, I had a good idea where it would have been stored: at the back of Kate's wardrobe, where she customarily hid my gifts.

I charged into the bedroom and pulled open the wooden door of the closet, revealing the suspended skins of Kate's previous life, when clothes had been an important part of who she was. I reached into the darkness, batting aside loose fabric, and allowed my fingers to trace the contours of the wood. Within seconds I prodded something soft and pliant that reminded me of Peter's beautiful new belly, something that yielded almost instantly to the touch. It had been wrapped in a sheet, and when I pulled it out and unmasked it, I discovered I was staring into the innocent glass eyes of the doll.

My hands started to shake, more out of relief, I think, that it *had* actually been a doll in the picture, and the more I shook, the more I imagined the thing laughing at me as it jostled up and down in the sweat of my trembling palms. It was disgustingly life-like, the skin buoyant with artificial colour, and I threw the monstrosity on the bed, tempted to tear the thing apart with my bare hands.

I took a deep breath and reminded myself to stay calm. Kate still had to be challenged and I needed to be in the right frame of mind to make her realise how toxic the situation had become.

I could still hear her mumbling something to Peter as the child lay in his crib and I moved stealthily in the direction of his room. I had no intention of upsetting the boy; he had done nothing to deserve any of this. He was as innocent now as he'd always been, though a small voice inside me, a voice whose honesty and candour I despised, began to wonder if such a thing could be true.

There was no time to ponder the matter now; it was an issue for another day, that would no doubt plague me in the weeks and months to come.

I stepped into Peter's room and held my breath. Kate had removed the boy's pyjamas and had her lips pressed up against the scar on his chest. She was muttering something barely audible into the swollen cicatrice on Peter's belly, the heat of her words vibrating against the wall of puckered skin.

I watched in disbelief, trying to discern what nonsense she was confessing to the scar. Had Peter gained weight since last I'd looked, or was it my imagination, exaggerating every single aspect of the moment, impeding rational thought? I could feel myself slipping into a mindset that could easily derail me, and I had to consciously drag myself back from the darkness that was pervading the room.

"Kate," I said, trying to maintain a level tone. "I'd like a word in the bedroom."

I turned and walked away before she could reply, hoping that she'd sense the urgency in my voice and quickly return Peter to his crib.

When she entered our bedroom, I was clutching the doll in my hands, determined to regain control.

"What the hell's going on?" I asked, finding it hard to keep my emotion in check.

She looked puzzled. "I bought a doll for Peter," she said. "But it frightened him a little, so I stashed it away till he's older."

She reached out a hand to take it from me, but I pulled the doll away before she could claim it. She looked perfectly calm, if a little dishevelled, and I wondered if I might have made a mistake. It was only a doll, after all; an ordinary, run-of-the-mill toy.

"What about the picture?" I said. "What the devil were you thinking, dressing them up to look the same?"

"I thought it might be cute," she said, smiling. "Peter and I get up to all kinds of silliness during the day."

I felt confused. Was it that simple? Had she merely been occupying the time during the hollows of those dull afternoons?

I could feel a nascent migraine coming on and my body was slick with sweat. I desperately wanted to believe her, but when I watched the calculated movement of her face I thought I saw something cold inhabiting her eyes.

"Can I go now?" she asked, sending the doll back into hiding behind her clothes.

I nodded and watched her coolly retreat from the room.

I sat on the edge of the bed and held my head in my hands, amazed by how heavy it felt. There was stuff in there that I couldn't dislodge, no matter how hard I tried, and I wondered if it had thrown me off course.

I picked myself up and moved to the top of the stairs, peering into Peter's bedroom as I walked past. There was a slice of moonlight triangulating the floor and I saw a pale shadow scuttle across the carpet, edging towards the baby's crib.

I felt a chill pass through my body and moved cautiously into the room, trying to convince myself that the thing I'd just seen didn't have an arm and teeth and hair.

Peter's chest rose slightly as he breathed and I felt a little of the panic recede. There was a Winnie the Pooh mobile above the crib, still rotating in the moonlight, and I knew implicitly that what I had seen had been the shadow of one of the animals on the floor.

I placed a hand on his chest and felt the reassuring warmth of his heart ticking peacefully inside. I pulled open his pyjamas and stared hard at the scar; watched it buckle as though something had burrowed underneath, revealing the bulge of an outstretched palm, indelicately cast in the skin.

𝕂

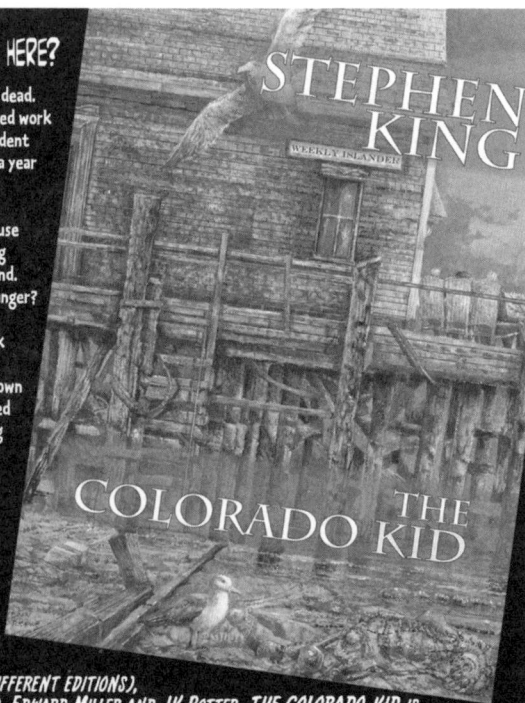

"The Last Testament Of Seamus Todd, Soldier Of The Queen", features in Graham Joyce's novel-in-progress about demons, and when he offered it to us for this special edition of Post-scripts we jumped at it. "It seemed to me to work as a stand-alone story and is actually a complete 'manuscript' composed by Todd and handed to the main protagonist of the novel before the soldier suffers his fate," Graham says. "I couldn't think of anyone less likely to be troubled by the 'nonsense' of ghost and demons than Todd, whose British army training and motto of Form Up, Move Out, Press On would equip him more than anyone to shrug off any kind of psychic disturbance."

The Last Testament Of Seamus Todd, Soldier Of The Queen

Graham Joyce

This is the last will and testament of me, I, Seamus Todd, ordinary soldier of the queen and very little else is my guess. Not that there is anything to laugh about in the way of *will* and that leaves only the *testament*. But which is honest, true, factual and everything I have seen with my own eyes. If I haven't seen it with my own eyes, or if I maybe just thought it or heard it said second-hand by another soldier or anyone else, then I have left it out. There's more than enough cheap talk and I don't want to add to it.

I done my twenty-two. Born in 1955 I joined the army at eighteen. Then the last couple of years haven't been so good, but I'm not complaining, that being my own fault and the few thousand pound give me by the army when I was discharged I have not used wisely.

This is my own slip-up and I don't like a moaner. Never have.

I don't have much to say about my time before the army but most of it weren't good. I never knew my father and my mother, bless her, was a bit simple. I can say that, she being my own Mum, though if another soldier were to say the same I would easily break his back. Even before I enlisted I heard things said about her and I always paid back the badmouth. All I know regarding my father was that he was a soldier. I don't know what regiment. The thing that steered me to the army was when one badmouth did say my father was not a soldier but an entire barracks. I paid back the badmouth for that, too, but I was touched by the Law for it. It was my probation officer at the time brought up the question of the military and I went sharpish to the recruitment office in Halford Street and the army saved me and squared me with my PO.

Though she died from a fall after drinking in 1988, I still won't have things said about my mother. I was given compassionate leave from serving in Belfast to come back for her funeral. I had a sister somewhere but she never even turned up. There was some talk of a half-brother, but if there was one, I never met him. The army was my family, and after the cremation of dear old Mum I went straight back and signed on for another seven.

I started off as a private in the Staffordshire Regiment and I worked my way up to Colour Sergeant. Three tours of duty in Northern Ireland and then joined the landing assault as a battle casualty replacement in the Falklands. I was already well seasoned when the Gulf War came along in '91. Most of my squaddies were little pink-nosed boys of eighteen or twenty-one. I was their big angry Daddy, and I looked after every one of them. They all said I was hard but fair. What else do you want? I stand by that. I looked after my boys. They knew it. I told them "loyalty and a sense of humour" is what I want, "but you can fuck the sense of humour" and it always got a laugh. I don't know why. Well, you're not laughing when you're under fire.

I had the tip of one finger shot off in South Armagh bandit country on patrol, while another soldier was telling me a joke about three nuns out picking mushrooms. Wedding finger, left hand. Lucky for me the IRA sniper was a shitty shot. Also broke my leg in the

Falklands, but this was in a game of football after we'd taken the islands back from the Argies. Slipped on sheep shit. That's the only injuries to report out of all my combat experience.

When the Gulf War kicked off it was just another posting, except that now I was looking after all my little lads, and it was my job to tell them how normal everything was. You know: war is normal.

And it is normal. That's why it's a paid job. You don't ask: why are we in the Gulf? Why are we in Ireland? Why are we in some sheep-shit South Atlantic island that no-one's ever heard of? You don't argue with the Queen. You form up. Move out. Press on.

And in January of '91 I came to be in the desert as a member of the coalition forces lined up against Saddam Hussein's Iraqi cohorts to drive them out of Kuwait. According to Saddam it was going to be "the mother of all wars" and him saying that put the wind up everyone. But that's not how it turned out.

We knew we were going long before Christmas. They haven't told you but you hear the drum. I can't explain. You're on active duty and there's a drum beat, an echo, maybe it's your own heart beating very quiet, and it thuds on until something happens or until you're stood down. Hear the beat, get the order. Form up. Move out. Press on.

With the heavy armour already at sea we were to be airlifted after Christmas so I was able to tell my boys: go shag your girlfriend and kiss your wife and get ready to go. It's what I always said and it always got a laugh. But the family men, those of them with little sprats in the homestead, there was always a quick switch off behind the light in their eyes. Yeh, better get the lad that new bike this year. Yeh, better get that little gal a big teddy bear.

But I didn't have that to think about, and no family to make Christmas with. Preferred my own company. Nuke a leg of turkey, pull in a crate of brown ale, feet up, watch the telly. I did get invites, I did. One or two of the lads would have me come and sit down to Christmas dinner with them and theirs. Poor old fucker's got nowhere to go type of thing. Nah, didn't want it. Only makes the evening darker when you had to get up and leave.

So Christmas day I'm feet up and supping beer from the bottle in my Mess watching the Queen's speech. Outside is definitely not a White Christmas. It's lashing it down with rain. I'm listening to her talking about looking back to the past and wondering if she's going to mention us lot off to the Gulf, and I don't know if she does or she doesn't because I fall asleep in my chair.

I'm woken by this tiny tapping. At first I think it's someone beating on the window with a coin or something, but I can't see anything. My empty bottle has fallen to the floor and the Queen has long finished. Some comedy programme is gagging away on the telly and I hear the tapping again but it's coming from the door. Well the upper half of my door is frosted glass so if anyone's jogged over to wish me a happy christmas I would see their shape through the glass and get ready to

thump them. But there's that sound again: a tinny little rapid tap tap tap.

I knuckle my eyes, get to my feet and open the door. But there's no-one there. Or at least no person there. Because I look down and I see what's making the noise. It's a crow. He's been tapping on the door with his beak, see.

I don't know why but it makes my skin flush to see this crow there, black as you like. His feathers are a mess. He's dishevelled by the rain. Then he lifts up his head and looks me right in the eye.

—What the fuck are you doing there? I say to him, out loud. What's goin' on then?

And he shits on my doorstep and hops over my foot, and inside.

It's a big crow. A very big crow. I'm standing there with the door held open, not knowing what to do. I want to leave the door open for it, but it's perishing outside and all the warmth from my gas fire is escaping. So I shut the door.

—That's sorted you, ain't it? Now what you gonna do?

Crow hops a bit further in. I'm scratching me head. Don't want a live bird in there for the rest of the day. The crow makes some clicking noises at me. Then it hops over to the telly.

Now my telly is already a beat up thing and the on-off switch is hanging out of the front panel by its wiring. Well maybe the crow thinks one of these exposed wires is a worm, because it goes for it, grabs a thin cable in its beak and it pulls; and then there's an almighty bang and smoke and sparks from the telly.

And I'm in my chair.

That's right, I'm back in my chair. The telly has blown up. There's no crow. Nowhere. Dreaming, haven't I? Dreaming.

Only one thing. *Only one thing, my son.* The door, though not open, is ajar. And there's that little worm of birdshit, just past the threshold. And you know what? That's two things.

I never told anyone this. I've written it down here in my will and testament, that's all. Because I stopped thinking about it, what happened on that Christmas Day. You can let a thing like that play on your mind. If you're weak. And if you're off to war, and you've got boys to look after, you don't want that shit playing on your mind and jogging your elbow. You don't want it.

I pushed it to the back of my mind. Anyway the drum was beating. Form up. Move out. Press on. Within a few days the tinsel and the Christmas cards and the Brazil nuts were all just another check-box on last year's calendar and we were in the Saudi desert.

Now the desert held no fear for me, but it wasn't the kind of fighting I was used to. Street to street, house to house, urban shadows that's me, and that's where I learned my Ps and Qs in Ireland; and that education served me well in Bosnia when I was the blue hat; or before that even your coarse terrain, yomping over the bog-fields of the Falkland Islands. Give me rough cover, half a shadow, I'm your man. But the flat trackless desert: not my arena.

Tanks for the desert is the thing. Line up your tanks. Get your air power to fuck over as many of the enemy's tanks as you can before you roll him up. It ain't complicated. But then when you do hit a settlement or defensive position you've got to have your infantry—me—keeping pace with the tanks in armoured Warriors, so's we can dismount and engage at the battle line, mopping up with bullet, grenade and bayonet. That's me. See that bayonet? Don't get to use it very often but I do love to keep it shiny and sharp. That's where I'm happy.

But this was mostly going to be settled by the tanks, not by a bayonet's length. And for the first time since World War One there was serious threat of gas and chemicals. We drilled and drilled and drilled, fixing those spooky chemical hoods in place. Stinking. Hear yourself heavy breathing. All your buddies bug-eyed, trying to see your face behind the mask. Get your jabs at the ready. That's not fighting. But you got to do it.

And it's the fucking boredom of it that can get to you.

We'd finished up the drill one evening and I was standing, dripping with sweat and getting my breath back from bellowing at the lads from behind the mask. The lads were dismissed and I was standing with my hands on my hips looking out at the sky over the flat desert sands.

—What you looking at Colour-Colour-Sar'nt? This was a lad called Dorky. Good lad but wouldn't shut up. Used to keep following me round like a little dog. Always asking questions. —What's this? What's that? —Come 'ere Dorky. Look out there. What d'you see?

—Nothing, Colour-Sar'nt. Nothin' there. Desert, only desert Colour-Sar'nt.

—Look again, son.

—Can't see anything. Nuffink.

—Look at that sky. You ever seen a sky that colour?

—No, Sar'nt.

—Not Sar'nt, Colour-Sar'nt you little toe-rag. What colour is it, Dorky?

—Pink, Colour-Sar'nt.

—It ain't pink you muppet. Look again.

A few of the other lads trudge by, clutching their sweaty chemical masks, wanting to know what we're looking at.

—Dorky says it's nothing, I says to 'em. Then he says it's pink, but I says it ain't pink. What colour is that sky?

—Lavender, says Chad, a black-country kid. Innit.

—No, ti'nt lavender, says Brewster, a Liverpool scally, good lad in a fight. Ti'nt lavender.

Next thing there's seven or eight lads looking into that nothing, trying to decide what colour that nothing is. The truth is I don't know what colour it is. It's the most beautiful sky I ever seen in my life and I don't know what colour to say.

—See that sky lads? That's why you joined the army. It ain't just to have it out with the Iraqis. It's so you'll see miraculous things. Like that sky.

And I walk away; leaving them scratching their heads. They don't

know if I'm taking the piss. Truth: I don't know either. Though I do remember thinking: look at the sky now lads, cos it's gonna get dark.

Waiting, drilling, waiting, drilling. Saddam has used gas against the Iranians and the Kurds and the marsh Arabs, so we're expecting him to fling a pot of gas in our faces. Real Soon Now, as they say. But it doesn't come. There are a few more sunsets while the air assault makes softening-up runs over the Iraqis occupying Kuwait. It turns out the enemy has no decent air assault to answer with and I'm already thinking this might be a short war.

Where is their air assault? Where is their artillery, lobbing gas and chemicals at us? This is supposed to be the biggest army in the Middle-East. What are they doing? Lying in their trenches and sharpening their swords? The waiting is getting our boys nervous. There's only so many times you can tell 'em to look at a pink sky. Lavender.

The serious aerial bombing starts in the middle of January and while that goes on we just have to train and wait. There are a few duels with the artillery but the only attackers are helicopters. The MLRS units are pumping out rockets and with these little bug things—unmanned RPVs—whining in the sky to send co-ordinates back to our computers so we can throw still more rockets I start to think: that's it mate. Your type of soldier is redundant, get cashiered, hang your boots up. See— there's nothing coming back. One sided war if they don't have the technology. Then at the end of January the Iraqis start to stir and they move across the Kuwait border and into Khafji. That don't last long. We're getting rumours that the Iraqi prisoners picked up in Khafji have no stomach for the fight.

By the third week of February the Iraqi divisions have all their supply lines across the Euphrates river bombed to fuck and they are low on food and water. Huge numbers of their tanks and artillery have been smashed. And we're still practising with masks and watching sunsets. It's all good news for us. The ground offensive might be easier than we first thought. But I don't like it. Not war, is it?

I never like it when it's too easy. If it's too easy, it ain't worth it. Ever.

Nobody is more relieved than me when they tell us we're on. Hear that drum? I don't have to be told. I've been listening to our artillery increase its bombardment every day. No-one has to tell me. We're going up the Wadi el Batine and then swing right into Kuwait city and even though my lads are looking a bit sick except for Brewster who is well up for it I'm laughing and singing *Wadi, wadi, we're going up the wadi* and my boys are going: *you're cracked Colour Sergeant you are.*

Not cracked. It's just that when I know that I'm doing what I'm supposed to be doing, that's when I'm happiest. Form up. Move out. Press on. 24th of February 1991 and the British 1st Armoured of which we are a part is rolling. Hear the noise of war engines. And guess what? It's overcast, cold and raining. British weather, in the desert. Staffs ride in the hull of Warriors, just

behind the tanks and even though the deserts are trackless we move, we bounce and we move.

I'm disappointed not to be part of the first wave. Yank marine forces have gone under cover of darkness to make paths through the minefields and barriers and first layers of Iraqi defensive positions. After sunrise I begin to hear the gun reports of tank engagement. What I don't know is that the Yanks and the French have struck north to slam the back door on the Iraqis. The enemy have no air reconnaissance by now so can't have known this. No reinforcements and no way out. They've been popped in the oven and we're just about to turn it up to Mark 200. How d'you like your turkey cooked?

It isn't until later in the first day that we swing back eastwards to engage Iraqi armoured troops around the Kuwait border. I have the strange feeling that the war is already over after the first day because we just keep going. Black puffs of smoke drift across the sands and the crump of engagement ahead isn't getting any nearer. We stop to mop up a few emplacements, but beside a few rounds fired off the resistance is feeble. We pick up a few of their troops—conscripts, kids trying to smile at us—and they are all passed back down the line as prisoners of war.

There is no conflict. We can't find it. Just deeper into the desert and thick black smoke billowing around, and a weird stench. I keep thinking: I can see the smoke, I can hear the guns, but where's the war?

We roll on for hours, past burned-out shells of tanks and beetled ar-moured vehicles, all Iraqi. Flame is still licking from some of the gun turrets, smoke is winding from the guts of engines. Metal is buckled and bent. Vehicles are lodged in the sand, cater-pillar wheels buried deep, and dust cov-ers them like they've been there for years. It all has the feel of a battle long over. The only thing that makes you certain it's recent is the occasional burned corpses of soldiers flung from a bombed vehicle. Or half a corpse still in a vehicle, like the bit of the sardine you can't get out of the corner of a sardine can. We put rounds into every burning tank we pass anyway, either with the 30mm Rarden cannon or we strafe them with the chain gun. Just to be sure. Well, not even that; more out of frustration of having nothing to shoot at.

Doesn't look much like there's going to be any kind of role for us boys. Not that I'm hungry for it, like some of the kids looking for action. I'll do it if it's there to be done, but I've learned enough about the book-keeping of war. You don't want to get yourself in the red column just by staying too long.

I'm in the turret with the driver. Weird phosphorescent flashes keep popping from miles up ahead, and they're followed by what I want to call a flutter; it's like your eye goes a-quiver for a moment. And there's a smell in the air, nothing like the usual reek of burn-ing and high-ex. And I don't like it. When it comes to combat I don't much like anything I haven't seen before.

Anyway I'm just thinking we're not going to see much action, and that this war is far off the radar when we come under fire. Mortar and small arms.

—Rag-heads, 'bout five hundred metres, quarter left, goes my driver Cummings, a snippy little hard-case Bristolian with shit tattoos all over his neck.

—Shove in that dip, quarter right.

There's a dune we try to snuggle in behind. Our vehicle stops dead in the sand and the engines power down. I drag my knuckles across the side of Cummings' head.

—Do not repeat do not let me hear you refer to the enemy as rag-heads towel-heads sand-niggers or any other fucking thing other than the fucking enemy, right Cummings? Right?

—Colour-Sar'nt!

They should know that by now. I won't have it. Not in the middle of combat. Down the pub, in the mess or in the whorehouse you can call 'em what the fuck you like. But not here. Won't have it.

—Why not? I ask him. Why fucking not?

Another mortar falls and there are a couple of pings as bullets strike our AV. The boys in the back think I'm mad. We're under fire and I'm giving them parade ground drill. But I know the mortars are well short and the bullets are spent when they hit the sides of the Warrior. —Come on! Let's hear it!

—Underestimation of enemy Col-our-Sar'nt, says Brewster at the top of the class.

He's going to say more but I cut him off. —Under-fucking-estimation of enemy! I don't know what we've got here but sitting just behind them is the National Republican Guard. More fucking highly educated than you are, Cummings. Crack fucking soldiers, you cunt. Loyal to Saddam. They are not towel heads rag-heads or sand-niggers, they are the fucking enemy and you will respect their capacity to blow your fucking balls off, right Cummings?

—Colour-Sar'nt! goes Cummings, red in the face. Another round of bullets ping the Warrior.

That's enough of that. All the lads in the back are looking at me, so I swing down and give 'em a nice big smile, like really I'm just lemonade. —Good lads. Now then, what we got?

Turns out there is a little emplacement dug into the sand, still active behind our front lines and this is just what we're here for. Clean up. Mrs Overalls. Get the marigold gloves on, out with the bleach and polish, make the world shine. Our infra-red should be able to tell us how many bodies they have dug in but it's on the fucking blink which is normal. All this gear works fine until you need it to run with sand in it; though I suspect these phosphorescent flashes might have something to do with the malfunction. Doesn't matter. Our AV is well equipped to take the enemy out.

The terrain suits us. There's a slight rise on our eastern flank so I can get a couple of lads out there to attack the position while we give covering fire with the cannon. Brewster and Dorky volunteer, as do one or two others. I give them the nod, and then for some reason—I don't know why—I decide I'll go and hold their hands. It's not that they need me. There's just stuff bothering me. Can't put my finger on it all.

I order the driver to power up and move on fifty yards to fire a couple of white phos grenades to make a smoke-screen so's we can drop out and flit over to get behind the rise, hopefully unnoticed. When we reach the rise we can see a burned out Iraqi tank on the sand maybe just another hundred yards away. We scope it out. There are bodies, or bits of bodies lying around it. No life. It's all clear. It's a bit of useful cover and we go up behind it to set up our gear to help the Warrior make its fire on the Iraqi bunker.

—Fucking hell, says Dorky.

He's looking at a torso nearby. Or at least I thought it was a torso. But it still has its arms and legs. It's a weird shape. Shrunk. Nasty.

—Never mind what's around you, I bark at him. Get operational!

But Brewster and Dorky are paralysed by this thing. Mesmerised. It's an effort for them to look away.

—Come on lads, I say, a deep low growl.

Training kicks in, they go to it, fumbling a bit, fidgety, hyper, but they set up. And I look at this thing, but out of the corner of my eye because I don't want the lads to see I'm freaked by it, too. And I am. I'm freaked.

It's a corpse—of a kind—of an Iraqi soldier spilled out of the tank. Part of his head's gone but most of the rest of him is there. Well I can't see hands and feet. None of that bothers me. I've seen enough bits of bodies in my time and after a while it's no different to what's in your burger. But this thing: it's a body but it's shrunk to maybe a third of the size it should be. It crossed my mind it might be a kid, but it's bearded and anyway it's not like it's a kid, it's like the whole thing has twisted like a plastic bag when you set fire to it. And it's left a spooky shadow behind, a man-shaped shadow on the sand.

The boys are set up and ready, but I've got to shift this bloody mess. I step over to the thing and I try to side foot it under the tank, out of eyesight, but my foot passes straight through part of it. Nothing turns my stomach. My guts are cast iron, but for the first time in years and years my bowels soften. Some of the thing sticks to my foot. I scrape sand and debris and push as much of it as I can under the tank.

I turn back. Dorky and Brewster are watching me now. —All set up lads?

—Colour-Sar'nt!

Brewster radios the Warrior and we watch the slow elevation of the cannon before it locks. There's a pause before the Warrior launches its bombardment of the Iraqi emplacement. Dorky watches the results through binoculars and reports what's happening. I have to make a mental effort not to think about this goo stuck to my boot.

—Give 'em a strafing.

—Chain gun! Brewster tells his radio.

There's not much more. After the cannon and chain gun has softened them up they come out and all we have to do is point our weapons. These are not Republican Guard. These are conscripts; they've had enough and they're stumbling out with their hands on their heads. They seem to think we're the Yanks. Their idea of being a prisoner is to try to talk to us in Iraqi.

After the prisoners are passed back down the line the mopping pattern is repeated. The only thing that's changed is the dust. The tanks and the armoured vehicles are kicking up so much dust and sand that it's getting hard to see further up ahead. We're proceeding pretty much by radio co-ordinates and infrared activity. We stop a couple of times to check out a destroyed tank or other vehicle and we keep spotting these shrunk plastic bodies, with their shadow-casts, and all the time I'm thinking: what weapon is it that shrinks a human being but doesn't destroy a tank? I mean the tanks are burned but the shell is intact. I have to break up little groups of boys who stand mesmerised over these shrunk bodies.

—Don't look at it lads. Press on.

About another ten kilometres ahead we get radio directed to another clear-up. Same as before: a few salvoes to loosen the sand around them then in we go. The Iraqis are pouring out like ants from a poisoned nest, but I don't want my boys to get complacent. There are always die-hards, and I want no rush. By the book, me, and I'm dedicated to bringing all my boys home with their trousers on.

The dust and the sand are being swirled around by a strong breeze coming from the east. It smells of spice and engine smoke and this other stuff I don't like, and it's choking so we have to go in now with scarves over our faces, just to stop your nose and mouth filling up. This time I peel off with five of my boys, Dorky and Brewster amongst them. From somewhere up ahead there's sniper fire coming at us, but it's being fired pretty wildly into the dust. We get down behind an escarpment.

They know the drill. I'm going out very wide; they're going to crawl on their bellies at spread intervals but stay in visual range, using the dust-storm as cover. Meanwhile I've got my other boys noising up the Warrior's chain gun to draw fire and support our attack.

I yomp off maybe three hundred metres wide. I can hear the report of the sniper as he fires on the Warrior, but I can't see him. The dust gets thicker. There's a strong breeze picking up and I can't tell how much of this dust is generated by vehicle movement and how much is a natural wind-blown sandstorm, but it's swirling and lashing about like a sand-lizard's tail.

I look across the line. The dust is so strong I can barely see Brewster, who is my nearest support. I wave at him. He sees me and I point to my eye, warning him to stay in visual range with me and the next man. I don't want to be shot by my own troops: happens all the time in combat. Brewster gives me the thumbs up to show he understands.

We make slow progress towards the Iraqi emplacement. They're still firing, infrequently and wildly. I have an instinct there's only one or two of them, maybe three hundred metres away. I'm going on my belly.

Then the dust whips up again suddenly and aggressively. You can actually see the sand in the air turning in spirals, a whip-o'-will, a dark thing, like a live creature, part smoke, part sand. And the dust is so thick I've lost sight of Brewster.

If he remembers his training he'll stay exactly where he is until we re-establish visual range. But at the moment I can't see more than maybe seven or eight metres ahead of me in the gritty yellow fog. We're all radio disarmed: nothing like somebody squawking through your set when you're on your belly six inches away from the enemy. Maybe I could use the radio safely with this wind and racket going on but I don't want to risk it. We wait. Behind the wind I can hear our artillery pounding the Iraqi dugouts a few miles ahead. Then I can't even hear that.

After a while the sandstorm begins to ease. I have a thin cotton scarf over my mouth and it's almost stiff with the dust logged in it. My eyes are stinging and sweat is dribbling along the curve of my spine. I'm scoping out the spot where I last saw Brewster, but even though the dust is clearing I can't see him or anyone else.

What I can see is the Iraqi dug-out, and I'm way nearer to it than I should have been. There's no activity. The dug-out has taken a direct hit and there are bodies spilled. There's still no sign of Brewster and should one single rifleman remain in the dug-out, I'm exposed.

I have two grenades. An L2 high-ex,

and a white phosphorous grenade. I decide to use the phos bomb because as well as clearing anything within 15 yards of where it lands it makes a good signal. I chuck it at the dug out and get down, keeping my eyes averted from the flash to avoid the after-dazzle. The thing goes off and the smoke rises pretty quickly. Anything coming out of the dug-out is going to walk straight into my line of fire.

But there's nothing there.

I hang in, still waiting to make eye-contact with any of my boys. Visibility in the dust is fluctuating at between maybe twenty to thirty yards, no more than that, and after the shock of my phos grenades everything is quiet. I can't even hear the artillery up ahead and the flyovers have stopped altogether. I decide to wake up the radio.

My radio, like all of them in our unit, is a piece of shit twenty years old and it's fucked and we've reported it fucked and got no replacement gear. I have to make several calls before someone in my Warrior picks me up.

—Who's that? I ask.

—Fox, where are you?

—I'm at the dug out. Where's Echo and Valiant? These are the call-signs for Brewster and Cummings: normal names are prohibited over the radio.

—They've lost you, Cobra.

—Did you see my flash?

—Flash?

—Phos bomb you fucking idiot. You couldn't fucking miss it. If you can't raise Echo and Valiant send me two other lads to clear this dug-out. This is

bad radio procedure. Normal conversation is also prohibited but we're on a closed net at short range and I'm getting mighty irritated.

—No flash, Cobra. Give me your last co-ordinates.

I sit back and wait. The thick yellow cloud of sand and dust is like a gas, a sulphurous fog, and I still can't see more than about thirty yards. No-one comes. I radio again.

—We can't find you, Cobra.

—For fuck's sake. I'm gonna lob my high-ex. Follow the fucking bang you useless twat!

—Colour-Sar'nt.

I do just that. If there was anything alive in the dug-out it's probably mince by now. I radio again.

—No bang, Colour-Sar'nt.

—What?

—No bang. We're looking. We're listening. Sit tight.

I wait for another half an hour. What bothers me is that there is no sound from anywhere in the desert. Pretty unusual I'd say, what with a war going on. The distant artillery has stopped. It doesn't make sense. I radio again but this time I can't get a signal at all.

My instincts convince me that the dug-out is clear up ahead. I do what I tell my boys never to do and I make a solo approach. Not because I'm feeling brave but because I'm bored. I'm in the middle of combat and I'm bored, and when I'm bored I start thinking too much and that scares me more than the enemy.

The dug-out is well sand-bagged and there is a big, black broken gun blasted half way over the sand bags. I can smell the oil and the ripped steel. I approach silently, slowly from the rear. The dug-out is clean. When I say clean, I mean there are no live enemy. Plenty of dead ones. Nothing done by my grenades though, because they're all shrunk, shrivelled bodies like I've seen before. Shrunk with their original shadows scorched into the dust. Scattered particles of my WP are still smoking, but no-one's going anywhere.

I kick over the mess cans and check round. There's nothing of useful intelligence and I need to return to my unit. The problem is I don't know where my unit is and my radio is still on the blink. I go outside the dug-out to climb the rise to see if I can get a better signal. Maybe ten yards from the sand-bags I hear a click.

Things that never happen in real life: you see those war movies, maybe Vietnam, where a soldier steps on a mine and they cut to the expression on his face as he realises what he's done. There's a pause. Boom!

Nah. Doesn't happen. You step on a modern mine and there's no pause and you've no face left to have an expression. You know nothing about it.

But I step on something and there's a loud click. I don't know what it is, but I can feel a metal plate under my foot. I've trodden on something and I've triggered a spring-release.

I have no idea what this is. It may be a mine, it may be an improvised booby trap. But I know that if I don't keep my foot down on it, it's going to blow my leg off, and maybe a lot more. The point is I'm stuck. I'm not going anywhere.

Now this is an interesting situation. With the yellow smog visibility is still down to about twenty yards or so, but should any Iraqis come stumbling through that dust I'm a dead man. Should I lift my foot I'm a dead man. I can't see what it is I've trodden on but I can certainly feel the hard metal shape under my size nine boot. Maybe it's a mine that has malfunctioned. Maybe it's some old piece of crap the Iraqis had left over from their desert war with Iran, and it's not going to blow. I have no way of knowing.

I feel a maggot of sweat run along my spine. My mouth is full of dust. Keeping my foot in place I get on the radio. Miraculously I patch through at the first attempt. —Cobra. Where are you?

—Listen carefully. I've stepped on a mine.

—Fuck! Are you all right.

—No, listen. It hasn't gone off. I've got my foot on it and I can't go anywhere or it will detonate.

—Fuck! Don't move your foot.

—You dick-head! I'm not moving my foot anywhere. But I need you to find me pronto. I need someone to work out how to get me out of this.

—Colour-Sar'nt. What are your co-ordinates?

—Exactly what I gave you last time.

—Can't be, Colour-Sar'nt. We've been all over there looking for you.

—Speak with Brewster. He was the last man I saw.

—Exactly what we did Colour-Sar'nt.

—Well fucking do it again! I'm getting a bit fucking warm out here, corporal!

—Colour-Sar'nt!

—I'll fire three rounds, wait fifteen seconds and then fire a further three rounds. You listen for me.

—Won't be easy in this noise, Colour.

And I'm thinking, what noise? There is no noise. The desert is completely silent. Then I realise at the back of Corporal Middleton's radio voice I can hear artillery booming. I end radio contact and I fire three rounds into the air. I count to fifteen and do the same again. I try to radio Middleton to get confirmation but all I get on the airwaves is angry static.

Hoping they can locate me from my gunfire I wait. With my hot foot on the mine.

In the heat and dust of the desert, in full combat gear, with the sweat trickling inside my helmet, my vest and in my groin, I wait and I wait. And no-one comes.

I'm on alert and my automatic rifle is primed in case an Iraqi might turn up out of the dust and spot me standing there. I think about getting down on one knee to give my limbs a break; but I'm afraid that the slightest easing of pressure from the spring-mechanism will detonate the mine. Eventually I have to do something and I do lower myself on one knee, but only by resting my gun arm across the thigh bearing over the mine and forcing my entire weight down on that leg.

I stay in this position for over two hours. The radio crackles with static but nothing else. At one point I lose my patience and bellow out loud. —Brewster! Where are you, you little shitehawk? Brewster!

Nothing. No-one. Not even a sound. My leg is cramping up badly so I return to my standing position. By now I've run through every possibility for getting myself out of this. I have the weight of my pack, equipment and my weapon, but I can't risk manipulating it all onto the mine in the hope that it is heavy enough. With gear weighing roughly 50lbs I even try to make a calculation, but I have no way of knowing what force I'm currently bearing on the mine under my foot. I reckon that if and when the boys turn up they will have the gear to clamp the mine, or to weight it, or to get me out of my boot somehow without the thing triggering.

I take off my helmet. Even though my head is shaved it's caked in sweat and grit. I have weird sensations running up and down my leg. A horrible feeling of lightness is in my foot, as if it's threatening to float up quite against all my intentions for it to stay bearing down on that metal plate. Then a Red Admiral comes by.

I mean a butterfly. One of those beautiful, rare ones you sometimes see in an English country garden. I didn't even know you got them in the desert and I think, well, there ain't much green round here for you is there? I'm glad to see it. It takes my mind off the situation for a few seconds as it flutters by. Then it turns back towards me and it settles on my wrist.

Beautiful. I wonder if this is the last thing I'm going to see. I do believe it drank my sweat from my wrist. It opens its wings and just stays there quite happy. There you are. Drinking sweat from a man with his foot on a mine. What's that all about?

That's not bad, I think. If that's the last thing I'm going to see, a Red Admiral. I can think of a lot of things lower down my list. Have you ever looked hard at one? They are strange. They look like they're looking back at you. Like they're holding this cloak open for you to see.

Rubbish, I know, but I start to think about keeping the Red Admiral alive.

—You don't wanna stay there too long, old pretty. You're in the wrong place. You don't wanna stay there.

I flex my hand, gently, but it doesn't move; it's still drinking my sweat. When it beats its wings to fly away I watch it go. I track it for several yards, to the vanishing point where the yellow dust closes in around me. But it seems to stay, fluttering in the air, the tiniest red dot; and then the red dot changes and I realise the red dot I was looking at isn't the tip of a butterfly's wing at all; it's the red dot of an Arab's *shemagh*, the traditional headscarf, and the Arab wearing it is making his way towards me.

I instantly sight my rifle on him. He doesn't miss a stride, but he does raise the palms of his hands towards me to show me he's unarmed. He certainly isn't dressed like a regular soldier. He wears a long flowing black *dishdasha* thing and he's barefoot. But I guess the Iraqis have auxiliary soldiers or a mili-

tia; whatever he is, I'm ready to drill him if he even looks at me wrong.

His red and white *shemagh* shrouds his face. He wears it over his head and high over his nose and mouth against the dust. All I can see is his eyes. Still showing me a clean pair of hands he draws up about five or six yards away, not looking the least worried by my machine gun trained on him.

I say I can see his eyes: that is, he has one eye, of the most piercing blue I've ever seen. The other eye is stitched closed. The stitches are clumsy, angry black threads. His robe is dusty and his *shemagh* is smirched and dirty. He peers hard at me with that one blue eye. Then he looks around him.

The Arab seems confused. He puts a hand to his forehead, as if trying to remember something.

—On the floor! I bark this command, gesturing at the sand with my machine gun. —Get down.

He laughs. Just a little snigger, before peering hard at me again.

—Down! Now!

He shakes his head quizzically. Then he lowers himself to the sand. He takes a squat position, clasping his hands in front of him. But I want him down on his arse and I bellow at him some more. —Down! Get down!

—If you wish, he says as if this is a game.

—Speak English? You speak English?

He looks confused. Then he nods a yes, before looking round quickly to all points of the compass, as if expecting reinforcements or something.

—What's your unit?

—Unit?

—What's your company?

He shakes his head, making out he doesn't understand.

—Are you a soldier of Iraq?

He shakes his head, no.

—I'm holding you prisoner. You understand? Prisoner.

He is actually taken aback by my remark. I mean he does that thing of jerking his head back in surprise at my words. He takes the *shemagh* scarf from his mouth and he smiles at me.

—Prisoner, I say again.

Again he looks puzzled. There is an expression on his face that makes me think of men I have seen who were concussed. I wonder if he's been wandering in this state. He certainly doesn't seem to know where he is, or what is at stake here. I think he might be retarded.

Finally he gestures at the mine beneath my boot. —You are in some difficulty.

His English is very good, though he speaks with a thick accent, like he has sand in his throat.

—You let me worry about that.

The Arab makes to stand up again.

—GET DOWN!

He sinks back down to the sand and spreads his arms wide. —I was trying to think how I might help you.

—Like I say, I'll worry about that. I've got people coming.

He laughs. Quite loud. —Who? Who is coming?

I flick on my radio and make the call. Still nothing but static. I give him a cold stare. —Where are you from?

Again he looks around him, all points compass. Though there is still nothing to see beyond the twenty yards radius to the dust curtain. —I don't know.

—You don't know. Dark when you left, was it?

—Pardon?

—Never mind. Joke.

—Ah! Joking is good . . . in your predicament.

—Where did you learn to speak English?

He rubs his chin. —I can't remember.

—Funny fucker, incha?

—*Insh allah*.

I'm only asking questions to establish the upper hand, to show him that I'm in control. Given the situation I don't feel in control and he seems to know that, too. —Name. What's your name?

He looks at the sky. —You couldn't pronounce it.

—Try me.

—It's many. And many don't like to repeat it.

He turns his one eye on me when he says this, and I don't know why but my skin flushes. I mean my skin ripples like the sand does when the wind moves it.

—Funny fucker, I say again.

We spend the next half an hour staring at each other in silence. My wristwatch tells me I've been there with my foot on the mine for seven hours. Soon it will be nightfall. The Arab makes no movement. But something about him has me scared. And I'm the one with the gun.

He breaks the silence. —Perhaps you should tell another joke.

—What?

—To improve your situation. Perhaps one of your jokes.

—Perhaps I should put a bullet through your head. That would be a good joke.

—Then how could I help you? I'm thinking of how to help you, but this is all I have come up with so far. And you should not underestimate the power of levity. Your situation is grave. You must work against it.

—Excuse me, I don't know why but I don't feel like telling any jokes right now.

—The war you are in the middle of, the Arab states casually, is only part of a larger war: which is the war declared by levity on gravity. Indeed gravity is what placed your foot in this difficult situation. Levity is what will raise you out of it.

I twist my lip into a sneer. —Are you taking the piss, you fucking rag-head?

He blinks at me with his one eye. —I don't understand this expression.

—No? Well fuck off.

I try the radio again. I'm starting to suspect the batteries are failing. The useless static makes me want to toss my radio into the sand, but I keep my head, and I keep my gun trained on the mocking Arab. I'm thirsty. My throat is choked with dust, and I need a piss pretty bad.

My cramping leg by now is in a desperate state. I can't feel my foot at all and I'm afraid that the slightest gust of air will lift my foot off the mine and release the spring underneath it. Worse, a kind of involuntary tremor has set into

my calf muscle. My shirt and my combat trousers are saturated with my own sweat. For the first time I actually begin to speculate how long I can hold to this. At some point I know I'm going to lose concentration and remove my foot. I keep my full weight on the mine, tapping the sand with my free left foot, bouncing lightly, just to work some feeling into my leg.

It's no good. I have to manipulate my cock out of my combat pants and take a piss on the sand. All while keeping the weight of one foot on the mine and levelling my machine gun at the Arab. He watches this operation with great interest. My piss foams and sizzles on the sand. Finally I manage to put my tackle away. I'm exhausted.

—It's very difficult for you, he says. Very difficult. I really think a joke would help.

I raise my machine gun and aim it right between his eyes. I'm very close to pulling the trigger. I want to. But it's against my principles, though he doesn't know that. He doesn't seem the slightest bit worried. He just keeps talking. —You know, God laughed this world into existence my friend. He saw the night and he laughed. His very last snort of laughter was to create man. We were made from the snot in His nose, from His laughing too much. Do you know that the prophet said *Keep your heart light at every moment, because when the heart is downcast the soul becomes blind.* Even now in your difficult situation, this is good advice.

—And you see, levity is the only thing we have in the face of the absurdity of death. Laughter is the cure for grief. But you know all this because you are a soldier and you have seen death. You have also killed. I know this. I can see into your heart.

He talks this way for an hour or more. I listen because it takes my mind off my situation. And after a while his voice becomes a kind of murmuring. I don't know how it happened, but without me seeing him get up he's on his feet and he's whispering these things in my ear. I must be tranced out because I didn't see him get up—wouldn't allow him to get up. But there he is, an inch away, whispering, and I can feel his breath in my ear as he speaks. The sky has turned dark. Dusk is coming to the desert. I look at my watch. I've been standing on the mine for over ten hours.

—I've decided I'm going to help you, he says, if you'll let me.

—Who are you?

He steps back, shakes his head. —I don't know. I've been trying to remember. All I can tell you is this: there was a white flash in the desert, an explosion and a terrible wind and there I was, wandering. And then I found you. I can give you a wish.

—Yeh you're a fucking genie.

He claps his hands and jumps, laughing. The laughter takes him over for a moment. His black *dishdasha* flaps as he laughs and in a split-second of dizziness I hallucinate him as a black bird hovering near me.

—There, a joke! A good one! It will help. If I am a djinn I can summon up a wind. But if I help you, you will never be rid of me. You understand that?

—Get me out of here, I say.

This next part is the hardest part to write. The Arab is gone and in his place is the fluttering red admiral. The butterfly settles on the sand where the Arab has been, and within a second a black crow flies down from the sky and eats the red admiral, and I know it is the same crow that I hallucinated a moment ago, and the same crow that had come into my room that Christmas Day before I left for the Gulf. It eats the butterfly and it grows before my eyes, twelve foot, thirty foot in the air and I could smell the stink of its hot black feathers and its birdshit and I see its yellow claws scrabbling the sand near my foot on the mine; I wants to shout: No! But already a screaming is coming across the sky.

—Incoming! I shout to no-one. It's a mortar or a rocket and it lands maybe thirty feet away and the blast lifts me up high into the air and blows me clean across the desert. I'm already flying backwards when I hear the mine detonate safely, and then I'm dumped on the desert floor.

I don't know what happens next because I come round in a field hospital with about 200 beds. I wake up and look around me and say —Where's my boys? Get my boots, I have to look after my boys.

Medic comes up to me and snatches a clip-board hanging on the end of my bed.—For you Tommy ze var is offer—

—Fuck off. Where's my boots?

—I'm serious, it's over. And not just for you.

He is serious, too. I've been unconscious for nearly three days and the fighting is done and dusted. I didn't know, but the Iraqis had retreated and we'd torched their entire fleeing army on the Road Of Death. I've missed it all.

I get a visit from the brass and later that day Brewster comes by. —I'd heard you were awake.

—Brewster! Who brought me in?

—They said you'd stepped on a mine. The whole unit was out looking for you. We lost radio contact. The unit had to press on but the Major left three of us behind to try to find you. Hours it was. Then some friendly fire came in. After that we found you.

—Friendly fire?

He smirked at me. —Yeh. It blew half your uniform off. We found you on your back giggling like a fucking drain, Colour.

—I don't fucking giggle.

—You was giggling like a fucking loony wiv no sister. There wasn't a scratch on ya but your tongue was hanging out and you were giving it the big tee-hee-hee.

—Fuck off Brewster.

—I'm tellin' you, Colour. And you had this rag on yer head.

He turns away and steps over to a cabinet at the end of the tent. Takes something out of the cabinet and brings it to the bed. It's a neatly folded, red-checked *shemagh*. I take it from his hand.—What happened to the Arab?

—Arab?

—The one who was wearing this? What happened to him?

—No, *you* was wearin' this.

I sink back into my pillow. The last thing I can remember is the Arab whispering in my ear, and then the blast of the incoming. That was it. Lights out.

Brewster is looking at me strange. —What happened? Where d'you get to?

—My fucking head is killin' me, Brewster.

—You want the medic, Colour?

—Nah, just a bit o' peace. All the boys sound?

—All present and correct. All relieved you're okay.

—Good boys, good boys.

We clasp hands and Brewster leaves the medic tent. Leaves me holding the scarf. I still have it. The scarf. The *shemagh*.

I didn't know it then but my army days were already numbered. It was true that the blast hadn't left a scratch on me—physically. But after what had happened I couldn't sleep properly and never have been able to since that day. I've taken all kinds of medication. Useless. And the lack of sleep led me to have headaches. I took even more medication for the headaches, and that led me to have bad dreams; so bad that I didn't even want to sleep.

My job relied on me being as fit as a flea. I couldn't ask any boy to do what I couldn't do. I hid it from myself for a while, but I suppose inside I knew it was all over. Then about a year after the Gulf War the Colonel called me in one day and started to talk to me about career counselling and all the wonderful opportunities that can lie ahead of a man when he leaves the forces. There was counselling; there was re-training; there was a house-purchase scheme. This wasn't like the old days when you used to get dumped out of the army with nowhere to go, he told me. I remember listening to it all in stony silence. When he'd had his say I stood up, saluted him and marched out of his office.

I wasn't discharged or cashiered or anything like that. I retired with full honours and with an army pension. I got work. Mostly in security. I had a job with Group 4 security for about three years. I was happy to take on night work since I couldn't sleep anyway.

I don't know how many times he visited me before I dropped to who he was. And anyway, that was his way: he would take over someone, maybe for just for a few hours, or maybe just for a minute or so. But he'd let me know. There would be something in what he said to me. Sometimes he would be quite open; sometimes he would give just a little hint, or a word or two to remind me of our moments together in the desert. Sometime he would play games, you know, fuck with my head. He liked to wink. That would be like a reminder of his one eye, the wink. The trouble was of course that you do get people who like to wink at you in the middle of a conversation, and I would think: ah, he's here. But I might have got it wrong, and

it was just someone winking. He knew that. He knew he was fucking with my head. It was his sense of humour. But for that reason I didn't like people winking at me, which I think is fair enough, given what I had to put up with. But other people just thought I was being cranky.

That day in the desert when I had my foot on the mine he'd told me that he'd always be with me. That was the price I paid.

I'd be in an interview for some shitty job as a night watchman for this or that corporation and the suit interviewing me would say I looked suitable or whatever and then he might wink. And I would have to look behind his eyes. But I'd have to make sure they couldn't see me staring.

It wasn't just winking. I'd go into a bar and there might be someone drinking alone there, you know, leaning against the bar, staring straight ahead, pint half-supped, fags and lighter lined up just so and he'd say, —Red admiral.

Or something that hearkened back to our desert encounter.

—What? I'd go. *What?*

And the fucker would look at me and then look away. And I'd know it was *him*. See. But I couldn't challenge the drinker at the bar because it would be his way to leave immediately. Go from behind the eyes. Because they are in and out as fast as you like.

Sometimes he would stay long enough though to have a conversation. But I could never be sure. The thing I could never work out: was he riding these people, or was he riding me?

I went to a shrink. My headaches were getting worse, my sleep was a mess, I had pains in my liver and other problems. When I told my quack about the sleep disorders and the nightmares he arranged for me to see the shrink, but it didn't go well. The first thing I said to the shrink was —Don't wink at me, I don't like being winked at.

—Why ever not?

—It don't matter why not, just don't wink at me and we'll be all right.

—I assure you I'm not the winking kind of psychiatrist.

—Good. We'll get along fine. What are you writing down?

—Notes. We make notes, it's one of the things we do.

—Listen, I'm not an uneducated squaddie, right? I'm a Colour Sergeant. Was. So stop with the notes, because I know that if I tell you what's on my mind I know exactly what you'll say, so there's no point to all of that, right?

—Oh? And what will I say?

—Don't fuck me around, you know, I know, we all know.

—Seamus, how can I help you?

—Just give me the medication. Just give it me.

I wasn't going to tell him. It's a short road from telling what happened to getting sectioned and put away. I'm not stupid. I never told him, never told the army doctors nor the quacks on civvy street. This here in writing is the first time I've mentioned it. There are some things you do not talk about.

My piss started to burn. Well I hadn't had a girlfriend in a long time but I went down the GUM clinic anyway.

Embarrassing thing was the doctor was a good looking bird, sort of Arabic herself, I don't know. She shoved that metal cocktail umbrella down my pipe and I nearly hit the roof. She winced herself, closed one eye, and I thought: *is it you?*

Nothing. Clean as a whistle. Just burning. Same with cum. I couldn't even have a J Arthur Rank without my spunk burning. There was something wrong me but they couldn't find out what it was.

I lost my job with Group 4. The lads called me "Don't wink" behind my back. I didn't mind that, but when one of them tried to take the piss out of me one day I broke his jaw. And his arm. And wrist. And I faced charges and I had to do a stretch. I was helped by an army lawyer and my previous clean record helped but I still had to do a stretch in Winson Green.

The Arab used to come to me in prison. Come as a guard, come as one of the other cons. There was another bloke in there from the Gulf, ex-para, hard-case. Clever bloke. Good lad. In the nick the ex-army boys used to stick together. No-one would fuck about with us. He used to talk a lot about the Gulf. Why we were there. Opened my eyes it did. At first I used to want him to shut up, but he wouldn't let it go.

—It gets better.

This is how he used to talk. He'd always say *it gets better* when he was about to tell you something he thought you didn't know. We were in the exercise yard one day.

—It gets better. Wait til you hear this. So Saddam Hussein is the big western ally, right? We've equipped him, sponsored him, trained him up, right? Fourth biggest army in the world. He thinks he'll steam into Kuwait no prob, right? No way his mates in the west are going to stop him. I mean Kuwait—not even a fuckin' democracy, right? Just a fuckin' royal family, like ours, owning everything and running the show. And it turns out, they've been stealing Iraq's oil.

—Give it a rest, Otto.

—The Kuwaitis, with western investment, have been drilling for the oil *at a slant*, angle, miles inside their own border but tapping the Iraqi oil reserves. Basic robbery.

—*I've heard of Arabs*, says Nobby, ex tank battalion, biggest thief on the planet, inside for Fraud *who could steal the bedsheets from under your sleeping body* . . .

—Yeh, listen Nobby cos it gets better. So you all know about the PR firm who sold the war to the American senate? Hill and Knowlton, the biggest fuck-off PR and Marketing outfit in the fucking world, they're funded millions and I mean millions by the super-rich Kuwaitis and the oil fat-cats to persuade the American public and the senate to go to war. They make news videos to make it look like reporting. They sell it like it's a bar of chocolate. They do everything. They even fake a story with a weeping fifteen year old girl who says she saw Iraqi soldiers dump 314 babies on the stone cold floor to make off with the incubators.

—That's old stuff, I say, we've heard all that.

—*What they do*, says Nobby, *what they do is get a giant fevver, right, a fevver, and they tickle you while you're sleepin'* . . .

—Yeh but what you haven't heard is this: that girl, that fifteen year old girl is a member of the Royal Family! Her Dad is only the ambassador to the United fucking States!

—*They start on the right side of you wiv the fevver, and when you roll over they lift up the sheet on that side* . . .

—It gets better. The senate was persuaded by just five votes, right? That means that if three senators had voted differently, there would have been no Desert Storm and none of us would have gone to war. Now then—

—*. . . then they nip round the other side of the bed with the fevver and they start working on you from that side* . . .

—Forget about all those senators who are invested in the oil business, here's three Democrats for you: one's a bible belt Christian and they've got him stitched up with a beautiful Kuwaiti boy; another is having a long term affair with a Kuwaiti princess, not the one who sobbed about the fake incubators, another one . . .

—*. . . so then you roll away from the sheet that side* . . .

—and your third Senator (this is all true, I'm not making this up, no fuckin' need) admits he voted the wrong way because he had a terrible headache that day.

—*. . . and that's it, they fuck off, you wake up hours later with no sheet underneath you. Fucking brilliant it is* . . .

—So that's it then: yanks go, Brits follow, baaaaaa baaaaa and we're out in the desert heavy breathing Depleted Uranium.

—What's that then Otto? I says.

—. . . *one fevver. Brilliant it is* . . .

—What? Depleted Uranium? That's another story mate. But you see what I'm saying? One PR job, two fucks and headache. So who is the cunts? Eh? Eh? Who?

And when he says this Otto doesn't wink, no, but he pulls one eyelid down with his forefinger and looks at me with one blue eye, and I know who it is talking to me. I don't know how long he's been there, sort of inside Otto, but it's him all right. I turn away.

—You all right Seamus?

—I'm all right Otto. Catch you later, son.

Otto has a way of trying to look after me. I don't need looking after, but he keeps checking up, see if I'm okay, all that. He tells me about Depleted Uranium. Tells me what it is. I didn't even know we were using it. Explains the flashes in the desert and the way those Iraqi corpses were all shrunk but their boots weren't burned. That had been bothering me for a long time. But with Otto there's always more. He reckons it can explain the illnesses I've been having these last few years. He reckons there's a lot of American soldiers been making legal claims, but their government isn't wearing it. Same as ours isn't wearing it.

I don't know. I just don't know.

Otto gets out of nick before me. I miss him. He's a good lad. He comes back and visits me once a week. He's got ideas about us starting our own security business after we get out.

But the migraines get worse, the internal pains get worse. When I do finally get paroled out, Otto is there to collect me. Takes me off to a pub called The Sandboy—yeh—for a slap-up lunch and a few pints in the pub, so we can talk about this security firm. We're going to call it AV Security to suggest armoured vehicle without saying it. We both know it's bollocks—ain't gonna happen. But we get pissed and talk about the nick and pretend like it is.

Out of the blue and after seven pints of flat Courage Bitter Otto goes — Believe in evil, do you Seamus? Do ya?

—Eh? I notice he can't keep his foot still.

—We got mugged in this last lot, mate. Turned over. Done up the arse.

—Leave it out, Otto.

—Look Seamus, my nerves are shot. Your health is fucked. What for? Makes no sense we were even there.

—Strewth. Supposed to be having a good time, ain't we?

Otto's hands are shaking. He taps the table with his box of ciggies. —Sorry mate. Drink up. One for the road, eh?

We never talk any more about AV Security. Otto gets a pay-out for his arthritis. He tries to help me with all the forms and paperwork and so on but the doctors seemed to think all my complaints are in my head, so I get nothing. Anyway, Otto sinks his money into a toy shop. He says he wants to see happy faces. He offers me a job "dealing with stock". I took one look at his "stock" and realise he's just being kind. Plus I don't see myself lining up boxes of moulded plastic soldiers on a shelf.

After that I slipped. I lived in some odd places. Hostels. Squats. Derelict buildings. Stone me, I even washed up at the Sally Army more than once. And the Arab showed up in these places more than ever before. He told me it was easier in these places for him to get inside someone for a minute or two. I always knew when he was about to take over someone, maybe a fellow inmate at the hostel, maybe the Salvation Army hostel director, maybe some tattooed psycho sharing the squat. A fuzzy grey shadow would appear, like soot everywhere, there's no other way to describe it. Then their faces would go luminous for a moment, just in a passing moment. And the Arab would be there, maybe dropping me the wink, just talking, always talking, like he was trying to teach me things. Tried to teach me Arabic he did, and older languages. Mathematics. Loads of stuff. I was no good at it. The migraines. Plus there was a particular thing he used to say, every time, every encounter, just to wind me up. I'm sure it was just to wind me up. Taunt me.

The terrible thing is that as I look back over the last few years, I don't know how I've lived. I can't remember most of it. It's a half life. Sometimes I do wonder if I died that day in the desert. Took my foot off the mine and died, and this is me dragging on my way over. I've no markers, you see. No co-ordinates. I'm adrift.

I see Otto sometimes. I go to his toy shop and he hands me a few quid, to help me get by. But I wonder if he's dead, too? Died in Desert Storm like I did. It would add up. This is limbo. I don't know. A beer doesn't taste the same. A cigarette doesn't taste the same. I don't know.

I was a soldier of the Queen. I am a soldier of the Queen. I have wept for myself in the dark.

Strange things happen. You might be standing in the doorway trying to hustle for a drink. I says, —I'm trying to get a cup o' tea—and there's this dapper gent, reckons he knows me. Of course he knows me. His face lights and it's the Arab. Puts me in a cab, pays the driver. Takes me to Go-point. What a place. It's crawling with ones just like the Arab. And there's this lovely girl. Antonia. She gets me writing. She gave me this exercise book to write in. Therapy. But I don't let anyone see what I've written here. No-one gets to see it. There's a good reason. Antonia asks to see it but I say, —No my darlin'. No.

I keep the exercise book wrapped inside the Arab's red *shemagh*.

Yes, sometimes I wonder if I am dead, and sometimes I wonder if I'm still in the desert with my foot on the mine. It could happen. I'm well trained. Maybe I've just been there for like twenty-four hours and I'm still waiting for my boys to find me. Like I'm tranced out but I'm still covering that mine, muscles locked into position, holding down that spring. It could be. It really could be. I'm well trained enough to make that happen. And maybe all these things that have gone on since Desert Storm are just things swimming inside my head. It would explain a lot.

So either I'm still alive somewhere with my foot on a mine; or I'm dead and for some reason I can't go over; or a third possibility is that it did all happen and what I'm left with is worse than the other two alternatives.

I think the Queen can answer my question. I think she is probably the only person on earth who can. If I could find a way to talk to her she would make it all make sense. I'm going down to Buckingham Palace. They can change the guards all they like. I'm going to chain myself to the railings and I'm going to ask the Queen to come down and have a chat.

I want to take my foot off the mine.

It's been too long. I'm tired, even with all my training, I'm tired.

I'm not writing any more. This is the end of my will and testament. I said I keep this wrapped in the *shemagh*. This is not to keep other people out but to keep the Arab in. If anyone ever reads this, the Arab will pass over to them. The Arab told me that.

Not that you can trust the Arab. There's that other thing he's always telling me, though I know he's a liar. He's just out to get a rise from me. Every time. I don't take the bait. Every time I see the Arab I know that at some point he's going to reach with his forefinger to pull the loose flap of skin under his one good eye, and he's going to say, —*Seamus, there was no mine.*

He's a liar. That Arab is a liar.

Ⓚ

Once upon a time Tubby Thackeray's silent comedies were hailed as the equal of Chaplin's and Keaton's, but now his name has been deleted from the history of the cinema. Some of his music-hall performances before he went to Hollywood were riotously controversial, and his last film was never released – but why have his entire career and all his films vanished from the record?

Simon Lester is a film critic thrown out of a job by a lawsuit against the magazine he helped to found. When he's commissioned to write a book about Thackeray and restore the comedian's reputation, it seems as if his own career is saved. His research takes him from Los Angeles to Amsterdam, from dusty archives to a hardcore movie studio. But his research leads to something far older than the cinema in its latest and most dangerous shape... .

THE GRIN OF THE DARK

RAMSEY CAMPBELL

INTRODUCTION BY MICHAEL MARSHALL SMITH

RAMSEY CAMPBELL HAS FOUND TERROR IN THE LORE OF CINEMA BEFORE - IN *THE PARASITE* AND *ANCIENT IMAGES* - AND NOW HE TURNS TO THE SILENT ERA. LON CHANEY ONCE INVITED US TO CONTEMPLATE OPENING OUR DOOR AT MIDNIGHT TO BE CONFRONTED BY A CLOWN. JUST HOPE YOU NEVER FIND TUBBY THACKERAY THERE OR, EVEN WORSE, ON YOUR TELEVISION OR YOUR COMPUTER.

"This seemed to be one of those stories that grew out of a random idea," Ramsey Campbell tells us, "the passing thought of the game that gives the tale its title, although the thought immediately grew more macabre, as such ideas delight in doing for me. I was struggling to come up with more of an anecdote about the writing, even if I sometimes feel the interest should be nowhere if not in the story itself, when it occurred to me that my mother used to play this game with babies. I offer this information, and my having forgotten it, for readers to interpret how they will."

Peep

Ramsey Campbell

I'm labouring up the steepest section of the hill above the promenade when the twins run ahead. At least we're past the main road by the railway station. "Don't cross—" I shout or rather gasp. Perhaps each of them thinks or pretends to think I'm addressing the other, because they don't slow down until they reach the first side street and dodge around the corner.

"Stay there," I pant. They're already out of sight, having crouched below the garden wall. I wonder if they're angry with me by association with their parents, since Geraldine wasn't bought a kite to replace the one she trampled to bits when yesterday's weather let her down. They did appear to relish watching teenage drivers speed along the promenade for at least a few minutes, which may mean they aren't punishing me for their boredom. In any case I ought to join in the game. "Where are those children?" I wonder as loudly as my climb leaves breath for. "Where can they be?"

I seem to glimpse an answering movement beyond a bush at the far end of the wall. No doubt a bird is hiding in the foliage, since the twins pop their heads up much closer. Their small plump eight-year-old faces are gleeful, but there's no need for me to feel they're sharing a joke only with each other. Then Geraldine cries "Peep."

Like a chick coming out of its shell, as Auntie Beryl used to say. I can do without remembering what else she said, but where has Geraldine learned this trick? Despite the August sunshine, a wind across the bay traces my backbone with a shiver. Before questioning Geraldine I should usher the children across the junction, and as I plod to the corner I wheeze "Hold my—"

There's no traffic up here. Nevertheless I'm dismayed that the twins dash across the side street and the next one to the road that begins on the summit, opposite the Catholic church with its green skullcap and giant hatpin of a cross. They stop outside my house, where they could be enjoying the view of the bay planted with turbines to farm

299

the wind. Though I follow as fast as I'm able, Gerald is dealing the marble bell-push a series of pokes by the time I step onto the mossy path. Catching my breath makes me sound harsh as I ask "Geraldine, who taught you that game?"

She giggles, and so does Gerald. "The old woman," he says.

I'm about to pursue this when Paula opens my front door. "Don't say that," she rebukes him.

Her face reddens, emphasising how her cropped hair has done the reverse. It's even paler by comparison with the twins' mops, so that I wonder if they're to blame. Before I can put my reluctant question, Gerald greets the aromas from the kitchen by demanding "What's for dinner?"

"We've made you lots of good things while you've been looking after grandpa."

The twins don't think much of at least some of this, although I presume the reference to me was intended to make them feel grown-up. They push past their mother and race into the lounge, jangling all the ornaments. "Careful," Paula calls less forcefully than I would prefer. "Share," she adds as I follow her to the kitchen, where she murmurs "What game were you quizzing them about?"

"You used to play it with babies. I'm not saying you. People did." I have a sudden image of Beryl thrusting her white face over the side of my cot, though if that ever happened, surely I wouldn't remember. "Peep," I explain and demonstrate by covering my eyes

before raising my face above my hand.

Paula's husband Bertie glances up from vigorously stirring vegetables in the wok he and Paula brought with them. "And what was your issue with that?"

Surely I misunderstood Gerald, which can be cleared up later. "Your two were playing it," I say. "A bit babyish at their age, do you think?"

"Good Lord, they're only children. Let them have their fun till they have to get serious like the rest of us," he says and cocks his head towards a squabble over television channels. "Any chance you could restore some balance in there? Everything's under control in here."

I'm perfectly capable of cooking a decent meal. I've had to be since Jo died. I feel as if I'm being told where to go and how to act in my own house. Still, I should help my remaining family, and so I bustle to the lounge, where the instant disappearance of a channel leaves the impression that a face dropped out of sight as I entered. Gerald has captured the remote control and is riffling through broadcasts. "Stop that now," I urge. "Settle on something."

They haven't even on the furniture. They're bouncing from chair to chair by way of the equally venerable sofa in their fight over the control. "I think someone older had better take charge," I say and hold out my hand until Gerald flings the control beside me on the sofa. The disagreement appears to be over two indistinguishably similar pro-grammes in which vaguely Oriental cartoon animals batter one another with multicoloured explosions and other garish displays of power. I propose watching real animals and offer a show set in a zoo for endangered species, but the response makes me feel like a member of one. My suggestion of alternating scenes from each chosen programme brings agreement, though only on dismissing the idea, and Geraldine capitulates to watching her brother's choice.

The onscreen clamour gives me no chance to repeat my question. When I try to sneak the volume down, the objections are deafening. I don't want Paula and her husband to conclude I'm useless—I mustn't give them any excuse to visit even less often—and so I hold my peace, if there can be said to be any in the room. The cartoon is still going off when we're summoned to dinner.

I do my best to act as I feel expected to behave. I consume every grain and shoot and chunk of my meal, however much it reminds me of the cartoon. When my example falls short of the twins I'm compelled to encourage them aloud—"Have a bit more or you won't get any bigger" and "That's lovely, just try it" and in some desperation "Eat up, it's good for you." Perhaps they're sick of hearing about healthy food at home. I feel clownishly false and even more observed than I did over the television. I'm quite relieved when the plates are scraped clean and consigned to the dishwasher.

I'd hoped the twins might have grown up sufficiently since Christmas to be prepared to go to bed before the adults, but apparently holidays rule, and the table is cleared for one of the games Gerald has insisted on bringing. Players take turns to insert plastic sticks in the base of a casket, and the loser is the one whose stick releases the lid and the contents, a wagging head that I suppose is meant to be a clown's, given its whiteness and shock of red hair and enlarged eyes and wide grin just as fixed. I almost knock the game to the floor when one of my shaky attempts to take care lets out the gleeful head, and then I have to feign amusement for the children's sake. At first I'm glad when Gerald is prevailed upon to let his sister choose a game.

It's Monopoly. I think only its potential length daunts me until the children's behaviour reminds me how my aunt would play. They sulk whenever a move goes against them and crow if one fails to benefit their twin, whereas Beryl would change any move she didn't like and say "Oh, let me have it" or simply watch to see whether anyone noticed. "Peep," she would say and lower her hand in front of her eyes if she caught us watching. My parents pretended that she didn't cheat, and so I kept quiet, even though she was more than alert to anyone else's mistakes. Eventually I try conceding tonight's game in the hope the other adults will, but it seems Paula's husband is too much of a stockbroker to relinquish even toy money. The late hour enlivens the twins or at any rate makes them more active, celebrating favourable moves by bouncing on the chairs. "Careful of my poor old furniture," I say, though I'm more dismayed by the reflection of their antics in the mirror that backs the dresser, just the top of one tousled red head or the other springing up among the doubled plates. I'm tired enough to fancy that an unkempt scalp rendered dusty by the glass keeps straying into view even while the twins are still or at least seated. Its owner would be at my back, but since nobody else looks, I won't. Somewhat earlier than midnight Bertie wins the game and sits back satisfied as the twins start sweeping hotels off the board in vexation. "I think someone's ready for bed," I remark.

"You go, then," says Gerald, and his sister giggles in agreement.

"Let grandpa have the bathroom first," says their mother.

Does she honestly believe I was referring to myself? "I won't be long," I promise, not least because I've had enough of mirrors. Having found my toothbrush amid the visiting clutter, I close my eyes while wielding it. "Empty now," I announce on the way to my room. In due course a squabble migrates from the bathroom to the bunks next door and eventually trails into silence. Once I've heard Paula and her husband share the bathroom, which is more than her mother and I ever did, there are just my thoughts to keep me awake.

I don't want to think about the last time I saw Beryl, but I can't help remembering when her playfulness turned unpleasant. It was Christmas Eve, and she'd helped or overseen my mother in making dozens of mince pies, which may have been why my mother

was sharper than usual with me. She told me not to touch the pies after she gave me one to taste. I was the twins' age and unable to resist. Halfway through a comedy show full of jokes I didn't understand I sneaked back to the kitchen. I'd taken just one surreptitious bite when I saw Beryl's face leaning around the night outside the window. She was at the door behind me, and I hid the pie in my mouth before turning to her. Her puffy whitish porous face that always put me in mind of dough seemed to widen with a grin that for a moment I imagined was affectionate. "Peep," she said.

Though it sounded almost playful, it was a warning or a threat of worse. Why did it daunt me so much when my offence had been so trivial? Perhaps I was simply aware that my parents had to put up with my mother's sister while wishing she didn't live so close. She always came to us on Christmas Day, and that year I spent it fearing that she might surprise me at some other crime, which made me feel in danger of committing one out of sheer nervousness. "Remember," she said that night, having delivered a doughy kiss that smeared me with lipstick and face powder. "Peep."

Either my parents found this amusing or they felt compelled to pretend. I tried to take refuge in bed and forget about Beryl, and so it seems little has changed in more than sixty years. At least I'm no longer walking to school past her house, apprehensive that she may peer around the spidery net curtains or inch the front door open like a lid. If I didn't see her in the house I grew afraid that she was hiding somewhere else, so that even encountering her in the street felt like a trap she'd set. Surely all this is too childish to bother me now, and when sleep abandons me to daylight I don't immediately know why I'm nervous.

It's the family, of course. I've been wakened by the twins quarrelling outside my room over who should waken me for breakfast. "You both did," I call and hurry to the bathroom to speed through my ablutions. Once the twins have begun to toy with the extravagant remains of their food I risk giving them an excuse to finish. "What shall we do today?" I ask, and meet their expectant gazes by adding "You used to like the beach."

That's phrased to let them claim to have outgrown it, but Gerald says "I've got no spade or bucket."

"I haven't," Geraldine competes.

"I'm sure replacements can be obtained if you're both going to make me proud to be seen out with you," I say and tell their parents "I'll be in charge if you've better things to do."

Bertie purses his thin prim lips and raises his pale eyebrows. "Nothing's better than bringing up your children."

I'm not sure how many rebukes this incorporates. Too often the way he and Paula are raising the twins seems designed to reprove how she was brought up. "I know my dad wouldn't have meant it like that," she says. "We could go and look at some properties, Bertie."

"You're thinking of moving closer," I urge.

Her husband seems surprised to have to donate even a word of explanation. "Investments."

"Just say if you don't see enough of us," says Paula.

Since I suspect she isn't speaking for all of them, I revert to silence. Once the twins have been prevailed upon to take turns loading the dishwasher so that nothing is broken, I usher them out of the house. "Be good for grandpa," Paula says, which earns her a husbandly frown. "Text if you need to," he tells them.

I should have thought mobile phones were too expensive for young children to take to the beach. I don't want to begin the outing with an argument, and so I lead them downhill by their impatient hands. I see the scrawny windmills twirling on the bay until we turn down the road that slopes to the beach. If I don't revive my question now I may never have the opportunity or the nerve. "You were going to tell me who taught you that game."

Gerald's small hot sticky hand wriggles in my fist. "What game?"

"You know." I'm not about to release their hands while we're passing a supermarket car park. I raise one shoulder and then the other to peer above them at the twins. "Peep," I remind them.

Once they've had enough of giggling Geraldine splutters "Mummy said we mustn't say."

"I don't think she quite meant that, do you? I'm sure she won't mind if you just say it to me when I've asked."

"I'll tell if you tell," Gerald informs his sister.

"That's a good idea, then you'll each just have done half. Do it in chorus if you like."

He gives me a derisive look of the kind I've too often seen his father turn on Paula. "I'll tell mummy if you say," he warns Geraldine.

I mustn't cause any more strife. I'm only reviving an issue that will surely go away if it's ignored. I escort the twins into a newsagent's shop hung with buckets and spades and associated paraphernalia, the sole establishment to preserve any sense of the seaside among the pubs and wine bars and charity shops. Once we've agreed on items the twins can bear to own I lead them to the beach.

The expanse of sand at the foot of the slipway from the promenade borders the mouth of the river. Except for us it's deserted, but not for long. The twins are seeing who can dump the most castles on the sand when it starts to grow populated. Bald youths tapestried with tattoos let their bullish dogs roam while children not much older than the twins drink cans of lager or roll some kind of cigarette to share, and boys who are barely teenage if even that race motorcycles along the muddy edge of the water. As the twins begin to argue over who's winning the sandcastle competition I reflect that at least they're behaving better than anybody else in sight. I feel as if I'm directing the thought at someone who's judging them, but nobody is peering over or under the railings on the promenade or out of the apartments across it. Nevertheless I feel overheard in declaring "I

think you've both done very well. I couldn't choose between you."

I've assumed the principle must be to treat them as equally as possible—even their names seem to try—but just now dissatisfaction is all they're sharing. "I'm bored of this," Gerald says and demolishes several of his rickety castles. "I want to swim."

"Have you brought your costumes?"

"They're in our room," says Geraldine. "I want to swim in a pool, not a mucky river."

"We haven't got a pool here any more. We'd have to go on the train."

"You can take us," Gerald says. "Dad and mum won't mind."

I'm undismayed to give up sitting on the insidiously damp sand or indeed to leave the loudly peopled beach once I've persuaded the twins not to abandon their buckets and spades. I feel as if the children are straining to lug me uphill except when they mime more exhaustion than I can afford to admit. They drop the beach toys in my hall together with a generous bounty of sand on the way to thundering upstairs. After a brief altercation they reappear and I lead them down to the train.

Before it leaves the two-platformed terminus we're joined by half a dozen rudely pubertal drinkers. At least they're at the far end of the carriage, but their uproar might as well not be. They're fondest of a terse all-purpose word. I ignore the performance as an example to the twins, but when they continue giggling I attempt to distract them with a game of I Spy: s for the sea on the bare horizon, though they're so tardy in participating that I let it stand for the next station; f for a field behind a suburban school, even if I'm fleetingly afraid that Gerald will reveal it represents the teenagers' favourite word; c for cars in their thousands occupying a retail park beside a motorway, because surely Geraldine could never have been thinking of the other syllable the drinkers favour; b for the banks that rise up on both sides of the train as it begins to burrow into Birkenhead . . . I don't mean it for Beryl, but here is her house.

Just one window is visible above the embankment on our side of the carriage: her bedroom window. I don't know if I'm more disturbed by this glimpse of the room where she died or by having forgotten that we would pass the house. Of course it's someone else's room now—I imagine that the house has been converted into flats—and the room has acquired a window box; the reddish tuft that sprouts above the sill must belong to a plant, however dusty it looks. That's all I've time to see through the grimy window before the bridge I used to cross on the way to school blocks the view. Soon a station lets the drinkers loose, and a tunnel conducts us to our stop.

The lift to the street is open at both ends. It shuts them when Geraldine pushes the button, her brother having been promised that he can operate the lift on our return, and then it gapes afresh. Since nobody appears I suspect Gerald, but he's too far from the controls. "Must have been having a yawn," I say, and the twins gaze at me as if I'm the cause. No wonder I'm relieved when the doors close and we're hoisted into daylight.

As we turn the corner that brings the swimming pool into view the twins are diverted by a cinema. "I want to see a film," Gerald announces.

"You'll have to make your minds up. I can't be in two places at once. I'm just me."

Once she and her brother have done giggling at some element of this Geraldine says "Grumpo."

I'm saddened to think she means me, especially since Gerald agrees, until I see it's the title of a film that's showing in the complex. "You need to be twelve to go in."

"No we don't," they duet, and Gerald adds "You can take us."

Because they're so insistent I seek support from the girl in the pay booth, only to be told I'm mistaken. She watches me ask "What would your parents say?"

"They'd let us," Geraldine assures me, and Gerald says "We watch fifteens at home."

Wouldn't the girl advise me if the film weren't suitable? I buy tickets and lead the way into a large dark auditorium. We're just in time to see the screen exhort the audience to switch off mobile phones, and I have the twins do so once they've used theirs to light the way along a row in the absence of an usherette. The certificate that precedes the film doesn't tell me why it bears that rating, but that's apparent soon enough. An irascible grandfather embarrasses his offspring with his forgetfulness and the class of his behaviour and especially

his language, which even features two appearances of the word I ignored most often on the train. The twins find him hilarious, as do all the children in the cinema except for one that keeps poking its head over the back of a seat several rows ahead. Or is it a child? It doesn't seem to be with anyone, and now it has stopped trying to surprise me with its antics and settles on peering at me over the seat. Just its pale fat face above the nose is visible, crowned and surrounded by an unkempt mass of hair. The flickering of the dimness makes it look eager to jerk up and reveal more of its features, though the light is insufficient to touch off the slightest glimmer in the eyes, which I can't distinguish. At last the oldster in the film saves his children from robbers with a display of martial arts, and his family accepts that he's as loveable as I presume we're expected to have found him. The lights go up as the credits start to climb the screen, and I crane forward for a good look at the child who's been troubling me. It has ducked into hiding, and I sidle past Geraldine to find it. "You're going the wrong way, grandpa," she calls, but neither this nor Gerald's mirth can distract me from the sight of the row, which is deserted.

Members of the audience stare at me as I trudge to the end of the aisle, where words rise up to tower over me, and plod back along the auditorium. By this time it's empty except for the twins and me, and it's ridiculous to fancy that if I glance over my shoulder I'll catch a head in the act of taking cover. "Nothing," I say like Grumpo, if less coarsely,

when Gerald asks what I'm looking for. I bustle the twins out of the cinema, and as soon as they revive their phones Gerald's goes off like an alarm.

In a moment Geraldine's restores equality. They read their messages, which consist of less than words, and return their calls. "Hello, mummy," Geraldine says. "We were in a film."

Her brother conveys the information and hands me the mobile. "Dad wants to speak to you."

"Bertie. Forgive me, should we have—"

"I hope you know we came to find you on the beach."

"Gerald didn't say. I do apologise if you—"

"I trust you're bringing them home now. To your house."

I don't understand why he thinks the addition is necessary. "I'm afraid we're in trouble," I inform the twins as Geraldine ends her call. I have to be reminded that it's Gerald's turn to control the lift at the railway station. At least our train reaches the platform as we do, and soon it emerges into the open, at which point I recall how close we are to Beryl's house. As the train passes it I turn to look. There's nothing at her window.

The tenant must have moved the window box. It does no good to wonder where the item that I glimpsed is now. I'm nervous enough by the time we arrive at the end of the line and I lead the twins or am led by them uphill. They seem more eager than I feel, perhaps because they've me to blame. I'm fumbling to extract my keys when

Paula's husband opens the front door as if it's his. Having given each of us a stare that settles on me, Bertie says "Dinner won't be long."

It sounds so much like a rebuke, and is backed up by so many trespassing smells, that I retort "I could have made it, you know."

"Could you?" Before I can rise to this challenge he adds "Don't you appreciate my cuisine and Paula's?"

"Your children don't seem to all that much," I'm provoked to respond and quote a favourite saying of Jo's. "It isn't seaside without fish and chips."

"I'm afraid we believe in raising them more healthily."

"Do you, Paula? In other words, not how your mother and I treated you?" When she only gazes sadly at me from the kitchen I say "It can't be very healthy if they hardly touch their food."

"It isn't very healthy for them to hear this kind of thing."

"Find something to watch for a few minutes," her husband tells them. "Maybe your grandfather can choose something suitable."

I feel silenced and dismissed. I follow the children into the lounge and insist on selecting the wildlife show. "I've got to watch as well," I say, even if it sounds like acknowledging a punishment. They greet the announcement of dinner without concealing their relief, although their enthusiasm falls short of the meal itself. When at last they've finished sprinkling cheese on their spaghetti they eat just the sauce, and hardly a leaf of their salad. Though I perform relishing all of

mine, I have a sense of being held responsible for their abstinence. I try not to glance at the mirror of the dresser, but whenever I fail there appear to be only the reflections of the family and me.

Once the twins have filled up with chocolate dessert, it's time for games. I vote against reviving the one in which the pallid head pops up, which means that Gerald vetoes his sister's choice of Monopoly. Eventually I remember the games stored in the cupboard under the stairs. The dark shape that rears up beyond the door is my shadow. As I take Snakes and Ladders off the pile I'm reminded of playing it with Paula and her mother, who would smile whenever Paula clapped her hands at having climbed a ladder. I've brought the game into the dining-room before I recall playing it with Beryl.

Was it our last game with her? It feels as if it should have been. Every time she cast a losing throw she moved one space ahead of it. "Can't get me," she would taunt the snakes. "You stay away from me, nasty squirmy things." I thought she was forbidding them to gobble her up as if she were one of her snacks between meals, the powdered sponge cakes that she'd grown more and more to resemble. Whenever she avoided a snake by expanding a move she peered at me out of the concealment of her puffed-up face. I felt challenged to react, and eventually I stopped my counter short of a snake. "Can't he count?" my aunt cried at once. "Go in the next box."

Once I'd descended the snake I complained "Auntie Beryl keeps going where she shouldn't."

"Don't you dare say I can't count. They knew how to teach us when I was at school." This was the start of a diatribe that left her panting and clutching her chest while her face tried on a range of shades of grey. "Look what you've done," my father muttered in my ear while my mother tried to calm her down. When Beryl recaptured her wheezing breath she insisted on finishing the game, staring hard at me every time she was forced to land on a snake. She lost, and glared at me as she said "Better never do anything wrong, even the tiniest thing. You don't know who'll be watching."

Of course I knew or feared I did. I wish I'd chosen another game to play with Paula and her family. Before long Gerald pretends one of his throws hasn't landed on a snake. "Fair play, now," I exhort, earning a scowl from Gerald and a look from his father that manages to be both disapproving and blank. Perhaps Geraldine misinterprets my comment, because soon she cheats too. "If we aren't going to play properly," I say without regarding anyone, "there's no point to the game." Not addressing somebody specific gives me a sense of including more people than are seated at the table, and no amount of glancing at the mirror can rid me of the impression. I've never been so glad to lose a game. "Will you excuse me?" I blurt as my chair stumbles backwards. "I've had quite a day. Time for bed."

My struggles to sleep only hold me awake. When at last the twins are coaxed up to their room and the adults retreat to theirs, I'm still attempting to fend off the memory of my final visit to my aunt's house. She was ill in bed, so shortly after the game of Snakes and Ladders that I felt responsible. She sent my mother out for cakes, though the remains of several were going stale in a box by her bed. There were crumbs on the coverlet and around her mouth, which looked swollen almost bloodlessly pale. I thought there was too much of her to be able to move until she dug her fingers into the bed and, having quivered into a sitting position that dislodged a musty shawl from her distended shoulders, reached for me. I took her hand as a preamble to begging forgiveness, but her cold spongy grasp felt as if it was on the way to becoming a substance other than flesh, which overwhelmed me with such panic that I couldn't speak. Perhaps she was aware of dying of her overloaded heart, since she fixed me with eyes that were practically buried in her face. "I'll be watching," she said and expelled a breath that sounded close to a word. It was almost too loose to include consonants—it seemed as soft as her hand—but it could have been "Peep." I was terrified that it might also be her last breath, since it had intensified her grip on me. Eventually she drew another rattling breath but gave no sign of relaxing her clutch. Her eyes held me as a time even longer than a nightmare seemed to ooze by before I heard my mother letting herself into the house, when I was able to snatch my hand free and dash for the stairs. In less than a week my aunt was dead.

If I didn't see her again, being afraid to was almost as bad. Now that she was gone I thought she could be anywhere and capable of reading all my thoughts, especially the ones I was ashamed to have. I believed that thinking of her might bring her, perhaps in yet worse a form. I'd gathered that the dead lost weight, but I wasn't anxious to imagine how. Wouldn't it let her move faster? All these fears kept me company at night into my adolescence, when for a while I was even more nervous of seeing her face over the end of my bed. That never happened, but when at last I fall uneasily asleep I wake to see a shock of red hair duck below the footboard.

I'm almost quick enough to disguise my shriek as mirth once I realise that the glimpse included two small heads. "Good God," Bertie shouts from downstairs, "who was that?"

"Only me," I call. "Just a dream."

The twins can't hide their giggles. "No, it was us," cries Geraldine.

At least I've headed them off from greeting me with Beryl's word. Their father and to a lesser extent Paula give me such probing looks over breakfast that I feel bound to regain some credibility as an adult by enquiring "How was your search for investments?"

"Unfinished business," Bertie says.

"We were too busy wondering where you could have got to," Paula says.

"I hope I'm allowed to redeem myself. Where would you two like to go today?"

"Shopping," Geraldine says at once.

"Yes, shopping," Gerald agrees louder.

"Make sure you keep your phones switched on," their father says and frowns at me. "Do you still not own one?"

"There aren't that many people for me to call."

Paula offers to lend me hers, but the handful of unfamiliar technology would just be another cause for concern. At least we don't need to pass my aunt's house—we can take a bus. The twins insist on sitting upstairs to watch the parade of small shops interrupted by derelict properties. Wreaths on a lamppost enshrine a teenage car thief before we cross a bridge into the docks. I won't let the flowers remind me of my aunt, whose house is the best part of a mile away. The heads I see ducking behind the reflection in the window of the back seats belong to children. However little good they're up to, I ignore them, and they remain entirely hidden as we make for the stairs at our stop.

The pedestrian precinct appears to lead to a cathedral on the far side of the foreshortened river. The street enclosed by shops is crowded, largely with young girls pushing their siblings in buggies, if the toddlers aren't their offspring. The twins bypass discount stores on the way to a shopping mall, where the tiled floor slopes up to a food court flanked by clothes shops. Twin marts called Boyz and Girlz face each other across tables occupied by pensioners eking out cups of tea and families demolishing the contents of polystyrene cartons. "I'll be in there," Geraldine declares and runs across to Girlz.

"Wait and we'll come—" I might as well not have commenced, since as I turn to Gerald he dodges into Boyz. "Stay in the shops. Call me when you need me," I shout so loud that a little girl at a table renders her mouth clownish with a misaimed cream cake. Geraldine doesn't falter, and I'm not sure if she heard. As she vanishes into the shop beyond the diners I hurry after her brother.

Boyz is full of parents indulging or haranguing their children. When I can't immediately locate Gerald in the noisy aisles I feel convicted of negligence. He's at the rear of the shop, removing fat shoes from boxy alcoves on the wall. "Don't go out whatever you do. I'm just going to see your sister doesn't either," I tell him.

I can't see her in the other shop. I'm sidling between the tables when I grasp that I could have had Gerald phone for me to speak to her. It's just as far to go back now, and so I find my way through an untidy maze of abandoned chairs to Girlz. Any number of those, correctly spelled, are jangling racks of hangers and my nerves while selecting clothes to dispute with their parents, but none of them is Geraldine. I flurry up and down the aisles, back and forth to another catacomb of footwear, but she's nowhere to be seen.

"Geraldine," I plead in the faded voice my exertions have left me. Perhaps it's best that I can't raise it, since she must be in another shop. I didn't actually see her entering this one. As I dash outside I'm seized by a panic that tastes like all the food in the court turned stale. I need to borrow Gerald's mobile, but the thought makes me wonder if the twins could be using their phones to play a game at my expense— to coordinate how they'll keep hiding from me. I stare about in a desperate attempt to locate Geraldine, and catch sight of the top of her head in the clothes store next to Girlz.

"Just you stay there," I pant as I flounder through the entrance. It's clear that she's playing a trick, because it's a shop for adults; indeed, all the dresses that flap on racks in the breeze of my haste seem designed for the older woman. She's crouching behind a waist-high cabinet close to the wall. The cabinet quivers a little at my approach, and she stirs as if she's preparing to bolt for some other cover. "That's enough, Geraldine," I say and make, I hope, not too ungentle a grab. My foot catches on an edge of carpet, however, and I sprawl across the cabinet. Before I can regain any balance my fingers lodge in the dusty reddish hair.

Is it a wig on a dummy head? It comes away in my hand, but it isn't all that does. I manage not to distinguish any features of the tattered whitish item that dangles from it, clinging to my fingers until I hurl the tangled mass at the wall. I'm struggling to back away when the rest of the head jerks up to confront me with its eyes and the holes into which they've sunk. I shut mine as I thrust myself away from the cabinet, emitting a noise I would never have expected to make other than in the worst dream.

I'm quiet by the time the rescuers

arrive to collect their children and me. It turns out that Geraldine was in a fitting room in Girlz. The twins forgot most of their differences so as to take charge, leading me out to a table where there seems to be an insistent smell of stale sponge cake. Nobody appears to have noticed anything wrong in the clothes shop except me. I'm given the front passenger seat in Bertie's car, which makes me feel like an overgrown child or put in a place of shame. The twins used their phones to communicate about me, having heard my cries, and to summon their parents. I gather that I'm especially to blame for refusing the loan of a mobile that would have prevented my losing the children and succumbing to panic.

I do my best to go along with this version of events. I apologise all the way home for being insufficiently advanced and hope the driver will decide this is enough. I help Paula make a salad, and eat up every slice of cold meat at dinner while I struggle to avoid thinking of another food. I let the children raid the cupboard under the stairs for games, although these keep us in the dining-room. Sitting with my back to the mirror doesn't convince me we're alone, and perhaps my efforts to behave normally are too evident. I've dropped the dice several times to check that nobody is lurking under the table when Paula suggests an early night for all.

As I lie in bed, striving to fend off thoughts that feel capable of bringing their subject to me in the dark, I hear fragments of an argument. The twins are asleep or at any rate quiet. I'm won-

dering whether to intervene as diplomatically as possible when Paula's husband says "It's one thing your father being such an old woman—"

"I've told you not to call him that."

"—but today breaks the deal. I won't have him acting like that with my children."

There's more, not least about how they aren't just his, but the disagreements grow more muted, and I'm still hearing what he called me. It makes me feel alone, not only in the bed that's twice the size I need but also in the room. Somehow I sleep, and look for the twins at the foot of the bed when I waken, but perhaps they've been advised to stay away. They're so subdued at breakfast that I'm not entirely surprised when Paula says "Dad, we're truly sorry but we have to go home. I'll come and see you again soon, I promise."

I refrain from asking Bertie whether he'll be returning in search of investments. Once all the suitcases have been wedged into the boot of the Jaguar I give the twins all the kisses they can stand, along with twenty pounds each that feels like buying affection, and deliver a token handshake to Paula's husband before competing with her for the longest hug. As I wave the car downhill while the children's faces dwindle in the rear window, I could imagine that the windmills on the bay are mimicking my gesture. I turn back to the house and am halted by the view into the dining-room.

The family didn't clear away their last game. It's Snakes and Ladders, and

I could imagine they left it for me to play with a companion. I slam the front door and hurry into the room. I'm not anxious to share the house with the reminder that the game brings. I stoop so fast to pick up the box from the floor that an ache tweaks my spine. As I straighten, it's almost enough to distract me from the sight of my head bobbing up in the mirror.

But it isn't in the mirror, nor is it my head. It's on the far side of the table, though it has left even more of its face elsewhere. It still has eyes, glinting deep in their holes. Perhaps it is indeed here for a game, and if I join in it may eventually tire of playing. I can think of no other way to deal with it. I drop the box and crouch painfully, and once my playmate imitates me I poke my head above the table as it does. "Peep," I cry, though I'm terrified to hear an answer. "Peep."

🝫

In the wake of their blissful sojourn in the city of Lamentable Moll, the intrepid sorcerers Bauchelain and Korbal Broach — along with their newly hired manservant, Emancipor Reese — have set out on the wide open seas aboard the sturdy Suncurl.

Alas, there's more baggage in the hold than meets the beady eyes of Suncurl's hapless crew, and once on the cursed sea-lane known as Laughter's End — the Red Road in which flows the blood of an Elder God — unseemly terrors are prodded awake, to the understated dismay of all.

It is said that it is not the destination that counts, but the journey itself. Such a noble, worthy sentiment. Aye, it is the journey that counts, especially when what counts is horror, murder, mischance and mayhem. For Bauchelain, Korbal Broach and Emancipor Reese, it is of course just one more night on the high seas, on a journey without end — and that counts for a lot.

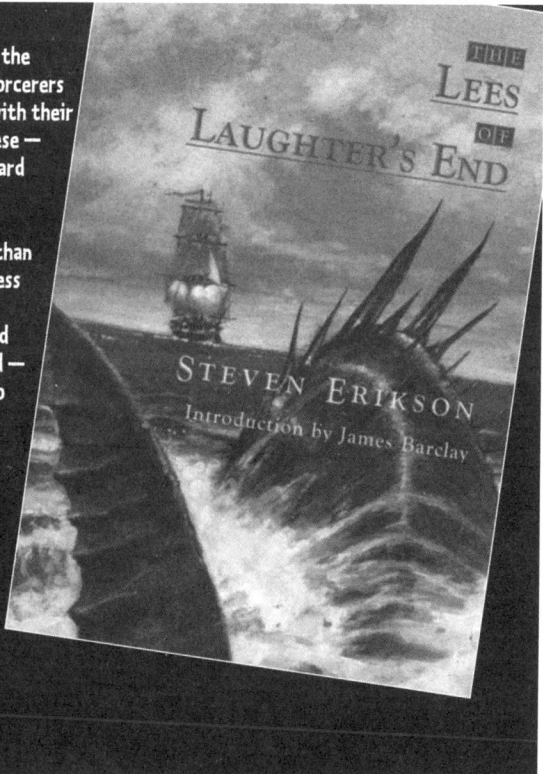

THE LEES OF LAUGHTER'S END

STEVEN ERIKSON

Introduction by James Barclay

"Years ago, long before I took up writing," Steven Erikson writes, "I spent long stretches of my summers working as an archaeologist, both digging sites and surveying vast areas of wilderness, looking for ancient places of habitation and the like. One of the great, unexpected discoveries on these projects was meeting locals—trappers, game wardens, bush pilots, Native Americans. A few beers, a campfire, and the stories started.

"Although I was not aware of it at the time, I was soaking this stuff up on all kinds of levels, and some of that eventually emerged in this modest tale here. There's a certain detail in 'This Rich Evil Sound' that had me cornered by a handful of disbelieving Americans a few years back, and to head things off this time round: yes, it can get cold enough on a winter night in Manitoba that trees will explode. Heard 'em myself, lying awake one night in a snow quincy just north of Redrock Lake—a lake frozen solid, by the way, nineteen or so feet at its deepest. Like the locals told me, ain't no fish in that lake, bud."

The Lees of Laughter's End, *Steve's new tale of that lovable duo Bauchelain and Korbal Broach, is now available from PS.*

This Rich Evil Sound

Steven Erikson

I'm not an old man. Sometimes the tracks old men think along are so deep cut nobody can see where they're going, maybe not even see the tracks themselves. But then I think that maybe there are different kinds of old. People say I should've been born a hundred years ago. Does that make me old in some way? They don't mean harm when they talk like that. It's just that they don't know me. I was in love with this girl, once, back in high school. Her name was Linda, and she was pretty popular, I guess. One day in the lunchroom I got down on one knee and sang for her a love song. One of my buddies had laid a dare on me—they sat at their table laughing and cheering. It was something I wanted to do anyway. No harm in it. The guys thought it was silly, but that's all right, too.

I know people make fun of me. I just look at things different from others. Before I got big I used to get in fights. There's always guys who don't like the way you look at things. They think it makes you weaker than them, maybe, and that's what they were trying to prove by fighting me. By the time I was fifteen they left me alone. They still figured me weak in my head, probably, but my body didn't look weak, not anymore.

I'm twenty now, so people have been leaving me alone for about five years. I don't mind. I like being alone. I quit school when I was sixteen, headed out into the bush. I spent the winter in northern Manitoba, nearly froze my feet off. I learned to lay trap lines from this Ojibwa Indian. He didn't know a word of English, except "nineteen seventy." I tried to teach him "nineteen eighty," because that was the year, but I don't think he ever got it. When I got back to Winnipeg I applied for and got a trapping license and that's what I've been doing ever since, out in Whiteshell Park.

In summers the park is full of people, so I head to Grassy River where it's quieter. But in the winter the only people in the park are rangers and trappers and old people who don't like the city and stay in their cabins. I don't mind running into those people, because we usually look at things the same way, and they don't make fun of me or anything.

This winter I was working Redrock Lake and the Whiteshell River. I'd heard from one of the rangers that Charlie Clark was wintering for the first time up at his cottage on Jessica Lake, so I decided to pay him a visit. Ever since they'd retired, Charlie and his wife had been spending the summers out here. But his wife died last summer, so he was all alone. I knew he'd be glad for some company.

I use a tent, but most trappers got cabins, because the years just pull at you and pretty soon a tent or quincy's too cold. It gets hard checking the lines when all your bones ache. Charlie wasn't a trapper, but I knew he'd understand and put me up for a couple days so I could dry out and get toasty. I'm pretty tough but I don't mind some luxury when I can get it.

Getting to Jessica Lake was easy. The Whiteshell River connects most of the lakes in the park. I broke camp an hour before dawn and walked the river. Winter's the quietest season. You're the only

thing moving, the only thing making any sound. You listen to your breath, to the backpack creaking in its straps, to the crunch of your snowshoes. You can sing songs to pass the time and your voice sounds beautiful. And you can think about things, taking all the time you want to, with nobody pushing you for answers. You can think as slow as you like, and the rest of the world, if it cares at all, just waits. No ticking clocks, just shadows all blue and soft and moving slower than you can see.

I reached the park highway by noon. They keep it ploughed for the cross-country skiers who come out from Winnipeg on warm weekends and for people like Charlie Clark.

I smelled woodsmoke long before I saw his cottage. There'd been a cold snap the last couple weeks. No snow, no wind, just that rich silence under a sundogged sky. The smoke hung in the air like it had no place to go, smelling bittersweet because it was black spruce. It's not a good wood to burn, since it goes fast and doesn't give off much heat. I figured Charlie was getting low on his wood supply. A few minutes later the cottage came into view, its windows lit.

I gave a shout just to warn him, then turned into the driveway. At the porch I unstrapped my snowshoes. Charlie had come to the window and was now trying to open the frozen door. He had to shove it hard a couple times before it swung free of its frame.

"Goddammit, Daniel, it's good to see you! Get in here!"

"You running low on wood, Charlie?" I asked as I stepped inside and Charlie closed the door behind me.

"Just one pile's getting down," Charlie said. "I cleared some black spruce from out back last summer. Just using it up. How the hell have you been?"

"Good." I took my backpack off, started stripping down some. "Thick pelts this winter."

Charlie shook his head, rubbing his brow. "Animals. They always know when it's gonna be a cold one. They always know, don't they?"

"Sure do," I said. We went into the den and sat down in front of the fireplace. The ranger had told me that Charlie had taken his wife's death pretty hard, and I could see that he didn't look too good. The skin of his face was pasty and yellow. And I saw that a shaking had come to his hands. "How you been, Charlie?" I asked, stretching my feet towards the fire.

"Strange winter, eh?" Charlie looked down, rubbing his forehead again. "I know this sounds funny, but I'm tasting metal these days." He squinted at me. "Can't really explain it, Daniel. But ever since the snows hit for real, I might as well be eating lead ten times a day, from the taste I'm tasting."

I glanced at him, then looked away. He was giving me this real troubled look. I stared at the fire. "Don't know," I finally said. "Maybe it's the lake water."

"Hell no, it isn't like that." He paused. "Had a heart attack last summer, did you know that?"

I shook my head. "Didn't hear anything about it. How bad was—"

"The doctor in the city—I forget his name, he took over when Bill retired, just a kid, really—he's been phoning me about once a week, asking me how I'm doing. So I tell him, but he says it's just psychological. He says there's no way somebody can taste a pacemaker. I suppose he knows what he's talking about." Charlie looked up at me and smiled. "But he was the one making the connection with the wind-up, not me, right? I just said to him, 'I keep tasting metal, Doc. How about that?' "

"And what did he say to that?"

"Psychological, like I told you."

"Oh yeah. Right." I studied the flames, listened to the snapping wood. It was burning real fast, that black spruce. For some reason I wanted it to slow down. It was burning too fast, just eating itself up and hardly any warmth reaching my feet. The way the wood spit out sparks bothered me, too, like words coming so quick all you can do is nod, answering everything "yes" no matter what you hear.

"Young people," Charlie said. "The ones in the city, like that doc." He looked at me. "The city people—can you figure them, Daniel?"

I laughed. "If I could maybe I wouldn't be here."

"You can't figure them, then?"

I shrugged. "They're just different, that's all. Like when things go quiet—they gotta make noise. So when they do something funny everybody laughs real loud, and it's not quiet anymore, and they get comfortable again. And winter, and the bush—well, they don't know what winter is, and they don't like the bush, the way it just swallows their noise. You couldn't laugh loud enough to keep that from happening, I bet."

Charlie was nodding. "Always questions, that's what I notice. Always 'why?' They ask 'why?' and then they answer themselves right away. 'Why?' 'Because.' Just like that. Making everything seem so simple. Know what I mean? And they're always so suspicious, especially about complicated things, like when I say I'm tasting metal. 'Why?' 'Psychological.' Just like that. I was a teacher, did you know that, Daniel?"

"Sure."

"Ten-year-old kids like that question. 'Why?' How old are you, Daniel?"

"Twenty," I said, feeling uncomfortable for some reason, maybe about the way he kept using my name. He made it sound strange, like it wasn't my own. I thought about what I'd said, about city people, and I wondered at how angry I got saying it.

Charlie was talking. "Me and Mary couldn't have kids, did you know that? It was a hard thing for her to accept. I didn't mind. I didn't mind at all. The Lord just didn't see fit, that's all."

The room should have felt cozy, with the bear rug between us and all the knick-knacks crowding the shelves, the mounted jack and the antlers on the walls, the easy chair deep and comfortable. But it didn't feel cozy. I put more black spruce on the fire, then pulled my chair closer to it. "Anybody else drop by?" I asked.

Charlie nodded. "Yeah, the strangest winter. And it's not just the taste in my mouth, either. When it was snowing

the ploughs used to come and clear the road a couple times a week. I'd go out and give them a wave, let them know I haven't run out of batteries or something." He laughed. "On the really cold days I flagged them down, gave them a thermos of hot chocolate. And you know, no matter if it was a different driver next week, I always got the thermos back. Sometimes we talked a bit. You know, just to keep the jaws greased. I told them about the buck, the one that comes across the lake every morning, right up to the cabin looking for food. And the very next week one of the drivers drops off two bales of hay. How about that?"

He'd been talking so fast I wondered if I'd missed something. "Charlie, what buck?"

He looked surprised. "I didn't tell you about the buck?"

"I don't think so."

Charlie's gaze returned to the fire. "Hasn't snowed in weeks. The ploughs stopped coming. Sometimes I swear I can hear them, way off down the road, so I go out, right? I go out and wait, figuring they're coming to check up on me. But they must be doing something else, cause they don't come. I can hear them, all right. They must be busy, right?"

"Sure." I stood. "Listen, I'm gonna get some other wood, if that's all right?"

"Fine. You go right ahead and get it, Daniel. That's fine by me. I got some birch out back."

"Great," I said.

Outside, I stood in front of the woodpile, holding Charlie's axe in my hands. I listened to the silence beyond the sounds of my breath. The muscles around my neck felt tight. I let the quiet sink into me, studied the grey trees beyond the clearing. Without leaves the trees all seemed to be standing alone, each one cut off from the others. The snow beneath them was like empty space, as if the roots and earth had been wiped away, leaving nothing behind.

My feet began to tingle. My toes had been frozen so many times there wasn't much feeling left in them anyway. All I had to do, I knew, was to get moving, but I just kept standing there, and the cold started working its way up my legs the way it does—picking out little areas, making them feel sort of wet, exposed. Then the feeling goes and there's just an empty patch. My knees went, then my thighs.

Behind me the backdoor opened. "Hey, Daniel?" The spell, or whatever it was, broke. I turned around. Charlie was standing just inside the door, clouds of vapor around his legs.

"Just thinking," I said to him, smiling.

"Thought you froze right up!" Charlie said, laughing. "Hurry up back inside. I got hot chocolate brewing."

"Right," I said, turning back to the woodpile. I began pulling out birch logs. To split them all I had to do was let the axe fall of its own weight—the logs seemed to almost jump apart. But the moving around brought the feeling back to my legs.

I piled wood on the back porch, then brought an armload inside. Charlie was in the kitchen, standing by the stove.

"They must be pretty busy, right?" he asked, stirring Fry's cocoa into a pot of simmering milk.

"Who?"

"The guys who clear the roads, like I was saying before. There's lots of side roads that probably need work, ones they couldn't get around to earlier, right? Can you believe this cold snap? All night long I can hear trees cracking. Exploding, you know? It's an eerie sound, all right. Can't say I like it. Do you like it, Daniel? I've been getting up at dawn and I make some coffee and sit in the rocker so I can look out over the lake.

"That's how I first saw the buck, looking out over the lake. He comes from the far side, every morning. Stumbling through the deep snow. Uses a different trail every time. Can you figure that?"

Charlie poured us cups of hot chocolate. We returned to the den. I set my cup down on the mantle and went to bring in the birch. The echo of the axe splitting the wood kept going through my head, making me think of what Charlie had been saying about exploding trees.

I stoked the fire, then sat down again. "That doc in the city," I said, "he's still phoning you every week?"

Charlie rubbed his face, then licked his lips. "I unplugged the phone. He kept saying the same old thing, over and over again." He leaned towards me and gestured for me to get closer. "Tell me, do you think my tongue's turning blue?" He poked out his tongue.

I looked at it, then sat back. "Hard to tell," I said. "Don't think so."

"I think so," Charlie said.

The heat coming from the birch logs made me push my chair back. I thought about the nights I'd spent alone, wrapped in my Woods arctic sleeping bag, watching my breath lay a sheet of ice on the nylon ceiling above me. I'd be filled with the silence, so filled and warm, with my thoughts going slow as they like to do. Then crack! A tree would explode. I'd jump, stare into the darkness, my heart pounding. Black spruce. It's the black spruce that explodes.

"I hope the ploughs come back," Charlie said. "We're running low on hay." He frowned suddenly. "Oh," he said, "I forgot." He climbed to his feet. "Come on, Daniel, let's look out over the lake."

I followed him to the large frosted window. We stood side by side and stared outward. I could see the buck's trails, shadowed blue. They stopped at a scuffed-up area just below the porch deck, maybe thirty feet away. The scuffed-up area was spattered with frozen blood, and off to one side lay the frosted carcass of the buck, half eaten.

"Wolves? Jesus, nobody's seen a wolf in this park for years."

Charlie asked, "Did you see the Northern Lights last night?"

"I'm usually asleep by seven," I said.

"From horizon to horizon, I've never seen them so big. They made a sound like, like wind on sand, falling all around. All around. It's so beautiful, Daniel. There's no real way to describe it, is there?"

"Not really. You're right in that." But I knew that sound, the voice behind the silence, the voice that pushed the silence into me. And I knew what that voice said, the single word over and over again. Alone, alone, alone.

"Only," Charlie continued, "only, there'd be this falling from the sky, right? And all these streams of colour. And deep in the forest, deep in the forest, Daniel. The trees kept on shattering. As if, for just last night, for just those few hours when I was standing out there, the world was made of glass. The thinnest glass. And the trees reaching upward. I don't know." Charlie turned to me, a terrible frown on his lined face. "Maybe the trees were made of glass, too. But all gnarled and bubbled and black. Trying to join the sky, but too rough." He turned back to the window. "Too rough. Just no way they could make it. They were reaching up, to where the colours played. Reaching. Then snapping. Like gunshots. I tell you, in certain lights you can see it—the blue on my tongue. Then the glass in the sky shattered, and there was this falling. Endless falling."

I nodded. "Like the world was made of glass." His words had left a pain inside me, a deep, spreading pain. "Too rough," I said, "wanting to play with the colours, all the colours. But too rough." The voice whispered its word in my head, and it hurt me.

"That buck," Charlie said, "he was so strong, so healthy. All his life. You could see that. He—I built this cabin with my own hands, Daniel, did you know that? He was strong, healthy. He'd been through hard times lately, but he was all right. Four wolves. I watched it all happen. That buck, running across the lake, full bore. I was sitting in this rocker, this one right here. They took him not twenty yards from here—you can see where he first went down. I'd been thinking about getting my bear rifle, but it was already too late. That's the way it looked anyway. But the buck," he shook his head, "that buck, he just got up and kept coming. You can see it—he dragged those wolves ten, fifteen yards. Dragged all of them."

"Son of a bitch," I said.

"He'd been so strong, all his life. He dragged them all right, but in the end it didn't matter. It didn't count for nothing. I just sat here, all this morning, watching them wolves eating. Funny, they kept walking around and around him, not knowing what to do, really. What to do with it all."

I stared at the carcass, at the gnawed ribs and purple ice-flecked meat. "They'll be back for more," I said. "They earned it."

"I'm thinking, Daniel, the same things over and over again. Funny how that happens, eh? I'm thinking about my rifle, and that taste filling my mouth. Metal. He'd been so strong, cut down just like that. And I'm thinking about this window, this one right in front of us, Daniel. Two panes each a quarter inch thick. How everything happened in absolute silence. And the

only sound I knew, I know, is something I feel more than hear. It's probably psychological, eh, Daniel? But there's this tingling, like glass chimes, and there's this humming—both coming from my chest. It's fading, I think, Daniel."

I shook my head, again and again, but he wasn't paying any attention to me. I didn't even know what I was saying no to, but in my head a voice kept asking, "Why?" Why? And Charlie, he kept answering me, he kept saying "Because, Daniel. Only because. Just because."

"The strangest winter," Charlie said. "No way to explain it, any of it. My tongue turning bluer and bluer, getting stained deeper and deeper every time, the doc telling me it's psychological—what the hell is that supposed to mean?"

We stood there for a long time, staring at the carcass. I wanted to cry, I wanted to shut my ears, stop the silence outside, never again let it in. But the tracks were cut too deep inside me. I'm not an old man. I don't think I'm very smart as far as young people go. I was never good at things they're good at. I'm not brave, and I'm sorry for that. I really am. I left Charlie that afternoon. I ran from him, across the lake, using one of the buck's trails. I pitched my tent on the other side of Jessica Lake. I could've gone farther but I didn't. I know it wasn't a tree shattering that woke me that night, made me jump up, staring into the darkness, heart pounding. I know that it wasn't a tree, and I'm sorry. Truly sorry. 𝕂

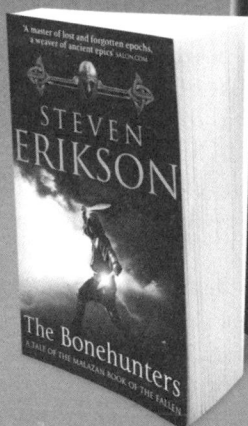

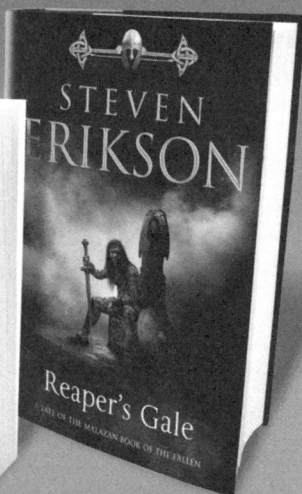

In November of 2006, while he was touring in London for Lisey's Story, *Stephen King had the most vivid dream of his adult life. "When I woke," he says, "I slid to the floor, glad to be awake and amazed that any human brain could hold such a powerful image.*

"I knew I had to write about it, I knew the story had to be short—no more than a vignette— and I knew I would never be able to do that image (God, don't let it be a vision) justice. Since then, I have seen the image replicated twice on American network TV—once in Jericho *and once in* 24. *Clearly I am not the only one haunted by this terrible possibility. But my mother used to say, 'Tell your dream and it won't come true.' Let's hope she was right." Indeed.*

Graduation Afternoon
Stephen King

Janice has never settled on the right word for the place where Buddy lives. It's too big to be called a house, too small to be an estate, and the name on the post at the foot of the driveway, Harborlights, gags her. It sounds like the name of a restaurant in New London, the kind where the special is always fish. She usually winds up just calling it "your place," as in "Let's go to your place and play tennis" or "Let's go to your place and go swimming."

It's pretty much the same deal with Buddy himself, she thinks, watching him trudge up the lawn toward the sound of shouts on the other side of the house, where the pool is. You didn't want to call your boyfriend Buddy, but when reverting to his real name meant Bruce, it left you with no real ground to stand on.

Or expressing feelings, that was that. She knew he wanted to hear her say she loved him, especially on his graduation day—surely a better present than the silver medallion she'd given him, although the medallion had set her back a teeth-clenching amount—but she couldn't do it. She couldn't bring herself to say, "I love you, Bruce." The best she could manage (and again with that interior clench) was "I'm awfully fond of you, Buddy." And even that sounded like a line out of a British musical comedy.

"You don't mind what she said, do you?" That was the last thing he'd asked her before heading up the lawn to change into his swim trunks. "That isn't why you're staying behind, is it?"

"No, just want to hit a few more. And look at the view." The house did have that going for it, and she could never get enough. Because you could see the whole New York city-scape from this side of the house, the buildings reduced to blue toys with sun gleaming on the highest windows. Janice thought that when it came to NYC, you could only get that sense of exqui-site stillness from a distance. It was a lie she loved.

"Because she's just my gran," he

went on. "You know her by now. If it enters her head, it exits her mouth."

"I know," Janice said. And she liked Buddy's gran, who made no effort to hide her snobbery. There it was, out and beating time to the music. They were the Hopes, came to Connecticut along with the rest of the Heavenly Host, thank you so much. She is Janice Gandolewski, who will have her own graduation day—from Fairhaven High—two weeks from now, after Buddy has left with his three best buddies to hike the Appalachian Trail.

She turns to the basket of balls, a slender girl of good height in denim shorts, sneakers, and a shell top. Her legs flex as she rises on tiptoe with each serve. She's good-looking and knows it, her knowing of the functional and non-fussy sort. She's smart, and knows it. Very few Fairhaven girls manage relationships with boys from the Academy—other than the usual we-all-know-where-we-are, quick-and-dirty Winter Carnival or Spring Fling weekends, that is—and she has done so in spite of the *ski* that trails after her wherever she goes, like a tin can tied to the bumper of a family sedan. She has managed this social hat-trick with Bruce Hope, also known as Buddy.

And when they were coming up from the basement media room after playing video games—most of the others still down there, and still with their mortarboards cocked back on their heads—they had overheard his gran, in the parlor with the other adults (because this was really *their* party; the kids would have their own tonight, first at Holy Now! out on Route 219, which had been fourwalled for the occasion by Jimmy Fredericks's Dad and Mom, pursuant to the mandatory designated-driver rule, and then later, at the beach, under a full June moon, could you give me spoon, do I hear swoon, is there a swoon in the house).

"That was Janice-Something-Unpronounceable," Gran was saying in her oddly piercing, oddly toneless deaf-lady voice. "She's very pretty, isn't she? A townie. Bruce's friend for now." She didn't quite call Janice Bruce's starter-model, but of course it was all in the tone.

She shrugs and hits a few more balls, legs flexing, racket reaching. The balls fly hard and true across the net, each touching down deep in the receiver's box on the far side.

They have in fact learned from each other, and she suspects that's what these things are about. What they are for. And Buddy has not, in truth, been that hard to teach. He respected her from the first—maybe a little too much. She had to teach him out of that—the pedestal-worship part of that. And she thinks he hasn't been that bad a lover, given the fact that kids are denied the finest of accommodations and the luxury of time when it comes to giving their bodies the food they come to want.

"We did the best we could," she says, and decides to go and swim with the others, let him show her off one final time. He thinks they'll have all summer before he goes off to Princeton and she goes to State, but she thinks not; she thinks part of the purpose of the upcoming Appalachian hike is to separate them as painlessly but as completely as possible. In this Janice senses not the hand of the hale-and-hearty, good-fellows-every-one father, or the somehow endearing snobbery of the grandmother—*a townie, Bruce's friend for now*—but the smiling and subtle practicality of the mother, whose one fear (it might as well be stamped on her lovely, unlined forehead) is that the townie girl with the tin can tied to the end of her name will get pregnant and trap her boy into the wrong marriage.

"It would be wrong, too," she murmurs as she wheels the basket of balls into the shed and flips the latch. Her friend Marcy keeps asking her what she seems in him at all—*Buddy*, she all but sneers, wrinkling her nose. *What do you do all weekend? Go to garden parties? To polo matches?*

In fact, they have been to a couple of polo matches, because Tom Hope still rides—although, Buddy confided, this was apt to be his last year if he didn't stop putting on weight. But they have also made love, some of it sweaty and intense. Sometimes, too, he makes her laugh. Less often, now—she has an idea that his capacity to surprise and amuse is far from infinite—but yes, he still does. He's a lean and narrow-headed boy who breaks the rich-kid-geek mold in interesting and sometimes very unexpected ways. Also he thinks the world of her, and that isn't entirely bad for a girl's self-image.

Still, she doesn't think he will resist the call of his essential nature forever. By the age of thirty-five or so, she guesses he will have lost most or all of his enthusiasm for eating pussy and will be more interested in collecting coins. Or refinishing Colonial rockers, like his father does out in the—ahem—carriage-house.

She walks slowly up the long acre of green grass, looking out toward the blue toys of the city dreaming in the far distance. Closer at hand are the sounds of shouts and splashing from the pool. Inside, Bruce's mother and father and gran and closest friends will be celebrating the one chick's high school graduation in their own way, at a formal tea. Tonight the kids will go out and party down in a more righteous mode. Alcohol and not a few tabs of X will be ingested. Club music will throb through big speakers. No one will play the country stuff Janice grew up with, but that's all right; she still knows where to find it.

When she graduates there will be a much smaller party, probably at Aunt Kay's restaurant, and of course she is bound for educational halls far less grand or traditional, but she has plans to go farther than she suspects Buddy goes even in his dreams. She will be a journalist. She will begin on the campus newspaper, and then will see where that takes her. One rung at a time, that's the way to do it. There are plenty of rungs on the ladder. She has talent to go along with her looks and unshowy self-confidence. She doesn't know how much, but she will find out. And there's luck.

That, too. She knows enough not to count on it, but also enough to know it tends to come down on the side of the young.

She reaches the stone-flagged patio and looks down the rolling acre of lawn to the double tennis court. It all looks very big and very rich, very *special*, but she is wise enough to know she is only eighteen. There may come a time when it all looks quite ordinary to her, even in the eye of her memory. Quite small. It is this sense of perspective before the fact that makes it all right for her to be Janice-Something-Unpronounceable, and a townie, and Bruce's friend for now. Buddy, with his narrow head and fragile ability to make her laugh at unexpected times. *He* has never made her feel small, probably knows she'd leave him the first time he ever tried.

She can go directly through the house to the pool and the changing rooms on the far side, but first she turns slightly to her left to once again look at the city across all those miles of blue afternoon distance. She has time to think, *It could be my city someday, I could call it home*, before an enormous spark lights up there, as if some God deep in the machinery had suddenly flicked His Bic.

She winces from the brilliance, which is at first like a thick, isolated stroke of lightning. And then the entire southern sky lights up a soundless lurid red. Formless bloodglare obliterates the buildings. Then for a moment they are there again, but ghostlike, as if seen through an interposing lens. A second

or a tenth of a second after that they are gone forever, and the red begins to take on the shape of a thousand newsreels, climbing and boiling.

It is silent, silent.

Bruce's mother comes out on the patio and stands next to her, shading her eyes. She is wearing a new blue dress. A tea-dress. Her shoulder brushes Janice's and they look south at the crimson mushroom climbing, eating up the blue. Smoke is rising from around the edges—dark purple in the sunshine—and then being pulled back in. The red of the fireball is too intense to look at, it will blind her, but Janice cannot look away. Water is gushing down her cheeks in broad warm streams, but she cannot look away.

"What's that?" Bruce's mother asks. "If it's some kind of advertising, it's in very poor taste!"

"It's a bomb," Janice says. Her voice seems to be coming from somewhere else. On a live feed from Hartford, maybe. Now huge black blisters are erupting in the red mushroom, giving it hideous features that shift and change—now a cat, now a dog, now Bobo the Demon Clown—grimacing across the miles above what used to be New York and is now a smelting furnace. "A nuke. And an almighty big one. No little dirty backpack model, or—"

Whap! Heat spreads upward and downward on the side of her face, and water flies from both of her eyes, and her head rocks. Bruce's Mom has just slapped her. And hard.

"Don't you even joke about that!" Bruce's mother commands. "There's nothing funny about that!"

Other people are joining them on the patio now, but they are little more than shades; Janice's vision has either been stolen by the brightness of the fireball, or the cloud has blotted out the sun. Maybe both.

"That's in very... poor... *TASTE!*" Each word rising. *Taste* comes out in a scream.

Someone says, "It's some kind of special effect, it has to be, or else we'd hear—"

But then the sound reaches them. It's like a boulder running down an endless stone flume. It shivers the glass along the south side of the house and sends birds up from the trees in whirling squadrons. It fills the day. And it doesn't stop. It's like an endless sonic boom. Janice sees Bruce's gran go walking slowly down the path that leads to the multi-car garage with her hands to her ears. She walks with her head down and her back bent and her butt sticking out, like a dispossessed warhag starting down a long refugee road. Something hangs down on the back of her dress, swinging from side to side, and Janice isn't surprised to note (with what vision she has left) that it's Gran's hearing aid.

"I want to wake up," a man says from behind Janice. He speaks in a querulous, pestering tone. "I want to wake up. Enough is enough."

Now the red cloud has grown to its full height and stands in boiling triumph where New York was ninety seconds ago, a dark red and purple toadstool that has burned a hole straight through this afternoon and all the afternoons to follow.

A breeze begins to push through. It is a hot breeze. It lifts the hair from the sides of her head, freeing her ears to hear that endless grinding boom even better. Janice stands watching, and thinks about hitting tennis balls, one after the other, all of them landing so close together you could have caught them in a roasting pan. That is pretty much how she writes. It is her talent. Or was.

She thinks about the hike Bruce and his friends won't be taking. She thinks about the party at Holy Now! they won't be attending tonight. She thinks about the records by Jay-Z and Beyonce and The Fray they won't be listening to—no loss there. And she thinks of the country music her Dad listens to in his pickup truck on his way to and from work. That's better, somehow. She will think of Patsy Cline or Skeeter Davis and in a little while she may be able to teach what is left of her eyes not to look.

☒

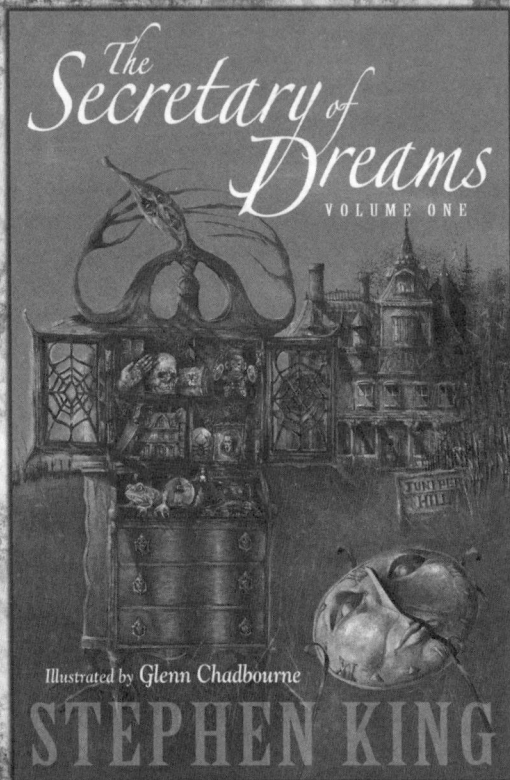

" 'Nothing Prepares You' is a cautionary tale about loss, and the consequences of loss," says Mark Morris. "It's a story I've had in my head for a long time, and is a very personal one in that a great many of the actual events and emotional situations which take place in the first half of the story are lifted from my observations, experiences and memories of my father's sudden death in 1988. My dad dropped dead at the age of forty-nine whilst playing golf, and I don't think a day goes by when I don't think about that, and more particularly about the odd, almost schizophrenic attitude human beings have towards their own lives.

"On the one hand we take life for granted—wishing precious days away because we're looking forward to some potentially pleasurable future event; full of plans and ambitions as if we're immortal—and on the other we're constantly aware of our own mortality, of the ephemeral nature of existence. The older I get, and the older my children get, the more acutely I feel the passage of time, and the more I come to realise that every one of us, in one way or another, is striving for some kind of meaning, or contentment, or inner peace."

Nothing Prepares You
Mark Morris

One: Martha

She was in the bath when the phone rang. She swore and stood up and stepped out awkwardly, reaching for the towel she'd dumped on the white-painted wicker chair, where Shaun sometimes sat and talked to her. She dried her feet quickly before throwing the towel around herself, but still left wet footprints on the wooden floor. If she didn't wipe them up quickly she knew they'd soak into the wood and stain it black. Which was a good reason—if freezing her arse off in the draughty hallway wasn't enough of one—to give the caller short shrift.

She reached the phone on the seventh ring, wishing that Shaun would hurry up and buy the new answer phone he'd been promising to get ever since their old one had given up the ghost last week. Snatching up the receiver she—not *too* querulously—said, "Hello?"

"Martha?"

She didn't recognise the voice at first, but there was still something about it, a bleakness to its tone, that gave her a feeling of what she could only describe as dread.

"Yes. Who's this?"

"It's me, Martha. Richard."

"Richard?"

Richard was Shaun's best friend. They had been best friends ever since starting school together, over thirty-five years ago.

"Are you sitting down, Martha?"

"Why?"

"I think you should sit down."

Richard's voice was shaky, close to breaking up. She could tell from his tone that something bad had happened. The only thing she didn't know was *how* bad.

"For fuck's sake, Richard," she snapped, fear making her angry, "just tell me."

"It's Shaun. He . . . we were playing squash, and . . . he seemed all right . . . but then he just . . . collapsed."

"Oh my God." Martha felt light-headed, almost as if she was a bit tipsy. "Is he all right?"

"He . . . he had a heart-attack. He died, Martha. I tried to save him, but . . ."

The room spun. Martha could no longer feel her legs. The water was turning cold on her shoulders, making her shiver. She clutched the towel tightly around her body and slid down the wall until she was squatting on her heels. She listened numbly as Richard's words dissolved into wracking sobs and knew that her life was over.

Shaun was in a private room. The walls were mint green. The window looked down on to the hospital car park. There was a curtain rail around the bed, but the curtains had been pulled back. The covers on the bed looked very clean, very crisp. They had been pulled up to Shaun's chest, but his arms were outside, which made the covers look uncomfortable, constricting. There was a chair beside the bed. Martha sat in it. Her right hand was clutching her handbag, the strap of which was over her right shoulder, but she didn't know why she'd brought it with her. Force of habit, she supposed.

Shaun's hair was combed funny. They'd given him a parting where he didn't normally have one. His lips and fingernails were blue, but apart from that he didn't look too bad. Except for that awful parting, of course. That horrified her in a way she could barely define, made her feel sick to her stomach. She reached out, surprised to see how much her hand was trembling, and lovingly re-arranged his hair. There, that was better.

She sat and stroked his cheek gently with the back of her hand. She stroked it and stroked it, over and over, not saying anything. His skin was cool, but not cold. She'd felt it colder. On winter walks. On the skidoo ride in Lapland when he'd leaned over and kissed her and told her how much he loved her. She realised his lack of coldness was giving her an absurd sense of hope, which all at once appalled her.

She couldn't say goodbye. She couldn't get the word out. She leaned over and kissed him—on the forehead, on the cheek, on the lips. She thought, *he'll never kiss me again*, and she sat back down with a little gasp, feeling as though something had broken inside her. Something brittle but flimsy, like a tiny, delicate egg, deep in her belly. She held his hand for a few seconds, but its limpness terrified her and she let it go again with a shudder. Later she couldn't remember leaving his bedside. She couldn't remember the moment when she had left him there on his own.

How *old was he?* That was the question all the neighbours asked her. They kept calling in, throughout the day, one after another, to see if she wanted anything.

Yes, she thought, *I want Shaun. And if I can't have him then I want to be dead too.*

"Forty-five," she'd tell them.

Forty-five. They'd all say it the same way. As if they were appalled. It was like they were auditioning for a play, like they all had the same lines to learn. *It's no age, is it?*

It was night. The sun had set on Shaun's last day. When it had risen that morning he had still been with her, full of life, and now he was gone. Less than four weeks ago the two of them had celebrated twenty-five years together.

"Wonder where we'll be in another twenty-five," he had said. "I'll be—my God—seventy then."

They had been in bed, warm and cosy after a nice meal, a bottle of wine, but she had repressed a shudder. "Ooh, don't."

He had laughed at her. "Seventy's not so old. Your dad's seventy, and he's still sprightly as a lamb."

"I know, but I still remember the night we met as clearly as if it was yesterday. The way time flies, it's scary."

"Time flies like an arrow," he had said solemnly, "whereas fruit flies like a banana."

"Idiot." She had giggled and turned her face up to his. "Kiss me you."

"Yes, ma'am."

His warm lips on hers. She closed her eyes, trying to remember. But the memory gave her no comfort. Only a yearning pain.

Eve arrived just after seven. Her father had been dead almost eight hours by then. Martha couldn't imagine how awful her train journey from Durham must have been, surrounded by people going about their usual lives. People who were laughing and joking. People chatting about soap operas and reality TV shows and celebrities. People disgorging office gossip, complaining about minor ailments, discussing plans for the weekend.

As soon as Eve stepped into the front room, pale and thin, stunned by what had happened, the neighbours melted away. Perhaps they didn't want to intrude on the personal grief of mother and daughter, or perhaps they were simply grateful to extricate themselves from the heavy pall of death in the air. Until now Martha had been tearless, and from the looks of her Eve had been too—her eyes were bright and flinty, her lips compressed, the muscles in her face taut. But as soon as the two women saw one another, it was like a switch being thrown. Eve spoke two small and broken words—"Oh, Mum"—and then they were clinging to each other, sobs tearing their way out of their chests and throats.

The next morning. Waking up with a red wine hangover. Shreds of fitful, messy dreams clinging to her mind, blurring her thoughts. Martha knew something was wrong, but for a blissful second she forgot what it was. Then she turned over in bed, and saw the pillow she had placed in the slight dip in the mattress where Shaun had laid nearly every night for the last twenty years, and where he would never lie again. And down they came, a rock-fall of memories, crushing her beneath an unendurable weight of futility and despair.

Shaun was dead. Her other half. Her beloved. The man she had chosen to spend her life with. The man she had always assumed she would grow old beside.

They had talked of buying a little cottage when they retired. Somewhere by the sea. They had talked of leisurely pub lunches, trips abroad, long walks on the beach, afternoons spent pottering in their garden. They had planned to do everything their currently busy lives prevented them from doing.

But now all that was gone. Snatched away. Now she would have to spend the rest of her years alone.

And what was the point in *that*? she thought fiercely. What was the point of *anything* any more? She mashed her face into her pillow, trying to blot everything out, wishing she could suffocate herself. She thought of Shaun lying in the hospital bed, pictured herself stroking his hair, holding his limp hand. She curled herself into a comma and began to cry again, loud retching sobs, as if she wanted to sick out her grief. If there was a God, how could he do this to her? How could he do this to Shaun? Shaun was a good man, a loving

husband and father. It didn't make sense. It wasn't fair! She felt a sudden and blazing surge of anger. She *hated* God! Hated God, and hated Shaun for leaving her. She hated Shaun and she loved him. She loved him so much she thought her heart would split in two.

Eve was in the kitchen. Sitting on a chair which was turned away from the breakfast table. She was slumped over, hair hanging down, obscuring her face. Her elbows were resting on her knees and Shaun's squash racket was clutched in her hands. She didn't look up when Martha entered, and at first Martha thought she was asleep. Then she saw her daughter's thin shoulders shaking beneath her night shirt, and she realised that Eve was crying. She saw tears dripping from beneath her curtain of hair and splashing—*plip plop*—on the floor between her long white feet.

Martha stood there, unable to offer comfort, unable to think of anything to say. Shaun was everywhere. His writing was on the calendar; his stoppered half-bottle of favourite Australian red was standing beside the spice rack; his Homer Simpson mug was on the draining board; the magnets he'd brought back from New York three years ago were attached to the fridge.

He was in the house. He surrounded her. She felt almost as if she could reach out and touch him . . . and yet he couldn't be more gone.

Eve looked up and pushed her long dark hair away from her face. She sniffed back her tears. She was nineteen years old. Slender and beautiful. Too thin, but perfect all the same. She had known her father for less than half his life. She would never now get the chance to know him better.

"Sorry," she said.

"What for?" asked Martha.

"I don't know . . . I just think maybe I should be stronger. For you."

Martha pulled out a chair and sat beside her daughter. "He was your dad. You're allowed to cry."

Eve hung her head. Her voice grew weepy again. "It's so unfair. Dad wasn't over-weight. He didn't smoke. He ate well. He took exercise. It's just so . . . fucking unfair."

Martha had never heard her daughter say "fuck" before. Even in her grief she was momentarily surprised by how it affected her. Instead of being shocked or disappointed she was moved by the depth of her daughter's feelings. "I know," she said, "I know."

"And I was thinking," Eve whispered. "Oh, it's so stupid . . . "

"Tell me."

"I was thinking . . . who's going to escort me up the aisle on my wedding day now that Dad's gone? I don't . . . I don't want anyone else to do it . . . "

Martha held her daughter to her and rocked her. For the second time, and not for the last, they clung together and wept.

M artha woke up facing the wall. She had no idea what time it was. She couldn't remember falling asleep. It was as if the hours had come unravelled, as

if the past few days and nights had blurred, one into the other.

She thought it might be dawn. The light was pearly, and the air was still, as if the day was waiting to break out. Had she taken some of the diazepam that one of her neighbours, pill-popping Margaret, had pressed into her hand with a wink and a nod, like a drug dealer on a telly programme? She didn't think so, but she might have done. Her head felt muzzy enough.

"Martha."

The word was softly spoken, the voice infinitely tender. Her heart leaped. He was here behind her, standing right beside the bed!

She felt a hand on her shoulder. A hand that tugged at her, pulling her gently but inexorably over on to her back. She opened her eyes to look up into the face of her beloved, wondering only briefly how she had known it was dawn if her eyes had been closed. She blinked up into the thin daylight, desperate to see him smiling down at her.

But there was no one there.

"Y ou'll see him again, you know."

Cath Isles sat across from her, nursing a cup of tea. Martha didn't know how many cups of tea she had drunk, and how many tears she had shed, in the five endless days since Shaun had gone. Enough to fill a river, she thought. A river of tea and tears. Had it *really* only been five days? What had she and Shaun been doing this time last week? She thought back, and remembered that they'd gone to that pasta place on Bridge Street. Then they'd got a DVD out and watched it cuddled up together on the settee. The memory was like a jolt in her gut, like a needle pushing its way under her skin. Little things kept affecting her in the same way. Earlier she'd remembered that they'd been due at Paul and Brigit's for dinner this coming Saturday, and her legs had turned to jelly. She'd had to grab at the wall to stop herself crumpling to the floor.

Cath Isles and her husband, John, had moved away from the street nearly ten years ago. Martha hadn't seen Cath for at least half that time, but she'd known that John had died because Cath had told her so in a Christmas card. John had been forty-two. He'd been about to head off in the car to pick their sixteen year-old daughter up from a party and had started to feel unwell. He'd sat on the settee and Cath had gone to fetch him a glass of water. When she came back he was lying on the floor, convulsing.

"I knew that was it straight away," she said. She was loud and brassy and laughed like a horse, but she wasn't laughing now. "He was bright blue. As blue as your jeans, pet." She pointed at Eve's denim-clad legs. "He'd only been to the doctor's for a check-up the week before and told he was fit as a fiddle."

"What did you mean when you said we'd see him again?" Eve asked. She had been into town two days before and come back with a bag full of books about life after death, reincarnation. She was reading one now called *The Dead Are Alive!* Martha thought it was a load of rubbish, but she hadn't said anything. If it gave Eve a bit of comfort then where was the harm?

"They come back to say goodbye," Cath said. "When I saw our John I were washing up and I looked out of the kitchen window, and there he was, walking down the garden path, clear as anything. It were weird cos I didn't think anything of it. I just thought, 'Oh, there's our John', and I went to the back door and opened it to let him in. And of course there were no one there."

Eve's eyes were wide. "Do you really think you saw him?"

"He were as real as you are," Cath said.

"Did you hear that, Mum?" said Eve. "Maybe we'll see Dad again. Wouldn't that be fantastic?"

"Mmm," Martha said.

You'll feel a lot better once you've got the funeral over with. That's what everyone kept telling her. Martha knew they were only trying to be kind, trying to be comforting, but she wanted to scream at them. In her head, she *was* screaming:

No I won't! It won't make me feel any better! I'll never feel better again! Because Shaun will still be gone! I'll still be alone! And nothing anyone can do will ever change that!

She was dreading the funeral. Dreading seeing people. Dreading them looking at her. Dreading their sympathy. That morning she woke with a rock in her throat and carried it with her throughout the day.

At the funeral home she and Eve, and their good friends, Nick and Gill, went in to see Shaun lying in his coffin. Eve made a sound, a stifled whimper, and covered her mouth with her hand. Nick just stood there, looking awkward and embarrassed. Gill went straight over and kissed Shaun on the cheek.

It didn't look like Shaun. It looked like a wax model of him. His hair was too feathery and his cheeks were too red and they'd dressed him in something that he wouldn't have been seen dead in, if it wasn't for the fact that he *had* been seen dead in it. It was a satiny gown, blue with a ruffed collar, like something a choir boy would wear. Martha was appalled. It made her feel as sick as the hair parting in the hospital.

Martha wondered whether she'd approved what Shaun was wearing, or even been consulted about it. She couldn't remember. Not that it mattered. It would all be ashes in an hour or so anyway.

The bluntness of that thought took her by surprise. It was another smack in the face, another punch in the belly. As she tottered, Eve ran and grabbed her and helped her into a chair. The undertaker, Mr Stokes, made her a cup of tea, which she had to drink before she could carry on.

Because that was what it was all about, wasn't it? Carrying on. Carrying on even though she felt like fading away, sinking into darkness. The day passed in a glassy haze. At the wake afterwards, she heard herself laughing, and it was like watching another person, a version of herself from last week when

Shaun had been alive and the world had still been full of colour and meaning.

In bed she curled up and talked to Shaun, whispering, pleading. "Please come back to me. Please don't leave me alone. I can't go on without you."

Two: Shaun

"**S**he's coming round," Dr Willis said.

"Is she okay?" asked Shaun.

"Vital signs are strong. Brain activity normal." Dr Willis smiled reassuringly. "She'll be fine. A bit disorientated and emotional at first, but she'll get over it."

Shaun sat at his wife's bedside and held her hand. The sensor pads had been removed from her forehead, the IVs removed, the machinery taken away. There was nothing here now to alarm her or make her anxious. The physical effects of her treatment were minimal (small red circles on her temples, a little bruising around the veins in her arms where the needles had gone in), and would fade quickly.

"Talk to her," the doctor said. "Lead her out of the darkness with your voice." He smiled at Shaun's uncertainty. "I'll give you some privacy. There's no rush. Take as much time as you need."

He left the room. Shaun watched Martha's eyeballs moving beneath her lids in REM sleep. She was restless, as though having a nightmare. Occasionally she murmured unintelligible words—although once or twice over the past ten days he was sure she had spoken his name.

Remembering what the doctor had said, he talked to her, murmured sweet nothings, told her over and over that he was here for her, that everything was okay.

Quite suddenly, an hour later, she opened her eyes and looked at him. He smiled. "Hi," he said.

At first she did nothing but stare, as though he was something fearful and astounding. He took her hand and stroked it gently.

"It's okay," he said, "it's really me. Welcome back, sweetheart."

Her free hand reached up uncertainly towards his face, wavered in the air. He took it, kissed it, pressed it to his cheek.

"I'm real," he told her. "I'm alive. Feel."

She looked terrified and bewildered and desperately, achingly hopeful. Her breath quickened, turned to gasps; her eyelids fluttered as she began to hyperventilate.

"Take it easy," Shaun said. "It's okay, you're safe. You're home."

She was panting now, and each time she did it sounded as if she was breathlessly chanting his name. Her eyes brimmed with tears.

He nodded, kept telling her, "It's me, Martha, I'm here, it's okay, it's really me."

She let out a sudden and heart-rending cry of relief and accumulated anguish. She gripped his shoulders with both hands, digging her fingers in, drawing a hiss of pain from him. She dragged him towards her, at the same time using him to drag herself upright.

She wrapped her arms around him, hugged him fiercely, pressed her face to his. She was crying now, and laughing at the same time. She screamed out his name, over and over.

Shaun had been told what to expect, but even so he felt overawed, even afraid, of her intensity, her fervour. "It's okay," he kept telling her, "it's okay, Martha, it's okay." But even as he said it, he couldn't help wondering whether he was trying to reassure his wife or merely convince himself.

"Oh, Shaun," she said, "oh, Shaun." She took his face in her hands, her fingers probing, exploring, skittering over his lips and cheeks, burying themselves in his hair. She kissed him on the mouth hard enough to hurt. A ravenous kiss, as if she was desperate for sustenance.

"**D**on't go," she said an hour later. Her voice was raspy with misuse and emotion. She looked exhausted, washed-out, but her eyes were avid.

"I thought you wanted a drink?"

"I do, but . . . don't go. Call for somebody."

"I can't," Shaun said. "No one would hear me." In truth he wanted a breather. Just a minute's respite from her stifling desperation.

"Don't go." Her voice small now, the frightened whimper of a child terrified of the dark.

"I'll only be a minute. Promise. I'll be back before you know." He gave her forehead the gentlest of kisses. Then he stood up and walked across the room to the door, trying not to look at the panic in her eyes.

When he got back she was weeping and shaking. The instant he stepped through the door she crumpled, head drooping forward, hands falling limp to her sides. He went to her and took her in his arms and she clamped herself to him.

"Hey," he said softly, "it's okay. I said I'd come back, didn't I?"

"Don't leave me," she wept. "Don't ever leave me again."

"How much do you remember now?" he asked.

They were at home. He'd shown her the brochure for the Clinic, and she'd looked through it with sheer incomprehension.

"I don't remember *any* of this," she said.

"Dr Willis says that's normal. He says it'll take a while to adjust. Apparently it's too much of a shock to the system if your real memories override your false memories too soon."

"False memories." She repeated the phrase as if it couldn't possibly be true. As if *this* was the fantasy, the dream, and her temporary, implanted memories were the world to which she would eventually, inevitably return.

"I know it's confusing," he said, "but in a few days I promise everything you've been through will seem like a bad dream. All you have to remember is that I'm here, I'm alive, and all the horrible stuff is over."

She was still staring at the brochure, still looking bewildered, disorientated. Shaun couldn't help feeling a brief pang of irritation. Why couldn't she just be happy? Wasn't this a dream come true? To have your loved one, who you thought was dead, miraculously restored? To be given your shattered life back? Okay, so he appreciated that something like this would take *some* adjusting to, but if it had been him he would have been dancing on the roof by now. Like waking up from a bad dream, he would initially have felt a bit shocked, a bit disorientated, but pretty soon after that, he was sure, would have come, first, the relief and then the most incredible, delirious happiness he had ever known.

But Martha was just sitting there, looking all panicky and upset, as if she was actually pissed off to be back in the real world.

"I don't get any of this," she said. "I don't understand why I would ever have agreed to it."

Suppressing a sigh, he said, "We saw an advert in the paper, remember? You'd been getting a bit... mortality angsty. Worrying about getting old. Losing sleep over it, in fact." He grimaced, as though he was the unwilling bearer of bad news. "To tell you the truth, M, it had become a bit of an obsession. You'd been talking about going to see a counsellor, maybe even getting some medication."

She shook her head. "I don't remember *any* of that."

"And then we saw the ad," he said. "Bereavement preparation. A new and effective means of coming to terms with your fears. They wanted...well, guinea pigs. They were offering a lot of money."

"Is that why you persuaded me to do it? For the money?"

"No!" He reacted as if stung, then forced himself to calm down. "The money was nice, but we both thought the treatment might be worth a shot. We discussed it. They told us there'd be no risk. They told us it would be tough, but that afterwards your fears would be gone, that you'd feel fantastic. Like your life had been renewed, like all your dreams had come true. They said there'd be a short period of adjustment, but no lasting psychological effects. *You* decided to go for it. I didn't persuade you. *You* decided."

"I don't remember," she repeated. "I don't remember any of it."

"It doesn't matter," he said, and gathered her in his arms once more. "The only thing that matters is that we're together, that I'm not dead, and that everything's okay. Just remember that, all right?"

"Yes," she whispered, "yes."

S he gazed at him across the table as if he was something incredible. She had been "back" for four days now. They had come to their favourite restaurant to celebrate what she called his "resurrection".

She was grinning from ear to ear. He felt a little discomfited by the way she was looking at him—by the way she *always* looked at him now. But at least she seemed happy, even if it was manically, almost unnaturally so.

"What are you going to have?" he asked.

"You."

Since she'd been back her sexual appetite had been voracious. "Most men would be grateful," she'd said, when he'd claimed last night that he was tired.

He tried to laugh. "I mean to eat."

She reached across the table and grasped his hands, clutching them tight. Ignoring his question, she said, "I'm so happy, Shaun. I still can't believe you're here with me. I feel like I've been born again."

He laughed, hoping it didn't sound too hollow. "I'm happy you're happy," he said.

"W here are you going?"

He turned at the door, bag in hand. He knew she didn't like him leaving her alone, but she'd been better about letting him out of her sight these past few days.

"Usual Saturday ritual," he said. "Just going to meet Rich for a game of squash, then a couple of drinks. I'll be back at lunchtime."

The colour drained from her face. "*No!*" she cried, panic-stricken.

"What?"

"I don't want you to go!"

He frowned. "Why not?"

"I don't want to lose you again."

"You're not going to lose me," he said. "I'll be back in a couple of hours."

"No!" she cried again. "That's what happened last time. Richard phoned me and told me . . . " Her face twisted in anguish. "I can't go through that again . . . I just . . . I can't . . . "

He tried to make light of it, but her clinginess was beginning to get to him. He felt he couldn't move, couldn't breathe, any more.

"But that wasn't real," he said. "That's not going to happen. I'm fit as a fiddle."

She threw herself at him, wrapped herself around him, clung on for dear life. "Don't go, Shaun," she pleaded. "Please, Shaun. Please say you won't go!"

H is secretary buzzed him.

"Yes, Lisa?"

"It's your wife again, Shaun."

He closed his eyes briefly. It was at least the eighth time Martha had called him today, and on each occasion it hadn't actually been *about* anything.

"Tell her I'm in a meeting. Tell her I've got meetings for the rest of the day. Tell her I'll see her tonight."

Lisa's voice was carefully bland. "Yes, Shaun," she said.

"W hat's the matter *now?*" Shaun asked.

He hadn't meant it to sound like that. Hadn't meant to sound as if he found his wife's behaviour tiresome.

She didn't seem to register his irritation, in any case. Just sat there, staring at nothing. Following her manic period of butterfly-like rapture a week or so before, she had now become increasingly uncommunicative, withdrawn, slothful. For the past couple of days she had done little but sit around the house, staring into space. She hadn't been eating properly, and her hair looked as though it was in need of a good wash.

Shaun wasn't sure what to do. He had spoken to Dr Willis yesterday, but the doctor had simply advised him to give Martha more time.

"The procedure affects different people in different ways," he had said glibly. "Her mood swings are merely part of the process."

Shaun had tried to be understanding. *Was* being understanding. He appreciated it was hard for her. But even he had his limits.

He sat opposite her, tried to get her to look at him.

"Talk to me," he said.

Her eyes were pink, and the skin around them was bruise-dark. Shaun didn't think he had ever seen anyone look so tired.

"I can't go through it again," she murmured.

"Can't go through what?"

"You. Dying on me. I can't bear to go through it again."

He smiled. "I'm not *going* to die on you."

"Yes you are. We *all* die."

"But not for a long time. We're going to get old together, you and me."

She shook her head as if he didn't understand. "It doesn't matter. Tomorrow. Next year. Fifty years. *It doesn't matter!* One day it's going to happen."

"But we can't live our lives worrying about it. We just have to enjoy ourselves while we can."

"You haven't seen the future," she said.

It came again, that flash of irritation; he couldn't help it. "Neither have you."

"Yes," she said, "I have."

A s soon as he stepped through the door he knew. It was something about the stillness of the house, something about the quality of the silence.

She must have guessed he'd try the bedroom first. There was the note on the bed:

Dear Shaun

First of all, I'm sorry, but I love you too much to just walk away. I have to make it final. It's the only way I can be sure I'll never have to go through it all again.

If I didn't love you so much, losing you wouldn't have been so hard. Please remember that, and please tell Eve I'm so sorry.

Believe me, I know exactly what you're going through.

Your Eternal Love
Martha

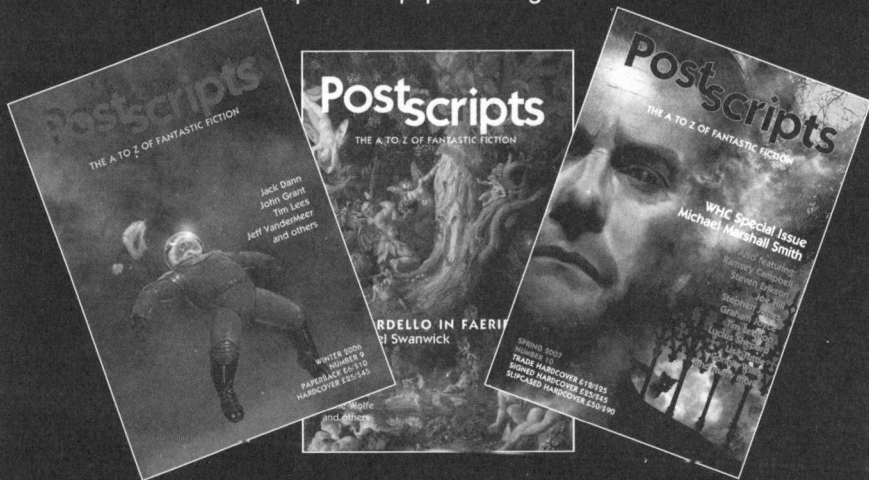

Lisa Tuttle sold her first short story in 1971; "Closet Dreams" is her 98th sale—we're putting it on record here that we'd like to have first shot at her hundredth! "For a long time," Lisa says, "I thought of myself as primarily a short story writer who just managed, with with great effort, to produce an occasional novel. But gradually that changed, and by 2001 I thought I might never write anything shorter than a novella."

When Lisa interviewed Roald Dahl back in 1981, he told her that after dedicating himself to the short story for twenty-five years he simply ran out of ideas. "I seem to have more ideas now than ever, now," she says, "but most of them need to be explored at length.

"Then, in 2006, I wrote three new stories. 'Closet Dreams' was the third, and my favourite, because it came suddenly, an unexpected gift, and I was able to write it very quickly, without a lot of agonizing, like taking dictation. Maybe I was channelling someone, but I hope not. I hope I just made it up."

Closet Dreams

Lisa Tuttle

Something terrible happened to me when I was a little girl.

I don't want to go into details. I had to do that far too often in the year after it happened, first telling the police everything I could remember in the (vain) hope it would help them catch the monster, then talking for hours and hours to all sorts of therapists, doctors, shrinks and specialists brought in to help me. Talking about it was supposed to help me understand what had happened, achieve closure, and move on.

I just wanted to forget—I thought that's what "putting it behind me" meant—but they said to do that, first I had to *remember*. I thought I did remember—in fact, I was sure I did— but they wouldn't believe what I told them. They said it was a fantasy, created to cover something I couldn't bear to admit. For my own good (and also,

to help the police catch that monster) I had to remember the truth.

So I racked my brain and forced myself to relive my darkest memories, giving them more and more specifics, suffering through every horrible moment a second, third and fourth time before belatedly realizing it wasn't the stuff the monster had done to me that they could not believe. There was nothing at all impossible about a single detail of my abduction, imprisonment and abuse, not even the sick particulars of what he called "playing." I had been an innocent; it was all new to me, but they were adults, professionals who had dealt with too many victims. It came as no surprise to them that there were monsters living among us, looking just like ordinary men, but really the worst kind of sexual predator.

The only thing they did not believe in was my escape. It could not have

342

happened the way I said. Surely I must see that?

But it had. When I understood what they were questioning, it made me first tearful and then mad. I was not a liar. Impossible or not, it had happened, and my presence there, telling them about it, ought to be proof enough.

One of them—her name escapes me, but she was an older lady who always wore turtle-neck sweaters or big scarves, and who reminded me a little of my granny with her high cheekbones, narrow blue eyes and gentle voice— told me that she knew I wasn't lying. What I had described was my own experience of the escape, and true on those terms—but all the same, I was a big girl now and I could surely understand that it could not have happened that way in actuality. She said I could think of it like a dream. The dream was my experience, what happened inside my brain while I was asleep, but something else was happening at the same time. Maybe, if we worked with the details of my dream, we might get some clues as to what that was.

She asked me to tell her something about my dreams. I told her there was only one. Ever since I'd escaped I'd had a recurring nightmare, night after night, unlike any dream I'd ever had before, twice as real and ten times more horrible.

It went like this: I'd come awake, in darkness too intense for seeing, my body aching, wooden floor hard beneath my naked body, the smell of dust and ancient varnish in my nose,

and my legs would jerk, a spasm of shock, before I returned to lying motionless again, eyes tightly shut, try-ing desperately, against all hope, to fall back into the safe oblivion of sleep. Sometimes it was only a matter of sec-onds before I woke again in my own bedroom, where the light was always left on for just such moments, but sometimes I would seemingly remain in that prison for hours before I could wake. Nothing ever happened; I never saw him; there was just the closet, and that was bad enough. The true horror of the dream was that it didn't seem like a dream, and so turned reality inside-out, stripping my illusory freedom from me.

When I was much younger I'd made the discovery that I guess most kids make, that if you can only manage to scream out loud when you're dream-ing—especially when you've started to realize that it *is* just a dream—you'll wake yourself up.

But I never tried that in the closet dream; I didn't dare. The monster had taught me not to scream. If I made any noise in the closet, any noise loud enough for him to hear from another room, he would tape my mouth shut, and tie my hands together behind my back.

I knew I was his prisoner. Before he did that, it wouldn't have occurred to me that I still had *some* freedom.

So I didn't scream.

I guess the closet dream didn't offer much scope for analysis. She tried to get me to recall other dreams, but when

I insisted I didn't have any, she didn't press. Instead, she told me that it wouldn't always be that way, and taught me some relaxation techniques that would make it easier to slip into an undisturbed sleep.

It wasn't only for my peace of mind that I kept having these sessions with psychiatrists. Anything I remembered might help the police.

Nobody but me knew what my abductor looked like. I'd done my best to describe him, but my descriptions, while detailed, were probably too personal, intimate and distorted by fear. I had no idea how an outsider would see him; I rarely even saw him dressed. I didn't know what he did for a living or where he lived.

I was his prisoner for nearly four months, but I'd been unconscious when he took me into his house, and all I knew of it, all I was ever allowed to see, was one bedroom, bathroom and closet. Under careful questioning from the police, with help from an architect, a very vague and general picture emerged: it was a single-story house on a quiet residential street, in a neighborhood that probably dated back to the 1940s or even earlier. (Nobody had used bathroom tiles like that since the 1950s; the small size of the closet dated it, and so did the thickness of the internal doors.) There were no houses like that in my parents' neighborhood, and all the newer subdivisions in the city could be ruled out, but that still left a lot of ground. It was even possible, since I had no idea how long I'd been unconscious in the back of his van after he

grabbed me, that the monster lived and worked in another town entirely.

I wanted to help them catch him, of course. So although I hated thinking about it, and wanted only to absorb myself back into my own life with my parents, friends and school, I made myself return, in memory, to my prison and concentrated on details, but what was most vivid to me—the smell of dusty varnish or the pictures I thought I could make out in the grain of the wood floor; a crack in the ceiling, or the low roaring surf sound made by the central air conditioning at night—did not supply any useful clues to the police.

Five mornings a week the monster left the house and stayed away all day. He would let me out to use the bathroom before he left, and then lock me into the closet. He'd fixed a sliding bolt on the outside of the big, heavy closet door, and once the door was shut and he slid the bolt home, I was trapped. But that was not enough for him: he added a padlock, to which he carried the only key. As he told me, if he didn't come home to let me out, I would *die* inside that closet, of hunger and thirst, so I had better pray nothing happened to him, because if it did, no one would ever find me.

That padlock wasn't his last word in security, either. He also locked the bedroom door, and before he left the house I always heard an electronic bleeping sound I recognized as being part of a security system. He had a burglar alarm, as well as locks on everything that could be secured shut.

All he left me with in the closet was a plastic bottle full of water, a blanket and a child's plastic potty that I couldn't bear to use. There was a light-fixture in the ceiling, but he'd removed the light-bulb, and the switch was on the other side of the locked door. At first I thought his decision to deprive me of light was just more of his meaningless cruelty, but later it occurred to me that it was just another example—like the padlock and the burglar alarm—of his overly-cautious nature. He'd even re-moved the wooden hanging rod from the closet, presumably afraid that I might have been able to wrench it loose and use it as a weapon against him. I might have scratched him with a broken light-bulb; big deal. It wouldn't have incapacitated him, but it might have hurt, and he wouldn't risk even the tini-est of hurts. He wanted total control.

So, all those daylight hours when I was locked into the closet, I was in the dark except for the light which seeped in around the edges of the door; mainly from the approximately three-quarters of an inch that was left between the bot-tom of the door and the floor. That was my window on the world. I thought it was larger than the gap beneath our doors at home; the police architect said it might have been because the carpet it had been cut to accommodate had been removed; alternatively, my captor might have replaced the original door because he didn't find it sturdy enough for the prison he had planned.

Whatever the reason, I was grateful that the gap was wide enough for me to look through. I would spend hours sometimes lying with my cheek flat against the floor peering sideways into the bedroom, not because it was inter-esting, but simply for the light and space that it offered in comparison to the tiny closet.

When I was in the closet, I could use my fingernails to scrape the dirt and varnish from the floorboards, or make pictures out of the shadows all around me; there was nothing else to look at except the dirty cream walls, and the most interesting thing there—the only thing that caught my eye and made me think—was a square outlined in silvery duct tape.

I knew what it was, because there was something very similar on one wall of my closet at home, and my parents had explained to me that it was only an access-hatch, so a plumber could get at the bathroom plumbing, in case it ever needed to be fixed.

Once that had been explained, and I knew it wasn't the entrance to a secret passage or a hidden room, it became uninteresting to me. In the monster's closet, though, a plumbing access-hatch took on a whole new glamour.

I thought it might be my way out. Even though I knew there was no win-dow in the bathroom, and the only door connected it to the bedroom—it was at least an escape from the closet. I wasn't sure an adult could crawl through what looked like a square-foot opening, but I knew I could manage; I didn't care if I left a little skin behind.

I peeled off the strips of tape, got my fingers into the gap and, with a little bit of effort, managed to pry out the square of painted sheetrock. But I didn't uncover a way out. There were pipes revealed in a space between the walls, but that was all. There was no opening into the bathroom, no space for a creature larger than a mouse to squeeze into. And I probably don't need to say that I didn't find anything useful left behind by a forgetful plumber; no tools or playthings or stale snacks.

I wept with disappointment, and then I sealed it up again—carefully enough, I hoped, that the monster would never notice what I'd done. After that, for the next thirteen weeks or so, I never touched it.

But I looked at it often, that small square that so resembled a secret hatchway, a closed-off window, a hidden opening to somewhere else. There was so little else to look at in the closet, and my longing, my need, for escape was so strong, that of course I was drawn back to it. For the first few days I kept my back to it, and flinched away even from the thought of it, because it had been such a let-down, but after a week or so I chose to forget what I knew about it, and pretended that it really *was* a way out of the closet, a secret that the monster didn't know.

My favorite thing to think about, and the only thing that could comfort me enough to let me fall asleep, was home. Going home again. Being safely back at home with my parents and my little brother and Puzzle the cat, surrounded by all my own familiar things in my bedroom. It wasn't like the relaxation techniques the psychiatrist suggested, thinking myself into a place I loved.

That didn't work. Just thinking about my home could make me cry, and bring me more rigidly awake on the hard floor in the dark narrow closet, too aware of all that I had lost, and how impossibly far away it was now. I had to do something else, I had to create a little routine, almost like a magic spell, a mental exercise that let me relax enough to sleep.

What I did was, I pretended I had never before stripped away the tape and lifted out that square of sheetrock in the wall. I was doing it for the first time. And this time, instead of pipes in a shallow cavity between two walls, I saw only darkness, a much deeper darkness than that which surrounded me in the closet, and which I knew was the opening to a tunnel.

It was kind of scary. I felt excited by the possibility of escape, but that dark entry into the unknown also frightened me. I didn't know where it went. Maybe it didn't go anywhere at all; maybe it would take me into even greater danger. But there was no real question about it; it looked like a way out, so of course I was going to take it.

I squeezed through the opening and crawled through darkness along a tunnel which ended abruptly in a blank wall. Only the wall was not entirely blank; when I ran my hands over it I could feel the faint outline of a square had been cut away—just like in the closet I'd escaped from, only at this end the tape was on the other side.

I gave it a good, hard punch and knocked out the piece of sheetrock, and then I crawled through, and found myself in another closet. Only this one was ordinary, familiar and friendly, with carpet comfy underfoot, clothes hanging down overhead, and when I grasped the smooth metal of the doorknob it turned easily in my hand and let me out into my own beloved bedroom.

After that, the fantasy could take different courses. Sometimes I rushed to find my parents. I might find them downstairs, awake and drinking coffee in the kitchen, or they might be asleep in their bed, and I'd crawl in beside them to be cuddled and comforted as they assured me there was nothing to fear, it was only a bad dream. At other times I just wandered around the house, rediscovering the ordinary domestic landscape, reclaiming it for my own, until finally I fell asleep.

My captivity continued, with little to distinguish one day from another until the time that I got sick. Then, the monster was so disgusted by me, or so fearful of contagion, that he hardly touched me for a couple of days; his abstinence was no sign of compassion. It didn't matter to him if I was vomiting, or shaking with feverish chills, I was locked into the closet and left to suffer alone as usual.

I tried to lose myself in my comfort-dream, but the fever made it difficult to concentrate on anything. Even in the well-rehearsed routine, I kept mentally losing my place, having to go back and start over again, continuously peeling the tape off the wall and prying out that square of sheetrock, again and again, until, finding it unexpectedly awkward to hold, I lost my grip and the thing came crashing down painfully on my foot.

It was only then, as I blinked away the reflexive tears and rubbed the soreness out of my foot, that I realized it had really happened: I wasn't just imagining it; in my feverish stupor I'd actually stood up, pulled off the tape and opened a hole in the wall.

And it really *was* a hole this time.

I stared, dumbfounded, not at pipes in a shallow cavity, but into blackness.

My heart began to pound. Fearful that I was just seeing things, I bent over and stuck my head into it, flinching a little, expecting to meet resistance. But my head went in, and my chest and arms ... I stretched forward and wriggled into the tunnel.

It was much lower than in my fantasy, not big enough to allow me to crawl. If I'd been a couple of years older or five pounds heavier I don't think I would have made it. Only because I was such a flat-chested, narrow-hipped, skinny little kid did I fit, and I had to wriggle and worm my way along like some legless creature.

I didn't care. I didn't think about getting stuck, and I didn't worry about the absolute, suffocating blackness stretching ahead. This was freedom. I kept my eyes shut and hauled myself forward on hands and elbows, pushing myself ahead with my toes. Somehow, I kept going, although the energy it took was immense, almost more than I possessed. I was drenched in sweat and gasping—the sound of my own breathing was like that of a monster in pursuit—but I didn't give up. I could not.

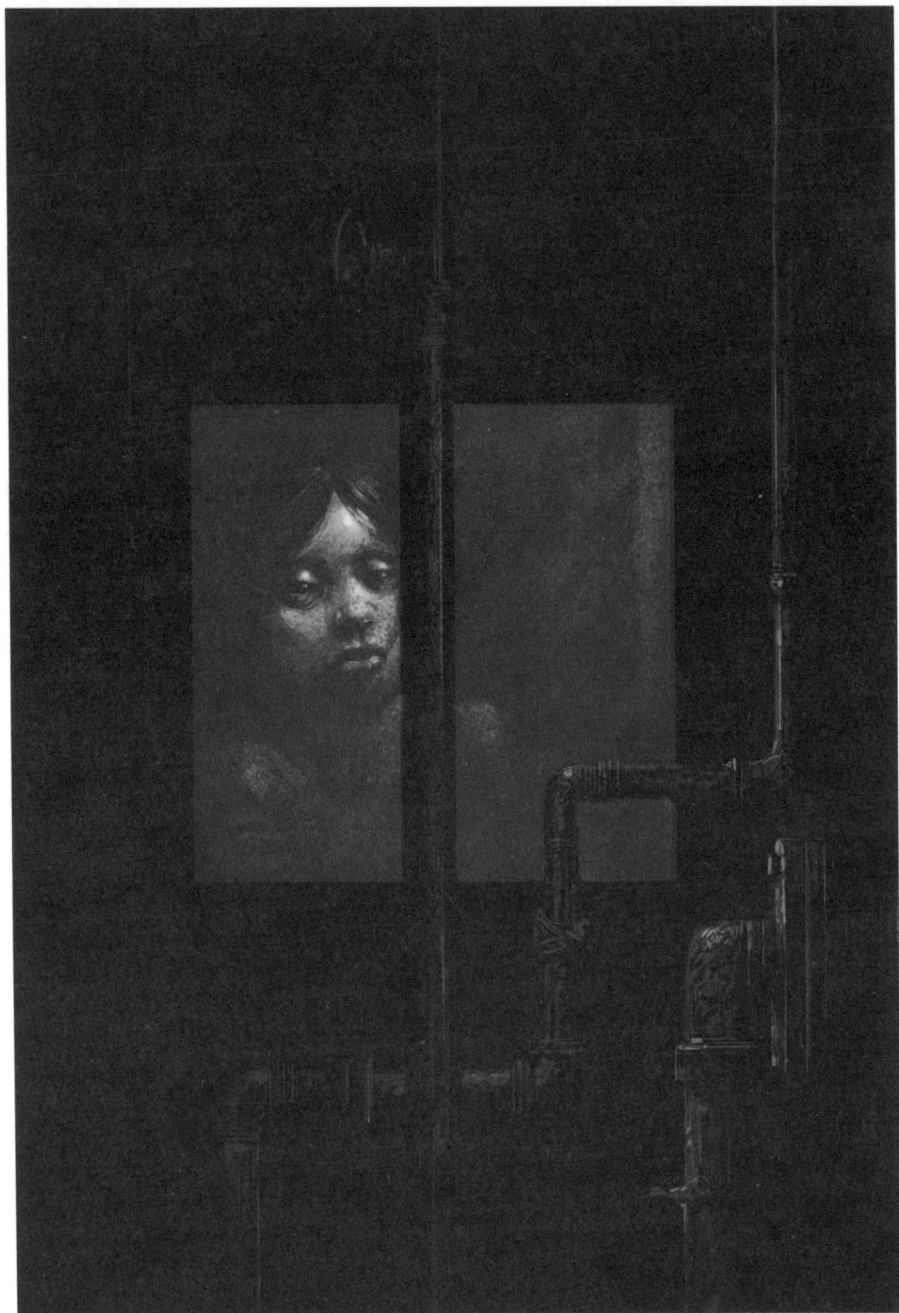

And then I came to the end, a blank wall. But that didn't worry me, because I'd already dreamed of this moment, and I knew what to do. I just had to knock out the bit of plasterboard. Nothing but tape held it in. One good punch would do it.

Only I was so weak from illness, from captivity, from the long, slow, journey through the dark, that I doubted I had a good punch in me. But I couldn't give up now. I braced my legs on either side of the tunnel and pushed with all my might, pushed so hard I thought my lungs would burst. I battered it with my fists, and heard the feeble sound of my useless blows like hollow laughter. Finally, trembling with exhaustion, sweating rivers, I hauled back, gathered all the power I had left, and launched myself forward, using my head as a battering ram.

And that did it. On the other side of the wall the tape tore away, and as the square of sheet-rock fell out and into my bedroom closet, so did I.

I was home. I was really and truly home at last.

I wanted to go running and calling for my mother, but first I stopped to repair the wall, carefully fitting the square of sheetrock back into place, and restoring the pieces of tape that had held it in, smoothing over the torn bits as best I could. It seemed important to do this, as if I might be drawn back along through the tunnel, back to that prison-house, if I didn't seal up the exit.

By the time I finished that, I was exhausted. I walked out of the closet, tottered across the room to my bed,

pulled back the sheet and lay down, naked as I was.

It was there, like that, my little brother found me a few hours later.

Even I knew my escape was impossible. At least, it could not have happened in the way I remembered. Just to be sure, my parents opened the plumbing access hatch in my closet, to prove that's all it was. There was no tunnel; no way in or out.

Yet I had come home.

My parents—and I guess the police, too—thought the monster had been frightened by my illness into believing I might die, and had brought me home. Maybe he'd picked the locks (we didn't have a burglar alarm), or maybe—because a small window in one of the upstairs bathrooms turned out to have been left unfastened—he'd carried me up a ladder and pushed me through. My "memory" was only a fevered, feverish dream.

Did it matter that I couldn't remember what really happened? My parents decided it did not, and that the excruciating regime of having to talk about my ordeal was only delaying my recovery, and they brought it to an end.

The years passed. I went to a new junior high, and then on to high school. I learned to drive. I started thinking about college. I didn't have a boyfriend, but it began to seem like a possibility. I'm not saying I forgot what had happened to me, but it was no longer fresh, it wasn't present, it belonged to the past, which became more and more blurred and distant as I struck out for adulthood and independence. The only thing that really bothered me, the real, continuing legacy of those few months when I'd been the monster's prisoner and plaything, were the dreams. Or, I should say, dream, because there was just the one, the closet dream.

Even after so many years, I did not have ordinary dreams. Night after night—and it was a rare night it did not happen—I fell asleep only to wake, suddenly, and find myself in that closet again. It was awful, but I kind of got used to it. You can get used to almost anything. So when it happened, I didn't panic, but tried practicing the relaxation techniques I'd been taught when I was younger, and eventually—sometimes it took just a few minutes, while other nights it seemed to take hours—I escaped back into sleep.

One Saturday, a few weeks before my seventeenth birthday, I happened to be in a part of town that was strange to me. I was looking for a summer job, and was on my way to a shopping mall I knew only by name, and somehow or other, because I wanted to avoid the freeways, I got a little lost. I saw a sign for a U-Tote-Em and pulled into the parking lot to figure it out. Although I had an indexed map book, I must have been looking on the wrong page; after a few hot, sweaty minutes of frustration I threw it down and got out of the car, deciding to go into the store to ask directions, and buy myself a drink to cool me down.

I had just taken a Dr. Pepper out of the refrigerator cabinet when some-thing made me look around. It was him. The monster was standing in the very next aisle, a loaf of white bread in one hand as he browsed a display of chips and dips.

My hands were colder than the bottle. My feet felt very far away from my head. I couldn't move, and I couldn't stop looking at him.

My attention made him look up. For a moment he just looked blank and kind of stupid, his lower lip thrust out and shining with saliva. Then his mouth snapped shut as he tensed up, and his eyes kind of bulged, and I knew that he'd recognized me, too.

I dropped the plastic bottle and ran. Somebody said something—I think it was the guy behind the counter—but I didn't stop. I didn't even pause, just hurled myself at the door and got out. I couldn't think about anything but escape; it never occurred to me that *he* might have had more to fear than I did, that I could have asked the guy behind the counter to call the police, or just dialed 911 myself on my cell. All that was too rational, and I was way too frightened to reason. The old animal brain, instinct, had taken over, and all I could think of was running away and hiding.

I was so out of my mind with fear that instead of going back to my car I turned in the other direction, ran around to the back of the store, then past the dry cleaner's next door, and hid myself, gasping for breath in the torrid afternoon heat, behind a dumpster.

Still panting with terror, shaking so much I could barely control my movements, I fumbled inside my purse, searching for my phone. My hands were so cold I couldn't feel a thing; impatient, I sank into a squat and dumped the contents on the gritty cement surface, found the little silver gadget and snatched it up.

Then I hesitated. Maybe I shouldn't call 911; that was supposed to be for emergencies only, wasn't it? Years ago the police had given me a phone number to call if I ever remembered something more or learned something that might give them a handle on the monster's identity. That number was pinned to the bulletin board in the kitchen where I saw it every single day. It was engraved on my memory still, although I'd never used it, I knew exactly what numbers to press. But when I tried, my fingers were still so stiff and clumsy with fear that I kept messing up.

I stopped and concentrated on calming myself. Looking around the side of the dumpster I could see a quiet, tree-lined residential street. It was an old neighborhood—you could tell that by the age of the trees, and the fact that it had sidewalks. I was gazing at this peaceful view, feeling my breath and pulse-rate going back to normal, when I caught another glimpse of the monster.

Immediately, I shrank back and held my breath, but he never looked up as he walked, hunched a little forward as he clutched a brown paper bag to his chest, eyes on the sidewalk in front of him. He never suspected my eyes were on him, and as I watched his jerky, shuffling progress—as if he wanted to run but didn't dare—I realized how much our

encounter had rattled him. All at once I was calmer. He must know I would call the police, and he was trying to get away, to hide. That he was on foot told me he must live nearby; probably the clerk in the convenience store would recognize him as a local, and the police would not have far to look for him.

But that was only if he stayed put. What if he was planning to leave? He might hurry home, grab a few things, jump in the car and lose himself in another city where he'd never be found.

I was filled with a righteous fury. I was not going to let him escape. He'd just passed out of sight when I decided to follow him.

I kept well back and off the sidewalk, darting in and out of the trees, keeping to the shade, not because I was afraid, but because I didn't want to alert him. I was determined to find out where he lived, to get his address and the license number of his car, and then I'd hand him over to the police.

After two blocks, he turned onto another street. I hung back, looking for the name of it, but the street sign was on the opposite corner where the lacy fronds of a mimosa tree hung down, obscuring it.

That didn't really matter. All I had to do was tell the police his house was two blocks off Montrose—was that the name? All at once I was uncertain of where I'd just been, the name of the thoroughfare the U-Tote-Em was on, where I'd left my car. But I could find my way back and meet the police there, just as soon as I saw which house the monster went in to.

So I hurried after, suddenly fearful that he might give me the slip, and I was just in time to see him going up the front walk of a single-story, pink-brick house, digging into his pocket for the key to the shiny black front door.

I made no effort to hide now, stopping directly across the street in the open, beneath the burning sun. I looked across at the raised curb-stone where the house number had been painted. But the paint had been laid down a long time ago and not renewed; black and white had together faded into the grey of the concrete, and I couldn't be sure after the first number—definitely a 2—if the next three were sixes, or eights, or some combination.

As he slipped the key into the lock the monster suddenly turned his head and stared across the street. He was facing me, looking right at me, and yet I had the impression he didn't see me watching him, because he didn't look scared or worried any more. In fact, he was smiling; a horrible, familiar smile that I knew all too well.

I raised the phone to summon the police, but my hand was empty. I grabbed for my purse, but it had gone, too. There was no canvas strap slung across my shoulder. As I groped for it, my fingers felt only skin: my own, naked flesh. Where were my clothes? How could I have come out without getting dressed?

The smells of dust and ancient varnish and my own sour sweat filled my nose and I began to tremble as I heard the sound of his key in the lock and woke from the dream that was my only freedom, and remembered.

Something terrible happened to me when I was a little girl.

It's still happening.

🐾